# all of my
## *heart*

### BECCA NEIL

Cover design and formatting by Destined Publishing

Cover art by @angki.s_ (Instagram)

Interior art by Elise LaValle (@art_by_elliel)

Edited by Sara Onstine

Proofread by Logan Sage Adams

Published by Destined Publishing

*To M,*
*I hope we find our way back to each other again.*

# content warning

THIS NOVEL INCLUDES THE following sensitive topics that may trigger reactions in some readers:

- Verbal and physical abuse of a minor (off page but referenced) and of a young adult (on page)

- cPTSD, PTSD, and trauma-induced anxiety

- Moderate to severe social anxiety

- Brief suicidal ideation without intent

- Parental abandonment (both current and in the past) not related to the MC's sexuality

- Brief descriptions of underage alcohol and drug use

- References to alcohol use and smoking

# prologue

## alex

"WHAT DO YOU THINK about when you go to sleep at night, Alex?"

"Hmm? What?"

"When you go to sleep? Do you just fall right to sleep, or do you, you know, think about something to help you?"

I blink and frown as I stare up at the bright blue sky. Next to me, Nico shifts uncomfortably, and I can tell he's about to apologize. He does that a lot, and it's the last thing I want. So I answer quickly with the first thought that comes to mind, even though it's not the entire truth. "Oh, um, well, I guess I just fall right to sleep. Doesn't everyone?"

I turn my head toward him. He's lying a foot or so away from me, staring up at the sky like I had been. A breeze blows through, ruffling his curly dark hair.

His expression tightens, and I see his chest rise and fall as he takes a deep breath. "I don't," he says. And I think he wants to say more, but then he hesitates.

"You were snoring away last time you slept over," I tease, and that earns me exactly the reaction I'd hoped for—he turns his head to look at me, rolling his beautiful green eyes, and then he sticks his tongue out at me.

I should probably have said something else, though, because despite his silly response and eye roll, his expression almost immediately turns sad. He shifts back to look up at the sky again as a frown settles on his lips.

"I sleep better at your house than at mine," he says after another few seconds. Then his voice gets much quieter. "When I'm at home, some nights it seems like I barely sleep at all."

"That's rough. I'm sorry."

"Sometimes when I play a story in my head, it helps. Distracts me. All those other voices stop screaming at me for a little while. Know what I mean?"

He knows I don't. But I nod anyway. "Yeah, I can see that."

I'm still staring at him, but he's looking at the sky. He bends his knees, his bare feet sliding through the thick grass, and he brings his hands back behind his head, the short sleeves of his shirt riding up toward his shoulders. The bruise on his upper arm—the one I noticed yesterday but hadn't said anything about—is just visible now. Deep purple and black.

I swallow and turn my head to look up at the sky again.

"What's your story about?" I ask.

He's quiet for several long seconds. Then he says, "This."

I almost snort a laugh, but instead, my chest tightens. "Your story is about us wasting our summer away doing nothing while we lie in the grass and stare up at the sky?"

"No," he says, and his voice sounds a little small when he adds, "Well, actually, sometimes it is."

A wave of guilt rushes through me, because I certainly hadn't meant to tease him. I start to apologize, but he continues before I can.

"We should go back. I'm gonna get in trouble if I don't get all my chores done."

"I can help you," I offer, but he shakes his head, which is his typical response.

"He won't like it if he knows I had you over." Nico pushes himself up on his elbows, and I catch him grimacing. "Besides, don't you have work this afternoon anyways?"

If only he knew I'd gladly drop all of my other responsibilities if it meant he wouldn't get in trouble. Still, I copy him, pushing myself up off the warm ground. I dust my palms on my shorts. "Yeah. Mom's getting ready for that big art show she's organizing in Omaha this weekend, and she needs me to help her pack up her truck this afternoon. She'll be gone all weekend."

"I can't believe she's leaving you home alone."

We stand up together and grab our shoes, then start walking down the hill, still barefoot. It's about half a mile back to his house, and then my house is another mile and a half down the road.

"She says I'm responsible enough now that I've been 'officially a teenager' for several months."

Nico laughs. "Has she *met* you?" He laughs again and then adds, "So, when's the party, and why haven't I been invited?"

I'm grinning, but I don't answer. There's no party, and he knows it. I am actually a pretty responsible kid, even with as much grief as I give my mom.

We pick our way down a pile of rocks, Nico following behind me. His house is visible in the distance, just beyond a sparse stand of trees. When we reach the bottom of the rocks, we stop and put our shoes back on, then we continue in silence.

There's an old, beat-up light-blue truck in the driveway, and as we get closer, I can hear music coming from inside the house. Some loud, crass heavy-metal rock stuff with lots of cursing. Nico walks a little slower, and when I glance over at him, his shoulders are tense.

"I thought he wasn't going to be home until later?" I ask quietly.

Nico shrugs but doesn't say anything.

We stop in the middle of the driveway, dirt kicking up as my shoes scuff into the ground. I hate this part the most, and I think he does too.

"Text me later," I say, and he knows what I actually mean. *Text me. Let me know you're okay and that that jackass hasn't hurt you more.* Or at least I think he knows. "I'll see you tomorrow."

"Yeah." Nico swallows hard and then shuffles off across the driveway toward his house, not looking back.

And I turn and shove my hands into my pockets as I start on my way back home.

*Five years later...*

# chapter one

## *nico*

I DON'T KNOW WHY I let Alex bring me here.

Tomorrow's our high school graduation, and so we're supposed to be celebrating or whatever. But I hate parties, and he knows it. There are too many people, and everything's too loud, and it's impossible to walk anywhere without bumping into someone. The whole place smells like weed and alcohol and sweaty teenagers.

And it's even worse because nearly as soon as we got here, he took off. I'm not even sure where he went. Maybe to go find Kimmy or Leela or that new girl who's been hanging off of him all the time at school.

My stomach sours at the thought, and I risk a quick glance up toward where he disappeared to however long ago, hoping to catch a glimpse of his bright-blue hair. At least he makes himself easy to spot. But he's not anywhere I can see.

The tickle of anxiety in the back of my mind just gets worse, and I feel a little sick.

I lower my eyes back to my clasped hands as my knee bounces up and down. Maybe I should just leave. Shoot him a text and head out. He can find a ride home later from someone else. I'm not the only one here who's sober. Maybe.

I'm just about to stand up and figure out how to escape when I hear my name. But it's not Alex's voice calling me.

"Hey, hey, hey, Nico!"

My stomach drops. I look up, but only because I need to prepare myself.

A few feet in front of me, Brandon Jones pushes his way through the half-drunk crowd, dragging his latest girlfriend along with him. Nya, I think her name is. She hangs on his arm as he stops in front of me, and I can smell the alcohol wafting off of them. It's almost as rotten as Brandon's sneer.

He laughs as he stumbles to a stop. "Nico the Freako. Didn't expect to see you here. Where's your other half? Off with someone who's actually willing to put out?" He laughs again, then takes a long swig of his drink before leaning over and whispering something into his date's ear. She glances at me and giggles.

I don't answer him. He's not looking for an answer anyway. He's just another asshole, like so many of the kids in school, and he'll just interpret anything I say in some weird, fucked-up way.

From the other side of the room, the music kicks up a notch—the volume louder and the bass shaking the walls. Cheers go up from the crowd. Thankfully, Brandon doesn't seem to care to waste any more time talking to me. He sneers at me again, then starts bouncing with the music, pulling his date away with him as they head back into the fray.

I push myself deeper into the small couch and look back down at my hands, trying not to panic. But I feel a familiar chill settling in me, my fingers tingling, as my heart starts to race unevenly.

Where the hell is Alex?

If he just wanted to come to this party to get wasted and laid, and if he just brought me along so I could drive him home after—

I shake my head, knowing that's not true. He wanted to come because tomorrow's graduation and everyone's here celebrating, and he wanted me to be here, too, so I wouldn't feel left out. I know that. Alex is my best friend, and he wouldn't use me like that.

But the knowledge doesn't help. The music is too loud, and there are too many people, and the smell of alcohol and weed is too much.

I need out. *Now.*

I lift my eyes, scanning the room. But I don't see him.

To my right, there's a slider door leading out to the backyard. I think there's a gate around the side. I can leave now, drive myself home and just crawl into bed, maybe even before my mom gets home from work. Then she won't have to be bothered to ask me how I'm feeling or whatever. And Alex can find his own way home. Maybe with whoever he's off dancing with or fucking right now.

A bitter taste floods my mouth, and even though the thought was only in my mind, I immediately walk it back. He's not like that. He's never done casual hookups, at least not as far as I know. He's barely even ever dated the whole time we've been friends.

So why the hell is my brain telling me that he's off in one of the upstairs bedrooms or locked in a bathroom somewhere in this much too large, much too loud house, getting laid?

I suddenly can't breathe, and my heart's jumping all over the place, making my chest feel tight.

Someone else comes up—someone I might sort of recognize, maybe from physics class. They offer me a beer, but I shake my head as I stand up. They're saying something to me, asking me some question, but the words are fuzzy and I'm done enough that I just need to get away.

I start toward the back door, knowing I won't survive trying to push through the dancing crowd to get out the front. But then a hand lands on my shoulder, and the world stops.

I screw my eyes shut, fighting against the panic rising up in my chest. Everything's dark and cold, and I can't move or see or breathe. And awful, stabbing pains seem to attack me from all angles.

I try to speak, to ask whoever's got their hand on my shoulder not to touch me—fuck it, don't they all know this by now?—and I try to get my feet to move, because the back door is only a few feet away. But I can't. I'm trapped, and it's painful.

Goddammit, Alex. Where the fuck are you?

"Nico! Hey, asshole, don't touch him!"

"What? I was just—"

The hand disappears from my shoulder, and there's some exchange that seems heated. I don't listen, though, because I'm gone, scrambling forward toward the mythical back door on feet that still hurt and muscles that tremble. My vision's blurry, but I manage to tug the door open.

The air outside hits me like a wave, and at least it's warm, but it's also ridiculously humid and stifling. I suck in two deep breaths before I continue, my head down, away from the noise and people. There is indeed a gate around the side of the house, and in only seconds, I'm there, fumbling with the latch. I hear Alex behind me just as I push the gate open.

"Nico! Hey, wait up! I'm sorry, I was just—"

"I'm going home," I cut in. I don't want to hear about whatever the hell he was doing. Whoever the hell he was kissing or dancing with or whatever. I don't want to hear it.

He reaches my side, and he doesn't try to argue with me or console me or convince me to head back into the house. In fact, he doesn't say anything at all. He just walks next to me silently. I'm not sure if that's what I want or not.

My car, an old silver sedan that barely runs most days, is parked quite a ways down the street, and we walk the whole way there without saying a word. Finally, when I go to pull out my keys, Alex steps in front of me.

"Hey, um, I'm sorry. Really. I went to go find—"

"It's fine. I just want to go home," I say, and I skirt around him to the driver's side door. He doesn't move from his spot, and I wonder if he's going to head back to the party. He can, of course. That's up to him. I just want to go home, anyway. But I stop, my head down, a familiar anger rising up in my chest. Although I know it's not real, I'm also powerless to stop it or to control the tone of my words, which come out harsh and scathing. "Are you coming? Or are you staying here?"

I hate that my chest constricts at the thought of him staying, because I don't want to imagine what he might do. My brain's already been toying with me enough. And it's really not like I've got any claim to him. He's not mine, and he's never given me any reason to believe he's gay or bi or anything other than straight. He can't know how I feel, either. I've never even hinted to him that I've had a crush on him since we were in middle school.

But there's also no way I can stay here. I shouldn't even have come in the first place.

"I'm, uh . . ." He hesitates, and I can almost see him, concern in his deep blue eyes as he shakes his head. "You'll be okay driving home? I kinda want to stay."

I shouldn't be mad. After all, it's my own stupid ass's fault for coming in the first place. So I nod, not trying to hide my scowl. "See you at graduation tomorrow."

"Yeah."

Without looking at him again, I get in the car, fasten my seat belt, and drive away, leaving Alex standing there along the curb. It's only when I'm glancing in the rearview mirror for the last time that I see he's holding two bottles of water in his hands, frowning as he watches my car disappear down the dimly lit road.

# chapter two

## *alex*

*Nico (10:53 p.m.):* Sorry

*Nico (10:53 p.m.):* Did you get home okay?

*Alex (10:54 p.m.):* yeah just got home. u ok?

Rather than send a longer text to explain what I didn't have the chance to tell him earlier, I stuff my phone back in my pocket and carefully shut the door behind me. Mom isn't sleeping, I'm sure. I think I saw the light on in the garage, where her art studio is, and I know she's been working on a commission for a big client in California. So I don't want to disturb her, either.

Honestly, I just want to sleep. Tomorrow's going to be a big day, and I'm tired.

I head into the kitchen and pour myself a glass of water, and then I jog upstairs to my bedroom. I chuckle as I see that my mom's set out my graduation robe and cap and the clothes she bought me to wear underneath—slacks and a nice dress shirt and tie. There's a little note on top, and I set my glass down on the nightstand next to my bed and then lean over and pick the note up.

*To my sunshine -*

*I know I say this a lot, but I'm so proud of you. I've got that meeting tomorrow morning in Omaha, so I have to leave early, but I'll be home on time to watch my <u>valedictorian</u> give his speech! I love you so much.*

*-Mom*

*PS - yes, you have to wear the tie. Humor me, would you?*

I shake my head, but I'm smiling, and I fold up the note, put it in my nightstand drawer, and carefully move the clothes to my desk chair. Then I grab some clean briefs and a towel and head to the bathroom for a quick shower to get the party smell off of me. I'm completely sober—unlike most of the people I was hanging out with tonight—but I have no desire to go to sleep smelling like alcohol and weed and sweat.

Ten minutes later, I crawl into bed, burrow under my comforter, and close my eyes. Almost immediately, I see that awful scene from the party—Nico, frozen and terrified, standing there with Shane next to him, his hand on Nico's shoulder.

My jaw clenches, and I open my eyes again and turn onto my side.

Fucking Shane. He *knows* Nico doesn't like to be touched. Hell, everyone does by now. Or at least everyone who's been around since Nico exploded on Mr. Adams in biology class freshman year.

Nico's not okay, and I'm an ass for letting him go home alone, especially when it was so obvious that he was spiraling. His anxiety always morphs into shortness and anger when it gets beyond his ability to control it anymore. And that's all my fault, too.

He didn't even really want to be there in the first place. Then I disappeared, off to find us some nonalcoholic drinks, which proved to be more difficult than I expected. By the time I returned, it was too late. Nico was already in the middle of a frozen panic, sent there by the noise and the crowd and Shane's hand on his shoulder. Doesn't matter what the hell Shane was trying to say to Nico. He knows. Fuck him if he forgot.

No one should forget.

I reach over and grab my phone from the nightstand. The screen is black, with no new notifications, meaning Nico hasn't returned my text. That in itself isn't terribly surprising—he tends to send messages and then put his phone down, especially after something stressful happens. But I almost want to call him because I'm sure he's talked himself into a bad enough place in the last three hours.

I'm such an idiot.

I unlock my phone and type out another quick text.

> Alex (11:19 p.m.): want to chat?

But even after several more minutes, I don't get any response. Again, not unexpected. However, I'm worried, and I want to connect with him in some way so I know he's okay before I go to bed. I hate how we left things earlier. I shouldn't have invited him in the first place, or I should have gone home with him instead of letting him leave alone while he was so anxious.

Sticking around at the party wasn't that fun anyway. The new girl, Jenna, who's really sweet but has been hanging all over me all week, kept trying to get me to go upstairs with her, which I was

really, really not interested in. On top of that, I was probably one
of the only ones who wasn't drinking, and watching everyone else
get shit-faced was just not a good time.

I should have known what to expect.

And if my mom ever found out I was even *at* a party like that, I'd
be grounded for the rest of my life. Or, well, since I've technically
been an adult for several months now, and I'm heading off to
college in three months, I guess she couldn't *really* punish me. But
she'd be disappointed. And that would be worse than anything
else.

Except maybe losing Nico as my best friend because I screwed
up. That would be the worst thing.

My hand tightens on my phone, and I close my eyes for a few
seconds. Then I blow out a breath, try to remind myself not to
worry too much—because Nico just put his phone down, like he
always does—and type out a longer text, so when he wakes up in
the middle of the night, like he also always does, he'll see it and
then he'll know I didn't abandon him.

I wish he always knew that by now, but I don't blame him.
Anxiety is a bitch. And his jackass ex-stepfather, who thankfully
isn't in the picture anymore, really did a number on him.

> *Alex (11:25 p.m.):* freaking Leela had no water or anything nonalcoholic. i had to hunt for a couple bottles of water for us. thats why i disappeared for so long. i hope u didnt worry it was anything else

I want to write more, but I know he hates it when I apologize,
so I hold back. Then I hit send, plug in my phone to charge, and
bury myself under the covers.

As soon as I close my eyes, I see his smile, bright and uninhibited, like it hasn't been in a long time. He laughs, and his green eyes light up. And even though it's just a picture in my head, it makes my heart flutter all the same.

I fall asleep to that image of his beautiful face, happy and carefree, like I have nearly every night for years now.

# chapter three

## *nico*

"So, MY FINAL WORDS to the class of twenty twenty-five, are these: Don't settle. Be unambiguously and unapologetically who you are. Be generous. Be ferocious. Be real. And most of all . . ."

I watch as Alex pauses. His eyes find mine, and he gives a tiny nod before he continues scanning the rows of graduating seniors in our class.

". . . most of all, be kind. Because kindness, above all else, is what the world needs more of."

That sentence stabs me in the gut for whatever reason. And it's one hundred percent Alex.

We haven't had a chance to talk yet, and since his mom is taking him to some fancy restaurant with his grandparents in Omaha tonight, I doubt we'll get to talk today at all. But I still feel guilty enough about last night—how I let my anxiety turn me panicked and scared and spiral into that uncontrolled anger, as it always does—so maybe it's better this way.

Everyone's clapping for him, and I join in. His eyes find mine again, just briefly, and it's probably because I know him so well, but I see the concern in them. I try to smile at him, to let him know it's fine. I'm fine. I'm not sure if he understands, though. He shifts his gaze out to where the audience sits, gives a little wave, and then moves away from the podium and back down to his seat in the first row with the student government leaders and salutatorians and whoever else is special enough to be sitting in the front.

I'm near the back. Not that there are that many of us in the graduating class since our school is pretty small, but I'm *not* anything special, and alphabetically, West is always close to last. So that's fine, too.

On my right is Claire Young, and on my left is Shane Wallace. The same Shane who touched my shoulder last night. He's been sitting next to me pretty stiffly the whole afternoon, and I figure I should probably tell him there are no hard feelings.

But I don't think I can talk to anyone right now anyway, so I keep my mouth shut.

They start calling us up to get our diplomas, and there's plenty of ruckus, with lots of cheering and screaming—both from the audience and from the other students. I try to just sit there in my seat, clapping politely after each name is called. But as it gets closer to my turn, the anxiety starts to get bad again. Well, I mean, it's always there anyway—any time that I'm not just at home alone or somewhere quiet with Alex—and it's been building all day as it is.

The rows in front of us get called up one at a time, and as I watch each of the other students head up to the stage and shake the principal's hand, my anxiety not-so-subtly reminds me that I'm going to have to do that, too.

I'm going to have to shake Mr. Williams's hand.

And fuck if that doesn't start to scare the shit out of me.

I'm trembling before I even realize it, and I pull my shoulders in a little tighter, trying to make myself even smaller than I already am. But the chairs next to me are too close, and I can't get away from everyone around me.

Fuck, I hate this feeling.

I keep telling myself it'll be fine. It's just a handshake. But then

I watch closer, and I see it's *not* just a handshake. Mr. Williams is also setting his other hand on the opposite shoulder of each of the students, like a half hug, as they shake hands and then pause for a photograph.

And if I watch even closer, I can see he squeezes each student's shoulder a little. I tear my eyes away, suddenly nauseous.

It's then that I see Alex again. He's back in his seat now in the front row, his bright-blue hair tucked neatly under his graduation cap, and he turns his head around to look at me just as the row ahead of me gets up and starts walking toward the stage. His eyes hold mine for several seconds, and I let myself stay there, with him. It's a place that's comfortable, and I can almost hear his voice whispering to me. *"I'm here. Don't worry. You can do this."* It's as though he's standing behind me, protecting me. He gives me a small smile, and I can feel that, too, even though we're at least fifty feet apart. *"I'm here. Don't worry. You can do this."*

Of course, just as my heart has slowed back down to something closer to its normal rhythm, Claire elbows me in the side.

"Nico, go. It's our turn," she says, her voice frustrated.

Immediately, I lose Alex's comforting gaze, and all that nauseating, buzzing anxiety returns full force. I stand up stiffly and somehow convince my feet to move to follow Shane down to the aisle and then up to the stage. My vision starts doing that thing where it blurs in and out, and when Claire accidentally bumps into me as we stop at the bottom of the steps, it's almost too much.

It would be awesome to *not* make a fool of myself right now. Really, really awesome. But Claire's quick apology doesn't stop the flood of every fucking negative emotion ever from gripping me.

"Shane Wallace!" the announcer calls, and in front of me, Shane jogs up the few steps onto the stage. I can't really see, thanks to my blurry vision, but I hear cheering and yelling from our classmates.

Another few long seconds pass, and I force my eyes back open as a woman I don't recognize touches my arm. I flinch away hard and run right into the stair railing, the solid metal jabbing me in the ribs. The woman doesn't even seem to notice.

"Nico? You're next. Remember, shake hands and get your photo taken with Mr. Williams, then head across to the center of the stage to get your diploma from Ms. Cox."

I don't get to process anything before I hear my name announced over the loud speaker.

"Nico West!"

I know it's only a second that I hesitate, but it feels like longer. My hand grips the railing, and I'm frozen, unable to move.

I can't do this.

I can't do this.

I can't—

"Nico! Woohoo! Yeah!" Alex's voice jumps out over all the other noises, including the loud voices screaming at me in my head.

Then, from behind me, Claire calls out, "Yeah, go, Nico!" And there's a chorus of other voices too.

And somehow, my feet move. I hold tight to the railing and take the stairs one at a time.

When I reach the top step, I force my eyes up. Mr. Williams is standing there, only about ten feet away, and he's got both of his hands tucked behind his back. He gives me a solid nod, and there's something in his eyes that helps me somehow. I walk the few steps over to him, but as I get closer, my shaking worsens. My hands ball up into fists.

I think I'm going to puke.

"Just stand as close as you feel comfortable, Nico. No handshake. We'll get the picture without it. Okay?"

My eyes dart back up to Mr. Williams, and he smiles knowingly at me and nods.

"Yeah, Nico!! Woohoo!" I hear Alex again, loud and clear and encouraging.

Did he tell Mr. Williams for me?

Slowly, I nod, and I step up a little closer, until I'm maybe about a foot or two away.

"Turn and smile for the photographer," Mr. Williams instructs, and I can do that.

There's a quick click.

"Congratulations, Nico. Ms. Cox will hand you your diploma." Mr. Williams takes a step back, away from me, and carefully motions to his right, for me to continue across the stage to where Ms. Cox stands.

"Thank you," I manage, and once again, I get my feet moving. Ms. Cox hands me my diploma, again with instructions that we can stand apart while taking the photo, and then I make my way off the stage to more screaming from Alex and the audience and the other students.

I can barely breathe, and my chest hurts. But god, I made it.

I made it. Somehow.

# chapter four

## *alex*

"OH, I JUST CAN'T get over it. I'm so stinking proud of you."

My mom pulls me in for yet *another* hug—probably the fifth or so since she and my grandparents found me out on the football field where the ceremony was held. I hug her back, smiling into her dark hair as I rest my chin on top of her head.

I want to thank her for everything, again. I mentioned her in my speech, but even that seems like it's not enough. She's been the best mom—infinitely supportive of me for, well, ever, really, even when I sort of broke her heart with the news that I wanted to go to California for college. She just took a few minutes to compose herself and then asked me what I needed to make that happen. And then, after I got accepted to Stanford on a full-ride scholarship, she added a line to her budget for travel expenses, telling me, "Don't even argue. There's no way I'm going to go months without seeing you. Thankfully, there are plenty of inexpensive flights from Omaha."

I pull back and look down at her, and I chuckle and shake my head at the tears in her eyes. She just swats at my shoulder.

"Don't laugh at me, I only cry so much—"

"—because you care," I cut in, finishing her statement for her. She smiles up at me while wiping a tear from her cheek.

"Darn you, thinking you're all cute."

"I *am* cute. You tell me that all the time," I tease, but then I hug her again. "I love you, Mom."

When she pulls back this time, she stares at me for another half second, and damn, her eyes are so filled with pride and love that it's almost overwhelming. She pats me on the arm and then turns to my grandparents, and they start discussing our plans for the evening. We're supposed to head to Omaha for reservations they made at some Japanese steakhouse, and I guess we have to leave pretty soon.

With a wave of unease, I realize I hadn't found Nico after the ceremony, and I look up and start scanning the field. It's crowded, though. Parents and family and students are all milling about everywhere, talking and congratulating and hugging. And it's maybe a bit loud and chaotic, despite the feelings of excitement and hope everyone seems to have.

I can't see Nico or his mom anywhere, and actually, as I look again, searching the edges of the crowd for any sign of my best friend, I remember that he'd mentioned last week he wasn't even sure his mom would be coming. Something about her having to work and not being able to get the afternoon off.

That immediately makes my stomach drop.

"So, we should get going, yeah?" My mom touches my arm to get my attention, almost as though she knows I'm elsewhere at the moment.

I shuffle my feet a bit as I turn back to her. "Um, yeah, just . . ." I shake my head and look back toward where the crowd is starting to migrate to the parking lot.

There are so many people.

He would have hated this. I find myself hoping he actually *is* already gone, so he escaped before the crowd got bad.

But then what kind of friend does that make me?

I swallow hard and nod as I resist the urge to pull my phone out of my pocket. "Yeah, yeah, we can go."

I'll just have to check in with him later.

My mom and grandparents start off toward the parking lot, following the slow shuffle of the crowd, as the sun begins to drop lower in the sky to the west. I walk alongside my mom, and she's rambling on and on about how wonderful the ceremony was or something.

"The speech by the blue-haired boy might have been the best part!" my grandpa pipes in jokingly, and that gets them all going again.

My mom, who's been listening to me practice my speech for weeks now, starts pulling out random lines and reciting them, including the couple of dumb jokes I managed to slip in, and everyone's happy and laughing as we make it to our cars. Except me.

My stupid hand is in my stupid pocket holding my stupid phone, and as soon as I'm in the truck with my seat belt on, I unlock my screen and open up my messenger app.

Nothing.

I frown, ignoring my mom as she climbs into the driver's seat.

> *Alex (5:43 p.m.):* hey

Nothing.

"Everything okay?" Mom asks, and I nod.

"Yeah, it's fine, I just missed saying bye to Nico," I explain. I'm still frowning, staring at my phone screen, waiting for him to text back.

"Oh." My mom starts driving, navigating carefully through the busy parking lot. She doesn't say anything for a few minutes until we're on the main highway heading out of the small town of Redland, Nebraska, where I've lived my whole life. Omaha is north about thirty minutes or so. "He's probably celebrating with his family tonight. Right?"

I close my eyes, and the knot in my stomach tightens. Her question is sort of a question and sort of not, like she already knows the truth but is hoping she's wrong.

"Um, no. I think his mom's working. His aunt was maybe going to be driving in, but he wasn't sure."

Mom doesn't answer this time, and after another few minutes of staring at my phone, I can't stand it anymore. I tap to bring up his number and then tap again to call. It rings five times before going to voicemail.

Holding back a curse, I close my eyes again and listen to his voice on the short recording.

"Hey, you've reached Nico. I'm not available right now, so leave me a message, and I'll call you back!"

There's a beep, and I hesitate, not sure what to say.

*I'm sorry. Are you okay? Call me, please. I'm worried about you. I'm an ass.*

All of that is true, and yet it's not anywhere near telling him what I'm really feeling.

"Hey, uh, it's me. Just checking in since I missed you after the ceremony. Call me?"

Dammit.

I pull the phone away from my ear and hit the red button to end the call. Then I look back up and ahead of us. The highway stretches on and on, and I let myself get distracted.

"Backfire," I say.

There's a quiet chuckle from my left, and the next time a car passes us going the other direction, my mom chimes in.

"Periwinkle."

"Greenbelt."

"Asteroid."

"Guzzle."

We toss words back and forth for a while, sometimes laughing at the absurdity of whatever comes. It's a game we've played for as long as I can remember—we take turns coming up with a word that starts with the first letter in the license plate of the oncoming car. And it's just distracting enough that I manage to loosen my grip on my phone slightly.

After a long stretch of no oncoming cars, however, my mom clears her throat, and I almost flinch. It's her tell—she wants to talk about something serious.

And I'm sure it's related to Nico.

"So, I've actually been meaning to ask," she says slowly, "because you never told me. What does Nico think about you taking off to California in September?"

It's like she's going right for the jugular with that question. I turn my head and look out the window as we pass over a narrow river. "He's fine."

"Alex."

"Mom."

I don't want to talk about it, and part of the reason is the heavy guilt in my chest.

Nico's not going to college. At least, he's repeatedly told me he's not planning to. He can't afford it, he can't ask his mom for help with student loans because *she* can't afford it and probably wouldn't really even want to try, and despite working his ass off to do the best he could in his classes, he didn't have stellar grades to get any scholarships like I did.

Of course, he's also repeatedly insisted I should do what's going to make me happy—what I've been wanting to for years. And what I've been wanting to do for years is to get out of Nebraska. I want to study astrophysics, and I want to do that somewhere near a beach, somewhere out on the West Coast.

We actually argued about it more than once after my acceptance letters started pouring in—Stanford on a full tuition-paid scholarship *plus* housing and food; UCLA with tuition covered; University of Washington, also a full ride; and a handful of others. I tried to convince him to come with me, and when he said there was no way that could work, I told him, fine, I'd stay. Commute to Lincoln and go to the University of Nebraska. I still remember him looking at me like I had two heads, staring at me for a good minute before he shut down and said there was no world in which I should stick around fucking Nowhere, Nebraska just for him.

And I wanted to tell him just how much I'd do for him and just how much he's meant to me for so long. But I said nothing then, and I've said nothing more about it since.

Because how the hell *could* it work out anyway?

I ended up choosing Stanford—how could I *not* accept a free education at one of the best universities in the country?—but I still feel sick when I think about leaving him behind.

"Is he really fine, Alex?" Mom asks. Her voice is soft, and I'm sure she already knows the answer.

"He says he is." I rest my elbow on the car door and turn to stare out the window. We're almost to Omaha, the rolling hills and agricultural fields giving way to suburbs and businesses. The view isn't interesting to me; I've watched out this same window on this same drive too many times now. But I pretend to be distracted by it as I hear my mom let out a short breath.

"It's going to be a big change for both of you," she says after a moment. That's not what she wants to say—I can hear *that* tone in her voice, too—and for a second, my stomach drops.

She probably knows.

We've never talked about anything much—dating, girls, boys,

sex ... There've been a few reminders here and there to not get anyone pregnant on accident and that porn doesn't necessarily depict reality. But she's never asked me specifically about my sexuality or hinted that she suspects I'm not straight.

I'm not even one hundred percent sure what I am. Bi, probably, or maybe even pan if I stop to think about it. But I'm also completely in love with my best friend and so not really interested in exploring anything else.

I swallow and keep my eyes trained outside the car.

She'd be accepting. I know it. She's been outspoken about supporting the LGBTQIA+ community for as long as I can remember, and I'm really not even sure why I haven't told her yet.

Maybe I should. Although I'm not sure how that would help right now, because it doesn't really matter. Nico's not into guys. I think.

I close my eyes as my stomach swoops again, not in a comfortable way. I actually have no idea whether he's into guys. Or girls. Or anyone else for that matter. He's never, *ever* commented on anyone of any gender. Not that I can remember. And I'm pretty sure I would remember.

I clear my throat. "I asked him to come with me. To California, I mean." It's a half admission, if she reads into it, and I'm suddenly even more nervous than when I was standing up on that stage about to start my speech not more than an hour and a half ago. I continue on, hoping to pull attention away from whatever I hadn't quite said. "He said he couldn't leave because he couldn't afford it and he's not going to college anyway. Said he was planning to stay here. He, uh, did get that job as an assistant at the library, although I think that's supposed to be temporary over the summer."

Mom is quiet again, and I risk a glance over at her. She's looking ahead but biting her lower lip. That's another tell of hers. She's trying to not say what she wants to. But she'll end up saying it. She *always* does, like she just can't get herself to hold back.

I turn back to the window, close my eyes, and take a long, accepting breath. Then, I say, "I don't know how to convince him, but the thought of leaving him here while I go . . ." I press my hand into my thigh to try and get my leg to stop its anxious bouncing. "It hurts. It hurts my heart."

That's the best I can do right now.

I've never told another soul, and I know I still really haven't. Or at least I haven't said the words out loud to her.

*I'm in love with Nico West.*

But her response, short as it is, tells me exactly as I suspected. She probably already knows.

"Oh, sweetie . . ." Her hand reaches over and covers mine on my thigh, and she squeezes gently. "Maybe you should talk to him about it again."

"Heh."

"No, I'm serious. When did you talk before? Maybe if . . ." She trails off for a minute before she does what she always does and starts troubleshooting, getting much too practical about things. "Rent in Palo Alto is impossibly expensive, but maybe if he saves up over the summer and then he's able to find a decent job out there, and maybe if he looks a little farther south for housing and works out a good budget . . ."

"It's impossible, Mom."

"Nothing's impossible—"

"—unless you don't try. I know, Mom. But—"

"Ohhh, and actually! Actually!" Her hand grips mine, and she lifts it up and then pats it back down on my thigh. "I know someone!"

"You . . . what?"

"I think she's in San Jose, not Palo Alto, but that's close enough, isn't it?"

I'm lost, and she knows it, but right then, the automated voice on her phone chimes in, telling her to exit the freeway. She's quiet while she follows the directions from Google Maps, navigating us into downtown Omaha and to the restaurant. I see my grandparents' car ahead of us now, turning into the parking lot, and we follow. After we pull into a parking spot a moment later and my mom kills the engine, she turns to me.

"I know a woman who's the director of an art collective based in the Bay Area. She's grown the collective to include hundreds of artists, and she runs events all year round and manages several galleries. She's always looking for reliable employees."

My chest tightens as my mom smiles at me, her expression a mixture of understanding, love, and encouragement, but also with a glint of something else. I think maybe it's concern, but she doesn't give me time to really figure it out.

"Talk to him, Alex. You don't want to have regrets. You don't want to always be wondering 'what if,' especially when it's something—or someone—so important to you. There are *always* solutions even—"

"—when they're not easy. I know, Mom." I drop my chin to my chest, and my hand automatically goes to my pocket so I can pull out my phone. "I'll talk to him about it. Hopefully tomorrow."

That seems to satisfy her, but when I look up at her, her eyes are still filled with what has to be concern. I force a smile and then hold up my phone. "Uh, can I meet you inside? I just want to send him another text, and I don't want to make Grandma and Grandpa wait."

She nods and then reaches over and ruffles my hair. "I love you."

"Love you, too, Mom."

After she leaves, I unlock the screen on my phone and open up my text messaging app. And my stupid heart skips a beat.

*Nico (6:21 p.m.):* Hey. Eat a shrimp for me. You owe me.

I laugh and shake my head, and my heart does it again as I grin and type back a quick response.

*Alex (6:27 p.m.):* ew never

He responds almost immediately this time, but it's just a series of silly emojis, followed by "Have fun. Tell your mom and grand-parents I said hi. Text me later."

I send a thumbs-up emoji back. Then I close my eyes for a count of five before I stuff my phone in my pocket, climb out of the car, lock the doors, and jog into the restaurant to meet up with my family.

# chapter five

*nico*

THE HUM OF THE ceiling fan in my room *should* help me sleep. That's what everyone's always told me—it's white noise or whatever. But it's never really helped. Very, very few things have ever really helped.

So, like I always have, I pretend. I close my eyes and curl up in my bed with my comforter pulled up past my shoulders and my back to the door, and I lie there quietly, breathing slowly and rhythmically, hoping I'll be able to drift off.

But I've been lying here for hours now. *Hours.* And every time I think I'm about to *finally* fall asleep, a fucking noise comes from the direction of my mom's room down the hallway.

*He's* here.

She probably thinks I don't know since she probably thinks I'm asleep and that I've been asleep for a while. But I hear them talking. My mom giggling. Him laughing. Her shushing him. Then other sounds that make my stomach knot up and bile rise in my throat.

As if today hadn't been fucking awful enough.

The third time I hear a thud against the wall connecting my room to hers, I can't take it anymore. Silently, I turn over, grab my phone from the nightstand, and push myself up off the bed. Then I slip on my socks and shoes, stuff my phone into the pocket of my pajama pants, and tiptoe out down the hallway.

A moment later, I'm outside, and I suck in a deep breath. My heart's racing, though I hadn't noticed it before. And I need *out of here.*

Of course, my car keys are still in the pocket of my jeans, which are on the floor in my room. And there's no fucking way I'm going back in the house now. Not knowing that that asshole is here. So I guess I'm walking.

The moon's not out, and there's no light to see by. But I don't need any light to know where I'm going.

I start off down the driveway, ignoring how much my hands are shaking as I pull my phone out. Alex apparently sent me a text message about two hours ago, and I swallow hard and then click to read it.

*Alex (11:04 p.m.):* i ate a shrimp. it was disgusting. never again. not even for u

I should laugh. It's funny as shit, after all, especially when I picture his face, grimacing in disgust as he chews. But I don't laugh. My stomach is still in knots, and I'm fighting against the nausea in my gut and the tension in my jaw.

Fucking asshole Patrick. What the fuck is he doing back with my mom? And why is she allowing it?

Tears sting my eyes as memories spanning almost the last decade jump at me. I want to scream out loud to try and push them away, but they come anyway, and there's nothing I can do about it. It happened so gradually, I don't blame my mom for missing it early on—Patrick's voice becoming harsher when he talked to me, then the slow buildup of physical stuff. Rough touches, like a sharp grab of my arm or shoulder, turned worse until it wasn't uncommon for him to hold me so hard he gave me bruises. He dragged me around by the hair more than once, yelling and cursing, and the time he shoved me up against the wall and punched a hole right next to my head should have been the last straw. But it wasn't until the day he actually hit me—a closed fist to my face and the first and only time I ever broke a bone—that my mom finally kicked him out.

That was four years ago. She told me "never again" when it happened. Hell, she had the divorce papers delivered to him at Omaha Correctional Center while he was serving his sentence for assaulting me. So I believed her.

I'm a fucking moron, I guess.

I clench my jaw and try harder to push all that stuff away, and I focus on my phone again as I turn from the driveway onto the main road.

*Nico (1:11 a.m.):* You home?

Please. Please respond.

*Alex (1:12 a.m.):* yeah

*Alex (1:12 a.m.):* whats up

The relief is instantaneous, and I stop, my shoes scuffing into the dirt along the shoulder of the road, as I close my eyes for a count of three. When I open my eyes again, my hands are shaking so badly I can barely text my response back.

> *Nico (1:13 a.m.):* Can I come over?

> *Alex (1:13 a.m.):* ofc

> *Alex (1:13 a.m.):* r u ok?

I stare at his texts for several seconds, the part of my brain that wants everything to be "normal" right now begging for me to tease him about his awful texting shorthand. But the question itself is too distracting, because the honest answer is a resounding *fuck no*.

So, rather than answering or teasing him, I stuff my phone back in my pocket, tuck my hands under my arms, and continue walking down the side of the road.

Alex and his mom live in the first of a row of houses along a little side street set back from the main road that runs through town. There's a single street lamp illuminating the corner, but it's still pretty dark, and as I turn onto his street and step up onto the sidewalk about twenty minutes later, I see a dim light coming from his bedroom window on the second floor. The porch light is also on.

Something about that eases the heavy dread that's been building in my chest on the walk from my house.

He opens the front door just as I reach the porch, like he's been waiting for me to arrive, and though I can see the questions and concern in his eyes, he ushers me inside without a word and then closes the door quietly behind me. I follow him upstairs and into his bedroom, and it's not until we're alone in his room that I finally let out a long, shuddering breath.

I won't cry, I tell myself. I'm not twelve anymore. I'm fucking eighteen years old. But hell if that resolve doesn't crumble the second his arms come around me and he pulls me up against him.

"What's going on? Are you okay?"

I just shake my head because no words will come right now, and I let myself relax into him. He murmurs something against the top of my head, and his arms tighten around me. It feels safe here, like I'm protected from everything.

And it's only because it's him. Alex. He's the only one who can touch me like this. The only one who can really touch me at all, actually. It's been this way for years, and Patrick is the whole reason why.

"Goddammit." The curse slips out as my arms come around Alex's waist.

Somehow, he knows.

He knows not to ask more right now and that I'm one wrong word away from falling apart. So he just hugs me and doesn't say anything for a bit, and when I finally pull away a few minutes later, he still doesn't question me. He just steps back and heads over to the closet and starts pulling down some extra pillows and blankets. Then he makes up a place for me to sleep on the floor next to his bed. Just like we used to do.

When he's done, he turns toward me, his eyes still full of worry. He looks ready to say something, but I shake my head and look down at the ground.

"Don't ask," I insist. "Please."

I'll tell him later. Tomorrow maybe. Or maybe he doesn't even need to fucking know.

He's leaving for college in a few months anyway. If I tell him, he'll just worry more. And I'd hate it if that made him decide *not* to go. Even though I absolutely hate the fact that he's leaving.

"Okay. Um . . ." His bed squeaks, and I look up. He's sitting on the edge of the bed, staring at his hands, which are clasped together in his lap. "So, um, you take the bed, and I'll sleep on the floor, and then tomorrow—"

"No, I can't take the bed."

"Don't argue," he says, glancing up at me with a smirk. "I ate a shrimp for you, so now *you* owe *me*."

Maybe it's because it's well past one in the morning after a long-ass day and my brain is already broken. Or maybe it's my emotional state. I don't know. But I can't connect the dots right away, and I just stare at him for several long seconds with what I know has to be a stupid expression on my face.

His smirk fades, and he blinks and looks down, biting at his lower lip. "I'm joking, of course. I just want you to be comfortable. I can sleep anywhere, you know that. But if you're having trouble sleeping, you'll be more comfortable on the bed. So, please take the bed."

We're usually not this awkward. Of course, I don't usually show up in the middle of the night asking to stay over with no explanation. But there's something else, too. Something in the way Alex is watching me. Something different in his eyes.

And in any case, I have no more energy and no more ability to argue. And I have been having trouble sleeping. And I *will* sleep better on the bed.

So I nod and drop my chin down to my chest again. "Yeah, okay. Thanks," I manage.

Alex pushes himself off the bed and heads over to his desk, where he starts rummaging through a drawer. A few seconds later, he's back, and he plugs an extra cell phone charger into the outlet right behind his nightstand. Because he's thoughtful like that. He plugs his phone into the other charger and sets it face down. Then he switches off the lamp on the nightstand, leaving only a few thin rays of light peeking in through the shutters, and he lowers himself to the floor with an exaggerated groan.

"It's been a day, huh?" he says, pulling the blanket over himself as he lies down.

I give a stiff nod and then slip my shoes off and climb into his bed. It's soft and warm. And it smells like him. Sort of woodsy and clean and masculine.

I turn over onto my side facing him and tug the dark-blue comforter all the way up to my chin. Then I take a long, deep breath. The exhale shudders, but for a different reason than it had earlier. And when I close my eyes this time, I don't feel that overpowering unease. It's the opposite, actually. I feel safe again. Safe and comfortable and all the things Alex always makes me feel.

"Thank you," I whisper into the dark.

I hear a quiet huff, followed by Alex's voice, which sounds softer than usual. "Good night, Nico."

# chapter six

## alex

MOM IS UP AND gone by the time I head downstairs in the morning. She's meeting with her framer in Lincoln to talk about her current commission, and then she has a client meeting in Omaha in the afternoon. I love my mom, but I'm secretly happy she's not home so I won't have to explain why Nico showed up on our doorstep at nearly one thirty in the morning, looking worse than I've seen him look in a long time.

Actually, I still don't even know why he's here. It had to have been bad for him to come over so late.

And, given the conversation I had with my mom yesterday—what I didn't really admit but sort of did—having Nico sleeping over in my room, even though nothing happened, might look a little sus. Nico definitely doesn't need my meddling mom to be interrogating him right now.

What he *will* need, though, when he eventually wakes up, is coffee and food. And those things are easy. I can do coffee. And we've got pancake mix and eggs.

So I shuffle around the kitchen, taking my time as I cook up breakfast. Then I plate everything, drenching his pancakes *and* scrambled eggs in syrup, just how he likes it, and I arrange our plates and coffees on a big tray and head back upstairs.

It's probably after nine now, but he's still out cold when I push the door open with my foot, balancing the tray carefully to make sure nothing spills. I pause in the doorway, and my heart skips a beat.

*He's asleep in my bed.*

Not that it means anything, other than the fact that he was too exhausted to argue with me last night.

But the sight of him there, tucked away under my comforter, relaxed and sleeping, with his head resting on my pillow—it does something to me.

I tear my eyes away, because I shouldn't be staring at him, and I cough lightly to clear my throat as I step into the room. He stirs, blinking his eyes open with a quiet groan, and I smile.

"Good morning, sleepyhead," I tease as I set the tray on my desk.

He groans and tugs the pillow up over his head. "Too early."

"That's why I brought coffee. And pancakes and eggs."

"Syrup?"

"A ridiculously excessive amount, just for you."

He groans again but pushes the pillow off his face, and my stomach drops as he turns his head to look at me. His cheeks are sunken, and his skin is pale, contrasting with the dark circles under his eyes.

Just how long has he been having trouble sleeping? And why does he look like he hasn't eaten in days?

I force a small smile and tilt my head toward the food. "You want?"

He hesitates, his eyes shifting to the tray on my desk. Then he bites his lip and pushes himself up to sit cross-legged. "Um, yeah. Thanks."

It feels like a win, even if it's just a small one.

I bring the whole tray over, and we both scoot back on the bed until our backs are against the wall. He laughs lightly as he picks up his plate.

"Barely enough syrup."

"Barely enough?" I fake-scoff, knowing he's joking. "There's more syrup on the plate than real food."

"Syrup *is* a real food," he argues as he cuts off a piece of one of the pancakes. He brings the plate up to his chin to keep himself from spilling, and he takes a bite, syrup dripping off the pancake. It's funny, and I laugh.

"Whatever," I say.

He turns his head toward me with a silly grin and sort of rolls his eyes before taking another bite. And just like that, my heart soars.

This is us. This has been us for a while now.

As soon as I think that thought, though, reality hits, and it's sobering as hell. I look back at my own plate, but my appetite is gone, even if I haven't yet eaten a single bite.

How much longer do we have? My brain automatically does the numbers and spits the answer back out: just over one hundred days. We have just over one hundred more days of this.

Unless I can convince him to come to California with me.

I force myself to eat, if only so he doesn't notice the look of existential dread that must have crossed my face. And the silence persists for a few minutes. It's not uncomfortable, thankfully, and I feel something like relief when he eats everything I've put on the plate and drinks his whole coffee.

I'm slower to eat than him, but that in itself isn't unusual. By the time I've finished, he's leaning back against the wall, his eyes closed lightly as he cradles his now-empty coffee mug in his hands.

I should say something about California. Start the conversation again, especially now that I'm armed with all the information from my mom's impromptu planning session in the car the night before. But there's still a funny feeling tickling the back of my mind, telling me now's not quite the right time. So I try something else instead.

"Wanna head out to the river today?" I ask as casually as I can. "The weather's supposed to be good, I think."

Platte River is just a couple of miles east of town, and even back before Nico got given his mom's old car when he turned sixteen, we used to walk or bike out there a lot, especially in the summer. There's a spot we found that's sort of "ours"—a small, sandy beach just about a quarter of a mile from the road, sheltered by a thick stand of trees—and despite the crowds of people that head out to the river every summer, our spot is hidden just enough that we're always the only ones there. That seems to suit Nico quite well.

I watch him, waiting for his answer, but he just opens his eyes to stare down at his mug, and his fingers begin tapping anxiously on the ceramic. Now the silence *is* uncomfortable, especially when he shakes his head and frowns but still doesn't answer.

"Oh. Alright. Did you have something else in mind? I don't have any plans, and—"

"I should go," he cuts in, though he doesn't move from his spot on my bed.

Confused, I shift to face him, sitting cross-legged, and he finally looks up at me. There's a sadness in his eyes that I can't stand, and it's the same as what I saw last night, when he let me hug him. I swallow back all the discomfort and emotions swirling around in my chest, and this time, it's me shaking my head.

"Don't go. Whatever it is, we can talk about it. Here, or at the river, or hell, wherever you want. Or we don't have to talk at all. That's fine, too. But don't go. Please."

His expression tightens, and he drops his eyes back to his hands. With a sudden flash of fear—fear that he's pulling away from me, even though the summer's not even really started yet—I scoot closer, part of my brain arguing that maybe I should just tell him how I feel. But that seems like an awful idea when I let myself think about it more, at least right now, in this heavy moment that's being held together by a thread.

His long, slender fingers wrap tighter around the mug, and he closes his eyes again, his lips pursed in a frown. The muscles in his jaw tremble. And I can't stand it.

I set my coffee and plate back on the tray next to his plate, then carefully reach over and take his mug from him. I move the entire tray to the floor next to the bed, and when everything's cleared off, I scoot back onto the bed, shimmying over until I'm next to him, our shoulders just barely touching.

Do friends do this? I don't really know. I don't do this with anyone besides him. So maybe the answer is no.

Still, I only hesitate when he flinches slightly as my arm comes up around his shoulders. "Nico?"

His body shakes, and he lets out some quiet sound—some uncertain, uneasy whimper—and leans into me.

He could have moved away. He could have jumped up from the bed, repeated his earlier "I should go," and left. But he didn't. He chose to lean on me instead.

That has to mean something.

I shut my eyes and squeeze his shoulder gently, and I take a long, slow breath. He'll talk when he's ready. I know this. Yet, I still have to hold myself back from asking him what happened last night. I let myself be distracted by his closeness, by the warmth of his body next to mine, by the feel of his curly hair brushing against my cheek.

We stay there like that for minutes. Or, at least, it seems like minutes. My brain is jumping all over the place, wondering what he's thinking, what he's feeling. I relish the closeness, but then there's also this overwhelming sadness in my heart because he's obviously hurting. I want to hug him, like he let me last night.

And I find myself wishing, yet again, that I could tell him how much he means to me.

God, what the hell is holding me back?

His shaking finally calms, and his body relaxes a little. And just as I'm about to say something, he slowly straightens up and scoots away. The space between us is only a few inches, but it feels much greater for some reason.

"Thanks," Nico says, and he crosses his arms over his chest like he's protecting himself from something. He seems to try to speak, but his mouth just closes again before any words come.

I watch him, waiting, but it's hard to see him struggle with whatever's on his mind. I'm no stranger to this mood of his—he tends to do exactly this when things get difficult. He gets quiet, brooding. He pulls away. He doesn't text back. He isolates, even more than normal.

But he *did* come here last night. He came to me rather than stay at home by himself.

Dammit. What happened?

"I have to go home, but I . . ." He shakes his head and closes his eyes. "My mom had s-someone over last night. I couldn't stand, uh, hearing them," he explains, though I can tell he's still holding something back.

I wish I knew what to say, but all that comes out of my mouth is "Oh, Yuck."

He doesn't laugh, and he seems to clench his jaw as he nods. "Yeah. I don't know if the . . . if the guy is still there."

"I'll come with you." It seems like the very least I can do. But Nico immediately rejects my suggestion.

"No. That's not a good idea. I don't—" He shuts his mouth and stops talking suddenly, almost as though he'd been slapped in the face, and my stomach drops. Pushing himself forward, Nico starts over. "I'll be fine. I'll just go. Thanks for the food and stuff."

He stands up, careful to not step on the tray sitting next to the bed, and he gathers his phone and then puts his shoes on.

I want to hop up after him, pull him back into another hug, tell him that whatever's bothering him—whatever's *really* bothering him—we can figure it out. But I can see him starting to spiral. The tension in his shoulders is growing, and his jaw is clenched again. When he stands back up after putting his shoes on, his hands have balled up into fists, which he holds tight against his sides.

I don't want him leaving like this.

I've never really known what to do or how to handle him when he starts to get upset. It always seems best just to let him go so he can calm down, because he always does. But this time, something's different. I don't know what it is, but I *do* know I can't let him leave.

So I shake my head and jump up after him as he turns toward the door. "Nico, wait. Please."

He stops, his shoulders slumped over so he looks even smaller than he is. "What?" he says, the sharpness of his tone halting me in my tracks.

Maybe I *should* just let him go. That's what he wants, after all. But as soon as I have the thought, I know it's wrong. I can't just let him go this time.

"I'm coming with you," I say with much more confidence than I feel, and before he can reply, I turn and head over to my dresser. "Give me a minute."

To my surprise, he doesn't move while I sift through the middle drawer to find a pair of comfortable sweats, tug them on, and then slip on a clean pair of socks and my tennis shoes. I grab my cell phone and stuff it in my pocket, and then I step ahead of him and pull the bedroom door open the rest of the way.

It's only then that I see his face. Tears escape from the corners of his eyes, although he's trying to blink them back, and his cheeks are tinged red.

"Y-you should stay here, Alex," he says quietly, all of the anger gone from his voice now.

I shake my head. "Not unless you're staying too."

There's a moment of hesitation. Then his fists loosen, and he turns his head to look at me.

"Can we just hang out here, then? Watch movies or something? I don't want to . . . go out."

"Yeah. Of course. Whatever you want."

He almost looks like he's going to laugh, but he doesn't, and instead, he nods and turns back to the bed. Without a word, he starts straightening the blanket and pillows. After a second where I allow myself to breathe, I head over to help.

# chapter seven

## *nico*

*Mom (6:15 p.m.):* Where are you?

*Mom (7:33 p.m.):* I made dinner

*Mom (7:59 p.m.):* I called twice with no answer. Did I raise you to be this rude? Really?

*Mom (9:21 p.m.):* It's late. Where the hell are you?

"Bro, your mom's calling *me*. Should I—"

"Don't answer," I cut in, and I sigh and unlock my phone. "She's been texting me all night, and I just . . ."

I shake my head, not wanting to elaborate, and I open up my text messaging app as Alex settles back on the couch opposite me with another bowl of popcorn. It's our third so far today.

*Nico (9:45 p.m.):* I'm at Alex's. Staying here tonight.

Maybe I should also tell her I'm not sure when I'm coming home because the walls of the house are much too thin and I can't really sleep while I can hear her fucking her abusive ex-husband in the room next to mine. Maybe she should know that I know. Maybe that would make her think twice about the choice she made to let him back into her life.

But I don't have the energy for it, and I've barely been holding myself together all day. And really, I don't want to think about it anymore.

So instead, I hit send on the text, power down my phone so I don't get any more notifications, and then shove the phone back into my pocket. I know I can't stay away forever, of course. I start work at the library on Monday, which is terrifying enough, and I don't have any clothes or my wallet or my car keys. Alex let me borrow a toothbrush this morning, but I'm still wearing my pajamas from the night before and I'll definitely need to shave by Monday morning.

Alex has been great, which isn't surprising—he's always great. But he's been even more considerate than usual today, like he knows there's more to the story of why I'm here than I told him this morning. It sort of makes me feel like the fucking asshole that I am, knowing that I'm not being totally honest with him. Yet I can't bring myself to start up a conversation about it.

It's not that I haven't had time, either. We did a whole lot of nothing *all* day. We watched movies, ordered a pizza for lunch, played video games and watched more movies, did a little yard work, which he apparently promised his mom he'd get done. We talked about stupid shit, like the next *Hollow Knight* game that's supposed to be coming out later in the year and the way the neighbor's dog barking sounds like it's an old man with a sore throat. He also told me about the place they had dinner the night before with his grandparents and attempted to describe how awful the shrimp he ate was. And when his mom got home and started to ask me how I was doing, he cut in and turned the conversation to her and her day, like he knew that I didn't want to have to lie.

Because I'm still not doing very fucking well.

And I still haven't even told him the *real* reason I came over last night or why I'm still here or why I need to stay again. But he obviously knows something's up, and he knows I don't want to talk about it.

Alex sets the bowl of popcorn between us and starts scrolling through the movie listings on his mom's Netflix account. We both nope right over a few that look too intense, and even Alex doesn't seem in the mood for some new mainstream horror flick, which surprises me. Instead, he stops on a documentary of all things.

"Oh, I wanted to watch this!" he blurts out, sitting up and motioning enthusiastically at the TV. He glances at me and then laughs when he sees my face. "Uh, I mean, what do you think? Too boring?"

It's a documentary on the James Webb Space Telescope, which launched a few years back. I only know that because Alex talked about it nonstop for weeks before the launch and made me sit with him to watch all the news coverage of the actual launch. Every time NASA publishes new images sent from the telescope, he's like a little kid again—bouncing up and down and talking about it for days. It's fucking adorable, though I've never told him that, of course.

"Looks interesting. I'm game," I say, and his eyes widen a bit in surprise.

"Really?"

"Yeah."

It won't be too boring, especially because I know it's something he's very interested in, although I'd probably normally tease him for it. Maybe that's where his surprise is coming from.

"Okay, sweet. Thanks," he says, and he clicks a button on the remote to start the documentary.

He's literally sitting on the edge of his seat for at least the first ten minutes, his eyes still wide and his hands perched on either side of him on the couch. Each time I glance over at him, his mouth is open slightly in awe, the wonder on his face clear and beautiful. I find myself watching him more than the TV.

About halfway through the documentary, after he's finally settled back against the couch, he turns to me and says, "You good still?"

I only nod, and then he grins broadly, brightening up the room as only he can.

"Great!" His smile doesn't fade as he looks back at the TV, and instead, he scoots closer to me, moving the now-empty popcorn bowl to the coffee table, and rests his arm along the back of the couch.

It would be weird, right? To move over and settle in that spot I was in earlier on his bed, with his arm around my shoulders? My chest tightens in an uncomfortable way, sort of. Maybe it's not so much uncomfortable as yearningly.

It felt good—to be held like that. Good, safe, protected. And I want that feeling again.

It's sort of dumb of me, I know. Friends don't cuddle. He only held me earlier because I needed the comfort. Now isn't the same. Yet I start to move anyway, telling myself it's okay to seek comfort in my friend. It's not anything related to my feelings for him, after all. Totally not.

I shift over a few inches, then a few more, until he tenses up with a sharp inhale. A harsh, rough wave of unease courses through me, and I freeze.

Yeah, this was an awful idea. Of course he's uncomfortable with it. Leave it to me to fuck up such a decent day.

Screwing my eyes shut, I immediately push myself up off the couch and stand. "I'm gonna go now," I mumble. I try to say more—at least something to thank him for letting me stay over—but there's a nausea rolling through my stomach, and I think I might vomit if I stick around much longer. And anyway, the buzz of anger is starting to tingle under my skin, which is exactly what I don't want to happen right now.

"What? Why?" he asks.

I hear the TV click off, the documentary going silent, and there's only the quiet hum of some classical music from his mom's art studio in the garage. I feel him stand up behind me, and my chest tightens. I want to lean back into him, ask him to wrap his arms around me. It's fucking frustrating, because I can't let myself do it.

But then his hand sets gently on my upper back, and the negative energy that had been building up seeps out of me.

God, I'm so fucking tired.

"Nico . . . um, I thought you were staying over again? It's late. You shouldn't go home now . . . ?"

The end of his sentence stalls out, like there was a question to it he couldn't quite finish. His hand feels heavy on my back now. Heavy but protective. Just like I wanted.

He'll let me lean on him again, won't he? If I turn around now, he'll hold me. He'll hug me. He'll let me cry against his chest. He'll listen if I tell him who was really over at my mom's house last night. He'll make up a bed on the floor again, and maybe this time, he'll even let me sleep there instead of insisting I take his bed.

Fuck. What I *really* want is for him to hold me while I sleep.

But I know that's not going to happen.

His hand rubs back and forth along my shoulders, and with a shudder, I let out a long, slow breath, my chin dropping down to my chest.

"Stay," Alex says, his voice soft now, like he knows I'm seriously considering it. "I've got pajamas you can borrow, and you can take the bed again. My mom doesn't mind you being here, really. And tomorrow's Sunday. She makes blueberry pancakes on Sundays."

I know this already. He knows I know. So I laugh and shake my head. "Bribing me with food? You really want me to stay that much?"

His hand settles, no longer moving, and he says quietly, "I just want you to be comfortable. You, uh, slept so well last night. I want whatever's best for you."

"And you think it's not best for me to go home?" I hear the edge in my own voice, as though I'm daring him to argue. I can't help it.

He doesn't back off, though. If anything, his hand presses into me just a little more, and it chases away some of the hurt rising up in me.

"I don't really know," he admits slowly. And how could he? I didn't tell him the truth. He takes a deep breath and continues. "But I got the impression you didn't want to go home. You're more than welcome to stay here. Anytime."

The tightness in my chest loosens, and even though I don't know what to say or do, that's suddenly okay. I let myself lean back a tiny bit, and he's there, his hand strong and solid, supporting me.

He moves closer.

Anyone else, and I'd be in a panic right now. Anyone other than him, I'd be shaking, dizzy, *out of here*. Anyone else.

But he's so close now that I can feel the warmth of his breath when he sighs. And I want him even closer. I lean back a tiny bit more, and I close my eyes.

"You take the bed tonight and I'll stay." My suggestion—my *negotiation*—seems weak, but it's the best I can do. It's true that I absolutely do not want to go home right now, and I really should tell him exactly why. Maybe I will. Later.

His hand drops away from my back, sending a chill through me, but then there's a soft huff, like he's laughing. "Deal," he says, amusement in his voice.

I love the sound.

Then he's moving, gathering up the popcorn bowl from the coffee table and our half-empty glasses of watery orange juice, the ice having melted long ago.

"Come on," he says, tilting his head toward the kitchen. "Help me with the dishes, then we'll head upstairs. My mom'll be happy if she doesn't have to clean up the kitchen when she's done painting for the night."

"Yeah, sure."

He gives me a smile, and his eyes linger on mine. His gaze is warm, as it always is, and I wonder what the hell I've done to deserve him as my best friend. He puts up with so much from me.

And now he's putting up with this, too—me staying here, uninvited. He seems to want me here. Like he's happy to have me.

I look away first and clear my throat, and he laughs lightly, though it almost sounds forced. He starts toward the kitchen, and I follow.

It's not until we're at the sink, starting to wash the dishes, that he finally breaks the silence with another laugh. Then he starts talking. "Bro, so, listen to this. I meant to tell you last week, and then with graduation and everything, I just spaced out. The painting my mom's doing right now, you won't believe it, it's for this client she has in California. He's some famous baseball player or something. Anyway, he's paying her, I dunno, thousands of dollars or something to paint a leaf!"

"A . . . leaf?"

"Yeah. Maybe we can peek in there later so you can see. Seriously, though, it's just a leaf! I mean, it's a freaking neat leaf with all this insane amount of detail, but still . . ."

He washes, I dry and put away, and all the while, he talks, describing this painting his mom is doing. And when he's exhausted that topic, he talks about something else for a while. It's comfortable, and it feels good.

And I'm so grateful for him that I might not even argue if he tries to make me take the bed after all when we finally go up to his room for the night.

# chapter eight

## alex

Monday mornings during senior year were the absolute worst. Our econ teacher, Mr. Replogle, had a penchant for giving us pop quizzes or making us read current political news—what a total shitshow—first thing in the morning every Monday.

But now that it's summer, I expect my relationship with Monday mornings will be much less shaky. I'm not working, except to help my mom when she needs it, so Monday mornings should just be like every other morning. Hell, I don't even have an alarm set anymore since I have nowhere to be and nothing to do.

I've rather conveniently forgotten that the same is not true for Nico, however. As the first Monday morning of the summer rolls around, Nico, who's been staying at my house all weekend, seems to have almost worked himself into a panic. It can't be later than six in the morning when he tumbles out of bed and nearly steps on me as he rushes out of the room and down the hallway, presumably to the bathroom.

By the time I roll over and push myself up into a sitting position several minutes later, he's back, looking pale and nauseous. He doesn't say anything as he crawls back into my bed and buries himself under the covers, but I get a whiff of a faint minty smell, like my toothpaste.

I decide not to ask if he's okay, since he's clearly not, and instead, I rub the sleep from my eyes and then reach up behind me and grab my phone. Six oh three. Way too early still.

"What time do you have to be at the library?" I ask. My brain isn't fully functional yet, and I vaguely remember him saying nine. But it could be earlier.

He tugs the blanket down under his chin, and his hair falls in messy curls over his forehead as his eyes meet mine. He looks like he might throw up. Or throw up *again*, since I'm fairly sure that was what just happened in the bathroom.

"Eight fifteen," he says, his voice scratchy.

I frown. "Oh. Okay. So then—"

"Eight thirty, actually, but I don't want to be late. So, eight fifteen."

"Ah, right. Do you want—"

"I need to go home to get clothes and my wallet and my car." He shakes his head and turns to look up at the ceiling, reaching up to brush his hair back from his forehead with a shaky hand. "Sorry," he whispers, and this time, there's clear shame in his voice.

I hate that. Or actually, it just makes me sad to hear because he knows it's okay. We've been there, done that enough times before. His anxiety makes him blurt things out, interrupt when other people are talking. And I can see how anxious he is now; he definitely doesn't need to apologize for it. Only, I'm not sure whether he's so anxious because he has to go home, which he's been avoiding for days now, or because he's not sure what the day is going to be like, starting his summer job.

It's probably both.

"I'll come with you," I promise, and I watch as his jaw ticks and his eyes close.

I one hundred percent expect him to say no, to tell me I should stay home and that he'll be fine. But instead, he gives the smallest nod. It's both a relief and a surprise.

I'm still barely awake, but I drag myself up anyway, take a few minutes in the bathroom, and then head downstairs to make coffee and toast up some bagels. I didn't ask him if he wanted anything to eat, and I'm not surprised when he comes downstairs about ten minutes later, takes one look at the bagel I made him, and then spins around and sprints back up the stairs to the bathroom.

By the time he comes back down fifteen minutes or so later, again bringing that faint whiff of minty toothpaste with him, I've eaten my own bagel and wrapped his up in a paper bag.

"Here," I say, offering the bag to him, "so you can eat it later, if you're feeling up to it."

He hesitates, his shoulders slumped, but then reaches out and takes the bag. "Thanks. I, um, can walk home. Alone. It's fine. I don't want you to have to . . ." He sighs as he trails off, and he looks up at me, frowning.

I can see him fighting himself right now—fighting against his awful anxiety—and I shake my head gently, doing the best I can to counter his frown with a small smile.

"It's cool, I don't mind," I say. Again, I expect an argument, another *no*, another *it's fine*. Given his level of anxiety, I also expect that familiar flicker of anger to start building in him. But he just stares at me for a second, the pain in his eyes tugging right at my heart, and then, he nods.

"Okay."

I let myself smile more, and then I pat him on the shoulder. "Give me five minutes to change."

"Yeah, sure." He sits at the table and picks up the coffee I made him, and I turn and jog up the stairs.

Thankfully, he's still there when I return less than five minutes later. I scribble a quick note for my mom to let her know where I am in case she's up early—we're weird like that and still leave each other handwritten notes rather than texting whenever we can—and he dumps out the rest of his coffee, grabs the bag with his bagel in it, and leads the way toward the front door.

It's already warm out, hinting at the heat wave I think we're supposed to be having this whole week, and it feels great. I follow Nico out of the house and down the sidewalk to the main road, and as we turn right, hugging the shoulder, I tilt my head back and let the sun warm my face.

Next to me, Nico is quiet, but his shoulders have loosened a bit, and the silence doesn't seem too tense. However, the closer we get to his house, the more I notice the tightness creeping back in. When we reach the end of his driveway, he stops and just stares down the long dirt road toward his house, his jaw clenched and his expression hard. I follow his gaze, confused, and then I see it—an old, light-blue pickup truck parked just next to Nico's car in front of the house.

A sharp pain lances through my chest. "Nico, what the—"

"So you see it, too, right?" Nico spins around, away from the house, shrinking in on himself. "Fucking hell, he's still here. He's still here." He drops into a crouch, the bag with his breakfast bagel falling to the ground and his head suddenly down between his knees as he takes several fast, shallow breaths. I'm pretty sure he's going to throw up again.

I kneel down next to him and don't even think twice before my arm goes up around his shoulders. Tension radiates off him, and I squeeze him gently. "Breathe. Deep, slow breaths."

"I can't take slow fuckin' breaths," he hisses. "Dammit. Dammit, I—I can't—I can't believe he's still here. Fuck!" He smashes a fist into the hard ground, then growls a few more choice curse words. And he's shaking. Badly. And still barely breathing.

I stand slowly, pulling him up with me, and then I hold him tightly to me. He doesn't fight it, and instead, his arms loop around my waist, and he clings to me, burying his head in my chest.

"Fuck," he says again, his voice muffled and raw.

A million questions come to my mind, but he's so upset right now that I'm scared to ask even the most obvious one. I have to, though, because I feel like I really need to know. Bracing myself for his backlash, I say, "Since when?"

"Friday night," he mumbles against me.

That explains a whole lot, especially why he showed up at my house at one thirty in the morning, looking like he'd been through the wringer. I hug him a little tighter, though I'm not sure what else to say right then, and so we just stand there for a few more minutes. When he eventually pulls away, he wipes his cheeks. His face is red, his eyes are puffy, and his shoulders are still tense. He keeps his back to the house and crosses his arms over his chest.

"I'll go," I say, without really thinking it through. "I'll grab your stuff, and then we can go back to my house so you can get changed. What all do you need? Your wallet, your—"

"No."

"Nico."

"Alex," he retorts, and he glances up at me very briefly before turning back around toward the house. He bites his lower lip. "W-wait here for me?"

I shake my head. "Let me come with you."

"No."

He starts to walk, stiffly but with purpose, and I follow him. Like hell I'm waiting here. He drops his chin but doesn't stop walking.

"Please stay here," he says, the rough words simmering with whatever anger is building in him.

"I'm not going to let him hurt you again. Not even a chance. I'm coming with you." I frown. "Please, Nico. I don't want you to go alone."

He stops and closes his eyes, and his hands fall to his sides and ball up into fists. Suddenly, he looks twelve again, about to pull away from me as he had in the beginning, when that asshole first started hurting him. He didn't really keep anything from me, though we also didn't talk about it too much. But as the bruises gradually got worse, so did his fear and anxiety and depression. He got quieter, and then, after that bastard Patrick finally hit Nico in the face and broke his nose, Nico started to have strong reactions to anyone touching him. His anxiety morphed, making him prone to irritability and anger. And his *social* anxiety ballooned into something almost unmanageable.

He seemed to only find solace in being alone, or in being alone *with me*. He let me hug him, comfort him.

He trusted me then. And I need him to trust me now, too.

"Come on," I say quietly, and I start walking, slowly, to give him a chance to catch up. His feet stutter a little as he gets moving, and then he's silent as we make our way up the driveway, our shoes kicking up dust.

The small one-story home has seen better days. I haven't been here in a while, but it looks rougher than I remember. The siding is faded, its medium-brown paint peeling, and one of the windows has a long crack in the glass, stretching all the way from the top right corner to the lower left. The fascia along the lower edge of the roof is rotted, and the gutter at the near side of the house has come loose, drooping down to show an overflow of dead leaves and other junk. And the garden under the front windows is full of dry weeds and a single dead rosebush.

I remember planting that rosebush with Nico as a present to his mom when we were ten. He saved up his allowance for months to buy it for her. She loved it.

And it was shortly after that when Patrick started coming around.

I swallow hard and glance over at Nico. He's staring at the ground, his expression still hardened and angry and scared. I step a little closer to him.

"In and out, okay?"

He nods. Then he blinks, long and slow. "I need clothes. And my wallet and keys. A-and maybe . . ." He shakes his head and then moves ahead of me, taking the porch steps two at a time.

I follow, unsure of what we're about to encounter but certain we're going to get through it together.

# chapter nine

## *nico*

PLEASE.

Please let them be sleeping.

Please let us get in and out without waking anyone.

Please, *for fuck's sake*, don't make me face him.

I pause in front of the door, Alex right behind me. I don't even know what I'm feeling or how to deal with any of it. I'm shaking and sick and angry and terrified. Mostly terrified. And I want to turn and run. Get as far away as I can.

But I can't do that. At least not yet.

Alex moves up even closer, his body nearly touching mine, and I feel his warmth. How he gives me so much strength and courage, how just his presence makes me feel safer, I'm not even sure. But I can't deny that I'm secretly glad he insisted on coming, despite the dark pit of shame in my stomach.

"I'm not going to let anything hurt you," he says quietly, as though he knows I need to hear it. Then, because he's just the best person ever, he adds, "Fuck him."

I almost laugh at the curse; I could probably count on one hand how many times I've heard Alex say the f-word. But the situation definitely calls for it. I turn my head and glance over my shoulder at him, and he shrugs with a half smile. Then he gets serious again.

"Ready?"

I nod, even though the answer's a definite *no*, and I reach out and turn the doorknob. My mom never locks up at night—small town, secluded house well off the main road, and all that—and I'm thankful for that right now as the door opens with only its usual squeak.

All the lights are off, and it's silent—two more points in our favor. I step inside ahead of Alex, and he follows right behind me, shutting the door quietly.

I've lived here my whole life, and yet, right now, the house feels completely unfamiliar. It's not. Not really, anyway. Nothing has really changed, except that the kitchen table is a mess, the sink is full of unwashed dishes, and there are empty beer bottles on the counter and coffee table. There's also a staleness in the air, a thick heaviness that stops me from moving.

"Come on, let's go," Alex whispers, and then—*god*—his hand sets low on my back. My heart skips a beat or maybe two, and when he presses into me with a gentle encouragement, heat rushes through me, fast and strong. It's a good distraction. A *very* good distraction.

I nod and blink back the feeling that I shouldn't be here, in my own home, and I get my feet to move. My room is right at the beginning of the hallway—another point for us, since we don't have to walk past Mom's room to get to mine. The door's open, even though I know I left it closed on Friday night, but I suppose that's better for us now. I walk in ahead of Alex, and he closes the door behind us, again. I head straight to the bed, stepping over the dirty laundry I left on the floor, and I grab my backpack, dump out all my notes and school folders and other things I don't need anymore, and turn back to Alex.

My heart's racing as our eyes meet, and before I can even ask the question that's on the tip of my tongue, he nods.

"Grab as much as you can now," Alex says, keeping his voice low. "Whatever you need for today, at least. We'll come back for more later in the week, when he's not here."

It hurts and doesn't at the same time, and I blink and look down at my shoes. "Your mom won't mind?"

"Of course not."

I know this. Laina Hayes has never been anything but extra nice to me and has always seemed to be happy to have me over. But I needed him to say it anyway. I look back up at him, and he gives me this knowing nod that's warm and caring.

"Really," he says, his tone taking on a softness I'm not sure I've ever heard before, even from him. He steps closer to me, and with a half smile that I can also see in his eyes, he adds, "I'll talk to her today, but I'm sure it won't be a problem. You shouldn't be here anymore if he's going to be here."

I just nod. He's right, after all. I swallow tightly and then step over to my dresser and start stuffing clothes into my backpack.

"Anything else you need that I can grab?" he asks in a low whisper, and I frown and glance over my shoulder at him as I shove a few pairs of briefs into my backpack.

"Uh, no. I—I'll get everything," I say, stumbling over the answer. It would feel weird to have him digging in my dirty jeans on the floor to get my keys and wallet. And the only other thing I want to make sure I have is buried in the back of my middle dresser drawer anyway.

I close the top drawer and open the middle one, and then I pull out a shopping bag that contains a set of new clothes—a pair of slacks, a belt, and a polo shirt—that I bought with what little money I managed to save up over the last few months. I stuff the bag in my backpack and frown, my shoulders tensing. Alex's eyes are still on me, I can feel them. Hopefully he's not really paying attention, though, because even *he* doesn't know my sketchbook exists.

I shift a little to block his view and then reach into the back left corner of the drawer, under a few neatly folded pairs of pants that I never wear because they don't fit me anymore, and grab my sketchbook and pencil bag. The pencils rattle around in the bag, and I flinch at the distinct noise.

Fuck. Please don't ask. Please don't ask.

Without turning around to look at him, I slide the sketchbook into the backmost compartment of my backpack, along with the pencil bag, which makes another of those traitorous rattling sounds. Then I zip up the compartment and spin around to finish packing. Alex backs up as I bend over to pick up my dirty jeans, and I fish around for a few seconds in the pockets to get my wallet and keys. The jeans get tossed right back on the floor when I'm done. They're not my favorite pair anyway.

Straightening up, I avoid Alex's gaze and let my eyes drift around the room. I don't *need* anything else. At least not today. And the clothes I grabbed should be enough for a few days. But it feels strange, like this is the last time I'll be here in this room. Like I'm getting kicked out. Like I really, *really* don't belong here anymore. And that feeling is almost painful.

Is it a coincidence that the day I graduated high school was the day my mom let that asshole back in her life?

I swallow hard and push the thought away as I sling the backpack over my shoulder.

"I think that's it. We can—"

A noise from the other room cuts me off, and I freeze as my heart seems to stop. There's low mumbling in a distinctly male voice, and I can't make out the words, but it doesn't even matter. I hear *him*. And the feeling of dread is even worse than it was the other night. Fear inches up my back and wraps itself around my throat, and I screw my eyes shut in some lame attempt to keep my panic down.

Spoiler: it doesn't work.

"Let's get the hell out of here," Alex hisses, and I agree with him, but my feet won't move. I'm trapped. Trapped with some vise gripping me, holding me in place, refusing to let go.

More words come from the other room, and this time I can make out my mom's voice mixed with *his*. The bed creaks. Heavy footsteps echo. A door slams.

"Nico!" Alex whisper-yells. "Come on!"

His hand grasps mine, and he gives a light squeeze that seems both comforting and like he's saying "pull yourself the fuck together." And when I still don't move, he forgoes the light encouragement and opts for dragging me out of the room.

Everything after that is a blur—a loud, messy blur. We manage to get out of the house and down the stairs to my car, Alex pulling me along behind him the whole way, before my mom catches up with us. Alex opens the passenger door for me and tells me to get in, that he'll drive, and he grabs my backpack and tosses it into the back seat as Mom throws open the front door.

I turn to look up at her, holding onto the car's doorframe for support. There's anger in her eyes and something else. Why the fuck is she mad at me? And when did that happen? I stare at her, scowling, and she stares right back, shaking her head.

"Get in," Alex urges, his hand once again settling on my back. "Come on, let's get out of here."

He's right. But I'm sick, and I'm stuck, wishing she could read my mind. She has to know why I'm leaving. Does she really not care *that* much?

"You fucking promised me!" I yell, because I can't help it. I can't hold it back. It's stupid, I know. But I need her to hear it. "You promised me he'd never be back!"

Her expression falters for a second, *only* for a second, and then she's frowning again, shaking her head at me in disapproval. She opens her mouth to speak, stepping outside of the house and onto the porch, but Alex moves in front of me so I can't see her, and his hands come up to my shoulders with another of those light squeezes.

"Hey, Nico," he says quietly, and I look up and meet his eyes. They're filled with concern and a soft understanding. "Let's go, okay? Let's go now."

"I . . ."

"I know," he says, his voice still gentle. My jaw trembles, and I look down at the ground. "You have every right to be mad. This is inexcusable. But now's not the time to talk to her about it, okay? Some other time, when, uh, when he's not here. Then you can talk to her. Okay? For now, right now, let's get back to my house. There's time. You can get changed, and—"

There's a noise behind him, more voices, and my eyes close as the air leaves my lungs again.

They're arguing. About me. And I hear Patrick's voice clear and loud and angry, a harshness to it.

"What's that little fucker doing here?"

"Pat, not right now."

"Fuck that, the kid needs to be reminded whose house this is and that he can't just—"

Whatever else that asshole says, I don't hear it, because Alex squeezes my shoulders and starts talking again, louder this time, so his voice drowns out the other sounds around me.

"Nico, look at me," he says, and I do. I lift my chin and open my eyes.

Fucking tears are sliding down my cheeks. Alex shakes his head slowly, and the muscles in his jaw twitch.

"We need to get going, okay? You're going to look at me, listen to my voice. Nothing else, okay?"

I nod.

"Get in the car now, here." And he guides me, his hands careful and light and gentle. I'm not even sure how it happens, but I'm suddenly sitting in the passenger seat of my car, handing him the keys. He takes my hand and gives it a squeeze. "Keep your eyes down. You don't even need to see that bastard, okay?"

I nod again. The door shuts, and not more than a few seconds later, Alex is climbing into the driver's seat. I still hear yelling, and the voices seem closer, louder, angrier. But Alex immediately starts talking again as though to keep my focus on him.

"I'm not sure when the last time I drove your car was," he says. He laughs a small, humorless laugh and starts up the car. "And remember last summer when I borrowed it because I needed to get groceries, but I got that flat tire right as I turned into the parking lot at the supermarket? Hah, just my luck, eh? Let's see if I can remember . . . it tends to stick a little . . ."

The car jerks into reverse, and I make the awful fucking mistake of lifting my eyes. I shouldn't have, though. I shouldn't have looked up, because the first thing I see is that jackass Patrick, standing at the bottom of the porch steps, his face red and his brown eyes flashing with rage.

Why the hell is he so mad at me? He's the one who punched *me* in the face. I never did anything to him except exist. In my own home. But the sight—his eyes, his anger, his fists balled up, flexing tightly like he's ready to take another swing at me—makes me fucking nauseous all over again, and I lower my head between my knees, trying desperately to force air into my lungs. It's not really working, though, and it's not until after Alex has shifted the car into drive and is flooring it down the driveway toward the road that I finally manage to suck in a breath. The air feels hot and sticky and stale, and I blow it out and take another deep breath and then another.

Alex's hand settles on my back, rubbing gently as I wheeze. It's maybe the only good thing so far this morning, knowing that he's here for me.

"Thanks," I mumble.

"Yeah, of course. You okay?"

His hand stops on my back. Please don't pull away. Please. I screw my eyes shut as the thought repeats in my head over and over. Please. Please.

Fuck all of this.

"No. Yes. I mean, I-I will be?"

His hand disappears, and I almost groan in protest, but the warmth returns a few seconds later, after the car turns from the driveway onto the main road.

"You will be," he repeats, and there's a softness to his voice as his palm presses into me, the touch both gentle and firm.

God, it's helping. It's helping so much. I wish I could just tell him that. I *should* just tell him that. But I'm not quite there yet, and I'm not really sure why.

I manage another deep breath, and this time, the air doesn't feel quite as thick.

# chapter ten

## *alex*

I'M NOT SURE HOW I manage to get us back to my house. The drive is short, but it's a blur. When we turn onto my street, Nico's panicked shaking gives way to his familiar anxiety-induced anger, and he finally lifts his head from his hands, his mouth set in a hard line as he stares ahead.

My hand stays on his back, though I'm not entirely sure whether it's really welcome. I move it only to shift the car into park once I pull into the driveway. Then I set it on his back again.

He doesn't say a word, and neither do I. His eyes remain trained forward, unfocused, and his breathing is stilted, every few breaths shuddering.

Have I ever seen him this upset? Probably. Things were really bad for a while just before Nico's mom finally kicked that asshole Patrick to the curb. Nico always had a bit of social anxiety and awkwardness, but then when things started to get worse, when the bruises started to appear, his anxiety turned not-so-gradually into something different—a reactivity to being touched, anger and tension that was sometimes impossible for him to control. It got worse in the months right after Patrick left, which didn't quite make sense to me. But in the last year or so, it's mostly leveled off, at least from my perspective. Or maybe it's just that it's more predictable to me now.

I mean, he's still reactive. He still hates being around too many people. Crowds, he's told me, are terrifying for him. And he still can't stand anyone touching him—except me. I'm thankful that I'm able to give him whatever it is he needs. Reassurance, at least. Especially when things are bad.

But this feels different. Something about this time is different. I know what it is, I think. And my heart hurts even more.

He was just forced to see his abuser—the man who put him in the hospital years ago. And his mom, of all people—the one person he should really be able to count on unconditionally—she was the one who forced this upon him. She was the one who let that bastard back in. She broke whatever promises she gave him and tossed them out like they were trash.

Hell, she essentially tossed him out, too.

I'm not sure I can even imagine how that feels to him.

I press my hand into his lower back, feeling him tense up. His eyes close, and he pulls in a sharp breath and holds it. And I feel it again—his shaking. Ignoring the pang in my chest, I rub his back gently, hoping it'll help, hoping it's somehow enough.

"You should get changed, yeah? Um, I mean, we can talk now if you need to, or—"

"No, I need to go." He opens his eyes, his gaze still unfocused and pained.

"Yeah, that's what I thought. But—"

"I only have a few minutes, and—and I . . ." With a sudden flinch, he squeezes his eyes shut, balls his hand up into a fist, and slams it down onto the dashboard. Hard. "Fuck! God fucking dammit!" The anger suddenly seeps from him as though he's too weak to hold onto it anymore, and he collapses forward, burying his head back in between his knees. His voice becomes small, filled with uncertainty, and he starts talking again, mumbling a stuttering mess of half-formed thoughts and questions into his hands. "Why . . . why the hell did he . . . ? And why did she . . . Alex, wh-why did she let him come back? Why did she . . . why did she choose him over me? Do I really mean that little to her? Does she really not want me there? I don't—I don't—I can't understand."

God, I wish I had all the answers for him. More than that, I wish I could change it all—fix the whole last hour, the whole last three days . . . the whole last few years. There's a lump in my throat, but I swallow past it and open my mouth to speak as he turns his head slightly to look up at me. He's not crying, somehow. But his eyes are red rimmed and his cheeks are flushed.

And he looks so sad, so broken. I want to fix that, too. I want to make him feel better and see just how loved he is. I want to gather him up in my arms and hold him.

It hurts that I can't do that right now.

"I don't know the answers," I admit quietly, and my stomach lurches as I watch his frown deepen. But then I let my hand rub up his back to his shoulders, and he closes his eyes with a sigh. It sounds like a relieved kind of sigh, almost, like . . . like my touch is soothing to him. So I repeat the motion, running my hand slowly down to his lower back and then up again. His sigh is even more distinct this time, and I can actually see some of the tension leave his shoulders. Gently, I clear my throat and say in a low voice, "I do know that you don't deserve to be treated like that. I'm not sure why your mom made that decision. I can't understand it, either. But you're welcome to stay here. Anytime and for as long as you need. My mom has said as much. So, you know, you don't have to, uh, worry about . . . that."

There's a moment where I think he's going to pull away or tense up again or something, but thankfully, he doesn't. In fact, he doesn't say anything at all. He just lets out another of those sighs and gives the tiniest nod. Then he straightens up and rakes a hand through his hair.

"I need to get changed and go so I'm not late."

"Yeah."

He swallows, takes a deep breath as though to reset himself, and then grabs his bag from the back seat, pushes open the door, and climbs out. I turn off the car, pocket his keys, and follow, trying to push away my unease.

He's still hurting. He's still in pain. And I wish I couldn't see it, since he's obviously trying to hide it. But I do see it. It's there. Maybe it wouldn't be obvious to anyone else. Maybe that's a good thing, since he has to go to work.

What I really want, though, is to be able to comfort him. To be able to hold him and hug him and kiss him. To help him navigate this. And to make sure he knows, always, that I'm here for him in whatever way he needs.

As I follow him into the house, two thoughts hit me, one after the other.

The first sends a warm shiver through me. I'm going to tell him. Tonight. Tonight, I'm going to tell him all the things that I've been keeping to myself the last few years. That he's more than just my best friend. That he's the most important person in the world to me. That I love him. That I'm in love with him.

And that I'll be here for him, always.

The second thought, however, turns that warm shiver into a cold shot of ice. My feet nearly miss the single step up onto the porch, and I grab the railing to hide my almost-stumble as Nico glances back at me over his shoulder, his green eyes narrowing slightly with curiosity.

I fake a grin and shrug my shoulders, and he frowns but turns forward as he opens up the front door.

I follow slowly, heaviness weighing down each of my steps. My second thought, the one I had right after the hopeful, beautiful thought of finally coming out and coming clean to my best friend, is that no, I absolutely can't tell him. Not right now. Because if me revealing my feelings to him makes anything any sort of awkward at all . . . if it would make him uncomfortable knowing how I feel . . . he'd have nowhere else to go.

And I can't do that to him. Especially not right now.

Mom wastes no time putting me to work after Nico gets changed and leaves. I suppose that's a good thing; otherwise, I'd just spend all day worrying about him. As it is, I can barely stay focused to get all the chores done, and it takes probably twice as long as it should.

We're having a big family thing next weekend. Relatives I've never met are coming in from all over the country. I'm not entirely sure what the occasion is, or if there even is an occasion, but Mom's excited. She says there'll be at least forty or fifty people here. Cousins, cousins of cousins, and cousins of other cousins, as well as my aunts and uncles and both sets of grandparents.

My dad isn't in the picture. He never really has been, actually. I guess he cheated on my mom when she was pregnant with me and then took off and never came back. His parents, however—Grandpa Joe and Grandma Kay—they've always been around. I see them at least once or twice a month, and the only reason they weren't at my graduation last week was because their motor home broke down on their way back to Omaha from their annual spring trip to Jackson Hole.

The big get-together means a lot of cleaning and organizing, especially since a few of the out-of-town guests will be staying here for a couple of days. So I keep myself busy most of the day. By the time afternoon rolls around, I've cleared out the downstairs bedroom, which we were using as storage for my mom's artwork and art supplies and prints; deep cleaned the downstairs bathroom and kitchen; and mowed the lawns in both the front yard and the backyard.

There'll be more to do tomorrow and the rest of the week, but what I did manage to get done seems like a good enough start. So I put the lawn mower away in the shed in the back and then head inside, pulling my phone out of my pocket as I go. My stomach sinks as I turn on the screen.

Nothing.

Still.

I mean, nothing from Nico. No texts or calls. The same as it's been all day.

I do have several other notifications, and I begrudgingly swipe through them as I walk across the living room and toward the garage. Jenna messaged me an hour ago, asking whether I wanted to go into Omaha with her tomorrow. And mom texted me to remind me to pick up dinner at five at The Rancher—her favorite restaurant going on forever now. Then I've got an email from a professor I connected with at Stanford. That seems pretty important, but since I'm in a hurry, I make a mental note to take a look at it later, when I have time to respond.

The one person I really wanted to hear from, though, he's been silent all day. Not that that's unlike him. In fact, it shouldn't even be surprising, really. It's just . . . well, I'm worried. More than usual.

I click on his name in my messaging app and reread the last couple of texts I sent him, shortly after he left my house this morning.

> *Alex (8:07 a.m.):* You're gonna do great to-day!

> *Alex (8:09 a.m.):* Let me know if you want me to meet you on your lunch break or any-thing. Otherwise, I'm just stuck doing chores today =P

I half expected him to respond just to ask if I'd been abducted or if someone had stolen my phone. I rarely use proper spelling and punctuation when I text, and Nico's always making fun of me for it.

But, nope. No teases, no taunts. Not even a quick thumbs-up emoji. Nothing.

And that's done nothing all day, especially right now, to ease my worry. He does tend to go silent when things are stressful or when he gets anxious, but I hope if things got too bad, he would have let me know.

I stuff my phone back in my pocket, trying to ignore the knot in the pit of my stomach, and I push the door open to the garage.

My mom's sitting on her stool in front of the huge canvas she's been working on for weeks now, just staring at it. She's got a paintbrush in her hand, and there's a small splotch of white paint on her cheek. I'm pretty sure she hasn't noticed me yet, and with a quiet laugh, I wonder how long I can stand here before she will.

I'm feeling too antsy to test that out, though, and so I shuffle my feet and knock lightly on the doorframe. "Hey, Mom, I'm heading out to grab dinner. Did you need anything else while I'm out?"

For a second, I think maybe she's not going to respond—that she's so focused she didn't even hear me. But then she turns her head with a quiet "hmm?"

I laugh out loud this time as I see her realize I'm standing there. She's got paint on her forehead, too, and three used paintbrushes tucked into her shirt pocket. I guess she's been in here painting as long as I was working around the house. That's my mom. I love her.

"I'm heading out to grab dinner," I repeat. "Do you need me to pick up anything else?"

"Oh, right, hmm . . ." She turns back to look at her painting again, her eyes scanning the massive four-foot-by-five-foot canvas. "Um, no, I don't think so. It's already dinnertime?"

"Almost."

"'Kay."

I shake my head and step all the way into the garage, holding the door handle to make sure it closes quietly behind me. "It's after four. Did you eat lunch?"

"Of course. Or . . ." She twists around toward me, her eyes narrowed like she's trying to remember. "Maybe?"

I give her a crooked smile. "You didn't, did you?"

"Yeah, maybe not," she admits, and she glances at her painting one last time as she stands up and stretches. "I'm actually . . . done, I think. It's done."

"Whoa, what? Really?"

"Yeah. I think so."

She smiles, and I can see the exhaustion in her eyes slowly replaced with the familiar glow of pride and joy she always has when she finishes a piece.

Her eyes wander across the painting, but she doesn't seem to be scrutinizing it. She seems to be taking it in—the whole of the canvas and her hours and hours of work. I follow her gaze, letting my eyes linger on all the details she's added since the last time I studied the painting—the soft dewdrop sitting just on the edge of the huge leaf, the little bits of sunshine glinting off the leaf's stem, the darker shades of green along the hint of the leaf's underside peeking out after the leaf curves. How she creates such realism, I'm not sure, but the whole painting has a sort of texture to it, a volume, like it's not just painted on a flat, two-dimensional canvas.

I wrap my arm around her shoulders. "It's really, really beautiful, Mom."

She leans her head against me with a long sigh, and we don't move for a minute or two. Finally, she straightens up and then turns to me, her nose wrinkled.

"You should shower before you go get dinner. You stink."

Laughing, I roll my eyes. "You smell like paint."

"Well, you smell like sweat and dirt. Did you mow the lawns?" She turns away from me and starts gathering up her paintbrushes and supplies.

"Yeah, I finished the downstairs bedroom and then did the mowing—"

"Nico's staying longer?" she asks, turning toward me abruptly. There's a question in her eyes, and I almost hear it before she says it. "Did you talk to him about . . . you know . . . things?"

My chest tightens as I stare at her. *Things.* Did I talk to him about *things*? No, Mom, because I was busy trying to keep him from panicking too much about—

"What happened? What is it?" She steps closer, her whole expression changing to concern. How the hell can she read me so well?

I shake my head and drop my eyes, not really wanting to get into everything. This morning, all I told her was that we went to get his clothes for work. I didn't mention Patrick or the sort of falling out with his mom or the fact that I basically offered for him to stay here indefinitely.

Guess I should have talked to her earlier.

"We didn't talk about California yet, if that's what you mean,"

I start. I know that's not all she means, but I keep going so she doesn't jump into a long speech about how it's better to be honest about things right away and talk about things sooner rather than later—a speech I've heard lots and lots of times. "There's stuff going on. At his house, I mean. And he needs to stay here for a while longer. I told him that was cool."

When I risk a look up, the concern in her eyes seems to bore right into me. I frown.

"Sorry I didn't mention it sooner, but I didn't think you'd mind. It's pretty . . . bad. He can't really . . . go home."

"Alex, what's going on?"

I shake my head and drop my eyes. She should know, though, because—

A wave of nausea rolls through me as I picture the scene from that morning. Patrick storming out onto the porch with his sneering face and god-awful mustache and beady brown eyes. He hasn't changed from the last time I saw him years ago. But this morning, the anger and hate in his expression were downright scary. And Nico's mom—she didn't look much more welcoming, either. I'm not sure I've ever seen her like that before.

Pursing my lips, I shake my head again and look back up. "Nico's stepfather is back. Patrick. The man who—"

"What?!"

God, I'm glad she interrupted me this time so I didn't have to finish that sentence. I just nod. "Apparently since Friday night, and his mom . . . Yeah, um, so he needs a place to stay. I told him he could stay here. I should have asked you first, but—"

"Of course he can stay here. As long as he needs to. I can't believe Cindy would . . ." She trails off, shaking her head. "You did the right thing, sweetie. He can stay for as long as he needs."

Relief hits me, even though I didn't really doubt she would say yes. I expect a much longer lecture on being upfront and honest and communicating better, but hopefully she'll let that wait until later, because I really should get going.

Her hand settles on my arm, and she gives me a light squeeze. When I lift my eyes, she's watching me with a kind, quiet smile.

"Thanks, Mom. I should . . ." I hike a thumb up, pointing back to the door, and she raises her eyebrows with a half smile.

"Shower first. You really do stink," she repeats, and she pats my arm this time and then steps away from me, heading back over to continue gathering her painting supplies. To my surprise, she doesn't mention needing to talk or that we should discuss honesty and communication or anything else that I know is on her mind. Instead, she just says, "I didn't order anything for Nico for dinner. I'll call Jack and update our order. He likes their burgers, right? Cheese and lettuce and pickles but no tomato or burger sauce?"

There's another lump in my throat, and maybe it's because my mom cares enough to know what Nico's order would be from her favorite restaurant. Or maybe it's because I appreciate her not grilling me right now. "Uh, yeah. And he likes the fries extra crispy."

"Right, yeah. Okay, I'll call and update the order."

"Thanks, Mom," I say, and I know my voice breaks, but I can't help it. I turn before she can see the stupid tears forming in my eyes. "I'll shower and then . . . yeah."

I expect her to stop me, call me out, ask what's wrong. Because that's her—that's what she does. But above the sound of my heart pounding in my ears, all I hear is a quiet "okay, sweetie" filled with kindness and love and understanding.

I blink as a tear slips out, but I manage to get through the door and close it behind me before I wipe my cheek.

# chapter eleven

*nico*

"ALRIGHT, I THINK THAT'S about it for today." Sharon Lenoway, the head librarian at the small public library where I'm working for the summer, stands up from her desk and gives me a tight smile. "Good start. You got a lot done, I think."

"Yeah. Yeah, thanks," I say. I try for a smile back, but it's probably more of a grimace, clouded in exhaustion and the constant ache in my chest I've been fighting since this morning.

Sharon doesn't seem to notice. Instead, she picks her cell phone up off the desk, grabs her purse, and then motions toward the front entrance. She starts talking as she walks, and I force myself to try to listen as I follow back a safe distance.

"So tomorrow and Wednesday will be about the same as today, I think."

She reaches the door and pulls it open, holding it for me, and she keeps talking, saying something about Thursday and the project I'll be working on with a huge batch of donated books we're getting in. But I have to work to keep myself from shrinking away, and her words float right on past me, drowned out by the sound of my heart pounding loudly in my ears. I slink by her, making myself as small as possible. Again, she's oblivious, and she keeps going as she locks the door.

"It shouldn't take more than a week or two, I think," she says. "But there are a lot of books, and you'll need to check them all for damage and missing pages, clean them, sort them, catalog them, label them. Oh, you know what? Maybe Caitlin will be able to help you if she's not too busy with the summer school kids."

I clear my throat and manage to force out a few words. "That's okay. I should be able to handle it." I fucking hate how my voice sounds all unsure. Raspy, too, like I'm out of breath. But I *am* out of breath, and I can't seem to take in enough air.

"Alright, good. You're a hard worker. I like that," she says. She turns to face me with a serious nod, looking at me like she's seeing me for the first time. "See you tomorrow?"

"Yeah. Uh, yeah. See you tomorrow." I wave awkwardly, which is weird because she's standing right next to me, and she gives an equally awkward smile as she goes to step around me. But then she's suddenly too close, suddenly coming toward me, suddenly some huge threat according to my *stupid fucking* brain, and I react before I can stop myself. With a flinch, I jump backward out of her way, nearly tripping over my own feet.

God, I'm a fucking idiot.

She stops, and her eyebrows arch.

"S-sorry, sorry. Um, yeah, so, I'll see you tomorrow," I repeat, and before she has a chance to say anything or to look more confused or annoyed or whatever, I train my eyes to the ground, shove my hands into my pockets, and start moving. My car is thankfully parked on the opposite side of the parking lot from hers, all the way off in the corner by itself, and I can't get away fast enough.

Halfway there, my legs start to feel like Jell-O, though the farther I get from the building, the less the ache in my chest hurts. I pull my car keys out of my pocket as I get closer to my car, and a minute later, I'm collapsing into the driver's seat, taking long, slow, deep breaths to steady myself.

Dammit, I need this job. It's probably the only job I could find that I can actually sort of handle. The library is quiet, not busy, and most people who come in are families with young children. I don't fucking panic and flinch away from young children.

But, hell. Pretending to be okay all day has been awful, and I'm done, barely holding myself together now that I no longer have to.

I let out something that resembles a laugh, or maybe it's a sob, and it resonates oddly in the interior of my small car. I'm shaking, too, and I'm so ready to go home, I can't even—

A stabbing pain shoots through my chest, fast and hot, and I close my eyes and hold my breath.

*Home.*

Right.

I *can't* go home. I don't even fucking *have* a home anymore, do I?

My hand finds my pocket again, and I wrap my fingers tightly around my cell phone as I try to block out all the terrible memories of that morning—the memories I've been desperately pushing away all day. But they surround me, suffocating me, pressing down on me.

I can't go home. I'm not welcome anymore. Mom doesn't want me there anymore. It's all so sudden that it's making me dizzy.

She texted earlier, just after my shift started. Said she'll pack up the rest of my stuff today and leave it in a box at the end of the driveway. She wants my room empty so she can, I dunno, use it for that asshole's extra shit or something. And when the month is over, my car insurance is canceled. And my cell phone plan.

*Keep the car and the phone*, her text said. *But you can pay your own bills now. You're an adult. Time you act like one.*

So fucking generous of her.

Patrick texted, too. He shouldn't even have my number, the fucking jackass, but he got it anyway, probably from Mom. He sent three messages, each of them short but threatening—a clear warning that I should stay away. His last message had some awful implication in it that what happened years ago was *my* fault. That him hitting me and my mom kicking him out were *my* fault.

I'm fucking lucky I didn't just lose it right then. I screenshot-ted the messages and then deleted them and blocked his number. Maybe that wasn't the smartest thing to do, I don't really know, but I didn't feel like I had any other choice.

As it is, I'm not sure how I *actually* made it through the day.

Well, maybe that's not entirely true. Maybe I do know how.

*You've got this today!*

God, Alex has no idea how much I needed that message earlier. He has no idea that I had to steal a few minutes every couple of hours today at work, go hide in the back office, take my phone out and open up my message app and read it over and over. He has no idea how much those few simple words helped remind me that even though I feel more alone than ever, he's still here. For me.

If not for him . . .

I let out a long, shuddering breath, and my stomach's in knots as I pull my phone out of my pocket, my eyes still screwed shut. The phone vibrates with a notification, sending an unwelcome chill down my spine.

*Please. Please be Alex. Please.*

The thought repeats in my head as I force my eyes open and glance down at the screen. A warmth floods through my chest and all the way down into my toes when I see his name pop up. I have two texts, and both are from him. Nothing else.

No angry, vitriolic messages from my mom and no unan-nounced, threatening texts from her asshole ex-husband.

Just two simple messages from my best friend.

With fingers that are much too stiff and shaky, I enter in my passcode to unlock my phone, and then I tap on his name. And for the first time probably all day, I smile.

> *Alex (5:11 p.m.):* dinner! when will u be home?

His eyes smile back at me—gorgeous blue eyes that somehow dance in the sunlight. He sent a picture, a selfie. He's standing outside his mom's truck, that wide, carefree grin on his face as he holds up a take-out bag from the local steakhouse.

And he's adorable. Fuck, I can barely stand it. His bright-blue hair is sticking up every which way, almost looking like he just woke up. The short strands are messy and out of place, and there's one curl that's dipping down over his forehead.

I can almost imagine running my fingers through his hair, straightening it out for him. It would be soft. Soft and smooth. And since he's a bit taller than me, I'd have to stretch up to reach. He'd steady me with his hands on my waist, and his cheek would brush against mine, his breath hot on my neck.

That's probably not how it would really happen. He'd probably swat me away and tell me to fix my own hair.

But I can pretend.

I purse my lips, ignoring the rush of heat low in my groin, and I send him a short text back.

> *Nico (5:13 p.m.):* On my way

> *Alex (5:14 p.m.):* rad! mom and i r setting up to eat outside. we'll wait for u

It shouldn't hit so hard, his last sentence. *we'll wait for u.* It shouldn't, but it does. It hits me right in the chest. That, coupled with the question in his earlier text—*when will u be home?*—and I'm shaking again.

*Home.*

They're waiting for me at home. Him and his mom. It's not my home; it's his. But hell if I can't pretend with this, too, right? I can pretend he's inviting me home, welcoming me *home*. With him.

I'd better start driving before I'm too much of a mess.

Alex's mom talks a lot. She's always analyzing things, giving advice, making sure Alex has everything he needs to succeed. And it's not that she micromanages. Just that she's, I dunno, *there*. She wants to make sure he's thought of all the options, that he's got all the opportunity, that he understands the ins and outs of everything.

Maybe that's why he's a freaking genius valedictorian who got a full-ride to Stanford.

So I shouldn't be surprised when she sits us both down for a "talk" after we've done the dishes. Alex returns my look with a shoulder shrug, though there's a flicker of something in his eyes that suggests he's maybe a little uneasy. But he motions to the kitchen table, and we both sit.

His mom takes a seat across from us and gives me a gentle smile that should put me at ease. But it doesn't, and my chest is suddenly tight as I hear echoes of words from that morning. *What's that little fucker doing here?* I see a flash of dark, angry eyes. A sneer. And my mom's texts, telling me I'm not welcome at home anymore.

Fuck. What if Alex's mom is about to tell me I'm not welcome here, either?

"I-I'm sorry, Ms. Hayes, I—" My hands wring together in my

lap as I stop talking, unsure what I was going to say or what I was even apologizing for. My heart's racing, and I close my eyes as my stomach churns.

"No, no, sweetie." The soft voice contradicts everything I've been hearing in my head, and I suck in a breath through gritted teeth as she continues. "You have absolutely nothing to apologize for. Alex told me what happened this morning. And I just wanted to make sure you know you're welcome here." She pauses, and I manage to lift my eyes back up. She's still got that gentle smile on her face. "You're always welcome, Nico. Okay?"

I'm not really sure and not really okay. But I give a small nod anyway, and her smile softens even more.

"I do have a few rules, but nothing much, and it's just so we're all happy, you know? First, no parties"—she gives Alex a glare, and he shrinks back into his seat sheepishly—"and no loud music or anything, please, because I *do* work from home most of the time. Pick up after yourself. We all respect each other and contribute to the chores, as I think you know already. Oh, and please, please, *please*, do not—"

"—leave the laundry in the washing machine overnight," Alex jumps in. "It's my mom's worst pet peeve. Or maybe her only pet peeve. Well, that and people who forget to put on their blinker when they're turning. She gets really mad about that."

Alex's mom rolls her eyes but then looks back at me with that soft smile.

"You are welcome here. No strings attached. No anything at all. Okay, sweetie?"

I lower my eyes as I nod slowly, and there's a moment where I wonder if it's too good to be true, really. Any time now, she'll laugh and say she's kidding. Rent's due on the first of the month or my ass is kicked to the curb.

But then she just starts talking again, her voice kind and sweet and caring.

"I usually go grocery shopping on Sundays. If you need anything, we keep a list on the fridge. You know Alex is allergic to cinnamon, so please be sure you don't bring anything in the house that has cinnamon in it. Oh, and I often need to back my truck up to the garage to load things from my studio, so park your car along the curb, not in the driveway, unless you're unloading groceries or something . . ."

She keeps going on for a few more minutes, similar things that are just common courtesy and expectations, and I risk a glance at Alex. He's watching me, his eyes soft and understanding, and he gives me a tiny smile and nod, like he's saying, "See, everything will be fine."

When his mom finishes, she looks from me to Alex and then back again, and something flickers in her smile.

"Okay," she says, setting both hands on the table and then pushing herself up to stand. "I'll let you two boys do whatever it is you're going to do. I'll be in the garage finalizing some paperwork and things for the framing company. Oh, Alex! Actually, can you help me out tomorrow? They called while you were picking up dinner and said they can get me in tomorrow. Do you already have plans?"

Alex seems to startle a little, as though he wasn't really listening to her question, and then he fidgets in his chair and shakes his head.

"Uh, Jenna asked me to go to Omaha with her tomorrow, but I hadn't responded yet. I can help you instead."

His tone is strange, but I figure it's probably just because he wasn't expecting the question.

"Are you sure?"

"Yeah. Of course."

"Okay. Great. We'll have to package the painting, and then we'll load it up and leave at nine. Sound good?"

Alex coughs a little and says, "Yeah, sure."

And there are some other words exchanged between them as I sit there, but my brain dissociates a bit, and it's not until several minutes later, I suspect, that Alex's hand sets gently on my arm.

"Hey, you okay?"

"Hmm?" I look up, and he's standing now, staring down at me with concern. His mom is nowhere to be seen. "Um, yeah. Sorry. I, uh . . . I'm tired, I guess."

His expression turns soft, and his blue eyes seem to study me as he squeezes my arm.

"You can rest, if you want. I've gotta return an email that I forgot about earlier. Then, I dunno. I'm kinda tired too. Mom kept me busy all day cleaning."

He steps back from me, pulling his hand away, and my stomach drops from the loss of contact. My earlier thoughts start to swirl around in my head as I watch him lift his hand up and run it through his hair with a sigh.

I look away and then push myself up to stand as well.

"Yeah, I should probably shower and change, then I might just crash. Today's been—"

FUCK.

I grab the table with both hands, and I feel Alex step a little closer to me.

"Nico?"

I shake my head, unable to speak. And as I close my eyes, I see the words again.

*Come get your shit*, she texted. *I'll leave the box at the end of the driveway.*

Had she really cleaned out my room? Gone through my things? Decided what I might want to keep and what was *trash*?

I try to remember what else was in my room, whether there was anything I actually really need, but I can't think straight. Which is probably why I do the fucking stupidest thing possible. I pull out my phone, unlock it, open up my message app to my mom's messages from earlier that day, and shove it over toward Alex without a word.

"What's . . ." He takes the phone from me, and there's a second or two of silence. Then he breathes a short, rough exhale. "Oh, shit. Nico, this is . . ."

Without finishing the thought, he sets my phone face down on the table and then he's wrapping me up in this warm hug that's just everything I need right now. I collapse into him, slipping my arms around his waist, and he holds me even tighter, murmuring quietly in my ear. I can't really hear whatever it is he's saying, but I feel the intent, like he's surrounding me with this protective bubble and assuring me I'm safe.

I close my eyes and let myself break down against him, not even trying to pretend that I'm okay anymore.

# chapter twelve

## alex

THE FLIMSY CARDBOARD BOX sitting in the passenger seat of my mom's truck is pitifully empty. I glanced in it when I picked it up a few minutes ago, and another quick look after I park back in the driveway at home shows that, yeah, there isn't much there. Some clothes, a few books, and a phone charger or something. That's it.

I wonder what his mom just threw out or didn't bother packing for him.

I shut off the truck's engine, but I don't get out right away. Instead, my eyes drift up to the second-story window. Soft light peeks out from behind the shutters, and I wonder if Nico's asleep yet.

Part of me hopes he is, because he looked so exhausted earlier. But then the selfish part of me hopes he's just lying in bed, waiting for me to get back so we can, I dunno, talk or something.

The way he hugged me after dinner . . . God, I can still feel it—his sadness and desperation, his pain, his need. He clung to me for several minutes, needing me to just hold him. Needing me to be there for him. And I did. Gladly.

But I feel like we should talk. I think there's more he hasn't told me, and there are definitely things I need to tell him, too. I need to be sure he really believes everything my mom said earlier, about how he's welcome here, no strings attached. And then there's the other stuff. We need to talk about California again. Especially now.

It's almost too heavy for me to even think about, the fact that *he just got kicked out of his home.* His mom kicked him out of his home. Right out on the street. If he hadn't come here . . . if my mom hadn't been so welcoming and open . . . what the hell would he have done? Would he be sleeping in his car right now?

My chest hurts, and I close my eyes for the briefest of moments. Then I take a deep breath, knowing the best thing I can do is to be there for him, and I open the door, grab the box from the passenger seat, and lock the truck before jogging along the walkway and up the porch steps.

It's still early—maybe only about seven thirty—and I can hear my mom humming to herself from the garage as I step inside the house. The rest of the house is quiet and dark. I slip my shoes off by the front door, poke my head into the garage briefly to tell my mom I'm back, and then head upstairs, tiptoeing quietly when I get to the hallway just in case Nico is already asleep.

The door's closed, and for the first time since Nico started staying here Friday night, I hesitate before entering. It's technically my room, yeah, but what if he needs or wants privacy? After a day like today, I'm not sure whether he'll want me to be close by or whether he might want to spend some time alone.

I glance back down the stairs. There's an extra bedroom now. The bed even has fresh sheets and pillows so it's ready for my cousins, who are coming in on Friday night and staying the week-end. I could let Nico have my room if he wants, and I could sleep in the extra room. Or vice versa.

Another thing we should talk about.

Not that I mind sleeping on the floor. I really actually don't. But every night now, I've had to argue with him about it.

Quietly, I shift the box under one arm and knock on the door.

There's no response, so I slowly turn the knob and push the door open. The light's on overhead, the ceiling fan humming as it does on the lowest setting, and Nico's curled up in the bed, his back to me and the blanket pulled up all the way to his shoulders.

I watch him for a few seconds, seeing the blanket shift slightly with each long, relaxed breath he takes. Even though he's facing away, I can see that the tension is gone from his shoulders, and I hope that means he's getting the rest he needs.

When I'm sure he's actually sleeping, I step inside the room, careful not to make any noise, and I set the box down by my desk, then go back to shut the door behind me.

I'm not tired—well, I mean, not *really* anyway—and so I sit in my chair at my desk and, as quietly as I can, open up my laptop. While it's turning on, I take my cell phone out of my pocket, not surprised to see a message from Jenna.

> *Jenna (7:31 p.m.):* Soooooooo tomorrow? Bowling and lunch with Leela and Shane. I'll drive. Pick u up at 10???

I frown as I stare at the screen for a minute. Jenna's . . . nice. She's sweet and pretty and smart, and although I know she wants a relationship—she's made that abundantly clear, especially after she had a few drinks on Thursday night at the pre-graduation party at Leela's parents' house—she's also been understanding when I've been wishy-washy about it. It's been bothering me for a while now, though, because I hate the feeling that I'm leading her on. She's a good person, and even though she's only been in town for a few months now, I appreciate her friendship.

I type out a short text in response.

*Alex (7:39 p.m.):* srry i cant, i have to help my mom tomorrow. raincheck for thurs?

*Jenna (7:39 p.m.):* Okay :)

*Jenna (7:40 p.m.):* Might just be u and me on Thursday, I think Leela has a thing

I'm glad she's not here to see my grimace, because if I agree to go knowing it will just be me and her, alone . . .

Ah, hell, I have no idea what I'm doing. Would that be suggesting to her that *yes*, I'm ready for and want more than to just hang out as friends?

I *almost* jump up and head downstairs to ask my mom, but I hesitate, stare at the phone for another few seconds, and then make a decision.

*Alex (7:42 p.m.):* sounds good, looking forward to it

Thursday, it is. Thursday, I'll tell her I like her as a friend. Nothing more. And I hope she'll be okay with that because I really do like having her as a friend.

She sends me back a smiley face emoji, which is better than a row of hearts or something, and I set my phone down and turn to my computer to take care of the other important thing I need to—emailing Dr. Ellis back.

I don't know why I'm nervous about it. Maybe it's just that this is another thing that's making California feel more real. I'm *really* moving to Palo Alto in just a few months. I'm *really* going to be living less than an hour from the beach and studying at one of the top universities in the world. And, if all goes well and I can make myself sound as smart as I've been told I am, I'm *really* going to be doing research with someone like Dr. John Ellis—acclaimed Nobel laureate, professor of particle physics and astrophysics, and Director of the W.W. Hansen Experimental Physics Laboratory at Stanford University.

I can't even believe he's given me the time he has, responding to each of my emails with what sounds like enthusiasm and encouragement. It seems unreal, and every time I email him, I feel even more unworthy.

Trying to be as quiet as I can so I don't wake Nico, I open up my email and reread his message from earlier today.

*Alex -*

*Hmm, interesting. I love that you integrated the theory on how dark matter affects space-time with the concepts of gravity and the formation of black holes. This is actually an evolving field, and while it's not the focus of my current research, I'm quite interested in chatting more about it. Tell me, how would you expect dark matter to behave as it approaches the event horizon of a supermassive black hole, given this theory of yours?*

*We should chat more about this in person when you're on campus. Were you planning to visit any earlier in the summer, or should I put a meeting on my calendar for mid-September?*

*- John*

My brain immediately switches gears, and I take his question about dark matter and black holes and run with it. I *do* have the awareness to type quietly, and more than once, I glance back behind me to make sure I haven't woken up Nico. But it feels good to let myself get lost for a bit in the theoretical—concepts that have me straining to really perceive them, even as I try to formulate a coherent response to Dr. Ellis's question.

I take my time, too, since I want to at least *try* to sound smart, and by the time I've finished what I hope is a thorough explanation of what I think dark matter might do as it nears the edges of a supermassive black hole, I've spent nearly three hours, read four new research articles published in top-ranked astrophysics journals, and rewritten and rethought my response multiple times.

I sit back, looking at the email one final time and grinning. I love this stuff, and I hope that even if I sound like an uneducated idiot to Dr. Ellis, he can hear the enthusiasm I have for it.

There don't appear to be any stupid typos in the email, and everything seems clear to me on my final read through, so I finish the email with a note that no, I do not have any plans to visit sooner than mid-September but that I'm really looking forward to talking in person then.

My stomach does a little anxious swoop when I hit the send button, but I'm smiling, and there's a part of my brain that's still racing with excitement for all the ideas I'd written down. I start to lean back in my chair when there's a low laugh behind me, and I startle and nearly fall backward, barely managing to catch myself by grabbing onto my desk.

Nico laughs again, though it sounds weak. "Did you write a whole novel or something?"

His voice is slow and deep with sleep, and when I turn around to face him, he's sitting up in the bed, his eyes half open and his hair falling in messy black curls over his forehead. He's got one of my

T-shirts on, and it's a size too big on his small frame, but it looks perfect. *He* looks perfect. Right there in my bed, wearing my shirt, just as he is.

I don't realize I'm staring until he quirks an eyebrow at me, and then I cough and tear my eyes away. "No, uh, no. Just . . . writing back to Dr. Ellis—that professor at Stanford."

"Oh."

I reach up and rub the back of my neck. "I might have gotten a little carried away, but I've got this theory on dark matter and black holes and gravity, and, well, he said he wanted to hear about it, so, uh . . . yeah."

My eyes meet Nico's again, and I'm not surprised to see him smirking at me. He blinks and then rubs his eyes and collapses back onto the bed, curling up and tugging the blanket around his shoulders.

I turn back to my computer, close the lid, and then stand up and face him, expecting to see him already asleep again. But he's not. He's staring at the box next to my desk, his jaw clenched.

"That's the stuff from my mom?" he asks, his voice rough.

"Yeah. There's clothes and some books. Not . . . too much."

I instantly regret saying that, though it's the truth, and I watch, my heart aching for him, as he pushes himself back up, climbs out of the bed, and shuffles across the room. Then, he lowers himself to the ground to sit cross-legged next to the box. I want to warn him, although I'm not sure what I want to warn him of, but I end up staying quiet as he reaches out and lifts the flaps open.

He blinks and looks down into the box, and his expression flickers with pain and then hardens.

I'm really not thinking too clearly now, but whatever. I push my chair back and quickly join him on the floor, slipping my arm around his shoulders. He's stiff, his body rigid with tension, and he doesn't immediately relax into me or seem to take comfort in my closeness like he had earlier in the day.

Maybe that's because he's probably thinking the same thing I am.

Everything in this box.

That's it.

That's all he has.

I close my eyes and squeeze his shoulders gently, and I feel him shudder as I whisper, "It'll be okay. It'll be okay, I promise. We'll figure everything out."

But he doesn't react or relax, and as I lean my head against his, feeling his whole body trembling, I realize I'm not really sure whether he even heard me.

# chapter thirteen

*nico*

*Mom (Tuesday, 10:39 p.m.):* Cell phone billing cycle is up on Saturday. Your line will be canceled then

*Mom (Wednesday, 11:14 a.m.):* You know, things didn't have to be this way

*Mom (Wednesday, 12:22 p.m.):* If you hadn't lied, we wouldn't be here now

*Mom (Wednesday, 12:25 p.m.):* Pat told me you took a swing at him first. You know he went to jail for months and lost his job because of that! What a shitty thing to do to someone who was always nice to you and just trying to take care of us both!

*Mom (6:59 a.m.):* Fine. You're going to ignore me, then maybe I'll just take the car back too. $500 for it. Due by June 1 or I'll report it stolen. It's still in my name. Stop being an entitled little ass

*Nico (7:40 a.m.):* I get paid next Friday (June 6). I'll give you the money then. Please don't report it stolen.

*Mom (7:42 a.m.):* Fine. Bring the money on or before next Friday and I'll give you the title. I'll be off work at 4

I stare at the message for a few minutes, my stomach in knots. Then I hit the power button to turn off the screen on my phone, toss it onto the bed next to me, and cover my face with my hands.

Today couldn't have started off any worse, and it's only 7:45 a.m.

How the fucking hell am I supposed to come up with five hundred dollars after only a week of work when I'm making minimum wage? I'm no math genius like Alex, but I'm not an idiot either, and I'm pretty sure after taxes, my first paycheck won't even *be* that much. And since I only have about forty bucks in my checking account right now, I have no idea how I'll get enough money. I kinda need that forty bucks anyway. I've been washing my only set of work clothes every night so far this week, hoping my boss doesn't realize I'm wearing the same polo shirt and slacks every day. Plus I need to put gas in my car. And apparently pay my cell phone bill and my car insurance.

But honestly, the financial shit isn't even the worst part. The worst part is this complete one eighty she's doing, treating me like a villain.

Fuck.

I *didn't* take a swing at him first. I was fucking thirteen years old. And he was *not* always nice to me. He was *never* nice to me. I'm glad that asshole went to jail and lost his job. He deserved that.

But it's that—the fact that she's letting herself believe him, believe his lies and whatever else he's telling her or she's making up on her own, turning me into this awful person—that's what really hurts the most.

I ignored her as long as I could, still pretending. Pretending she wasn't actually texting me those baseless accusations. Pretending she wasn't being someone completely different. I still haven't shown any of those texts to Alex, even.

But I couldn't ignore her anymore after her message this morning. I can't let her report my car as stolen. I can't have it taken away, and I don't want any trouble with the police.

I roll over onto my stomach with a groan and bury my head into the pillow.

And that doesn't even make me happy because the pillow doesn't smell like Alex. It's not his.

Tuesday night, I moved into the downstairs bedroom—the one he cleaned up and prepped for his cousins, who are showing up tomorrow evening. It was dumb, kinda—to have me move down here for just a few days, since I'll be moving back up into his room tomorrow and staying up there for the weekend. But we got into yet another argument over who would be sleeping in his bed, and I just couldn't convince him that I'd be okay sleeping on the floor. So rather than make him sleep on the floor *again*—which just feels wrong because it's *his* room—I sort of . . . kicked myself out.

Of course, I haven't slept well at all the last couple of nights, either, like my body just *knows* he's not nearby. And being tired certainly hasn't helped me deal with all this added stress of my mom's texts.

I should probably share them with him. He's smart. Maybe he can help me come up with a way to get the extra money without having to basically hand over my entire paycheck or beg her to give me more time.

I turn over and sit up, intending to get dressed and maybe force myself to eat something before work. Instead, my eyes land on my backpack, which I shoved down to the corner of the bed last night.

Without thinking, I reach down and grab it, yanking it up to the head of the bed with me. Then I unzip the back compartment, pull out my sketchbook and pencils, and flip to one of the few clean pages left in the book.

I'm not an artist. Not really, anyway. And I don't even want to be one. The thought of ever sharing my drawings with anyone actually makes me feel sick. But sketching does help calm me sometimes, especially when I'm just too in my head and can't seem to get myself out. I close my eyes, trying to pull up an image of something soothing, like . . . like Alex's hand on my back, comforting me when we were together in my car on Monday morning. I can still feel it, and I try to channel that feeling as I start to sketch, first a rough outline and then adding more and more detail.

That freckle he's got right next to his knuckle on his right hand.

The wrinkles in my shirt as his hand moves slowly, gently across my back.

The *softness* of it all.

A tear falls down my cheek, and I hate it. I hate it so much that I reach up and swipe it away, but another comes anyway. Why the hell is this making me cry? And what time is it, anyway? Am I going to be late for work now?

I flip over my cell phone and glance at the screen as the time lights up. 8:03 a.m.

Dammit.

I groan, slamming the sketchbook closed. Then I shove it under the pillow, along with my pencil, drag myself out of bed, grab my rewashed clothes from the laundry basket Alex's mom is letting me use, and trudge off to the bathroom to get ready for work. All that anxiety I thought I banished with my sketching has returned as this equally uncomfortable, slowly simmering anger, and I'm not even really sure why.

"So, the thing that most people probably don't know about these book drives is that we don't *actually* keep most of the books." Sharon pushes a laptop over in front of me and hits the power button. She continues talking while the computer boots up, her hands much too animated for my liking, though I manage not to flinch away. "There will be a ton of duplicates, a bunch of books in poor condition or with pages ripped out or writing inside. Then a bunch of books we just don't expect will ever get checked out."

I scoot my chair over a little to give her room as she inputs a password into the computer and then clicks a few buttons to open up a spreadsheet.

"We'll probably only keep about ten percent of the books, honestly," she admits. "For the rest, we've been lucky to partner with a bookstore owner in Omaha the last couple of years. He buys and resells all the books we don't keep. That's why this fundraiser and all these donated books are really important; even if the books themselves don't make it to the shelves, the library ends up with a lot of money."

I nod tightly and look up across the room at the stacks and stacks of boxes lining the far wall. There are probably thousands of books in those boxes. They'll be my job for the next however-long it takes.

I clear my throat. "So, how do I decide which ones to keep?" It seems like a decent-enough question. But Sharon gives me a look that isn't really inviting, and I shrink back into my seat as she continues without directly answering me.

"What you need to do first is sort all of the books. Enter every one into this spreadsheet, regardless of whether it's a duplicate or it's obviously trash," she says.

I'm shaking, though I don't know why. It's been this way all morning. Off and on—shaking and anger and even this random stabbing headache that comes and goes. I clench my jaw and try not to outwardly react or show her how much I'm struggling.

She goes over all of the information I have to enter into the spreadsheet. Then, after she's repeated that information twice, she explains the sorting process she wants me to follow. I write down a few notes as she talks, if only to give myself something to focus on, and then she leaves me so I can get started.

Despite the overwhelming volume of books for me to sort, I find myself actually enjoying the work. It's tedious, yeah, but I get into a sort of rhythm with it, and it passes the time. More importantly, I have to keep myself engaged with the work, and there's not really any room for my mind to wander to the dark place it wants to go.

In fact, I don't even realize how much time has passed until there's a quiet knock at the door.

My eyes dart up, and I see Caitlin, the library assistant, standing in the doorway. She smiles at me as she tucks a short lock of her jet-black hair behind her ear, and then she scans the piles of books I've unboxed and begun to sort. When her eyes meet mine again, she laughs lightly and shakes her head.

"I'm really not at all jealous you've got this job this year rather than me. Although I can't say my group of summer school students is much better," Caitlin jokes easily, stepping into the room. She stops at the end of the table where I'm working, still a good few feet away, and picks up one of the books I just added to the pile for nonfiction books in good condition.

As always, my entire body tenses up at her closeness. Hell, even my chest feels tight, and it's suddenly difficult to breathe. It fucking sucks, and I hate it, especially now. I swallow hard, trying to push the feeling away, because I need to. Caitlin is my work colleague, even if this job is only for the summer, and the last thing I need is to do something idiotic enough that she complains about me to Sharon. I need to keep this job. Now more than ever.

But my stomach twists up into a knot anyway, and I shrink down into my chair. I can't stop it, and I can't hide it. Fucking anxiety.

Unlike Sharon, Caitlin seems to notice my discomfort. She purses her lips and tilts her head slightly, and then she smiles again, although it's maybe a bit more reserved than her first smile.

"Um, I came in to tell you it's time for your lunch break, actually. Sharon says maybe you lost track of the time? And I don't know if you brought lunch or anything, but several of the kids didn't show up today, so we've got extra sandwiches and bags of chips and stuff. It's all in the activity room. Feel free to grab whatever you want."

"Oh, uh, yeah, thanks," I mumble. She's right that I lost track of time. I also didn't bring lunch and sort of planned to just keep working through lunchtime, really. That sounded a lot safer than taking a break and allowing my mind time to wander and think. But my hand shifts into my pocket, and I grip my phone, remembering that it buzzed several times earlier.

Maybe Alex texted.

I haven't spoken with him at all today.

He wasn't awake when I left his house, and I've been working nonstop since I got here, trying to put a dent in the mass of books.

So maybe I *should* take a break, even if just for a few minutes. I can check my texts, or hell, maybe I can even call him. My fingers tighten on my phone at the thought of hearing his voice, and suddenly, lunch sounds like a really, really good idea after all.

I force myself to look back up at Caitlin. "Thanks," I repeat, and I cough to clear my throat, hating the way I sound so unsure all the time. I try a little harder to sound more normal. "I think I'll try one of those sandwiches."

She gives me a small smile and nod and turns to leave, but then she stops and faces me again. She seems like maybe she wants to ask me something, maybe something she knows she really shouldn't. But when I tear my eyes away, pretending to get back to work studying the spreadsheet, she just lets out a long sigh, and I hear her footsteps moving away, toward the door.

My stomach churns anyway, even though she's moving farther away, putting space between us, and I grip my phone tighter in my pocket as the footsteps stop.

"I am really glad to have you here this summer," she says quietly, and even though it makes no sense at all, her comment causes my stomach to hurt more. I shrink down again but force myself to look over at her. She's watching me, and there's something maybe a little too knowing about her expression. "I hope you feel comfortable enough. This is actually a pretty decent place to work. And it's quiet most of the time, as you've probably seen. Sharon can seem like kind of a hard-ass, but she's a good boss, too. And she cares about this library a lot. So, um, just, you know, do your best at whatever she asks you to do, and if you have any questions, don't be afraid to ask."

She sounds kind and genuine enough. But all I can do is nod and force out another quick "thanks."

After she disappears through the open door, I turn back to the computer, save the file I was working on, and then push myself to my feet. I pick out half a turkey sandwich from the platter in the activity room and grab an apple as well, and I head out the side door. There's a small courtyard with a lawn where the fifteen or so summer school students have all gathered, chatting or playing on their phones while they eat. Caitlin is sitting with a group of the younger kids—maybe six- or seven-year-olds—and when she sees me, she gives me a bright grin and small wave before focusing back on the conversation the students are having.

There are a few benches positioned around the courtyard, but most are already occupied by library patrons or the couple of parent volunteers helping with the group of students. I walk as quickly and unobtrusively as I can through the courtyard to the single unoccupied bench, which is thankfully off in one corner by itself and is right under a nice, large oak tree that provides a good amount of shade.

I'm sort of hungry but really sort of not. So rather than force myself to eat, I just set the plate with my sandwich and apple next to me on the bench and finally pull my phone out of my pocket, trying to ignore as my stomach knots itself up in the most uncomfortable way.

It's like this every day now, every time I take out my phone to look at my messages. Because even though I already blocked his number, it could still be *him*. Patrick. Somehow, Patrick could be contacting me again. Threatening me. Accusing me.

Or it could be my mom, which would maybe be worse.

This morning was bad enough. Her messages from the last three days were bad enough. I don't even know what I'd do if she messaged me with more accusations or demands.

But I guess it's my lucky day after all, because the name that pops up on the screen isn't *Mom* or *Unknown Number* or anything like that.

It's *Alex*. And there's a series of several messages, the first one just a tongue-out emoji. I pull my legs up onto the bench to sit cross-legged, and my smile grows slowly as I read every word.

> *Alex (9:38 a.m.):* bro i just woke up

> *Alex (9:40 a.m.):* wut the heck with this heat

> *Alex (9:45 a.m.):* so (stay with me here, this is going to get long) dr ellis emailed me back

> *Alex (9:55 a.m.):* sorry, mom called me to help her get something down from the hall closet

> *Alex (9:58 a.m.):* so long story short, dr ellis wants to connect me with a visiting professor who will be at stanford for the next two years. theyre collaborating on a project and this other professor has a background in supermassive black holes and is *now* studying dark matter as well (which is why theyre coming to work with dr ellis for a time)

> *Alex (10:02 a.m.):* he asked if he could send them our email communications

> *Alex (10:03 a.m.):* im freaking out here. i told him yes of course

*Alex (10:04 a.m.):* thats not crazy, right? cuz now im scared my ideas are dumb. im just a kid, i dont know anything =P

I can almost hear his voice in that last message, and despite all of his uncertainty, it makes me feel even better. The most recent messages he sent were just about twenty minutes ago.

*Alex (12:02 p.m.):* tonight. u and me. harleys. im buying

*Alex (12:02 p.m.):* theyve got a new mint chip flavor and u have to try it

I can't not laugh. Alex and his obsession with mint chip. He *knows* how I'm going to respond, too.

*Nico (12:26 p.m.):* Nothing will ever beat Harley's chocolate peanut butter brownie

I hit send and wait for only a few seconds before his reply comes back.

*Alex (12:26 p.m.):* i dunno man. mint chip.

*Alex (12:27 p.m.):* u on lunch?

My stomach growls, and I glance down at my sandwich. I should eat.

As soon as I have the thought, I feel nauseous, and I swallow back the emptiness in my stomach as I click on Alex's name to call him. The phone rings just once before he answers, and the sounds coming through the phone speaker are immediately loud and jarring.

"Hey, Nico, one sec." Alex sounds flustered or something, but I answer with a quick "okay" and wait. There are some other muffled sounds, and then I hear Alex's voice. After another moment, the background noise fades a bit. "There, hopefully I can hear you now."

"Where are you?" I'm trying to remember if he had something planned for today, but if he told me about it, I can't recall.

"Lando's Lanes," he says, and as though he needs to clarify, he quickly continues. "I'm here with Jenna, but it's super loud and busy. We almost didn't even get a lane. They're having some tournament that's taking up over half of the lanes, and there's music and stuff."

"Oh. Right."

Lando's Lanes is the bowling alley he and some of his other friends like to go to in Omaha. I've been once. Never again. I forgot he was going with Jenna today. I try not to let my stomach sour at the thought of him spending all afternoon with her.

My sandwich looks even less appetizing now, and I gaze out over the lawn as he starts talking again.

"How's the project going? The donated books, right? That started today?"

"Yeah. It's, um, it's good, really. Distracting." I have the sudden urge to tell him about my mom's texts, to admit to him how much I'm struggling, because I could sure as hell use his reassurance and calmness and logic to keep all my panic at bay. But he's out. With

Jenna. And that doesn't really seem like a topic to bring up right now. So instead, I force a laugh, which I hope he hears as genuine. "There are thousands of books, you wouldn't believe it. Some of them are weird, too. One of the boxes I just sorted through had a complete box set of how-to books on 'the Japanese art of decluttering.'"

Alex laughs, and that sound alone makes me glad I called him. I close my eyes and let the warmth of his reaction wash over me.

"Seriously, an entire box set?"

"Yep."

"Bro, I wonder who donated that? Maybe Mr. Jensen or—oh! I know—"

"—Mrs. Hanover!"

Alex is laughing again. "Hah, yep! It had to have been her," he cackles, and now I'm smiling, too.

And my nausea is gone. Just like that.

God, I can't even believe how much better he makes me feel. Even just hearing his voice.

His laugh dies after another few seconds, but he's still chuckling as he says, "I should head back in. Jenna probably just bowled another strike. She's kicking my ass. You're up for ice cream tonight, though, yeah? I should be back before you're off work."

"Um, yeah. Ice cream sounds good." I manage to ignore that part of my heart that's suddenly really jealous of him and Jenna spending time out together, though I still feel the ache. It's another reminder that although he's my best friend, he's not *mine*. Maybe I'm not really ignoring it, though. Maybe I'm just lying to myself and pretending more, because there's a sharp pang in my chest, and even though I fight against the urge, I can't stop myself. My voice drops to some quiet, soft tone as I close my eyes and say, "I can't wait to see you tonight."

It's the fucking truth, anyway, and he *is* my best friend. So it doesn't have to mean a damn thing, except . . . I know it does.

He doesn't respond right away, though I hear him clear his throat with a light cough. And when he does speak, he's oddly stuttering over his words, and his voice is hesitant. "Y-yeah. Yeah, yeah, me too. Um, I . . . can't wait, either."

My eyes open, and I look out across the lawn to where Caitlin and the kids are all starting to get up. Their lunchtime is over, I guess, and that means mine probably is too. I frown down at my uneaten sandwich, my stomach now a mixed bag of butterflies and uncertainty.

"Cool. See you then," I say.

"Yeah."

There's another awkward pause, and I lower my legs down to the ground. "Bye."

"Bye."

I wait for a second before hanging up, and then I drop my chin, wondering what the hell I just fucked up.

# chapter fourteen

## *alex*

WHAT ... JUST HAPPENED?

I'm standing outside the entrance to the bowling alley in Omaha, staring down at the now-blank screen of my cell phone. My head's spinning, and there's a funny tingle in my chest. He called me, which he never does. And then ... then he said, *"I can't wait to see you tonight."*

I can hear the words as if he were standing right next to me. And it's not really the words so much as his tone, soft and with almost some sort of yearning to it. God, I must have imagined it. That's the only explanation, right?

*No, it's not.*

I shake my head, which I realize probably looks strange if there's anyone watching me. But I don't really care. And yeah, that's not the only explanation. There are plenty of other equally possible explanations. Like maybe he just *really* misses his best friend. Or *really* wants Harley's ice cream. Or maybe he's tired from work.

Or maybe ...

My brain backfires in the most spectacular way as I imagine him getting home tonight, walking through the door, coming straight over to me. Then he hugs me, his arms wrapping up around my neck, and his lips find mine.

I hear his voice, clear and wanting. *"I missed you."* The words are whispered against my mouth, and then he kisses me again, his lips soft and pliant and warm.

It's almost too real, this scene that's one hundred percent a product of my overactive imagination. And it's not the first time I've envisioned it. Or something like it. But it might be the first time I've wondered if maybe it could actually happen.

Now is *not* the time or place to be letting myself think about these things, though. Not here, outside the bowling alley, when Jenna is inside waiting for me. Besides, the real explanation for Nico's odd tone is probably just that he's tired and overwhelmed at work. I'm sure he's just looking forward to some quiet time with his best friend. And some ice cream. That's all. It wouldn't be anything more than that.

I let out a long breath and shove my phone in my pocket, willing my brain to quiet down. Then I turn around and head back inside the bowling alley. Jenna stands up as I reach our lane, pushing one of her long, thick black braids back over her shoulder. She grins at me, looking as smug as ever, a teasing glint in her dark-brown eyes.

My head's still spinning, and my heart's still racing, but I force a smile. "Lemme guess, you got another strike?"

"Sure did!" she says, her whole face lighting up, and she steps closer to grab my hand. "Come on, your turn!"

Her fingers close around mine, and she leads me over to the ball return. It's strange and yet not, because she's been doing little things like this the whole time we've been here. Taking my hand, leaning on my shoulder. Hell, she even gave me a much-too-familiar celebratory hug when *I* actually got a strike during the first frame. It's obvious what she's trying to do, and I don't blame her, I guess. She's never been subtle that she likes me. But since I've never been clear to her about my own feelings, she can't really know that I'm not on the same page as her.

I was supposed to fix that today. I promised myself I'd be honest with her about it. And after Nico's phone call, it feels different. Her touch doesn't seem as innocuous anymore. In fact, it's kind of making me uncomfortable now.

I swallow hard and stop. "Jenna . . ."

She looks up at me, her hand tightening around mine, and there's something different in her eyes that's almost hungry. Not really, actually, but for a second, that's what I feel, especially when she loosens her fingers from around mine and starts trailing them up my forearm.

"Hmm?" she asks, her lips pursed into a playful half smile.

And that's really too much now. A sharp shudder runs through me—and it's not pleasant.

I pull my arm away and step back, shaking my head. "Um, can we talk? I think maybe I, uh, need to be more honest with you about . . . things."

She bites her lip as her expression shifts to something much more serious, and then she clasps her hands together in front of her and nods. "Yeah. Sure. Um . . ." She blinks, lowering her eyes, and then motions to the seats next to us. "Is this something we can talk about here? Or should we maybe head out to my car for some privacy?"

That's a good question, though I'm not really sure what the right answer is.

I glance up around the bowling alley, and I'm reminded how loud and busy it is here today. Which automatically makes me think about Nico and how he absolutely hated it here the one time we came together. I can't remember the occasion, maybe it was a birthday party or something.

"Alex?"

"Hmm?" My eyes snap back to hers, and she's watching me now, her eyebrows raised. "Oh, right, um . . . Either should be fine."

"Okay."

She sits and although there are enough seats so that I wouldn't have to sit directly next to her, it suddenly seems like it's even louder in here, and I realize I *would* have to sit directly next to her for her to hear me. I frown.

"Actually—"

She stands up abruptly, shaking her head. "Yeah, it's too loud in here. Come on. I was going to kick your ass anyway. We'll just say I won." She slips off her bowling shoes and puts her sneakers back on, and I copy her. Then we drop off the bowling shoes at the desk at the front before heading outside.

She's quiet as she leads the way, not to her car, but out across the parking lot in the opposite direction. She's walking fast, her head down, and she glances back at me when I jog a few steps to keep up. With a tight smile, she slows her pace a little and says, "I wanted to go to the RiverFront after we were done bowling. Better than sitting in my car, right? And it'll be quiet there."

"Oh, yeah, sure," I agree, and I continue to follow her as she heads down Harney Street for a couple of blocks and then cuts across the short grass toward Conagra Lake, a small, man-made lake right alongside the Missouri River in east Omaha.

I've only been here once before, but Jenna seems to know her way around like she's much more familiar with the place than me. She leads us down to the sidewalk that runs along the outside of the lake and then around to the north end before veering off a side path and up to a small enclave formed around a hexagonal bench.

"I used to come here a lot," she explains as she takes a seat on the bench, pulling her legs up to sit cross-legged. "Before we moved. Or, before we moved *again*, I mean." She pauses for a second and then pats the bench next to her. "Sit. It's really kind of perfect right here."

I run a hand nervously through my hair, but I go ahead and take a seat next to her on the bench. The wooden panels of the bench are warm from the sun, and I fold my legs up to sit like she is, facing the lake. I feel her looking at me for a second, and I turn my head to meet her gaze.

She's more reserved than normal, and I realize she probably has some idea of what I want to talk about, given how I pulled away from her at the bowling alley. But she just flashes me a small smile and then looks back out to the lake.

"I don't know if I ever told you . . ." she starts, and she sets one hand down on the bench close to mine, though she doesn't touch me. "When I was a freshman, we moved from New Hampshire to Kansas City. Then partway through my junior year, we moved again to Omaha. We actually lived in the apartments right over there." She points off in the general direction of the southwest and then frowns. "It was only a year before we moved again, just back at the beginning of March. I guess it was okay, since I hadn't been here that long. Mom still works here in the city. Dad works from home. They wanted to buy a house, since it seems like they're finally settling down and done moving around the country. You know, now that *I* graduated and am ready to head off to college." She laughs sardonically, and there's just enough sadness in her voice that I move my hand over to cover hers.

"That sounds really rough, all that moving around," I say, squeezing her hand gently. Maybe that's counter to what I should be doing, especially with what I need to talk to her about, but I'm trying to be about as platonic as I can about it. And she does seem like she really needs a friend.

But when I lift my eyes to her face, she's staring at our hands with her eyebrows narrowed and her lips pursed.

"Alex, I thought . . . ?"

I huff a quiet laugh and pull my hand away. "Sorry, yeah, I, um . . . You sounded sad, and I . . ." I clasp my hands in front of me and drop my eyes. "I should talk now, huh?"

"Probably."

I hate this. I've dated once before. Or twice, sort of, but the second was a blind date with a friend's cousin who was only in town for a week and so it didn't go anywhere. And Jenna and I are not even dating, though I know she wants us to be. Still, this feels oddly like I'm breaking up with her, and I don't like it.

I close my eyes. "I, um, really like hanging out with you," I start, trying to choose my words carefully. And I'm gearing up to keep going when she lets out a long, drawn-out sigh. Frowning, I turn to look at her again. She's got her knees pulled up to her chest now, her chin resting on them. Her braids hang down to frame her face as she stares out at the lake.

"You really like hanging out with me, *but* . . . ?" She blinks and tilts her head to look at me, and there's an edge to her expression now, an emotional distance she didn't have before. "Let me guess. I'm not your type? Or maybe it's that you don't really want to do a long-distance relationship since you're leaving for California soon? Or maybe you just want to be friends? It's one of those, right?"

I start to open my mouth to respond—with what, I don't even know—but then she shakes her head and turns to look out at the water.

"Don't worry. I'm used to it. I've heard every excuse in the book. I know how it is. I just really thought . . ." She doesn't finish her sentence, and I'm shaking my head as I turn to face her fully this time.

"What did you think?" I ask. I don't really even expect an answer. She's obviously been hurt and led on before, and hell, I'm not really any better than any of those other guys, am I?

She smiles, but now there's almost a bitterness to it. "I really thought you were different, I guess. I thought you were honest.

And I thought you liked me, too."

"I do! I-I mean, I . . ."

"You like me, *as a friend*," she finishes for me.

I close my eyes again and groan, realizing how awful I sound right now. "Well, yeah, but—"

"It's okay. Like I said, I'm used to it."

"It's not okay. I should have told you sooner," I argue. "I just didn't know how to."

Her eyebrows lift in tandem as she turns her head toward me. "You didn't know *how* to? Alex, come on now. That's pretty weak, isn't it? I thought you were supposed to be some genius or something."

I drop my eyes, and my stomach clenches. She's right. It's a pretty lame excuse, and I'm not even sure what the truth is at this point. Why *had* I led her on?

Shaking my head, I say, "I'm sorry. The truth is, I've known you wanted more than friendship for a while now, but—"

"I wasn't exactly hiding it."

"No. You weren't. This is . . . this is on me. I, um . . ."

There's a quiet hum from next to me, and when I glance up at her, her eyes are a little wide and her expression softer.

I frown. "What?"

She bites her lower lip and then takes a deep breath. "You're . . . not . . . attracted to me," she says slowly, although that just confuses me more.

"What? No, that's not it. I mean, I think you're really pretty. Beautiful, actually. And you're nice and fun to be around and—"

"Oh, so you're *not* gay?" she cuts in.

Both of my eyes slam shut, and I shake my head, realizing this just got even more complicated. "I'm not. I'm not gay. I . . ." Fuck. This was *not* what I planned when I decided I wanted to be honest with her. But here we are, and . . . and she's my friend, and a good person. And after how I've hurt her, I should show her some trust. Right? I swallow hard, ignoring the queasiness in my stomach as I finally come out and say the words that I've only admitted to myself in my head. "I'm not gay. I-I'm bi. I think. I mean, I am. Or maybe pan. I'm not really sure, it's, um, hard to define exactly. But I do . . . find you attractive."

She's quiet for a minute, and when I finally convince myself to open my eyes, she gives me this small smile that's soft and kind. I tear my gaze away and stare back down at my hands, clasped tightly together in my lap.

"You're the first person I've ever told that," I say. "I think my mom might kind of know, but I've never actually, you know, told anyone before. So, um . . . yeah."

This time, it's her hand that comes over to cover mine, and it feels different than her touch back at the bowling alley. It feels like it's meant to comfort. With a gentle squeeze, she says, "Thank you for telling me." Then in a slightly teasing tone, she adds, "Although that doesn't really explain why you don't want to date *me*, does it?"

I laugh lightly, shaking my head, and she pulls her hand away and stares back out toward the lake. I follow her gaze, wondering if she's expecting me to explain more. I'm not sure I can, though, and as the silence stretches on between us, she scoots just a little closer.

Then, after a few more minutes, she says, "I'm cool with just being friends."

I tilt my head to look at her. "Yeah?"

"Yeah." She glances at me, smiles, and then bumps me with her shoulder playfully. "Besides, long-distance relationships do kinda suck, and there's no way I'm following you out to Cali."

That makes me laugh—partly because it's funny, but more with relief. She laughs, too, and stands up and offers me her hand.

"Come on," she says. "We didn't have lunch yet, and you're

buying."

"Oh, I am?" There's a warmth in my chest as I take her hand, and it's not awkward or uncomfortable this time.

"Yup. You totally owe me now." She winks and lets go of my hand as soon as I'm standing. "Follow me. I know just the place."

She starts off back down the path toward the lake, and I hesitate for only a second before jogging after her to catch up.

# chapter fifteen

*nico*

I'M SOME WEIRD BALL of nervous energy when I pull up outside Alex's house after work. My fingers are buzzing, and I can't seem to stop my jaw from clenching. The phone conversation I had with Alex has been replaying in my head for the last few hours, and I've got myself pretty convinced that my awkward fuckup has probably just ruined the only good thing in my life right now—our friendship.

And that scares the hell out of me.

I turn off my car and pick up my phone from its spot on the passenger seat, flipping it screen up. But it's the same as it has been since my lunch break was over. No new messages. Not from Alex or from my mom or from anyone else.

The screen is just blank.

And that also scares the hell out of me.

He always texts me in the afternoon. All week long, he's been texting me random things—pictures or memes or just rows of emojis. Every day this week, I've known what I'm coming "home" to. What's going to be on the table for dinner. Whether his mom's got chores for us to do. Whether he wants to do something or has plans.

So his silence this afternoon seems much, much too loud.

With a short breath that barely fills my lungs, I stuff the phone into my pocket and stare up toward the house. The empty hollowness in my stomach reminds me that I haven't eaten all day, which also reminds me that we're supposed to get ice cream tonight, maybe after dinner. And that reminds me how I'm really, really lucky to have a place to live.

Fuck it all if I've screwed that up by being honest with my best friend for once.

*"I can't wait to see you tonight."*

Fuck me. Why had I let that slip?

I close my eyes and force a longer breath. Then I climb out of my car and head inside.

His mom is in the kitchen, stirring the contents of a large pot over the stove, and she smiles and waves me over.

"Perfect timing! Alex is up in his room, and I need a taste tester. Here," she says, and she grabs a clean spoon from the drawer next to her and dips it into the pot. "Broccoli cheddar soup. It's a new recipe, and I'm not sure whether I added enough cheese."

Even though I've been living here for almost a week now and I've known Alex's mom for years, I'm still thrown off by how she just seems to have welcomed me right into the family. She's treating me with more kindness and respect than my own mom maybe ever has. And for a few seconds, I can't really get my feet to move as the weight of that realization settles on my shoulders.

Then she smiles at me again and holds out the spoon. "I think maybe it needs a little more cheddar. What do you think?"

"Um, yeah, I-I can help," I stutter, and my feet unstick as I manage to make my way through the living room into the kitchen. I take a deep breath as I approach, pulling my hands from my pockets. "I'm not sure I've had broccoli cheddar soup before," I admit.

"Oh, well, even better." I stop next to her, and I'm just failing miserably at ignoring the warmth spreading through my chest at her kindness. She hands me the spoon, then adds, "Let me know if you like it. It's one of my favorite soups, but Alex isn't too big a fan. So I'll have more reason to make it if you like it too."

It's all too much again, her kindness and generosity, and my hand starts to shake. I quickly try to hide it by forcing the spoon up to my mouth.

I don't like broccoli. I never have. And my stomach isn't really in the mood for anything, despite how hungry I am. But the soup tastes so good—thick, creamy, and flavorful with the distinct tang of sharp cheddar—that I just nod. "It's perfect just how it is. Alex is wrong to not like this."

That earns me a bright smile, and his mom resumes stirring the soup and then switches off the heat. "Maybe you can convince him to eat it, then," she says with a chuckle. "Dinner is in five minutes. I just need to heat the bread a bit. Can you tell Alex? I'm not sure what he's doing upstairs. He's been up there all afternoon."

"Uh, yeah, sure." I set the spoon in the sink as she starts to get dishes down from the cupboard. Usually Alex would be down here to set the table for her, and the fact that he isn't makes all the nervousness I was feeling earlier come right back as I turn and make my way up the stairs to Alex's room.

The door's shut, which isn't really normal, either. Usually he leaves it cracked open a few inches.

I stop just outside, and the knots in my stomach twist as I lift my hand and knock gently. "Alex?"

There are some muffled noises—a drawer closing, maybe, and his bed squeaks. Then he calls out, "Uh, yeah, hang on, just—just one sec . . ."

A moment later, he's *unlocking* the door, which makes even less sense, until I see him. Then . . . fuck.

Heat rushes straight to my groin as he peeks his head out

around the edge of the door. He's flushed, his cheeks red and his hair messy and ruffled. And his eyes are some weird combination of deep but unfocused. He runs a hand through his hair, which doesn't really straighten it, and he continues hiding partly behind his door as he forces a smile.

"H-hey, Nico. Shoot, sorry, I, um . . . I lost track of time. I was just . . ."

I *know* what the fuck he was doing. And I'm in trouble if he glances down. My fucking slacks won't hide a thing. Stupid work clothes. Dammit.

I tilt my head in the general direction of the kitchen and mumble, "Your mom says dinner's ready in five minutes."

"Uh, yeah. Cool. Okay." He runs his hand through his hair again as he blows out a breath. "'Kay, and uh, then we'll get ice cream?"

"Sure, yeah."

"Okay."

"Okay."

Fuck, this is awkward.

I shove my hands into my pockets and turn away, heading back toward the stairs so I can go get changed out of my work clothes, but I can't get the image of his flushed cheeks out of my head. As I reach the stairs, I glance back over my shoulder, and my stomach swoops. He's watching me, his eyes intense and his hand gripping the doorframe as he bites at his lower lip.

What . . . the fuck? Is he staring at my ass? No way.

I clear my throat, and his eyes dart up to meet mine. He forces another smile and then a laugh, but it's so obviously fake, I can't even figure out how to react.

"Uh, five minutes, you said?" he asks, shifting uncomfortably.

I nod. "Yeah."

He gives me another of those tight, forced smiles and holds

my gaze for several much-too-long seconds. Then he mumbles something I can't hear and quickly disappears back into his room, shutting the door behind him.

I'm even more confused than before.

Dinner is another half hour of awkward.

Thankfully, his mom carries the conversation most of the time, chatting with both of us about who's arriving tomorrow and when. She's made up some loose schedule for the weekend as well, and she shares several lists with us—one of all the things she's going to be cooking, then also a grocery list and another list detailing all the furniture that needs to be rearranged and how she wants the tables set up outside.

Alex barely looks at me the whole time.

I manage to eat a little, and my opinion that the soup is perfect still stands. But I find myself feeling nauseous the first time my eyes meet Alex's because his cheeks immediately turn pink, and he tears his gaze away.

When dinner is over, he offers to do the dishes, and his mom, who seems to be just distracted enough that she doesn't notice the weirdness between the two of us, thanks him and disappears upstairs.

And me . . . I just sit there for a few minutes, staring at my hands, wondering how the hell I should be acting right now.

I'm suddenly exhausted, and though we'd agreed to get ice cream, I can't see this awkwardness going away enough for us to do something that "normal." Maybe I'm wrong, but even now, he's not talking to me. He's just doing the dishes. Quickly and quietly and without looking over at me.

I glance up, letting myself watch him. His shoulders are tense, and he's scrubbing the soup pot with a bit of extra muscle that it really shouldn't need.

Guilt hits me then, because for whatever reason—maybe what I said and how I said it earlier on the phone, maybe something else, I don't really know—my presence here is making him uncomfortable. He shouldn't be uncomfortable in his own house, even *if* I interrupted what I think I interrupted upstairs. I shrink lower in my seat and look away, down the hall toward the bedroom I've been staying in.

"I'm s-sorry," I say, my voice breaking on the second word.

"What?" The clinking of dishes stops, but I can't get myself to look at him.

I drop my hands to my lap and rub my palms on my jeans, shaking my head. "I'm sorry."

He doesn't reply right away, but I feel him come back to the table, and then he pulls out the chair next to me and sits. "Why are you sorry?"

I shrug, and my chest feels tight. I keep rubbing my hands on my jeans, back and forth, back and forth. They're not sweaty or anything, but I can't seem to stop.

"Nico, hey, what's going on?" When I don't answer, his hand settles on top of mine, and I close my eyes as my movement finally stills. "I should be the one saying sorry," he continues. "I've been, um . . . well . . ." He lets out a weak laugh and slowly pulls his hand back. "I had a weird day today, and I've just been in my head a lot this afternoon. I, um . . . I finally told Jenna that I just want to be friends . . ."

He trails off in some way that seems to suggest he's got more to say, but he stops there, and when I look up at him, he's just staring at the table, his jaw tight and one hand absently rubbing the back of his neck. He swallows and glances sideways at me. Again, I get the sense he has more to say, but he stays quiet.

I blink and lower my eyes back to my hands. I want to ask more about Jenna, but it's pretty clear he doesn't want to talk about it. So instead, I just say, "I had a weird day too."

"Yeah?"

"Yeah."

"Work?"

"N-no, kinda. Work was okay. But I . . ." I pause and clench my teeth. I'm so fucking scared to say something wrong and mess things up more that I can't even get myself to say anything at all. He's obviously weirded out by what I told him on the phone, or he wouldn't be acting like this.

My hands ball up into fists, and I screw my eyes shut. I can't fuck this up *more*. I can't. I have to be okay. I have to stop making him uncomfortable. I can't slip up like that again.

Without warning, his flushed cheeks pop back into my mind. Flushed cheeks tinged pink, and with a thin sheen of sweat. And . . . breathless. He was breathless, his lips slightly parted as he tried to hide how fast he was breathing. Then his eyes, dark and intense, staring at me as I walked away. The . . . damn, the *arousal* in them. Shit. Shit. Shit.

What the fuck does it even mean?

"My mom's going to make me pay her for the car, or she'll report it stolen," I blurt out, because my jeans are suddenly too tight and I need to think of something—*anything*—else. "I have until June 6 to come up with five hundred dollars."

"What?! What the . . . No. Nico, that's . . ."

"Fucked up, right?" I push my chair back and pick up my bowl to move it to the sink, needing to put a little distance between us. But he follows me. Of course he follows me.

"How much do you . . . *Five hundred* dollars?"

I nod as I rinse out the bowl and put it in the dishwasher. "I get my first paycheck that day, but it won't be enough."

"Yeah, um . . . Shit."

"Yeah."

He's standing close, right next to me, leaning back against the counter. And I wish he'd just hold me. I wish he'd wrap an arm around my waist and pull me up against him and whisper that everything's going to be okay. Tell me I haven't fucked up and that he'll be here and that I've got a home here. I wish. But even though he's close enough that I can feel the heat of his body, he doesn't move, and whatever this awkward shit is between us just seems to grow.

I dry my hands on a dish towel and then stuff them into my pockets. "I don't know what to do," I mumble. Then, against my better judgment, I pull out my phone, open it to my mom's text from earlier in the day, and hand it to him.

His fingers brush mine, sending a rush of heat through me, but he seems to pull away quickly. Or maybe that's me imagining it. In any case, I shove my hands back into my pockets and stare down at the floor as he silently reads the texts from my mom.

I only know he's done when he blows out a long breath, sets my phone on the counter, and then hesitates for a second before stepping closer.

Please.

"Nico, I . . . God, that's so messed up," he says, his voice low and rough.

Please.

I close my eyes as my chest tightens.

Please help me.

He's going to. I can feel it. He's moving closer, and he'll hug me and make everything that much better, despite how fucked up it all is and despite how much *I* fucked up.

Just when I'm sure he's about to touch me, about to hold me

and make me feel protected and safe, he scuffs his foot into the floor and backs away several steps. "I, um, have some money from graduation and helping out my mom," he says. "Would that help you? How much do you need?"

I can't answer because I can't really breathe. I just shake my head. Then I turn and grab my phone, stuff it back into my pocket, and push away from the counter, too confused and too tired to deal with life anymore today.

"I'm going to bed," I tell him, and I start walking toward my bedroom, shrinking in on myself more with every step.

There's part of me that's still expecting him to follow—to come after me and stop me and remind me that we're supposed to go get ice cream. Harley's. Because mint chip.

But there's another part of me that knows that's not going to happen.

I make it all the way to the bedroom, and it's not until I shut the door behind me and collapse onto the bed that the little bit of hope I had disappears.

# chapter sixteen

## *alex*

I CAN'T SLEEP.

Every time I close my eyes, all I see is Nico shaking his head and walking away from me in the kitchen, his shoulders slumped in defeat. It's been hours, yet I can still *feel* the pain—his pain—when I failed him. He confided in me. He shared those texts from his mom with me, showing me even more of the awful shit she was throwing at him. And when he needed me the most, when he needed me to be there for him and help him, I failed, too embarrassed or guilty or whatever the hell is wrong with me right now to let myself comfort him.

I check my phone for the millionth time, but the last few messages I sent him are still unanswered.

> *Alex (7:15 p.m.):* im sorry i was being weird. r u ok?

> *Alex (8:23 p.m.):* i can still grab ice cream if u want. harleys is open until 10

> *Alex (11:44 p.m.):* r u awake?

He'd usually text me back after that last one, no matter his mood. An eye-roll emoji and something sarcastic, like *No, I'm totally asleep. See? Snoring away for hours now.*

So maybe that means he is asleep. Or maybe he's even more upset than I imagined.

And that means I really, really need to figure out how to fix this—whatever *this* is. So, I lie there staring at the wall as more hours pass, trying to think of something.

I come up with absolutely *nothing*.

I could help him with the money, sure. I did get quite a bit from my grandparents for graduation, and I've been saving almost everything for the last few years when I've worked for my mom. But he already turned that down once. Plus I'm pretty sure that's not the whole problem. Or even *most* of the problem. It's something else too.

Like the fact that he needed me to be there for him, and I . . . couldn't.

My chest tightens, and I roll onto my back to stare at the ceiling a bit, just for a change of scenery. That doesn't exactly help, though. It just rewinds the day a little more, back to the moment right before he knocked on my door to tell me dinner was ready.

I was lying here just like this, my knees bent up, stroking myself while I pictured him leaning over me, his hand on my dick, then his tongue—

"Ah, fuck."

I lift an arm up and muffle another curse into my elbow, but I can't stop my dick from responding. I'm already hard, and the images in my head just keep coming, even as I try to stop them. Nico lifting his beautiful green eyes to look at me, his lips stretching around my cock, then his hand following up and down as he bobs his head to take me in all the way. His cheeks are flushed, his eyes dilated, and—*god*—his mouth pops off me long enough for him to whisper in a low, hoarse voice, "Come for me, Alex."

With a groan, I bend one knee up and reach down to slip my hand under the waistband of my briefs, unable to resist the urge to finish what I started earlier. A sharp breath escapes me as I slide my palm down my length and then wrap my fingers around the base of my shaft. I try to push away the thoughts of him, but I fail at that too. It's *his* hand, *his* mouth, *his* heat.

"God," I hiss into my elbow, screwing my eyes closed. My fist moves, pumping slowly at first. Slowly and then a little faster and a little faster as the pleasure and tension build. There's a familiar tingle, like a warm shiver racing down my spine, and I groan again, pushing my head back into my pillow.

*"That's it. Come for me, Alex."*

Ah, hell.

My hips jerk up off the bed as my dick starts to throb with my release, warm liquid shooting out onto my stomach, and I turn my head to the side to muffle a moan against my arm.

I lie there for several minutes afterward, coming down from that high as my breathing slows back to normal. There's a layer of guilt wrapped around me, and I can't make myself move to go get cleaned up. It seems bad of me—wrong to have been picturing my best friend pleasuring me as I jerk off. And it's even worse because that's a big part of why I failed him earlier.

It felt too awkward.

He interrupted me when he knocked on my door. Then I saw it in his eyes. He *knew* what I'd been doing.

Not that I have any shame about masturbating. Not really. But when I'm jerking off to mental images of him with his hand and mouth on my cock, his voice whispering dirty words of encouragement, his tongue sliding up my slit, tasting me . . . and then I'm too embarrassed that he caught me in the act to give him the comfort he *needs* later, with everything he's going through . . .

Hell, those texts from his mom . . .

And not just that, but also having to deal with work, starting this new job when it's hard for him to even be around people thanks to his awful anxiety. Then having to live with the fact that he was basically kicked out onto the street, yelled at and chased out of his home by the man who abused him for years . . .

I couldn't even help him. God, what the hell kind of best friend am I?

I blow out a long breath, and even though my body still feels weak and shaky from my climax, I manage to pull myself up out of bed, wipe the cum off my stomach with a T-shirt that's in my laundry basket, and then sneak down the hallway to the bathroom to clean up better.

A few minutes later, I'm crawling back into bed, under the comforter, and I swallow and turn over to face the wall, closing my eyes.

I see him again, tense and unsure, his eyes filled with pain. He was nearly begging me to help him, and I was too distracted and embarrassed to see it, to act, to give him the support he needed.

I see him again, walking away.

And I screw my eyes shut.

*Never again.*

There's a conviction to my thought, and on impulse, I turn over and grab my phone from the nightstand. I set an alarm for seven, which—dammit—is only about three hours from now. Then I type out another text.

> *Alex (3:57 a.m.):* I can't wait to see you in the morning

I don't give myself a chance to worry about whether that's the right thing to say. I hit send, set the phone down, and roll back over to face the wall, pulling the comforter all the way up to my chin. Then I close my eyes and try to convince myself to fall asleep.

My alarm goes off right at seven. I'm not sure how much sleep I actually managed, but I drag myself out of bed without hitting snooze, take a quick shower, and get dressed. By the time I'm heading down the stairs, it's easily about seven twenty, and I'm hoping I still have enough time to make breakfast before Nico wakes up.

He didn't text me back, which isn't unexpected. Hopefully he's just been sleeping. But I'm still worried, and I still hate how I hadn't handled things well last night. All of yesterday, actually.

He deserves better from his best friend. And I will do better.

Starting with food.

"You're up early!" My mom's standing in the kitchen, leaning back against the counter and sipping from a cup of coffee as I jog down the stairs.

She's right. This is much earlier than I've been getting up since summer started. But I just shrug as I approach.

"I wanted to get going early today," I say. "Lots to do before this afternoon."

I stop just on the other side of the kitchen island as she eyes me with that . . . look. I'm not sure how to describe it. It has to be something only moms are capable of. Her eyes seem to see right through me, right into the heart of what's bothering me. Which isn't cool because I'm not ready to talk about anything yet. I frown and look down at the floor, avoiding her gaze.

"Today *is* busy," she agrees, her voice soft. "But if you need to talk, about *anything*, you know I'm never too busy for you, right?"

I know that, and her words remind me that yesterday was about more than just Nico. My conversation with Jenna is still weighing on me, too, and yeah, it would be really nice to have someone to talk to about that. That's for later, though. Right now, I have something I need to do, and what will likely be an emotional coming out conversation with my mom isn't it.

I lift my eyes and force a tight smile. "I might take you up on that later," I say, and she smiles and nods.

"Just as long as you know—"

"—that I can talk to you about anything. Yeah, Mom, I know." My smile loosens a bit, and she seems to chuckle as she sets down her coffee mug and then pushes away from the counter.

"I need to get to the grocery store and then start cooking. Jerry and Thelma will be here probably around three. They're staying in the extra bedroom for the weekend. Then Erica and Corrine are expecting to get here sometime before dinner. They'll take the pull-out couch."

I nod, even though I'm not sure I can remember exactly who Jerry and Thelma or Erica and Corrine are. Cousins, probably. "Sounds good. I'm just going to make some breakfast for Nico and then—" She gives me a look again, her eyebrows lifting up in tandem, but I ignore her this time and continue. "And *then*, I'll get started on the last of the laundry, changing the sheets and blankets and stuff in the extra bedroom, and the other chores on your list."

There's a moment where I see her wanting to ask—her tells are too easy to identify by now. But she holds back and then nods and picks up a piece of paper from the counter. "Anything you want me to add to this shopping list before I go?"

"Dr. Pepper?"

She rolls her eyes and swats at me as I come around the island to get started cooking. It's a bit of a running joke between us, because shortly after I was diagnosed with an allergy to cinnamon when I was maybe two years old or so, I started obsessing over every can of Dr. Pepper I saw. She says she thinks I just liked the color of the cans or something, since I was much too young to drink it, but because of my newly diagnosed allergy and the uncertainty around exactly what foods and beverages contain cinnamon, she banned Dr. Pepper and all other types of pop from the house.

"Seriously, is there anything you need?" She slips her arm around my waist and hugs me, and I look down at her and shake my head.

"No, I don't think so. I'll text you if I think of anything."

"Okay," she says, and she gives me another squeeze. "I love you."

"Love you, too, Mom."

She seems to hesitate for a second, but then releases me from her hug, pats me on the arm, and grabs her keys and purse off the table. She's out the door and gone before I even have the griddle out for the pancakes. Then, it's quiet.

Which is bad for my mind.

It wanders.

It wanders way back to the summer before that jackass Patrick showed up in Nico's life. We were ten, and there was one weekday when I got to sleep over at his house. That didn't happen often because his mom worked a lot; usually we had sleepovers at my house. But this particular time I remember because we built a fort out of couch cushions in his living room, and that was where we slept. And in the morning, we woke up to the smell of pancakes and eggs. I remember Nico jumping up and grinning and shaking my shoulder. Telling me to get up because his mom just made the best breakfast *ever*.

That was the first time I saw him smother his whole plate—eggs and all—in syrup.

And the first time my heart raced to see his smile.

What I wouldn't give to see that smile again this morning . . .

Just as I finish cooking, I hear the door to the downstairs bedroom open with a quiet creak, and my eyes dart up. He doesn't see me right away. He just steps out into the hallway, tucking his gray polo shirt into his slacks, and he starts shuffling in my direction. When he reaches the end of the hallway, he finally looks up, and then he freezes when he sees me.

There's no smile on his face, which just means I'm going to have to work to put it there, and yet my heart races all the same as he blinks and holds my gaze.

Did he read my texts? I wish I knew.

I clear my throat and try for a smile myself. "Hey."

He hesitates but then continues on his way toward me, running a hand through his hair. "Hey. You're up early." There's a note of something to his voice and clear tension in his shoulders, and I wish I could take it all away. I wish he had no reason for that tension to even be there in the first place.

"I couldn't sleep last night," I admit.

He stops at the kitchen table, and his eyes finally shift from me to the stovetop. He stares at the food for several seconds, then looks back up at me. "Yeah, I couldn't either."

Guilt rams into me, and I frown as I drop my eyes. I know he doesn't really like it when I apologize, but I need to own this, so I make myself look back up at him. "I'm sorry. I feel like I wasn't a great friend yesterday, and I hate that—" I pause as he shakes his head, the pain in his eyes now clear and deep.

"It's not you," he mumbles, gripping the chair in front of him. "It's me. I'm fucked up, Alex. My *life* is fucked up. That's not your fault."

"Maybe not, but I feel like I made things worse instead of better yesterday, and I didn't mean to. So I'm sorry," I repeat.

He frowns and holds my gaze for another few seconds. And god, my heart can't stand it. His eyes are so beautiful that I let myself get lost for the briefest of moments.

I want to just come right out and tell him. I want to tell him how beautiful he is, how much he means to me, how much I hate to see him hurting. I want to tell him all of that and more. And maybe, *maybe* I would if we weren't short on time this morning.

But he has to leave in maybe fifteen or twenty minutes, and he still has an entire plate of syrup-drenched breakfast foods to eat.

So instead, I say the words silently—the *I love you* that I know is true—and then I smile.

"I made breakfast."

He's still looking at me, his beautiful eyes studying me as he bites his lower lip, and it's only after another few seconds that he finally blinks and shifts his gaze to the food on the stovetop. "I . . . could eat."

A small smile.

I'm gifted with a small, brief smile that flickers at the corners of his lips before he lifts his eyes to me and adds, "If there's enough syrup."

A huge grin breaks out across my face, and I laugh. "There is."

He holds my gaze again, and this time, his smile seems to spread just enough that his eyes twinkle a little. It's not quite the smile I'm hoping for—that smile of his that I just know can light up the whole room. But it's getting there. And that's good enough for right now.

# chapter seventeen

## *nico*

I SCREW MY EYES shut as I hold the phone up to my ear, listening to it ring once, twice, three times. Just when I think she's not going to answer, the next ring cuts short, and her voice attacks me through the phone's speaker.

"I hope you're calling to tell me you have my money," she spats, and my stomach drops.

I push my head back against the headrest and open my eyes, staring out the front windshield of my car across the now-empty parking lot of the library.

"Not until next Friday, like I told you."

"Well, what do you want, then? You're not getting another extension. I need the money."

"And you think I fucking don't?!" I can't hold it back. I *meant* to. I tried. I fully intended to stay levelheaded and calm. But it's impossible. "I'm hanging on by a thread here, Mom. I have *forty dollars* to my name, and I'm wearing the same fucking set of clothes to work every day because I can't afford anything else right now. And next Friday, I'll get my *first* paycheck, and it probably won't even be enough, and you're expecting me to hand it all over like I don't need the money to *live*. What the fuck, Mom?"

She doesn't respond, which is probably a good thing. I take a breath to try to steady myself, and then I continue. "I was just calling because I'd really like to keep my cell number if possible. But that requires you to call T-Mobile and authorize it since you're the current—"

"No."

My hand balls up into a fist, and I press it down into my thigh hard. "But—"

"You asked, I answered. My answer is no."

"Wh-why?" I stutter, and my jaw clenches tight. I should probably just hang up now. It's not worth it, is it? To try to convince her of this? I should just hang up and make sure I've copied all of my contacts and everything before my line is canceled and I've lost my number. But I can't understand her hostility, and it's tearing me up. "Why are you being like this, Mom? I-I don't understand."

She sighs audibly—a sharp, frustrated sound, and then she grumbles, "I'm busy. I don't have time for this. Figure the phone stuff out for yourself. And get me my money by next Friday."

And then the line goes silent.

I pull the phone away from my ear and glare at it, gripping the plastic case so tight my fingers go white. The anger sizzling in my chest feels hot and uncontrolled, and I don't like that. I force myself to move, to set the phone down gently on the passenger seat, fasten my seat belt, and start the car. Then I force myself to make the drive back to Alex's house, following every speed limit sign and stopping completely at each stop sign.

The anger doesn't really fade, though maybe part of it does, because by the time I turn onto his street and see multiple cars parked outside along the curb—his cousins, I'm sure—I'm overcome by a new sort of numbness. It spreads through my chest and down into my toes. And it's cold.

I shiver, despite the heat of the late May afternoon, and I park my car behind an expensive-looking newer Jeep with a vanity plate that reads *OMYDOG*. I should get out and go inside, but instead, I just sit there and let my eyes wander up to Alex's window on the second story.

He texted me earlier, around lunch time, when I was on the phone with T-Mobile, trying to get things sorted out for my cell phone. He'd been sending texts all morning long. Emojis and memes and pictures of all the food his mom was cooking. Then, at just about 12:30 p.m., he sent a text that said *I can't wait to see you tonight*.

And I'm fucking confused as hell.

Last night after dinner was awful enough. I don't think I slept much. Periodically getting texts from him all night long hadn't helped, especially the one he sent at four in the morning or whatever god-awful time that was.

*I can't wait to see you in the morning.*

Why was he up at four in the morning? And . . . why was he thinking about me?

Now this text, too.

It feels like he's trying to tell me something—because why else would he use that *exact* wording?—but that can't be true. Can it?

I'm too tired, though. I'm too tired to think about it more or worry about it or try to make sense of it.

And now I've got the shit from my mom swirling around in my head. Plus, if I'm going to not be an awful guest, I'm going to have to sit and eat dinner with a table full of people I don't know and smile and talk and pretend that everything is okay. Which it's not.

I'm usually good at pretending. But I'm also just fucking exhausted.

This might be a really, really horrible night.

With a deep breath, I try to push everything down, somewhere that no one, not even Alex, will see. Then I stuff my phone and keys in my pocket, climb out of the car, and head inside.

As soon as I open the door, all my resolve drains away. They're loud. Whoever they are. There's laughing and chatter and too many unknown voices. My racing heart backfires, and it's annoying and painful, the pounding in my chest. I almost can't move for a moment, and I just stand there in the doorway as the voices continue.

Then I hear my name. It's Alex's mom, but I can't look up. Why can't I look up?

"Oh, good, Nico, you're home. Come on over here and say hello! These are my cousins, Jerry and—"

Alex's voice cuts in, a clear reprimand in his tone. "Mom, not now."

I swallow hard and force myself to lift my eyes. Alex is on his way over to me, his eyes full of concern. He mouths a quick "sorry" and then stops right in front of me, blocking my view of everyone else, and offers me a small smile.

"Sorry, my mom's just excited to have everyone here. Are you . . ." His smile falters as he studies me, and I lower my eyes back to the floor. I feel him turn away, and then he says, "Mom, I'll be back in a few minutes. Nico and I are heading upstairs for a bit. Okay?"

There's no verbal response, but his hand settles low on my back, warm and solid, and he guides me forward, to the stairs. A moment later, we're in his room, and he shuts the door behind us.

"Sorry about that. My mom, uh, well, she's had a few glasses of wine this afternoon. She gets kinda forgetful when she's tipsy."

"Yeah, um . . . it's okay."

He mumbles something that's a little too quiet for me to hear, but then his hand is there again, on my lower back. "You look tired. Here, sit," he says softly, and he presses his hand into me, helping me move toward the bed. "Do you, um, want to talk? What . . . what happened? Did something happen?"

My stomach churns as I lower myself to sit on the edge of the bed. He sits next to me, and I close my eyes, wishing, just like I had last night. Wishing he'd touch me again, hold me, comfort me.

And this time, he doesn't back away. He scoots closer until his shoulder is touching mine, and then his hand settles carefully on my upper back.

"Nico?"

He rubs gently along my back, the motion slow and light, and I let out a shuddering breath and lean into him as a wave of relief saps the last of my energy.

"I'm just so tired." My head drops onto his shoulder, and I close my eyes. His hand continues to stroke along my back and up around my shoulders until he's holding me. And it feels so good, just like I knew it would. I sigh and relax into him. "This is good, though."

There's a quiet chuckle. "Yeah?"

"Mm-hmm." My voice is muffled as I bury my head in his shoulder, and for half a second, he seems to tense a little. But then his arm tightens around me, and he chuckles again.

"Good. I'm glad," he says. I'm probably imagining how soft and low his voice has gotten. And how he gently lays his head on top of mine. And his tenderness as his hand caresses up and down my arm.

But if I'm not imagining it, this has to be the best way to spend time after work.

I sigh into him and pull my feet up onto the bed as I kick off my shoes. And he keeps holding me as I start talking quietly. I tell him how exhausting work was and how awful my mom was on the phone. I tell him how I'm worried I might lose my phone number and how everything feels so hopeless sometimes, like I don't even know which way is up or how to move forward from here.

He just listens and keeps holding me, and when I'm done, he

takes a long breath. His voice is filled with that same softness I might have been imagining earlier as he promises me I'm not alone and that he's here for me. Then he quietly suggests that if I'm not feeling like I can or want to socialize tonight, he can bring some dinner up.

But I'm too tired to eat, even. I feel him frown when I tell him that, and I quickly walk it back. Maybe I can manage, I say. And when he asks if I'm sure, I nod and say "yeah."

I can try, anyway. I can try and pretend for a little bit longer. For him.

Dinner is fucking horrible. I mean, not the food, although I'm really not hungry enough to enjoy it, and I only eat most of what's on my plate because I know Alex is watching. But the conversation is hard to be around. Alex's cousins seem nice enough, but they're all drinking, and it's kinda noisy and high-energy. It's not bad, really.

It's just me.

I can't handle things, like loud, lively conversation with people I don't know. Especially tonight. I'm on edge the whole time. Pretending hard. Pretending not to flinch every time someone laughs too loudly. Pretending to be engaged. Pretending not to be sick to my stomach.

It's fucking awful.

As soon as I finish, I thank Alex's mom and excuse myself. Then I retreat upstairs to shower and get ready for bed, even more exhausted now than I was earlier.

It's nearly midnight by the time Alex comes upstairs and the house starts to quiet down. I'm lying on the bed, as I have been for the last few hours, just scrolling on my phone.

He's smiling, like he'd been enjoying all the laughter and everything, and there's a moment when he stops and our eyes meet that I let his smile wash over me. It feels warm, and I try again. For him.

"Dude, look at this," I say, and I turn my phone toward him as the video I was watching starts to replay. It's nothing important. Just a short video of a little gray cat being silly and rolling slowly down a flight of stairs. But Alex steps closer as his eyes shift away from me, and his face lights up even more as the video plays.

"God, that's just—"

"—fucking adorable, right?"

He grins again and nods, and I lower the phone and shut off the screen. Alex steps over to his dresser and pulls out some pajama pants and a T-shirt, and I slowly sit up, my arms complaining from the effort.

"I'll be right back," he starts, and then he glances toward the closet. "I think I still have the extra pillows and blankets and stuff, if my mom didn't steal them for Jerry and Thelma. I'll check in a sec."

His eyes meet mine, and there's a flicker of something in them, but it's gone too quickly. Then he nods and disappears out the door and down the hallway to get changed and ready for bed, I guess.

I drop my phone on the bed and push myself to my feet, ignoring the exhaustion and brief dizziness that come with standing up. Then I head to the closet. I probably should have made up the bed on the floor earlier, but if I hurry now, maybe he won't argue with me when I insist on sleeping on the floor.

I roll my eyes at the thought. Of course he's going to argue with me. Because that's who he is.

The pillows and blankets are still in there, neatly folded and arranged on the shelf in the closet, and I pull them all down and have just started unfolding the thick comforter to lay it out for my bed when the door opens behind me. I glance back over my shoulder.

"Almost done."

He shuts the door. "Ah, thanks. You didn't have to do that."

The implication is there—he's planning to take the floor. He knows it, and he knows I know it.

I narrow my eyes at him. "Nope. Not this time."

He gives me a look and then steps in and starts to take over, setting one of the pillows right near the nightstand. "I'm sleeping on the floor. You're taking the bed." He says this like it's just the law or something, and part of me feels some weird tingle of warmth at his no-nonsense tone.

The other part of me gets angry.

"No chance." I push myself in front of him to grab the second pillow, but he nabs it first.

"You sleep better in the bed, remember?" he says, even as I snatch the pillow away from him. He lets go, but his eyes are fucking beautiful. Shining with amusement or something.

I'm not really amused.

Or maybe I am.

I'm not sure.

I turn my back to him and set the pillow down on top of the other one. "Yeah, but it's your bed. I'm not taking it away from you again."

"You're not sleeping on the floor, either," he says, using that same tone as though he's stating some undeniable fact.

A shiver runs down my spine, and I bite my lip as I ignore him, fluffing the pillows and then grabbing for the second blanket. His hand encircles my wrist, and I pause and lift my eyes to meet his.

"Take the bed. Please," he says.

"No."

"Nico."

"Alex."

"That's not going to work this time."

"And you're not sleeping on the floor in your own room."

"You're not sleeping on the floor, either," he repeats. "My room, my rules."

I twist my wrist to pull it away from him. "Then I guess we're just both sleeping in the bed," I spit out, calling his bluff.

Or, that was my intention.

His cheeks turn bright fucking red. And it's adorable as hell.

But then he does the thing I don't expect. He nods. "Yeah, okay. It's big enough for both of us."

What the fuck. "Yeah. Totally."

"Yep."

"Uh-huh."

He moves in front of me, his face still bright red, and he grabs the two pillows from the ground and tosses them up onto the bed. Then he leans over and straightens them, and if I wasn't so distracted by this little game of chicken we appear to be playing, I might notice how nicely the thin cotton plaid of his pajama pants stretches over his ass.

Aw, hell, who am I kidding? I totally notice anyway.

Alex straightens up then and blows out a breath as he stares at the bed before glancing back at me. He seems much less sure of himself when our eyes meet again, and he reaches up to run a hand through his hair. "Which, uh, side do you want?"

I shrug, but I feel my cheeks heat up, and I quickly look away, back to the bed. My phone's sitting there, the screen now blank, and I step around Alex, pick it up, and set it on the nightstand. And since there's no way I'm backing out now, I go ahead and crawl onto the bed and under the covers, scooting all the way over until I'm right up against the wall, my back to him.

I close my eyes and hold the blanket up to my chin, and he clears his throat, turns out the light, and climbs into the bed after me.

"Good night, Nico," he says into the dark.

"Good night, Alex."

There's a pause, and then his voice is gentle and quiet when he adds, "I can't wait to see you in the morning."

A soft warmth surrounds me, and I hold my breath for a second before letting it out slowly. Then I swallow and say, "Yeah. Me too."

He shifts a little behind me, and then I just hear his quiet, rhythmic breathing. And I close my eyes and try to fall asleep.

# chapter eighteen

## alex

NICO'S IN MY BED.

Nico's in my bed, *with me*. He's not two feet away, and my heart hasn't stopped hammering in my chest for a while now, at least since he blurted out that we should both sleep in the bed. Together.

And now here we are. Although I'm not sure whether I'm going to be able to sleep. My whole body seems to be on fire, and I've got the urge to turn over and scoot closer and gather him up in my arms. I can picture it and feel it, and it's all I can do to keep myself from acting on it.

I try to relax, try to keep my breathing level and deep, if for no other reason than I don't want him to sense how tense I am. After what might be a half hour or so, I hear him exhale a long, deep breath, and not more than a few minutes later, he shifts a bit, his body heat moving closer. His soft snoring stays rhythmic and slow.

Very carefully, I turn over until I'm facing him, and then I bite back a smile as contentedness washes over me. He's lying on his back just about in the middle of the bed now, and even through the darkness, I can see how beautiful he is. His eyes are closed lightly, his long, dark lashes contrasting against his pale skin, and he looks so relaxed, so comfortable.

My heart is urging me, too. To hold him. To hug him. To chase away anything bad that might bother him in his dreams and do everything in my power to help him feel safe and loved.

After everything he's been through, he deserves that. He deserves to feel loved.

I hope I've shown him that today—not only that I care about him but also that he's worthy of everything he wants and needs. I hope he knows.

He mumbles something quietly in his sleep and shifts again, and when I open my eyes, he's facing away from me, though he's still much closer than he had been at first.

I smile and whisper, "Sleep well." Then I close my eyes as I settle deeper into my spot.

I bury my face into something soft, something dreamy and pleasant, and I inhale deeply. The faint scent of vanilla makes a smile tease at my lips, and I hum as I nuzzle in a little more. "Mmm."

A warm solidness is pressed flush against my chest, and I'm not really thinking, still waking up from whatever pleasant dreams I was having, as my arm slides around and pulls the warmth up against me tighter.

It feels like *him*, though I'm sure it can't be, and in my half-awake state, I marvel at how perfectly we fit together. Like I always knew we would. I stay there for several long moments, breathing him in, feeling his warmth, sure I'm going to wake up for real any second.

It's only after I bury my face into his neck as my hand starts to caress upward that he tenses.

He.

Him.

Nico.

I . . . Holy crap.

"Shit, Nico, I—I'm sorry." My mind seems to finally catch up with my body, and I realize that I *am* awake and I *am* holding him, cuddled up against his back with my arm wrapped around his torso, my palm flattened against his chest over the top of his T-shirt. I go to pull away, but his hand grabs mine, and he presses it into him.

"Please. Please . . . stay." He swallows audibly, and I feel him shudder into me. "Please."

God.

His hand is gripping mine tightly, and tension pulls his shoulders inward as he shrinks a little. But he shrinks *back into me,* not away, and I close my eyes and lower myself back into my spot on the bed.

He wants me to stay. Here. Holding him. He wants me to hold him. Just like this.

He's warm. And . . . god, we do fit perfectly together.

Is this supposed to be platonic?

Holy hell, what am I doing?

"Okay," I say, and I inhale and exhale a slow breath as he sort of tugs me back into that place I found a few moments ago that was so comfortable, holding him tightly against me with my hand on his chest and my face buried in his hair. My legs are slightly bent, and the curve of his ass sits right at the top of my thighs.

Ah, damn. I'm not sure if this really *is* okay.

But then some of his tension seems to leave him, and he shifts a tiny bit, stretching one of his legs out to wedge it between mine. And that's even better. I inhale again slowly. He smells faintly of vanilla, and he's so warm, and this is so perfect.

"Thank you," he breathes, his voice barely audible.

"Yeah. Yeah, of course."

I nuzzle the back of his neck slightly, like I had earlier when I thought I was asleep, and god, how I want to kiss him. But I stop myself. Instead, I close my eyes and tighten my arm around him, humming quietly against his skin. "Mmm, is this okay?"

He takes a long, slow breath in and lets it out, and the tiny tremor in his body fades, along with all the rest of the tension in his shoulders. "Yeah," he whispers. "It's . . . it's perfect."

My heart flutters, and I wonder if he can feel me smiling against him. "Okay. Cool. Um, good night again."

He doesn't say anything this time, but he takes another of those long breaths, and his hand comes up to cover mine on his chest.

It *is* perfect. I'm really not sure there's ever been anything more perfect.

I lie there quietly for what seems like a long time, just holding him. I doubt I can sleep like this, but he falls back into a gentle sleep within only a few minutes, his body relaxed into mine, his breathing deep and slow. And my heart feels full and grateful.

I blink my eyes open in the darkness, and from the thin strings of light poking through the shutters, I can see the outline of his body, the gentle rise and fall of his chest. He has to trust me so much to let me be this close, to hold him like this.

It's overwhelming to think about how much he's giving to just being *here* with me, especially knowing how much he's been hurt, both in the past and now.

I let my arm tighten around him again, and I close my eyes and settle my cheek against the back of his neck.

"Thank *you*," I whisper on a quiet breath. Then I let the feel of his heart beating under my palm lull me off to sleep.

# chapter nineteen

## *nico*

WHEN I WAKE UP Saturday morning, the first thing I feel is him. His hand on my chest, his warm breath on my neck, his leg resting over mine. He's still holding me just like he was when I fell asleep however-many hours ago that was, and there's a gentleness to it, a tenderness that I just *know* I'm not imagining this time.

I love it.

I lie still, not wanting to wake him. It was one thing to ask him—god, I practically begged him, didn't I?—when it was the middle of the night. When he rolled over into me and then wrapped me up in his arms, cradling my body in his. It was one thing to ask then, but it'll be something completely different when he wakes up now, the room bright with the morning's light, his family showing up early for the weekend-long party.

I can already hear noises from downstairs. Talking and dishes clinking and furniture being moved around. His mom will come up here soon if he's not awake, reminding him she needs him to help with things. She probably needs my help, too, to set up outside or cook or run to the store.

I don't realize I'm holding my breath until his hand presses lightly into my chest and then slides downward to my stomach.

"Mmm, Nico . . ."

I figure he's not really awake fully or he would have pulled away, cursing another apology like he did last night. But that's not what happens. At all. Instead, he burrows his face into my neck and inhales deeply with another contended hum. His leg straightens just enough that his foot plays with mine for a second, and then he caresses back up my chest with his hand, still pressing lightly into me.

"Did you sleep okay?" he mumbles against me. "What time is it?"

"Dunno," I answer, too distracted to say much else.

He chuckles, and it's even more distracting then, feeling his whole body shake with his quiet laugh. "You don't know if you slept okay, or you don't know what time it is?" he teases, and then he nuzzles my neck, which sends a jolt of heat through me. I almost moan when he does it again, pulling me back against him more at the same time. "I slept really well," he murmurs, and his voice becomes a little quieter and deeper when he says, "I hope you did, too."

Holy fuck, what is all of this?

"I did."

There's another chuckle, and he squeezes me gently. "Good." He hums, and then takes a long, slow breath before pushing himself away with a groan.

I turn over to watch him as he scoots to the edge of the bed, sits, and reaches for his phone.

"Shoot. It's after eight thirty already," he says, frowning and running a hand through his hair as he stands up. "Mom's probably panicking right about now. I think I was supposed to be downstairs to help her like an hour ago."

He pauses as our eyes meet, and his cheeks flush, a smile teasing at his lips.

God, he's so fucking adorable.

I purse my lips, knowing I'm taking yet another stupid risk that I probably shouldn't, and I reach my hand out toward him. "Just five more minutes . . . ?"

I *need* him to say yes. I don't even know why. I just *need* it. So when his smile softens and he nods, a shiver of relief courses through me, warm and hopeful and something else that feels . . . good.

His eyes stay on mine as he quietly climbs back into the bed, and then I roll over while he pulls the comforter back up over us, settles down behind me, and wraps one strong arm around my midsection. I whimper, because I guess I love to embarrass the hell out of myself. But he just does that thing where he hums and snuggles in closer, sliding his leg over mine and his hand up my chest.

This isn't what guys who are just friends do. I'm about ninety-eight percent sure of that. But I also don't care to worry about what that means right now because, fuck, it's just so good.

"This is what you wanted?" he says against me, his breath warm on my skin.

"Mm-hmm."

"'Kay."

And that's it. He stays there with me, holding me for some time that I'm about ninety-eight percent sure is much longer than five minutes.

The rest of Saturday morning is a blur of activity that I'm actually proud of myself for navigating. Alex and I get out of bed sometime after nine, and we get dressed and head downstairs. His mom is already cooking breakfast, and his cousins—the ones who had stayed overnight last night—are up and chatting as they help to rearrange the furniture.

I'm not hungry, but Alex convinces me to eat *something*, and so, after a quick breakfast of a banana and a glass of milk, I volunteer to be the one to do the grocery run. Alex's mom is still cooking a huge breakfast, since some other cousins and family members are supposed to be arriving soon—all the more reason for me to get the fuck out of there. But she hands me a list of a bunch of last-minute things she forgot to get the day before, along with a wad of cash, and then I head out.

I stop at the grocery store first, glad that it's not really busy and thankful, as always, that self-checkout exists. After I finish up there, I head over to Green's Bakery and pick up her order of custom cakes, croissants, and fresh rolls. Again, it's not busy, and I manage through whatever short, awkward conversation happens with the single employee at the register while I wait.

I'm heading back out to my car, awkwardly balancing four large bakery boxes in my arms, when I hear someone call out my name from behind me.

"Hey, Nico!"

I freeze, my whole body going rigid as I try not to panic. It's not even a voice I immediately recognize, which means it's not my mom's or that asshole Patrick's or any of those jerks from school who always bullied me and teased me and whatever the fuck else. But it *is* familiar.

I'm still painfully far away from my car—at least twenty or thirty feet—and now I can't even move.

"You look like you could use some help. Want me to get the door to your car for you?"

The voice is closer now, just to my left, and I force myself to turn and look, even though my brain is screaming at me to run.

Jenna stands a couple of feet away, her hands on her hips and her eyebrows arched. I just stare at her like an idiot for several seconds before I realize she's waiting for me to answer, and then I swallow tightly and shake my head.

"N-no. No, thanks. I got it." Which is a stupid answer, because of course it'll be difficult and awkward for me to try to open the door myself and of course it would be easier if she helped me.

Jenna laughs as though she knows exactly what I'm thinking. "Okay, suit yourself," she says, her tone playful.

She doesn't go away, though, and instead, she follows me as I walk the rest of the way to my car. Her following me certainly doesn't help my anxiety, and it's all I can do to not snap at her to please, for fuck's sake, leave me alone.

"Sure you don't want some help?" she asks again when I stop at the passenger side door, frowning.

I suddenly feel quite small and nauseous, and I wonder why the hell I can't just be normal. Any normal person would just say yes, please and thank you, and go on with their day. But for me, she's already too close, even with as perfectly nonthreatening as she is. My heart races, and I fight a familiar feeling of lightheadedness.

"Um . . ." I intend to try to be nice, to say just that—yes, please and thank you. But I don't get the chance, because she steps up around me to my car.

"Here, really, let me help. Okay?" Her hand is on the door handle now, and she's looking at me with kindness in her eyes and a smile on her lips.

God, how fucking awkward am I? I push back all the fear wanting to swallow me up, and I manage a nod. "Yeah, 'kay, thanks."

She smiles brightly at me and turns to open the car door. Then, rather than let me continue to be awkward and try to fit all of the boxes through the door at once, she steps up to me and takes off the top box to move it to the car. She repeats that once more until I'm left holding the bottom two boxes, then she moves out of my way to let me finish loading the boxes into the front seat.

After I close the door, I barely stop myself from backing away or flinching or shrinking into myself. Instead, I just shove my hands into my pockets and mumble another "thank you." She's biting her lower lip and studying me intently when I finally manage to look up.

"You're welcome," she says quietly. Then she adds, "Are you okay? You look a little pale. Or, you know, paler than normal."

I laugh. Kind of. It feels almost like a laugh, and she gives me a half smile as she laughs too. "I'm trying to be okay," I say, which is probably about as honest as I can be.

"I can respect that." She backs up a step as though maybe she's sensed that's what I need, I'm not sure. But it's one hundred percent the truth, anyway, and some of the tension immediately leaves my shoulders. "Is there a party?" she asks, tilting her head toward my car and the boxes from the bakery.

I shake my head but then nod, and she gives me another of those skeptical looks, her eyebrows raised. I groan inwardly. I just want to leave, not have more conversation. "S-sorry, um. It's at Alex's. A family thing. I'm just helping."

"Oh, right." She nods thoughtfully. "He mentioned something on Thursday about a family reunion thing."

Thursday? With the hell that's been this last week, it takes me a second to catch up. Thursday . . . was a fucking mess of a day. But I remember that he went with Jenna into Omaha on Thursday, and then when I got off work . . .

God. Right. *Thursday.*

Thursday evening. Alex's flushed cheeks and unfocused eyes when I knocked on his door. The way he was slightly out of breath. The way he stared at my ass as I walked away.

I shouldn't be thinking about this now, but I can't seem to stop myself. Heat rushes up into my cheeks, and I quickly drop my gaze, cursing inwardly.

Fucking hell, Alex.

"Uh, y-yeah. So, um, thanks for your help. I should go now," I stammer, forcing the words out as I take a step backward.

"Okay, yeah. I should head back anyway. My parents are waiting for me. Um, tell Alex I said hi? I hope he's doing okay."

There's concern in her voice, and I can't help looking up at her. She seems shy suddenly, and she tucks one of her long braids back behind her ear, her expression some combination of soft and kind that almost reminds me of Alex's mom.

I must look confused, however, because she just sort of shakes her head and then says, "He was feeling a little off on Thursday, maybe? I dunno. I just worry, you know? He's a good friend."

*"I finally told Jenna that I just want to be friends . . ."*

I blink back whatever emotions are jumping around in my chest as I remember Alex's words from Thursday—words I was too off-balance to have processed when he said them that night. My heart does something weird, its rhythm stumbling around the wrong way.

Just because he's not interested in a relationship with her doesn't mean he *is* interested in something from me.

But my heart sure as hell wants to think it does.

I force a small smile and nod. "Yeah, he's fine," I say. Then I clear my throat and try for a little more, overcome by some need to reassure her. "He's doing well. He's excited about this weekend. I'll be sure to tell him you said hi."

"Good, thank you." Jenna gives me another of those soft smiles, and her eyes linger on me for a few more seconds, like she's studying me again. Then she sort of laughs and drops her eyes. "I'll see you around, Nico. Have fun at the party without me." She glances back up at me through her long lashes, grinning in a silly way this time.

I manage to actually smile for real, or at least in a way that doesn't feel quite so forced. "I'll be hiding in Alex's room, probably. Too many people," I say with an exaggerated grimace that quickly morphs back into a smile when she giggles and nods.

"Yeah, fair enough." She tips her head back the way we came a few minutes ago. "I gotta go."

"Yeah, me too."

She turns and leaves, and I take a few long breaths, surprised to find that I'm maybe, actually sort of okay. My heart is still beating unsteadily, and I have to consciously unclench my jaw. But that sense of panic, the need to retreat, the simmering anger that always comes along with my anxiety—they all aren't quite as bad as usual.

I take one more careful breath, and then I jog around to the driver's side of my car, hop in, and get on my way back to Alex's house. I have no doubt I *will* be hiding out in his bedroom for most of the day, especially because I'm suddenly tired on top of everything else.

But something inside me feels almost a little stronger or braver or maybe a little bigger.

Because I survived. Not just this conversation with Jenna, but this whole week.

It's not much. But for a brief moment, I feel maybe a little less fucked-up and broken than I usually do. And that's something I haven't felt in a really long time.

# chapter twenty

## *alex*

"ASTROPHYSICS, HUH? SO YOU'RE going to be, what, a rocket scientist or something?" Blaire—my . . . mom's uncle's stepson? I think?—takes a swig of his beer and then leans back in his chair at the outside table. We just all finished eating dinner, and the conversation around the table remains lively, as it's been all day.

Several other people sitting around us stop talking and turn to look at me, like they're also interested in my answer. The woman sitting on the other side of Blaire—whose name might be Wanda, I can't really remember—swats at his shoulder.

"No, remember? Laina told us it's like that Neil-what's-his-name guy—the guy who does those TV shows you used to watch with Damian. Studying the universe and stuff." Maybe-Wanda turns to me with a smile. "Right, honey?"

"Uh, yeah. Right. Um, it's mostly studying the physics of the universe—how the universe started, what stars are made of, black holes, gravity, dark matter." I might have lost most of them as soon as I mentioned dark matter, but I keep talking for a bit. It's helping me stay distracted anyway, and I love talking about this stuff.

One of my cousins—Pierre—actually just started working on his PhD in some physics-related field, and he joins in the conversation when I mention a research paper I read describing how gravity affects space-time. We get into a fun back-and-forth, and I'm just about to counter something he says about a theory on antigravitons when my mom's hand sets on my shoulder. I twist and glance up at her.

"Come help me clean up?" she asks, her eyes happy but tired.

I nod and smile, then excuse myself from the group and follow her inside. The house is a mess. Stacks of pots and pans fill the sink, and the trash can overflows with paper plates and plastic cups. The furniture is all wonky, too, and there's a toddler asleep on the couch, her iPad still playing some kid's TV show with the volume set low.

My aunt Tammy, who drove in this afternoon from Kansas, is in the kitchen putting away some of the leftovers, and she lights up when she sees me.

"Alexander Hayes, my how you've grown," she says, opening her arms for a hug. "It's been too long, kiddo."

"Hi, Aunt Tammy." I give her a hug, and she squeezes me tightly before pulling back to look up at me.

"Off to Stanford at the end of the summer. I can't believe it." She glances past me to my mom. "I always told you he was smart, didn't I?"

I hear my mom laugh, and Aunt Tammy releases me and turns back to the counter, where she starts rebagging the remains of a bowl of potato chips.

My mom steps over to the sink and opens up the dishwasher. "I was just going to load these dishes. Do you mind taking out the trash, sweetie?"

"No problem, Mom." But instead of getting the trash taken out, I move to the sink next to her. "You should go sit outside and have fun. I'll do the dishes and finish up here. You, too, Aunt Tammy."

It doesn't take too much to convince them, and not more than a couple of minutes later, I'm by myself in the kitchen. I get started. I load the dishwasher, wash the few extras that won't fit, and then I wipe down the counters, put away the last of the snacks and desserts that were left out, and take out the trash. By the time I'm finished, our guests have started filtering out family by family. Most of them will be back for another round tomorrow, but some are headed home.

There are a ton of hugs that come along with all the goodbyes, and I'm embarrassed but grateful when more than a few relatives I don't really remember ever meeting before secretly slip me some twenty dollar bills as extra graduation gifts. I spend a little more time helping get the furniture back in place so the cousins who are staying over have the pull-out couch to sleep on. Then, when my mom is settled into a conversation with Erica over a glass of wine, I excuse myself to go upstairs.

*Finally.*

It's not quite as late as last night, but I still pause at the closed door to my bedroom. Will he be asleep already? And if he is, will he be in the bed or on the floor?

Our paths only crossed a few times today. After everyone started to get here, he pretty much disappeared upstairs, and I saw him mostly when I came up here to bring him food and check on him.

But I've been thinking about him all day long. Whenever there was any lull in the conversation or I had a moment to myself, and even when anyone would mention me going off to college, my thoughts immediately strayed to him.

I'm shaking a little as I lift my hand to knock quietly, and then I open the door slowly. The light is off, though the ceiling fan is on, its rhythmic click and hum the only sound in the room. My eyes adjust quickly as I step inside, and my heart jumps in my chest.

He's in my bed again, his head resting on one of the extra pillows we pulled out of the closet yesterday. His back is to me, and

I don't think he's sleeping because I can see a tiny bit of tension in his shoulders. But he doesn't move.

I want to head directly to him, crawl into bed behind him and run my hands up his back to massage away that tension, then gather him up in my arms like the night before . . . But I need a quick shower first and to change my clothes and brush my teeth. So I tiptoe over to my dresser and pull out a clean T-shirt and pair of briefs. Then I disappear back down the hallway to the bathroom, rush through a shower and my bedtime routine, and sneak back in as quietly as I can, closing the door behind me.

I set my cell phone next to his on the nightstand and slowly sit on the edge of the bed. Despite how last night and this morning went, I can't just slip into bed without asking first. Can I?

I shift so I can see him. His eyes are closed, but there's tension in his jaw, too, and my stomach drops a little.

"Nico?" I whisper, even though I know he's awake.

The ceiling fan continues to click as the room stays silent for a count of three. Then his eyes screw shut tighter.

"Hmm?"

"I'll sleep on the floor again if—"

"No."

I huff a relieved laugh. "Okay. You're sure?"

He doesn't answer, but when I slip under the covers and lie down, he almost immediately scoots backward until we're touching, his back pressing up against my chest. I close my eyes as I let my hand land gently on his shoulder before caressing down his arm, slowing when I come in contact with the bare skin just above his elbow.

"God," he breathes, his voice so low and muffled I almost don't hear it.

I bend forward just slightly to rest my forehead against him, try-ing to manage all of the overwhelming sensations racing through me. My thumb rubs gently back and forth along his skin, the warmth turning hotter when he lets out another short, ragged breath. Then I pause before pressing my cheek into his hair.

It's all so good and perfect, and I finally let my hand slip down his elbow the rest of the way, around to his waist, and then upward to find its place on his chest again. Like this morning. And like this morning, he makes another contended sound, somewhere between a whimper and a sigh.

I smile into him. "Mmm, good?"

"Yeah," he says on another long, slow breath. Then—*god*—he snuggles back into me even a little more, wiggling until he's settled comfortably. Or something. And his hand covers mine on his chest, warm and soft.

We lie there for a while, just like the night before, and though he's relaxed, I feel him holding onto something, like he won't let his breathing steady out completely. I take another long, full breath and then press him into me more, tightening my arm around him, and he sighs.

I imagine it's a happy sigh. I imagine he's happy. Really, actually happy. Not that pretend happy he thinks I don't usually see.

"Did you have a good day?" I ask finally, keeping my voice low.

"Mm-hmm." He tilts his head a little, and that brings my cheek almost in contact with his. "I beat Nightmare King Grimm again."

"Damn."

"Yeah. He's so fucking fast."

"Did you use Sharp Shadow?"

"It's the only way. Sharp Shadow and Unbreakable Strength."

"Hmm."

His fingers caress along the back of my hand before settling again. "And, um, I managed to get a quote on car insurance. It wasn't quite as bad as I was expecting."

"Oh yeah?"

"Yeah."

I think maybe he's going to elaborate, but he doesn't. He just presses his hand into mine and sighs one more time. Then his fingers restart their gentle caress, tracing some pattern with a light, almost teasing touch.

My skin is on fire, I'm sure of it.

Sparks race up my arm and into my chest, their warmth spreading all the way down into my toes. I swallow back a groan, and I turn and bury my face into his hair as I shift my hips back a few inches. I swear I almost hear him huff a laugh, but that's probably just my imagination. He keeps up the motion, his fingers light and soft, though his breathing seems to slow and deepen as the minutes pass.

It's comforting in a way I've never really known before, holding my best friend like this and feeling the trust he has in me.

It's also more than arousing, though I try my best to ignore my reaction and remind myself that this is . . . I mean, I *think* this is supposed to be platonic.

I'm just about to, I dunno, implode or something from the overload of incredible sensations when his fingers slide up mine and stop, his palm flattening against the back of my hand. He clears his throat lightly. "Um, h-how about you?" he asks.

"Me? What?"

"Your day. Was it good?"

"Oh, hmm."

Before I can answer, Nico starts touching the back of my hand with just the tips of his fingers again, drawing little swirls and circles this time, and I can't hold back. I let out some quiet little sound, a moan maybe, that rumbles in the back of my throat. And I pull him tighter against my chest and press my cheek to him.

"It was good. Mmm, much better now, though."

He doesn't stop. He doesn't hesitate or tense up or pull away.

Instead, he nods and says, "Yeah. For sure," his voice a little rough.

Which sends all the wrong signals to the lower half of my body.

*God.*

*Is* this supposed to be platonic?

Because if it is, I'm failing. Miserably.

# chapter twenty-one

## nico

"UGHHHH. IT'S MORNING? ALREADY?"

"Mm-hmm, yeah. Fuck, sorry."

I twist around in Alex's arms, ignoring as he grumbles another something about how he really hates Mondays, and I reach over him to the nightstand to shut off the alarm on my phone. It *is* actually too early, and I should probably tell him I deliberately set my Monday morning alarm to fifteen minutes earlier than I needed to get up just so we could waste a little time cuddling before I had to go to work.

Though, on second thought, maybe I should keep that to myself.

I hit the snooze button on my phone and then hesitate. I'm sort of sprawled out half on top of him now, one hand in the middle of his chest and one of my legs somehow wedged between his. As I pause, trying to decide whether and where to move, his hand, which had been up covering his eyes to block out the sunlight, shifts to my shoulder and squeezes gently before rubbing lightly down to my elbow.

Shuddering, I drop my head to his chest. "Alex, ah, fuck . . ." I mumble against him, my breath warming his shirt.

"Hmm?"

He repeats the motion, his hand drifting up to my shoulder and then back down to my elbow, and I groan again as I lower myself on top of him. There's something much more intimate about this position, and with a wave of anxiety, I realize maybe *this* will be the point where he says *okay, enough*. He hasn't shied away from anything this whole weekend—and we've spent a lot of time snuggled up together in bed. But now, I'm lying *on top* of him, my knee between his legs and my fingers flexing into his waist.

Fuck, his chest is solid.

I'm distracted for a moment as I turn to press my cheek into the hard planes of his pecs. I hear his breath hitch when my hand drifts up his side a few inches, and I can't help it. I close my eyes and curl up right there—right there with my head on his chest.

It's so fucking comfortable.

"I hit snooze," I say, and he groans quietly and seems to inhale deeply as he buries his face in my hair.

"Mmm, good. It's too early. And this is good. Staying right here."

"Yeah."

His hand slips around to my back, rubbing slow circles over the top of my shirt. After a moment, he shifts a tiny bit, and his other hand finds its place on my back, too, low in the curve of my waist just above my ass.

"Nico?"

"Hmm?"

"This is what you want?" he asks softly, both of his arms tightening around me.

I nod into his chest, but I can't stop myself as I start to tremble.

*He's* what I want.

This intimacy is what I want.

These feelings of safety and protection, care and tenderness, gentle trust. Love. Those are what I want.

Fuck.

I'm suddenly terrified to move, to say the wrong words. And so I just breathe a quiet "yes" against him.

He hesitates, and then he runs his hand gently up and down my back and asks, "Is this . . . *all* you want?"

I squeeze my eyes shut, but I still can't move. I don't know what he's really asking, though it would be easy to assume, wouldn't it? But I'm not in a position to assume because if I fuck this up—

Shit. Shit, shit, shit.

"It . . . it doesn't matter what I want," I counter, my voice faltering. His hand still rubs up and down my back in the softest of strokes, and I feel him shake his head, his cheek pressing into my hair.

"It matters to me," he whispers, low and warm and soothing. I want to cry, especially when he adds, "*You* matter to me."

"Alex . . ." I can't finish the sentence. Hell, I can't even start it. Because that just sounded like something of a confession to me . . . like Alex was confessing to having feelings for me. And I have no idea how to respond.

Why the fuck can't he just come out and say it? If that's what he's trying to tell me. *"Bro, I'm gay, and I like you."* Simple.

Totally simple.

*Not.*

It's not really that simple, and I know it. Otherwise, I'd have done it years ago.

Right?

I hold my breath for another moment, my heart pounding in my chest. Then I grip his shirt tighter, and I blurt out, "I-I like you. I'm gay, a-and I like you. And this isn't all I want. I want more." There. I said it instead. Now he can freak out and kick me out and— "Fuck. Sorry. Dammit."

I pull away, scooting off of him and turning to face the wall.

A tear slips down my cheek, and I reach up to wipe it away as I shrink into myself, my chest tight. I don't know why the fuck I said that. I shouldn't have. I shouldn't have said it, and I shouldn't even be here, in bed with him, taking all this comfort he's giving me without anything to give him in return.

I'm such a fucking asshole.

Another tear slides down my cheek, but I ignore it this time.

The silence behind me is terrifying, and I'm about to excuse myself and figure out how to crawl out of bed around him when the mattress shifts. He gets up, and I hear his footsteps as he moves quietly toward the door.

Then there's a click as he locks it.

A few seconds later, he crawls back into bed, and he scoots up right behind me.

"Nico, can I hold you again?" he asks, his voice a low whisper that sounds even less sure than I feel.

Something stirs in my chest, though, as I realize what he's asking me.

I nod, and as his arm slips around me, pulling me up against him, a tiny whimper escapes my throat. God, what the fuck is happening now?

My back is flush against his chest, in the same position we've been cuddling in and sleeping in all weekend, and he does that thing that makes me feel so good where he nuzzles the back of my neck. I close my eyes and let out a long, shuddering sigh.

"This is okay? I don't want to make you uncomfortable," he says quietly, his breath warm on my neck. When I nod, he squeezes me gently, murmuring "good," and I hold myself as still as possible as he starts talking softly. "I-I'm bisexual. And, um, I . . . I like you, too. I've liked you for a long time, I was just too scared to tell you. You're my best friend, and I was scared, you know?"

I hear him swallow nervously, and his hand caresses lightly

down my chest to my stomach. I'm still too fucking terrified to respond or even let myself think about what he just said. And I'm not sure how the hell he can act so calm.

I move my hand to cover his, and he sucks in a breath and presses his forehead into me.

"I've been wanting to tell you," he continues. "But with everything going on, there was never a good time, and . . ."

". . . and things kept getting more complicated?" I finish for him.

He nods. "Yeah. Yeah, for sure." He pauses, and I can feel the uncertainty in his next words. "Um . . . did you really mean what you said? Do you really want more? With *me*?"

Here's where I should lie.

I'm a broken, worthless piece of shit, and he deserves so much better than anything I could ever give him or anything I've ever given him. I should pull away, make up some lame excuse, and then go get ready for work. I should probably pack up my shit, too, because I'm sure I've overstayed my welcome here.

But I don't do that.

Instead, I lie there in his arms, tense and unsure, trying to figure out how to respond.

"Sorry, I didn't mean to make you uncomfortable," Alex says quietly after another moment. He's still holding me, his hand now unmoving on my stomach.

I shake my head. "You didn't. I'm just . . . I'm scared," I admit, though I don't tell him exactly what I'm scared about.

There's a touch on my neck that feels different than before. Warm and soft and pliant, brushing gently along my skin. I only realize it's his lips when he hums against me. He starts to move his hand a little lower, and I moan quietly, pressing my head into my pillow as I feel the tiniest tease of his fingertips on my stomach, curling up under the hem of my shirt. He pauses.

"Is this okay?" he breathes, his lips still against my neck. "I've wanted to touch you for so long."

My cock stirs at his words, despite all the reservations and guilt I still have, and when his lips part and his hot, wet tongue touches my neck, I groan with want. I twist around in his arms, and his hand slips under my shirt, smoothing along my waist and then my lower back. One of my legs comes up over the top of his, and he responds by sliding his knee between my thighs.

"Holy fuck," I hiss.

He just groans in response, rubbing his foot down along my calf as his hand flattens against my back, warm and sure and steady.

I shift a bit more, needing to feel his body pressed against mine, and it's just as good as I've imagined. My chest tightens as I reach up, cup his cheek, and tug him down to me.

I've never kissed anyone before.

But I need him now like I need air to breathe.

He's confident and bold, and he brings his mouth to mine like he's done it a thousand times before. His lips caress and soothe with a pressure that's exactly right. I groan deep in my throat and then melt into him, kissing him back again and again. It's fucking perfect.

When we finally part, both breathing hard, it's like he can't stand it. He makes some sound of protest and then pushes himself up onto one elbow, leans over me, and captures my lips again, slower this time, as his leg slides between mine. He's gentle, even though I can feel his hard length pressing against my thigh.

He hums quietly and pulls back, and his hand comes up to trace along my jaw. "God, that was amazing." I open my eyes to see him, and I swallow hard when our eyes meet. He's looking at me with so much care and gentleness that it's almost overwhelming. "Nico, you're—"

I slip both hands up around to the back of his neck and pull him down, cutting off whatever he was going to say. He comes right to me, pressing his lips back to mine, though he's even more careful, soft, sensual. His hand slides around to my waist and then upward slightly, taking my shirt with it, and I moan into him.

Fuck, this *is* amazing. My heart's racing with the most incredible rhythm, and I'm warm and tingly all over.

He just starts to deepen the kiss in a new way—his tongue peeking out to run along my bottom lip—when my fucking alarm goes off from the nightstand again. Its annoying buzz turns into a pulsing tune that's too awful to be ignored.

With a groan, he breaks the kiss and rolls over away from me to grab my phone. "Snooze or stop?" he asks, his voice rough.

I can't breathe, and I'm hot and too overwhelmed to think, so I just screw my eyes shut and reach out with a grumble. "Lemme see." The phone lands in my hand, and I force my eyes back open with a groan. "Ugh, I gotta get up now," I mutter as I swipe to turn the alarm off.

I toss the phone onto the bed between us and cover my eyes with my arm. And not more than a second later, he's pulling me up against him again, his lips finding my neck and then my jaw and my cheek. It's light, and there's something almost joyful about how he's touching me. I find myself smiling, even as I feign another grumble and pretend to try to push him away.

He laughs against me, a puff of air warming my neck. Then he kisses that same spot and hums something quiet. I stop pushing him away and just curl up in his arms. My whole body shudders as his arms tighten around me and he places more soft kisses on my neck.

I can hear his heart thrumming hard, and I know mine's doing the same thing.

"I meant what I said," he breathes between kisses, and he stops with his lips lingering against my skin as I grip his shirt. He shifts to settle me more on his chest, and then he buries his head in my hair and inhales deeply. "I'm sorry I hid this from you. I've wanted to tell you for so long. I hope we can talk more later. Sorry I kinda, um, mauled you."

I laugh as my chest tightens, and I shake my head. "Don't be sorry about that. It was fucking incredible."

I should say something else. After all, we both just came out to each other. And he kissed me. Or I kissed him. Whatever. We kissed.

God, we fucking kissed.

It was the most amazing thing I've ever felt.

Some massive weight seems to disappear from my shoulders, and I breathe in a deep, uninhibited breath and cling to him as I let it out.

"I have to go to work now," I say quietly.

"Yeah."

I push up so I can see him, my hands resting on his chest. His eyes are soft, and he brings a hand up to cup my cheek.

"Meet me for lunch?" I ask.

He smiles, his face lighting up, and then he nods and leans in to kiss my forehead.

Fuck, that's even better than him kissing my neck.

"I'm helping my mom out most of the day today," he says. "Cleaning and then running some errands for her. But I'll skip out around noon and bring lunch. Will that work?"

"Mm-hmm, yeah."

"Good."

I still don't want to move, but after another minute, I manage to drag myself up off of him and grab my clothes to get changed. I'm just at the door when I glance back over my shoulder. His eyes dart up to mine, his cheeks turning red, and I can't help smirking at him.

"You *were* checking out my ass the other day."

The red in his cheeks turns even darker, and he shakes his head and runs a hand through his hair as he stammers, "N-no. No, I, um, I was just—"

"—checking out my ass," I finish for him, grinning. He's got his mouth parted as he stares at me, his hand now rubbing the back of his neck. I huff a laugh, feeling that odd joyfulness again that I'd felt from him earlier. "Maybe I'll let you *really* check it out later," I tease, turning back to the door with another smirk. I hear him suck in a breath.

"God, Nico," he hisses, and the next thing I know, he's wrapping his arms around me, pulling me back into him. His lips find my neck, and he murmurs, "I can't wait," his breath hot against my skin.

I laugh again and turn around in his arms, and then he presses me up against the door and kisses me.

I'm totally going to be late to work, I just know it. But when his tongue pushes into my mouth for the first time, I really, really can't bring myself to care all that much.

# chapter twenty-two

## *alex*

Nico kissed me.

He came out to me, he told me he likes me, and then he kissed me.

With something that sounds embarrassingly like a lovesick sigh, I flop down on my back in bed, my whole body buzzing with some odd energy that I've never felt before. I reach up and touch my lips, laughing at the stupid smile I can't seem to wipe off my face.

I can still feel the warmth of his mouth on mine, the way he was so tentative and yet not as he pulled me to him and pressed our lips together, how he fit so perfectly in my arms. I can still feel it all, and it makes my smile even bigger, giddy with anticipation and joy.

I laugh again and let my hand drop down to my stomach as I close my eyes. His cocky grin taunts me, and I see him as he was just before he left to get changed. How he glanced over his shoulder and teased me for checking out his ass, his green eyes sparkling.

I want *more* of that. For him, and for me.

Rolling over onto my stomach, I grab my cell phone from the nightstand. He just left to go to work a few minutes ago, and he's probably still driving into town, but I open up my messaging app anyway and start typing a quick message.

*Alex (8:14 a.m.):* how long is ur lunch break? at 12, yeah?

I click send, and since I'm fairly sure he won't respond right away, I set the phone back down and lie there for a few more minutes, smiling into my pillow like an idiot. I'm still grinning ten or fifteen minutes later when I finally drag myself back out of bed, throw on some clothes—just a plain gray T-shirt and an old, comfy pair of jeans—and then settle at my desk to check my email.

It probably takes me a good half hour to get caught up with the few school-related things that I put off over the weekend—filling out some housing forms and returning some emails. When I'm finished, I sit back in my chair and eye my email inbox again. A few lines down is the message chain I have going with Dr. Ellis, and now also with Dr. Millan, the visiting professor Dr. Ellis added to the conversation. It's grown to over twenty-five emails back and forth, and Dr. Ellis's latest email asked to set up a meeting for the three of us when I get to Palo Alto in September.

He wants to meet me. And he says he'll have an undergraduate research position available in the fall. It's unreal and exciting, and I can't wait.

But then, for the first time that morning, my stomach sinks.

Nico won't be there. As things are right now, I'll be heading to California without him.

That reminder hits me hard, and I frown and spin around in my chair, my eyes immediately landing on my phone. It's still sitting on the nightstand, face up, and there's a text message notification visible on the screen.

I push up to my feet and step over to the nightstand to grab my phone, expecting to see some brief response from him. But instead, the words *Message not delivered* stare back up at me from the screen.

*Message not delivered.*

Confused, I tap on the notification and start to retype my message from earlier. But I stop after typing just the first word, and my stomach sinks even further.

God, I'd completely forgotten.

It won't matter if I try again; the message won't go through. His mom canceled his phone line. I think he said it would have been shut off on Saturday.

I let out a long breath and sit down on the edge of my bed, still staring at the last few messages we sent to each other. I scroll through the texts, the knot in my stomach tightening.

I don't know how I forgot that he's basically homeless right now. If my mom wasn't letting him stay here, he'd have nowhere to go. And he's got no money; he told me that the other day when he showed me those messages from his mom. He has to hand everything he does have over to her on Friday if he wants to keep his car, which he sort of needs to get to town for work.

The joy and light from the morning dim back into a heaviness sitting square on my shoulders, and I stuff my phone into my pocket as I turn to look at my open laptop sitting on my desk.

I'm supposed to leave for California soon—just a little over three months from now. But how can I? How can I possibly leave him behind?

There's a quiet knock at the door, and my mom's voice follows. "Hey, sweetie. Are you up?"

I cough to clear my throat. "Yeah, yeah, just a sec." With one last glance at my phone, I push myself back up to my feet. Then I slip my phone into the pocket of my jeans and open up the door.

My mom's there on the other side, her arms crossed over her chest and her usual kind smile on her face. "Sorry, I know it's early, but I thought I heard you up. Do you think you can help me with—" She stops and frowns, tilting her head slightly. "What's wrong?"

My jaw tightens, but I don't say anything right away. I just hold her gaze for a few seconds and then drop my eyes to the ground, trying to figure out what and how much to tell her. If anything.

I shift and lean a little more against the door, running a hand through my hair. "Um, well, it's just . . ."

My heart aches with both longing and worry as I see Nico's beautiful eyes again, and I swallow back the lump in my throat. I can't even tell her the good stuff; I can't tell her Nico kissed me, told me he likes me, told me he wants something more with me. Though we didn't talk about it, I got the sense he hasn't come out to anyone else. And he definitely didn't give me permission to tell my mom. So, even though I'm sure she'll be happy for both of us, I can't say anything about that.

I guess I can tell her about all the rest, though.

Biting at my lower lip, I lift my eyes. She's watching me, both of her eyebrows raised in anticipation and concern. It's pretty easy to see she wants to say something more but that she's waiting for me first.

"I, um . . ." I remember our conversation on graduation night—my mom said she had a friend in San Jose who might have a job for Nico. She was ready to help me *us*—figure it out, if only I could convince Nico to give it a shot. But that's the problem. I haven't even brought it up again. There hasn't been any opportunity. Not with everything that's happened.

I close my eyes and drop my chin to my chest.

It would be too much to even ask of him right now. Wouldn't it?

"What's bothering you, sweetie? It's . . . something with Nico?"

This time, I laugh without humor and shake my head. Of course she would immediately figure out where my mind is. "Yeah. Yeah, I'm just, um—" The words still stick in my throat, and so I motion toward the stairs. "What did you need help with? Maybe, um, we can talk while we work?"

Her eyes narrow slightly, but then she nods. "Okay, sure." She turns to start down the stairs, and I follow. "The rental company will be here in about twenty minutes to pick up the chairs and tables. I need help moving them from the backyard out into the driveway."

"Sounds good."

She leads the way down the stairs, through the now-empty house, and out into the backyard, and together, silently, we get started. We fold up the tables and chairs she rented for the weekend and then move them in through the house, through the garage, and into the driveway. We're maybe a third of the way done when I finally get up the courage to speak.

"So, um, I don't think I told you about the most recent email I got from Dr. Ellis." I pause, a folded plastic chair under each arm, as Mom walks ahead of me through the slider door into the house.

"Oh, no, you didn't. Good news?"

"Yeah, pretty good, actually." We angle around the coffee table and to the open door to the garage. "He said he has an undergraduate research position available starting in the fall. He didn't specifically say it was mine, but I think that was the implication."

Mom steps into the garage and stops, resting her two chairs on the ground as she turns back to face me.

"That's incredible, sweetie, but that's—"

"—not what's bothering me, yeah," I cut in, dropping my eyes again. "I was trying to get there. Um . . ."

Why it's so hard for me to talk about, I'm not sure. My mom is so good at helping to find solutions to just about every problem, and I'm sure this won't be any different. When I glance back up at her, her expression is soft and knowing, and I have to look away.

"I'm really, *really* excited about it. But . . ."

"But . . . Nico?"

I nod, and for whatever reason, I still can't look at her. So instead, I continue the rest of the way to the driveway and set down the two chairs I brought out. It's warm already, and the air is thick with humidity. Off to the west, dark clouds are rolling in, and I frown as I study the sky. It's going to rain later.

A bead of sweat drips down my temple, and I reach up to wipe it away as my mom moves alongside me and stacks her chairs on top of mine.

"Come on," she says, her hand touching my shoulder. "We've got more to do, and they'll be here soon."

I follow silently, and we get another dozen or so chairs moved as I start talking. Carefully—because I'm still not entirely sure how much I can tell her without violating Nico's privacy—I start back about a week ago. I explain the text messages he showed me from his mom, how his cell phone is shut off and he'll have to get a new number, how his mom is making him buy his car from her. And I can tell she wants to cut in, but I keep going because I need to get it all out now.

I tell her how I know I should talk to him about coming to California with me, but how that seems almost insensitive of me or something, given his current financial situation. And just as I set down another couple of chairs, my voice breaks.

"I-I don't know if I can leave without him, Mom."

Her arms wrap around my waist almost immediately, and I return the hug, lowering my head to her shoulder as my body shudders.

"Oh, sweetie, I know it seems hopeless, but I'm sure if you just talk to him—"

"It's not that easy," I cut in, shaking my head against her. I let out a sharp breath, and all the rest of what I need to say comes pouring out. "I can't pressure him like that. If I tell him the truth, if I tell him how much my heart breaks when I even *think* about leaving him behind, that's only going to put more pressure on him when he's already struggling so much to just get by! I can't . . . I can't do that. It's not fair to him."

She laughs quietly, though it's warm and understanding, and her arms tighten around my waist. "Alex, sweetie, you know what's not fair to him?" she asks slowly.

I groan. "Don't say it's not fair to him to not give him the choice. You *know* it's not that simple. He's got . . . he's got *nothing*, and he can't just . . ." I pull back, and my eyes meet hers. "You know how hard it is for him. His anxiety . . ."

"I know," she says with a gentle nod. She reaches up and wipes a tear from my cheek, but I shrink back, pulling away and shoving my hands into my pockets.

I shouldn't be so embarrassed to be crying in front of her, but I am. It probably doesn't help that I've done nothing to hide how I really feel about Nico, and I realize she just has to know the truth by now, if she didn't already.

She stays where she is, but I can feel her eyes on me as I turn around and hastily swipe at my cheeks. Then she steps up behind me, and her hand settles on my back.

"I know how hard this is, sweetie. And I understand your reasoning. You're right that he's facing so many challenges—more than all the financial stuff that's come up this week." Her hand drops away, and she steps in front of me, lifts both hands to cup my cheeks, and tilts my chin up slightly so I'm looking at her. "But you have to give him the opportunity to make the decision for himself. And if you don't tell him . . ." She pauses as her smile softens. "If you don't tell him how you feel and what you want, how can he know it's even a possibility?"

I close my eyes and drop my chin back down, sniffling. She's right, of course. "But the cost of living there . . ." I argue lamely.

"Alex." Her hands slide down to my shoulders, and she squeezes gently. "It's a lot, I know. But you know what I'm going to say."

I nod. "There are *always* solutions, even to the really hard problems."

"Exactly. But you have to talk to him. Tell him how you feel, tell him what you want. And then, if he's up for it, you two can figure out whatever the solution is, *together*. You have to give him the choice, and because he maybe doesn't know or maybe doesn't believe it's even possible, you have to convince him that he *does* have a choice. That he *is* capable and he *can* do it, *if* that's what he wants."

My heart stutters in my chest as I nod again. "You're right."

"I usually am."

I roll my eyes.

She laughs, patting my shoulder. "Come on, we've got a few more trips, and they'll be here any minute."

With a deep breath, I follow her back through the door to the garage to get the rest of the chairs.

# chapter twenty-three

*nico*

"So, you're what, about halfway done?" Sharon stands in the doorway, her eyes narrowed at the boxes of books remaining along the far wall. The books I've sorted and catalogued are stacked neatly along the other wall.

"Um, yeah. I think that's about right." I try to sit up straight, and I close the book I just finished flipping through to check for damage—an old biochemistry textbook that was grouped with several other older textbooks.

"I expect you to finish by Thursday, at the latest," Sharon says, and I nod quickly as her gaze meets mine. Her eyes are intense and filled with skepticism, but I manage another nod that I hope is more convincing.

I feel oddly confident that I *can* indeed finish by Thursday, or even Wednesday, and so I tell her that. "It won't be a problem."

She stares at me for several seconds, her expression unreadable, until I feel uncomfortable enough that I pull my gaze away and shrink down in my chair. I thought I'd been doing a decent job, but Sharon tends to always look like she's angry. At least, that's how she is when she's interacting with me.

I sit there awkwardly for another few seconds, and then Sharon hums.

"Well, keep it up. When you're done with this, I'll give you the criteria for what we keep versus what gets recycled and what gets sold to the bookstore in Omaha. You can go through your spreadsheet and sort everything so we can send an invoice and then box up the books. You're moving right along here. Good job."

A spark of pride flares in my chest at her praise, and I lift my eyes in surprise. "Th-thank you."

She gives a stiff nod but then points a finger at me with a frown. "Make sure you go on break today. Twelve to one. Take the full hour. Got it?"

I nod quickly. I fully intended to take my entire lunch hour today, and the reason why almost makes me smile.

Sharon gives me a look but doesn't say anything else, and she spins on her heel and leaves the room.

When I'm finally alone again, I close my eyes and exhale a slow, shuddering breath, trying to let the tension out of my shoulders. I handled that well. Maybe. I don't think things are really getting easier—all of my anxiety is still here with me, all the time. But I *do* think I'm getting better at holding myself together when I really need to, including when I'm interacting with my boss.

With another long breath, I get back to work, keeping an eye on the clock in the lower right corner of the laptop. 11:42 a.m.

Soon.

He'll be here soon.

*I hope.*

Butterflies flutter around in my stomach, and I find myself glancing toward the door every minute or so, overcome by a sort of eager anticipation. I'm not sure I've ever felt like this before. In fact, I'm certain I haven't, and when I glance up again at 11:58 a.m. and see him standing there in the doorway, his hand raised to knock, a wave of the most amazing warmth crashes into me.

He's here. He came.

"Hey," he says, lowering his hand as he steps in the room.

"Hey." I'm grinning, and I can't stop it. I don't think I want to, though. It feels good. And that's also something I'm not used to.

Alex shoves both of his hands in his pockets as he stares at me. His eyes look almost stormy, but he's also smiling, maybe a little more tentatively than I am. That might be a first.

"The librarian lady said you were back here and to make sure you took your whole break today," he says, arching his eyebrows.

Damn, he looks adorable like that.

"So, I thought we could grab tacos at Del Sol and then head to Harley's for that ice cream we didn't get last week, if we have time?" He's still staring at me, and when I don't respond, his smile deepens, and he laughs quietly. "Yo, Nico, you there?"

I bite my lower lip and nod slowly, and his eyes dart down to my lips as his cheeks turn the most perfect shade of pink. Fuck me.

"Yeah. That sounds good," I manage, and I tear my gaze away long enough to save the file I was working on, close the laptop, and stand up. When I look back at him, his eyes meet mine with this soft, caring expression, and he smiles and tips his head.

"Ready?"

"Yeah."

"I'll drive."

"'Kay."

A few minutes later, he pulls his mom's truck into a parking spot in front of Del Sol, a taco place just a few blocks from the library. The rain is coming down pretty hard, so we hurry in, managing to not get too wet. I claim a table for us in the corner—thankful that it's not busy—and Alex steps up to the counter to order us some tacos.

I have the briefest flicker of shame when I see him pull out his wallet to pay, but he glances over his shoulder at me and grins reassuringly like he knows exactly what I'm thinking. His grin brightens up the whole room, I fucking swear, and all that shame turns into something warm and wonderful. Heat races up into my cheeks, and I lower my eyes.

A moment later, he sets two bottles of water on the table and slips into the seat across from mine. "It'll be just a few minutes, they said."

"Cool. Um, thanks for—" I wave a hand toward the counter, and he nods.

"Yeah, no problem." He pushes one of the bottles of water across to me. "So, um, how was your morning?"

"Fine. You?"

He purses his lips and stares at me for a long second before nodding. "Fine, yeah. I, uh, helped my mom move the chairs and tables from the backyard, and that's it, really."

"Sounds boring."

He shrugs, and I open my bottle of water just as one of the staff brings over two huge plates filled with various types of street tacos—chicken, steak, tofu, veggie, and even . . . Narrowing my eyes, I lean forward to get a better look.

"Is that . . . *shrimp*?"

My eyes dart up to see Alex grinning at me. "Yup. Just for you."

I laugh and roll my eyes. "Bro, *why*?"

"Are you telling me you don't *actually* like shrimp?" His eyes are fucking gleaming now, and he reaches to the plate in front of him and grabs one of the chicken tacos.

"You know I don't," I counter.

He fake-scoffs, his eyes still bright, and he just grins through his chewing as he stares at me, his gaze warm and familiar. My breath catches in my throat, and I feel my cheeks heating up again. Or more. Maybe they never cooled off.

Alex tips his head toward the plate in front of me. "Someone's got to eat it, and it's not going to be me."

The challenge isn't really one I care to beat, and so, despite Alex's huff, I pick up one of the veggie tacos instead. The two corn tortillas are stuffed with black beans, roasted zucchini, peppers, onions, and cilantro, and even though I thought I wasn't hungry, I find myself shoving the small taco in my mouth and taking a huge bite.

It's really, really good, and I finish in only a few more bites as Alex downs his chicken taco and one of the steak tacos. We talk a little more between bites, not about anything consequential, but the longer we're together, the more I just want to drop the tacos, grab his hand, drag him back out to his mom's truck, and disappear with him into the back seat so we can continue where we left off this morning.

His lips look so fucking kissable, and I find myself staring at them after I've eaten my third taco. Without meaning to, my tongue peeks out of my mouth and wets my own lips, and I hear him suck in a breath. My eyes shift back up to his, my heart pounding, and he takes a long, slow breath, leans in, and says, "Done eating?"

I nod eagerly, and he holds my gaze for another couple of seconds, then he nods, too, and hops up to head to the counter. A minute later, he returns with a take-out box. We both move the remaining tacos to the box, and then together, we jog out through the rain to the truck. The doors unlock as we approach, and I almost laugh as he glances around before grabbing the handle for the rear passenger side door. He yanks it open and nods at me.

"Tinted windows in the back," he says with a silly grin, and I laugh and jump in the truck ahead of him.

His hand finds my back as he follows me in, and as soon as the door closes behind us, he quickly sets the take-out box in the front seat and grabs me around the waist, pulling me over into his lap. His lips find mine, and he kisses me once and then again and again, like he's been waiting all day to devour me. Without losing contact, I shift to straddle him, settling on top of his thighs, and he groans into the kiss as his hands start to roam across my back. He untucks my shirt and slips a hand up underneath, and I break the kiss, dropping my forehead to his shoulder as his soft skin caresses mine.

"Ah, god. Fuck, that's good."

"Mm-hmm," he hums in response, and his lips graze my temple as he holds me against him, his hand now sliding all the way up my back to my shoulders. His other arm is around my waist, and he pulls my hips closer with a groan. "Oh, fuck," he hisses, his breath hot on my cheek.

I laugh at his curse, though I'm fighting not to be too over-whelmed by everything myself. I can feel his cock through his jeans, hard and hot and pressing into my upper thigh. It's a lot, and every bit of this is new to me.

It feels incredible. Comfortable. Right.

And fucking good.

Wanting more of that pressure, wanting to feel his arousal and know it's because of *me*, I grind my hips down into him. I gasp at the sensation, and at the same time, he throws his head back and groans. God, I love that sound.

I turn my head, breathing hard as I grind into him again. "You keep making that noise," I whisper, pressing a kiss to the spot right at the base of his neck. "I like it. *A lot.*"

"Nico . . ." His breathing is ragged as both of his hands shift to my hips, his fingers flexing into me like he wants to pull me down onto him more. "You . . . keep doing things that make me make that noise," he murmurs, breathless and rough. "Mmm, and god, I like it, too."

I straighten up a little, frame his face with my hands, and lower my mouth back to his. It's all heat and softness this time, and when both of his arms slip back around my waist, I can't stop the shiver that runs all the way down into my toes. I pull away, breathing hard, and rest my forehead against his.

Some urgent need to apologize bubbles up in my chest, but I manage to push it away as his lips graze my cheek.

"Ice cream?" he asks, though he doesn't sound super interested in it.

Neither am I. I shake my head and settle into him more, my arms wrapped loosely around his neck. I don't wanna move from this spot.

A quiet laugh rumbles in his chest, and then he breathes in deeply, burying his face into the crook of my neck. His lips find my skin, and he starts covering me in light, airy, teasing kisses.

We don't say anything else. I think we don't really need to right now.

And I'm happy to just bask in this feeling for as long as I can.

# chapter twenty-four

## *alex*

"OH, YOU'RE BACK ALREADY?" my mom asks, her light footsteps coming down the stairs behind me.

"Yeah, Nico's break was just an hour." I quickly find a place in the fridge for the leftover tacos Nico and I didn't eat at lunch, and then I close the fridge and turn around just as my mom stops on the other side of the island in the kitchen. She's wearing what looks like her hiking clothes, complete with a pair of loose-fitting gray hiking pants and a long-sleeve tech shirt. The smell of bug repellant plus sunscreen hits my nose, and I narrow my eyes and motion at her clothes with a grimace. "Are you going hiking? It's still pouring rain. I think it's supposed to rain all afternoon. And I don't think you have to worry about bugs or the sun . . ."

She grins and rests her hands on the counter. "Aunt Tammy managed to find a spot for her RV at the campgrounds at Platte River and decided to stay the week. She invited me to stay with her, since Bruce had to head back home for work. I don't have anything lined up for this week, so it seems like as good a week as any to take off. You don't mind, do you? I'll be close by if you need anything. She's coming to pick me up in a few minutes, so I can leave you the truck."

"Okay, yeah. But the rain . . . ?"

She waves me off dismissively, like a little rain can't possibly stop her and Tammy from adventuring. I guess it never really has before, though this isn't just "a little rain." Then she starts listing all the leftovers still in the fridge from the weekend, ending with what almost sounds like a threat that Nico and I had better clean everything out by the time she gets back (although she's not entirely sure when that will be), or else . . . !

While she talks, she moves around the island toward me, and when she's finished, she stops in front of me, setting her hands on my shoulders. Her eyes study mine intently, and I see the concern in them, an extension of our conversation that morning. I blink and look down, overcome by an emotion that feels like guilt or shame, even though I'm not sure what it's really about. She immediately pulls me in for a hug. No words, no more helpful advice or suggestions or explanations. No long-winded, one-sided discussion telling me again to just "talk to him, sweetie."

She knows I know.

And so, she just hugs me.

I let myself hug her back, taking comfort in the embrace. And because I haven't *really* said the actual words to her yet, I feel like I can't let her leave without finally being honest with her. Completely honest, so there's no more wondering or uncertainty anymore. No more vague "my heart hurts."

My eyes screw shut. I'm not sure why I'm scared, since I'm about ninety-six percent sure she already knows anyway, but I still hold her tighter as I start talking.

"Mom, I need to tell you something." I muffle the words into her hair, as though that will soften the blow. "I . . . I'm . . . I'm bisexual. And I, um . . . Nico . . . I really like him. I-I'm sorry. I'm sorry I didn't tell you sooner and sorry I—"

She shakes her head and squeezes me harder. "Shh, I don't want to hear any apologies because there's nothing to be sorry for." She pulls back, and her hands find my cheeks. I can barely look her in the eye, but I manage to hold her gaze for a few seconds. She's smiling softly, and she studies me, her expression filled with so much love and acceptance. Then she brings me back in for another hug, squeezing me so tightly I can barely breathe.

"Mom . . ." I huff out on a forced breath.

"Shh, you're fine. You're not dying. Let your mama hug you." She laughs into me and sniffles at the same time, then places a kiss on my temple. "I love you so much, Alex. Nothing will ever change that. *Nothing*. You got it?"

I nod, clinging to her now as I try not to cry. I'm not doing a great job of it, but that's okay, I guess. She kisses my temple again and then leans back to look at me. Her thumbs come up and gently brush the tears from my cheeks, even though she's got tears of her own still.

"So . . . do I need to give you another talk about safe sex?"

"God, no, Mom, we're not—"

"Because you know, you still need to think about—"

There's a loud knock at the door, cutting her off. *Thank god.* She stares at me for an extra second, and I quickly shake my head again, my face on fire. "No talk needed, Mom. Hurry up now, you don't want to make Tammy wait."

She gives me a half smile and a small nod, blinking back more of her own tears. "Yeah, okay," she says quietly, and her hands slip down to my shoulders and squeeze me gently. "Can you grab my suitcase from my room? I've gotta get my backpack and trekking poles from the garage."

I nod and, before she can say anything else, spin around and jog toward the stairs, now aware of just how much and how unsteadily my heart is racing.

"Tell me one more time why you're forcing me to watch this?" Nico leans forward, picks a single kernel of popcorn from the bowl, and tosses it in his mouth before settling back up against me, his head resting on my shoulder. On the TV screen in front of us, the camera's focus shifts from a ringing phone hanging on the wall to the two teens walking slowly down the hallway toward it—the opening scene of *The Ring*.

I shift so my arm is around his shoulders. "Because it's a modern classic and one of the best horror films ever," I argue. "I can't believe we haven't watched it together before."

"I can. Remember when you made me watch that one movie with you when we were like twelve, and I didn't sleep for like two weeks. What was it?"

"Ohhhhhh, yeah. *Hereditary*." I laugh and shake my head a little. "That movie is sick. Still one of my favorites. We were, uh, kinda young to watch it, though. I'm surprised my mom let me rent it."

"Did she even know?"

I shrug, because I don't really remember, and Nico scoffs but settles into me more, his hand sliding slowly across my stomach to my opposite hip. This closeness is just incredible, and I lean my head to rest on top of his, savoring every second of it.

The movie goes on, with plenty of jump-scares that Nico either cackles at or actually reacts to, tensing and holding me tighter. I love it—both seeing him happy and having him be so close. We finish off the bowl of popcorn about halfway through, and as the end credits start to roll, Nico finally shifts a bit, pulling his legs up onto the couch and then stretching out and lying down facing the TV with his head in my lap.

He's quiet as I gently stroke his hair, my fingers sliding through his dark curls, and when I lean forward to grab the remote so I can turn off the TV a few minutes later, he mumbles something about being comfortable and not wanting to move.

And I totally agree.

We stay like that for a while, only the sounds of rain and an occasional rumble of thunder from somewhere far off breaking the silence. I close my eyes and just . . . be.

I like this. Actually, no, I *love* this. I love how perfectly he fits against me—whether we're hugging, spooning in bed, cuddling on the couch, or like this, with his head in my lap. And I love how much he trusts me, how there's not even an ounce of tension in him right now.

"Nico?"

"Hmm?" His voice is heavy, the single syllable drawn out, as though he's right on the brink of sleep.

I stroke his hair again, letting my fingers drift down to brush along the smooth skin of his neck, and he breathes in a little deeper. I don't really know what I wanted to say. Maybe I just wanted to hear his voice. So I let my fingers wander along his neck to his shoulder and then back. And I ask softly, "Are you still comfortable?"

"Mmm, very."

My heart soars. "Good."

It's probably another fifteen minutes or more before he moves, and then he just rolls over onto his back, his eyes half closed, and tilts his head to rest on my stomach. I love that even more, because then I can see his beautiful face.

He must notice me studying him, or maybe he sees my smile, because he blinks lazily and then asks, "What?" His eyes close again, and he cuddles up into me more as I gently trace my fingertips along his forehead, brushing back his hair.

"I just . . . I feel so lucky to have this. With you," I say, my voice quiet and thick with emotion.

Nico blinks his eyes back open and looks up at me, his expression soft and sleepy. As he holds my gaze, I touch his forehead, my heart full and my chest warm. Something flickers in his expression, some deep emotion that's gone faster than I can interpret it, and he finally looks away again, yawns, and closes his eyes.

"Ready to head to bed?" I ask.

He nods weakly and then pushes up onto one arm, scooting closer to me in the process. I hold my breath as he stops, his lips now only inches from mine. His eyes dart down to my mouth, and then his cheeks redden, which just makes him look even more beautiful. I let out a slow breath and then dip down to brush my lips against his perfectly pink cheek.

"You head on up. I'll be there in just a couple minutes."

I kiss his cheek one more time, and we both stand. Then he disappears up the stairs while I spend a few minutes tidying everything up. After the front and back doors are locked and all the lights are out, I head up after him.

The door to my bedroom is halfway open, light spilling out into the otherwise dark hallway, and I pause in the doorway to drink in the sight in front of me. Nico's leaning over across the bed, pulling the comforter back, the thin cotton of his gray sleep short stretched just enough to show off his ass—his tight, perfectly shaped ass that I've been admiring much too openly for the last week or so.

"You're doing that on purpose," I say, my voice low and gravelly. I step inside the room and close the door behind me as he pauses and glances over his shoulder, his eyebrows raised as if in challenge.

"Doing what?" He smirks and arches his back so his shorts stretch even more over his perfect curves. "I'm just getting the bed ready."

"So innocently."

"Yep." He brings one knee up onto the bed, reaching over to, I dunno, fluff his pillow or something.

My dick throbs, and I do my best to hold back a groan as he pulls his other knee up onto the bed, too, so he's on all fours, his ass *right there*, taunting me.

It's not lost on me that we're supposed to talk tonight. I mean, *I'm* supposed to start a conversation about California with him. But, damn . . .

I take another step closer, and hell if he doesn't pause again, glance back at me, and then wiggle his ass in the air with another of those teasing smirks.

"The bed's alllllllll ready," he says, grinning. Then he bites at his lower lip, which makes even more blood rush to my groin. "You coming?"

This time, I do groan, loudly, and I shake my head as I close the rest of the distance to the bed. He rolls over, laughing, that beautiful pink tinge back in his cheeks, and he pats the bed next to him, still grinning at me. With a sigh, I climb in and wriggle under the covers.

I'm barely settled when he scoots over toward me, his hand landing right in the middle of my chest. There's a rush, a thrill, a pulse of joy as his palm flattens against me, and I suck in a deep breath, watching him stare down at where he's touching me. He only pauses there for a few seconds, but then there's a slow transformation as his joy and silliness turn into tension, his eyes narrowing and becoming serious for a moment. He frowns and looks up at me, his jaw clenching.

I want to say something, because he suddenly looks like he needs some sort of reassurance. But no words will come. So I just give him a soft smile and lift my hand to his elbow, letting my fingers drift leisurely down his forearm. He studies me for what seems like a long time, although it's probably only a few more seconds, and then he purses his lips. His shoulders relax, and he slowly scoots closer, his hand running gently up my chest to my neck. When his skin touches mine, I close my eyes with a sigh and slip my arm around his waist, pulling him in tight. His cheek presses against my chest, and I feel the warmth of his breath through my shirt. I dip my head with a muffled groan, burying my face into his hair.

He takes a clear, measured breath and then another, each one affecting me just as much as the last. Then he mumbles, "I should probably sleep soon."

I want to shake my head, slip my hand under the hem of his shirt, tease my fingers along the sensitive skin of his lower back. I want to hear him gasp or moan or exhale a rough breath, my name on his lips. I want to thrust my hips forward against him, find some relief, some pressure or friction or whatever the hell else will help. I'm achingly hard, and my body is screaming at me to do *something*.

But there's also something holding me back. Something in his tone, maybe. Or something in the way he's pressing his hand into me now . . . like he's about to fall apart and the only thing keeping him together is that contact.

And we still haven't talked. There's so much to talk about, and I can't keep putting it off forever.

So instead of letting myself go and giving in to arousal and lust and all the other things I'm feeling, I breathe a kiss into his hair and allow my fingers to caress slowly along his forearm again. "You're tired?" I ask.

"Mmm, yeah," he hums. "But I'm also just really, really fucking comfortable right here."

That makes me smile, and I press another kiss into his hair. "Good."

He tilts his head back and looks up at me, his eyes sleepy. I lift my hand and brush the back of my fingers against his cheek, my eyes not leaving his, and he leans into the touch in a quiet approval.

I try to talk, *again*. Yet I can't seem to force myself to start the conversation. It didn't go well last time, when I tried to convince him months ago to come to California with me, and there's a huge part of me that doesn't want to ruin the moment—this beautiful, wonderful moment where I can just *feel* how much we're meant to be together.

Dammit.

That thought hits me square in the chest, and all the air leaves my lungs as I continue to hold his gaze. I repeat the touch, caressing his cheek as lightly as I can, and then I close my eyes, lean forward, and rest my forehead against his.

"I like this." My hand drifts back down to his forearm. "I want this—*us*—to, um, to be ... something."

He tenses, his hand pressing into me and his body going rigid. But he doesn't say anything.

*Why doesn't he say anything?*

My heart's racing, and not in the good way it was earlier. I swallow hard, and with every ounce of courage I can muster, I continue. "Nico, I don't want to go without you. To California, I mean. I want ... I want you to come with me."

My words are ineloquent, but I hope my intention is clear. And I hope they'll at least jump-start a deeper conversation—a conversation I've been avoiding for too long.

That's not what happens, though. Instead, he does what I should probably have expected, knowing him as well as I do—he pushes away from me. He sits and scoots back until he's up against the wall, and then he pulls his legs in to sit cross-legged, clasps his hands together in his lap, and stares down at them, his hair falling loosely over his forehead.

It's painful to know that retreating is still his go-to response, even with everything that's happened in the last few days, and it feels like our conversation from months ago all over again, even though he hasn't said a word yet.

I give myself a second and then another, my heart aching as I try to decide what to do. I could give him space, offer to go sleep on the couch or in the extra room. Or I could backtrack, tell him not to worry, we can talk about it another time. Or I could double down. Gently, of course.

When he screws his eyes and clenches his jaw so hard I see the muscles in his neck tighten, my decision is made for me.

I *can't* back away from this. And I think I don't actually want to, anyway.

We need to talk, even if it's just me letting him know exactly where I stand and what I want and how important he is to me.

Slowly, I push myself up and then shift so I'm right in front of him, also sitting cross-legged. Then I reach out and gently cover both of his hands with mine. He's tense and shaking, which fills me with a sadness I don't even try to deny.

"Nico, I meant what I said this morning and just now," I start. I squeeze his hands lightly and force myself to continue, needing to get everything out in the open. "I care about you. A lot. Romantically or whatever, yeah, but also, you're my best friend. Even if you didn't like me back, I . . . I still couldn't imagine leaving you here. I know we talked about this before, but I just can't . . . I can't leave you here, I can't leave without you, especially now. And I don't *want* to. Whatever it is, whatever reason you're unsure, we can figure it out. Or we can at least talk about it . . . Please, Nico. Please, let's talk about it."

I finally stop my stupid ramble, and I wait for any response from him. But he's still tense and silent, just staring at our hands in his lap. And with each second that ticks by, another sharp pain stabs through my chest.

Hell, maybe I've read this all wrong.

Maybe he doesn't want what I do. Maybe he's not as into this as me. Maybe he hates the idea of moving to California so much that he's willing to give this up.

Or maybe I'm not wrong at all. Maybe he just can't see a future, no matter how hard he tries.

When he still stays quiet, I try not to hurt, not to pull away myself. But it's hard, especially when his smile from just a few minutes ago pops back into my head. Bright and joyful and teasing, like I hadn't seen in so, so long.

I shouldn't have said anything. I shouldn't have taken away that light and happiness *both* of us worked so hard for.

With a rush of guilt, I hold his hands tighter and blurt out, "I-I'm sorry. I really didn't mean to upset you. We were having such a good time, and—"

"Don't apologize," he cuts in, a familiar edge to his voice. He pulls his hands away and covers his face, muffling a few curse words. Then he shakes his head. "You shouldn't apologize. Nothing is your fault. It's me. It's that I just can't—"

He stops himself, and I can actually see him trembling now. I reach out toward him, wanting to comfort him, but he shakes his head again and shrinks back away from me.

"I'm . . . I'm doing that stupid thing where I start to get anxious and then angry," he mumbles. "And I *really* don't want to snap at you, because that's not fair to you. I don't know how to stop it, though. I want to stop it. I want it *all* to just fucking stop. I—fucking hell, I hate this."

He moves suddenly, pushing away from the wall and scrambling past me off the bed. I twist around, watching as he heads straight for the door, his shoulders hunched and his whole body stiff.

"Nico, wait, wait. Please," I call out, jumping to my feet. I stumble after him as he throws the door open and starts toward the stairs.

God, this wasn't what I wanted. Not at all.

While I'm pretty sure he knows that, at least on some level, I also know he's not able to really think straight when he gets like this. Which is why I can't let him just retreat this time. Something feels different, too. More urgent.

I make it through the doorway just in time to see him pause at the top of the stairs, and I hurry over and stop at his side, facing him. He's staring down the narrow stairway, darkness passing over his face. For a second, I track his gaze down the steep flight of wooden steps that disappear into blackness, and my stomach drops.

"*I want it all to just fucking stop.*"

No. No, he's *not* thinking what my brain is telling me he's thinking. He wouldn't think that. He wouldn't . . . he wouldn't *do* that.

*Would he?*

In an instant, my hand shoots out, my palm flattening right against the middle of his chest.

I'm wrong. *I have to be.* But something tells me that I can't just ignore this.

I press my hand into his chest harder, and he lifts his eyes to look at me. He hasn't really been crying, but his eyes look red and puffy in the dim light of the hallway. I shake my head gently.

"Nico, don't . . ." I hesitate, fear rattling me, taking my voice. "Please," I force out, and I physically push him back a step. "*Please* don't."

He narrows his eyes at me for a second, and I can almost feel the moment his simmering anger starts to fade. Then, with a sharp breath, he backs up another step. "I-I wasn't going to."

I nod and step in front of him, though I can't seem to get myself to breathe right. "Please don't, ever," I whisper, my voice now hoarse and rough with emotion. The fact that he knew what I was thinking suggests *he* was thinking about it, too. And maybe that's what has me shaking now. I slip my arms carefully around his waist, and he doesn't object as I pull him up against me. "Please don't, ever."

On my repeated words, his whole body shudders, and he collapses into me, shivering and shaking his head and mumbling something else I can't understand.

I'm really not sure what just happened—whether his mind *really* went to the place I think it did—but I hope to hell I never see that look in his eyes ever, ever again.

# chapter twenty-five

*nico*

ALEX HOLDS ME IN the hallway for several minutes, and then he gently turns me around and guides me back to his room. I'm feeling numb. Maybe. And in a way, that's much better than whatever the fuck just happened out there.

He talks quietly to me, soft words that soothe the uncertainty still buzzing around in my head. He doesn't say he's sorry again, but I can hear the apology and regret in his voice anyway, like a heavy guilt he's carrying. Like it's his fault I stopped at the top of the stairs, bombarded by the sudden thought of how throwing myself down them would be a good way to just be . . . *done*.

Fuck, I'm more broken than I thought I was.

Once I'm safely back in bed, tucked under the covers, Alex disappears, returning less than a minute later with a glass of water. He helps me drink, then sets the glass down on the nightstand, crawls into bed, and carefully gathers me back up in his arms.

"I wasn't going to," I repeat for him, and for me.

I really wasn't. It really was just a fleeting thought. Brought on by my anxiety or whatever.

With a frown, I close my eyes and rest my head against his chest, my hand flat on his stomach. His hand comes up to cover mine, and I feel him breathe a kiss into my hair. There's a tiny flicker of warmth that comes with it, but it's just a fraction of what I felt earlier.

"I didn't mean to upset you," he says softly, though I can hear the pain and guilt in his voice. And I hate that.

"It's not your fault." I shake my head. "It's *me*. It's always me. You were just trying to talk. I shouldn't have gotten so upset. I'm sorry. A-and I . . ." I'm so tired, and my words fizzle out as I sigh and bury my head in his chest. "I just want to sleep now."

"Yeah. Yeah, okay," he agrees, and his arm moves to wrap around me, holding me to him. "This is okay, right? I can hold you?" he asks.

I nod. "Yeah."

"Good, good." He squeezes me gently and then whispers, "You're safe here, Nico. You're safe with me. Always."

I feel like an ass, because even though I absolutely needed to hear those words, I don't respond. Just like how I didn't respond to him earlier when he was pouring his heart out to me. All of those words he said—everything about him not wanting to leave me behind, not wanting to go to California without me—they all mean so much, and I can still hear his sincerity, his compassion, his vulnerability. Yet, in the moment, I just froze up, and every bit of bliss I felt from our playful flirting seeped away with the reminder that he's leaving soon.

And now . . . Well, now, I'm just too confused to talk. Too confused and numb and tired.

I close my eyes and try to relax against him, letting his embrace surround me with the most gentle warmth.

But my mind won't stop running itself in circles, racing between here and California. Incomplete thoughts batter me, beating me with reminders of how little I have.

No home.

No real job.

No money.

No family.

And when he's gone, I'll also have no friends.

I'm worthless. Broken. A mess.

And pretty soon, I'll be depressingly alone.

No wonder the stairs seemed like an option for those few seconds there.

I tense up at the thought, a sick nausea making my stomach turn, and he's there, his hand rubbing my back and his warm breath in my hair.

"Shh. Rest now. I'm here. It's okay," he murmurs, but those words just make me feel even less steady.

Because it's not okay. I'm not okay. And I wish I knew how to fix myself.

I don't say anything, but I shake my head and push back a little to look up at him. His gaze is filled with concern, and his eyes flit down to my lips briefly before he dips down and kisses me. It's tender and sweet and warm, with a gentleness that makes me feel safe. I melt into it, glad that ugly numbness is gone so I can feel him again. He's tentative, careful, but at the same time, there's nothing unsure about it.

And when he breaks the kiss a moment later, chasing it with a light press of his lips against my cheek, his hand shifts to my lower back, and he tugs me closer.

He's right to hold me like this, like he's scared I'm going to take off. I do feel myself wanting to pull away. The strong buzz of anxiety tingles beneath my skin, along with a deep stab of irritability that I know will turn into anger all too soon. And then there's the exhaustion, too. My body's so tired and weak, I'm not even sure how I'm still awake. It's late, and somehow, I'm going to have to get up in the morning and go to work. Because I can't miss a day or be late. I can't risk screwing this up.

But I can't risk screwing up what he and I have together, either. He's so important to me, just like he said I am to him. And if I don't tell him that . . .

I quickly turn over to face away from him. I can't be looking at him while I say whatever the hell is going to come out of my mouth right now. He lets me shift, but his arm stays firmly around my midsection, and his lips brush against the back of my neck.

I screw my eyes shut, my stomach churning.

"I'm fucking messed up, Alex," I blurt out, the words escaping on a ragged breath.

"No. No, you're not, you're—"

"I *am*. I've been messed up since we were kids. You know that. And what happened just now? It scared the hell out of me. My brain was screaming at me to—"

Fuck, I don't want to talk about the stairs. Not right now.

I start over. "I *do* want this—*us*—to be something. I want it more than anything. But I'm fucking broken as shit. I can't even have a normal conversation about this with you right now. I lose my shit, get anxious and angry. How the fuck can we have a normal relationship when I can't communicate? And how can I go to California with you? How would that possibly work? I'd need a job—one that will work around my inability to just fucking *be* when there are other people around—and a place to live that doesn't cost me my entire salary every month. I can't see that happening."

I don't feel any better having said all of that, though I've managed to not start shaking again.

But Alex must have heard something totally different from what I actually said, because there's a quiet huff of a laugh, and I feel him smiling against my skin. Then he's kissing my neck, and he props himself up on one elbow so he's leaning over me, his hand roaming up my chest and back down as his lips work their way along my jawline toward my mouth.

"Didn't you hear what I said?" I grumble.

His body presses up against mine, and his free hand comes up to tilt my chin toward him. Then he's kissing me again. Another of those tender, slow, sweet kisses.

"You said, and I quote"—he pulls back enough to study my eyes, a soft smile on his face—"'I do want this—*us*—to be something. I want it more than anything.'" He dips back down to kiss me. "That's what I heard."

Fucking Alex. Fucking optimistic, confident Alex.

I fucking love him.

"I said more than that."

"Eh, details."

"*Important* details."

He shrugs, but he's still smiling that soft, kind smile, his eyes caring and bright. I frown at him, about to argue again, even though I know he's just messing with me, but he stops me by shaking his head.

Then he lowers his mouth to mine for another gentle kiss.

I wake up the next morning well before my alarm is supposed to go off, and even though I try to go back to sleep, I can't.

Alex lies right behind me, holding me. His embrace is just as warm and comforting as it has been the last few days. Even in his sleep, he makes me feel safe. At some point overnight, his hand slipped under my shirt and his top leg wedged between mine, and it's so intimate and familiar now that it's helped to chase away most of my anxiety for most of the night.

Because of that, I've been able to think a little without the constant barrage of negative thoughts telling me the future Alex seems to want is impossible. I've even been able to hear his words with more clarity and less emotion blowing everything out of proportion. And I wonder if maybe, just *maybe*, we really can figure something out.

I'd need a job—one that I could handle, even on a bad day. That's the biggest problem I see.

But that's going to be a problem no matter where I am. Here or California or anywhere else. My current job is temporary, and when the summer is up, I'll have nothing.

I blink my eyes open and just stare across the room at Alex's neat desk, his laptop sitting there open but with a blank screen. On the wall behind the desk is a corkboard with a bunch of random pinups. His acceptance letter to Stanford is front and center.

I remember the day he told me about it and the simultaneous joy and sadness that overwhelmed me because I was so fucking proud of him and yet devastated at the same time.

I already knew I wasn't going to college. I'd known for years.

I did try.

Everyone probably thinks I didn't, but they're wrong.

I *did* try. I thought if I could do decently in school, maybe I'd get loans or a scholarship or something need-based. And Alex helped me as much as he could when I struggled, especially in math and science. But even with how hard I studied and studied, I can't take tests for shit, and by the time sophomore year was done, the school counselor basically told me it would be a waste to even apply. No colleges would take me.

I worked my ass off to graduate anyway, though I'm not sure how much that matters now. I'm not really employable. I have few relevant skills and very little experience, and I don't know how I could possibly change that in just three months.

My stomach knots up, and I take a long, slow, deep breath,

trying to steady myself. Alex believes in me. He's told me as much. Believing in myself, though . . . I guess I'm just not there yet.

Behind me, Alex shifts slightly.

"Mmm, you're up early." His voice is thick with sleep, but his lips press into my neck as he starts to flutter kisses along my skin.

"Yeah. I woke up and couldn't go back to sleep." I inhale sharply as he kisses a particularly sensitive spot.

"What were you thinking about?" he asks softly, his lips still touching my neck.

"Mmm." With a hum, I tilt my head slightly to give him better access. "I was . . . I was thinking about—" I gasp, and all other thoughts vanish as his hand slides low along my stomach and his foot rubs up to my ankle and then calf. "Ah, fuck, do that again."

"Hmm . . . Do what?"

I don't answer. Instead, I reach back and grasp his hip to hold him to me as I grind into his thigh. The pressure and friction are delicious, and I groan and arch back into him.

"Ah, god." There's a hot breath on my neck, and his hand presses insistently into my stomach, teasing at the low waistband of my sleep shorts. Any lower and he'd need to ask for permission first.

I fucking want him to.

His hot mouth skims along the back of my neck, stopping to suck and kiss just under my ear. I grind against his thigh again with an obscene moan, and his cock throbs against my ass in response. He lowers his head to my shoulder with another groan and rocks his hips forward, his hand still on my stomach, pressing me back and holding my ass against him.

Holy . . . fuck.

"That, Alex, that. Do that. Again."

"You sure?"

"Fuck yes. Do it. Now." I can't help how demanding my tone

is, and I'm glad it doesn't seem to faze him. He groans, and his cock thrusts against my ass again, rock hard and hot.

"That? That's what you want?"

"Yeah," I pant. "Yeah. Again."

He does as I ask, grunting with each rock of his hips, and I close my eyes and arch my back slowly and deliberately with his rhythm, feeling every inch of his length slide against me. It's fucking *perfect*. He hisses out several expletives, which I secretly smile at, and his palm flattens low on my stomach, his fingers slipping under my shorts and then under the waistband of my briefs.

"Mmm, can I—"

"Fuck, yes."

He laughs. "You don't even know what I was going to ask."

"It doesn't matter. The answer is yes." I let go of his hip and slide my hand up and back into his hair, my fingers threading through the short strands, and I encourage him as I arch back into him again and again. I'm hard and aching, and I need him. Now.

His fingertips trace a path downward, confident and sure, and he slows as the backs of his knuckles graze along my length. *God.* My skin's on fire, and I'm throbbing with want. I screw my eyes shut, rock back into him, and moan, loud and breathless and rough. Still, he takes his time, rubbing his cock against my ass while his fingers work their way to the base of my shaft and lower. He wraps his hand around me for the first time and groans. Then, rather than stroking me, his hand continues lower until he's cupping my balls gently. Hot tendrils of fire shoot all the way down into my toes, and I gasp as my hips jerk forward.

"Sh-shit. Oh god. Holy fuck, Alex." I reach down, and with a groan of relief, I push my shorts and briefs down in front, freeing my hard cock.

He gives my balls another gentle squeeze, and then his hand moves upward to grip my shaft with the perfect amount of pressure.

"Like this?" he breathes against my neck, and he strokes me slowly, rocking against me with the same rhythm.

We both moan.

"Yesssss," I hiss in approval. "Just like—yeah."

"God, you're perfect, Nico. This is—this is perfect."

I cry out as his thumb brushes over my slit, spreading the drop of precum leaking from me.

"Perfect," he breathes again, the single word sending a rush of heat straight to my groin, and he pumps my cock faster.

"Keep . . . keep going."

There's another hot puff on my neck. "You mean"—he pants—"you don't want me to just stop. Right now. When you're . . . so . . . close. Ah fuck, fuck, I'm—"

He grunts as he thrusts against me one more time, then his body goes rigid and his hips jerk as he comes. His hand's still wrapped around the base of my dick, still stroking me, even as he groans through the last throb of his release.

"Alex . . ." I gasp his name, my voice needy and rough, and I feel his mouth on my neck, his breaths hot and fast.

"I'm here. I'm here," he says, and he kisses my neck and then my cheek. And when I tilt my head toward him, he captures my lips in a wet, messy kiss. I moan, and he pulls back, breathing hard, his hand pumping my cock faster now. "Come. Come for me, Nico," he whispers on a ragged breath.

And fuck, that's what I needed. His voice, his touch, his *every-thing*. Hot pleasure and ache pool in my balls and cock, and I'm done for. I moan as I come hard, my shaft throbbing with each pulse of my release.

His lips are on mine again, worshipping me with soft, tender kisses as his hand releases my dick and caresses slowly back up my stomach. "Beautiful," he breathes. "Beautiful and sexy."

I'm too sated to speak, and I just lean back into him, breathing hard, my head tilted toward him so he can keep kissing me. That's exactly what he does, too—he kisses me gently and slowly until we're both breathing normally. Then he lowers his head to my shoulder with a quiet laugh.

"Is that . . . what you were thinking about?"

"Mmm, god, what?"

He chuckles, slides his leg out from between mine, and then tugs me over so I'm facing him. My shorts are still pushed down in front, and there's a mess on my stomach and shirt. But he doesn't seem to care about that at all. He brushes a kiss on my forehead, then lowers his mouth to mine again. The kiss is short but sweet and so tender.

I feel . . . loved. Loved and whole. At least right here in this moment.

I break away, dropping my chin, and he places another kiss on my forehead, wraps his arms around me, and pulls me into him, burying his head into the crook of my neck. He breathes in deeply and hums a soft sigh. My heart stutters.

I don't think I want to leave this moment. Ever.

We lie there together for a few minutes, then he pushes up onto one elbow and leans down to kiss my forehead again. When he straightens back up, his eyes study me softly.

"When I woke up," he says, "I asked you what you were thinking about. You were about to tell me. And then . . . we got distracted." He arches his eyebrows, smirking.

Fucking adorable.

I grin and shake my head, and I reach up and push back the hair that's fallen over his forehead. "It definitely wasn't that, though I think that was just about the best way to wake up, ever."

"I can agree with that."

He's watching me intently, the emotion in his eyes tempered by a flicker of concern. I inhale slowly and deeply.

"The truth—I was, um, thinking about college. You going to college, I mean. And California, and . . . jobs for me. And how I . . ." I shake my head and look away, unable to finish.

"And how *we* could make things work . . . ?"

I force a small laugh. "I didn't get that far."

"Oh?"

"Yeah. You distracted me."

He fake-scoffs. "I distracted you, huh?" He reaches up and touches my chin, tilting my head back so our eyes meet. His expression is full of softness and understanding. With a small smile, he leans in and kisses me. "I'd love to meet you for lunch again. And then I'd love if you'd let me take you out for ice cream after work. And then, I'd really love if we could take some time to talk about, um, what you were thinking about and maybe . . . about last night, too." His hand finds my forearm, and he caresses up and down as his eyes study mine. "Please."

I swallow hard and nod, ignoring the flicker of uncertainty in my chest. "Okay. Yeah, I'd like that too."

"Good." His grin lights up, and it's fucking gorgeous. He's fucking gorgeous.

I stare at him for a few seconds, then I blink and reach down to pull up my shorts as I roll over away from him. "I, uh, should get cleaned up and changed. I don't want to be late to work."

"Yeah, of course. And now I've got *a ton* of laundry to do," Alex mock-complains. I glance over my shoulder at him with a crooked smile and start to stand, but his arm catches me around the waist. He tugs me back to him. "One more kiss first?"

Ah, fuck. He's too perfect.

"Okay, but just one," I tease, touching my fingertips to his chin as I lean down to meet him.

He grins again. "That's all I'm asking for."

We kiss, slow and deep. And probably more than just once.

# chapter twenty-six

## *alex*

WHILE NICO SHOWERS AND gets ready for work, I rush through a quick shower of my own in the downstairs bathroom, throw on a clean pair of sweatpants and a T-shirt, and make us coffee and a small breakfast. It all feels a bit domestic, but I can't deny I sort of love that.

Just as I set our plates on the table, he comes jogging down the stairs, tucking his polo shirt into his slacks. His dark hair is still slightly damp, the longer strands starting to curl at the ends, and as he pauses at the bottom of the steps, a thick lock falls down over his forehead, contrasting with his pale skin.

God, he's just gorgeous.

My heart leaps as I watch him finish tucking in his shirt, and when he glances up at me, his deep green eyes sparkling, my whole body tingles with the memory of what we did in bed not more than twenty minutes ago.

Hell, I *need* to kiss him right now.

I push myself away from the table and start toward him. As soon as I'm close enough, my arms slip around his waist, and I pull him against my chest. He's grinning, and his eyes are bright and happy. It's warm and perfect, and god, I love this.

*I love him.*

I can't believe my luck. I can't believe he's here with me and mine and in this as much as I am. I shake my head and purse my lips, trying to hold back my smile.

"What?" He crooks an eyebrow at me and shifts his hands up from my hips to my chest. Then he stretches up so his mouth is nearly touching mine. His grin almost looks cocky now, and I love that, too.

I bring my mouth even closer. "It's you," I say on a breath. My lips just barely brush his, and he closes his eyes and lets out the most arousing and needy little moan. "You're gorgeous," I whisper against him, and then I kiss him again in that same playful way.

He shakes his head. "You're just saying that because of what we did in bed."

"No, I—"

"You remember?" he cuts in, smirking up at me with a mischievous glint in his eyes. His hands slide the rest of the way up my chest, and his fingers tease along my neck. He stretches up until his lips are nearly touching mine, and he whispers, "Remember how you jerked me off while rubbing one out against my ass?"

I gulp, and heat rushes to my cheeks as Nico presses his hips forward into me. With a laugh, he closes the rest of that gap between us and kisses me. He holds me to him and deepens the kiss briefly, his tongue dipping into my mouth to taste me, before he pulls back, grinning.

"It was hot as fuck," he whispers. "I loved it."

My heart's pounding now, and my dick throbs with want, apparently ready for a second round. I groan and lower my mouth to his again, capturing his lips in a kiss that's much different from our light, teasing touches from a few moments ago.

There's a need and a hunger to it that I can't really hide, and I'm having a hard time not dragging him back upstairs. But he has to go to work, and I want him to have time to eat. So, after another few seconds, I pull back. He whimpers in protest and chases the kiss with another touch of his lips to mine.

I loosen my arms from around him and gaze down at him, letting myself get lost. His red, swollen lips taunt me, and his eyes are half-lidded with bliss. I smile softly and lean down one more time for one more kiss. Brief and much more chaste.

Then I force myself to step back, and I tip my head toward the table. "Hungry? It's not much, I know you're in a hurry," I say. "Just some scrambled eggs and then we had strawberries and cantaloupe. Unfortunately, we're out of syrup, so no pancakes today," I add with a smirk.

Nico rolls his eyes, but he's still grinning.

And god, that grin. It might just be making me fall even harder.

I motion to the table. "A-after you."

He purses his lips and shakes his head, and his eyes stay locked on mine as he says, his voice totally serious, "You first. It's my turn to admire *your* ass for once."

"What the—Nico!"

He laughs, and it makes this perfect moment even more perfect to see the pure delight in his eyes. I love it. Damn.

"Come on, now," he argues, though the façade of seriousness is completely gone. "You got all intimate with my ass earlier. Give me a little eye candy, at least?"

I'm still too stunned at his bold banter, and I can't form any words to respond. He just grins at me again, then takes my hand and pulls me along with him to the table.

I'd love to be able to say I didn't fret all day about the discussion Nico and I are supposed to have tonight. Unfortunately, that would be a lie. I'm not at all immune to worrying, and my brain is quite adept at running around in circles and overthinking things.

Fortunately, though, I'm also my mom's son.

After I get back from lunch, which was perfect in every way and ended with a quiet kiss stolen under an old oak tree at the back of the library courtyard, I sit down at the kitchen table with my laptop, a notepad, and a pencil, and I start planning.

I love math and numbers, and I've spent plenty of time watching my mom budget. But I've never had to make a budget myself, even if it's not a budget *for* myself.

It's not easy, especially because I have no frame of reference for most things. How much money does a single guy actually *need* for food each month? What about rent? Utilities? Extras? God, Nico's still wearing the same set of clothes to work every day.

And I can't answer what's probably the most important question—what can he do for work? How much money can he realistically expect to bring in every month? The minimum wage is higher in California than here in Nebraska, sure. But that doesn't necessarily negate the increased cost of living. In fact, it almost certainly doesn't.

There are so many uncertainties, and by the time I have a rough outline, I'll admit that it's hard to feel as optimistic as I had earlier in the day.

I'm about ninety-five percent sure my mom will be out hiking with Aunt Tammy or something—probably somewhere with no cell signal—but I text her anyway because if I'm going to try to convince Nico that this is something he can do, I'm going to have to believe in it myself first. And that means my numbers need to make at least *some* sense.

*Alex (2:34 p.m.):* hey mom call me when u can

I start typing out a second text to explain a bit more, but before I can even get the first few words out, the phone vibrates and begins to ring. Her name pops up on the screen. I swipe to answer and bring the phone to my ear.

"Hey, Mom."

"Hi, sweetie. Is everything okay?" she asks, breathing hard.

"Yeah," I answer automatically, although that's probably not the entire truth. "Well, I mean, I hope so. It's just . . ." I pause to take a deep breath and steady myself.

Muffled sounds in the background—birds chirping and the roar of a river, maybe—suggest my mom is at least outside, if not out hiking, and I immediately feel bad for interrupting her getaway with Aunt Tammy for something I should be able to figure out myself. But I know she wants to help, and she's always told me not to hesitate to ask for help when I need it. I open my eyes and look back down at the notes I scribbled onto the notepad. All those numbers that just don't add up. Then I try again.

"So, um, Nico and I are going to talk tonight. About California, I mean. And I wanted to get a jump on a budget, because I'm hoping to show him how it'll be possible for us to figure it out. But, uh, the numbers aren't . . . looking good, and I could use some help. Do you have a few minutes?"

"Ohhhh, hmm. Yeah, of course. Just give me a sec." There's some quiet talking, and I can hear Aunt Tammy's voice, though I can't make out her words. Then my mom's voice becomes clear again. "Okay, sweetie. I've got a few minutes here. Tell me what you've worked out so far."

We talk for much more than a few minutes, and I explain everything I've outlined to her. She's quiet while she listens, and when I'm done, she's quiet for another moment. I'm just about to ask her what she thinks when I hear her take a deep breath and clear her throat.

"You're, um, missing a few budget items on there still," she starts, and I can hear how reluctant she is. My stomach drops as she continues. "Um, he'll need to budget for health insurance, unless he finds a job that includes it or can get on Medicaid or whatever's available in California, and your numbers for car insurance are probably off because it sounds like you used the quote he just got?"

"Uh, yeah."

"The cost will be much higher in California. And you'd need to budget for gas for his car, too, which is hard to do if we don't know how much he'll be driving. Gas is much more expensive there, especially in the Bay Area."

My stomach knots up even more as she keeps talking, discussing each of the expenses I noted and explaining why each one might be incorrect or underestimated. When she stops talking after another few minutes, I'm *not* feeling better. In fact, I'm feeling worse. Especially when she quietly adds, "And don't forget to deduct estimated taxes from his paycheck. Whatever he's receiving, they'll take taxes out first. So even if he's making twenty bucks an hour, it won't mean that much in take-home pay."

"Uh, yeah. Right. Right." It's hard to keep the uncertainty and disappointment from my voice, and I know she hears it, because she immediately starts up again.

"But there are always ways to cut expenses, too, and I think you can find them. Maybe he can find a roommate to split the cost of rent, or—"

"Mom," I cut in, shaking my head, "he won't be able to have a roommate."

"Dammit, that's right," she mumbles, and I hear a muffled voice on the other end of the line. "Yeah, Tam, sorry. One more minute, okay? . . . Okay, sweetie, so, I know this looks really tough, but here's what you need to do, okay?"

She rambles on for another couple of minutes, explaining to

me how to trim the budget and then how to figure out just how good of a job he'd need to make enough money. She reminds me that he'll have an entire three months of work here to save up and explains how that money could be used to give him a buffer the first couple of months while he works out the kinks in his actual budget. And she also mentions all the savings *I* have, too.

"You can remind him that you're in this together," she suggests softly, "and that he's not totally on his own to figure it out. You have to live on campus the first year, since Stanford requires it, but after that, you'll have options on that front, too."

"That's true." I stare at the numbers on the page in front of me and then turn back to my laptop to do a quick search for a take-home pay calculator.

"It won't be easy, Alex, but—"

"—the best things in life never are," I finish for her with a light laugh. "Yeah. I just . . . I need to know it's possible. And it seems like it'll just be a matter of finding him the right job and housing situation."

I almost feel her nod through the phone. "Exactly, sweetie. It can be done. And in fact, remember that I mentioned that friend I have? She's in San Jose, I think."

"Oh, right, um, she has an art gallery or something?"

"She owns quite a few, actually. And she runs a collective of several hundred artists. If Nico decides he wants to give this thing a shot, I can contact her and see if she's looking for an employee. Not all jobs are client-facing, and I'm sure he'll be able to find something."

"That would be great, Mom. Thank you. I'll keep playing with these numbers, and we'll just have to find something that works."

"The two of you can do it," she says, and this time, I hear a confidence in her voice that gives me a little more hope.

"Yeah. We'll figure it out."

"Let me know how it goes later, okay, sweetie?"

"Sure, Mom. Thanks again. Love you."

"Love you too."

I hang up, set my phone down next to me, and turn back to my laptop, determined to get these numbers to work, even if it takes me the rest of the afternoon.

# chapter twenty-seven

*nico*

"WAIT, WAIT, WAIT." I shut the passenger side door to the truck and turn around as Alex meets me along the sidewalk. "So if *I* get a waffle cone, does that mean—"

"Oh, shit," he cuts in, frowning. He runs a hand through his hair with a sigh and then pulls out his phone. "I, uh . . . I actually don't know. Maybe it's fine?"

I step closer as he opens up a browser tab and googles our question. We both groan as the search results pop up. He scrolls for a second, skimming the summaries under each of the links. Then he sighs in frustration and shoves his phone back into his pocket.

"So . . . how do you feel about cake cones?" he asks, grimacing as he looks back up at me. He's about due for a haircut and a touch-up, if he's going to keep it dyed blue—his natural blond is showing through at the roots, and it's getting a little too long for his neat style. And now it's messy too. I want to reach up and brush it back into place, but I manage to keep my hands to myself.

Instead, I shrug and pretend to think on it. "Hmm, I dunno. How long did it say we'd have to wait?"

"Really? Really, Nico?!"

"I'm just weighing all of my options," I tease with a smirk. "I mean, you're asking me to choose between a waffle cone and kissing . . . I'm really not sure. It's a *huge* sacrifice."

He groans again, but there's a small smile tugging at his lips. I can tell he almost wants to swat at me, but he doesn't do it. He just shakes his head and turns to look toward the ice cream shop down the street. There's a line out the door, and all of the tables outside are filled with loud groups, mostly people our age. I immediately recognize a bunch of them from school, including several guys whom I'm not too fond of.

I blow out a breath and drop my eyes to the sidewalk, trying to ignore the rush of uncomfortable feelings and memories. Voices calling me names. *Nico the Freako. Punching Bag.* Other things. Worse things.

Suddenly, even my light tease about Alex's cinnamon allergy doesn't feel good.

I bite my lip and lift my eyes up just as he glances back at me, his expression tight. "I'm kidding, of course," I say, and he nods.

"Yeah, I know."

"I'll take whatever type of cone you usually get. What did you call it?"

"A cake cone." He looks down at his shoes and scuffs the toe of one into the ground. "I'm sorry, uh . . . That's something I hadn't really thought about before, you know? I hate to ask you to—"

"—make a tiny adjustment to my eating habits so we can be together safely?" With a smile, I reach out and brush my fingers against his. It's a tiny gesture, but the need to reassure him is strong. I link my pinkie with his for just a second before letting my hand drop back to my side. "It's fine. Really."

He lifts his eyes and then holds my gaze for a count of five. His cautious smile fades into a grimace. "You won't be saying that when you have to turn down a cinnamon roll. Or snickerdoodles. Apple pie. A lot of desserts, actually. And curry. Mole. Barbacoa. Oh, and Coke and Dr. Pepper."

"Damn."

"Yeah. Eating out can be kind of a minefield. That's probably one of the reasons my mom cooks so much. She can substitute for other spices when she's cooking, and there's no, uh, cross-contamination, I guess you'd call it."

I just nod, and together, Alex and I start down the street toward Harley's. Each step closer makes my chest tighten more, and an uncomfortable buzzing starts in my fingers. It's familiar, accompanied by a growing irritation in the back of my mind.

I fucking hate it.

Alex's hand touches my back briefly, as though he can sense the change. He probably can. And though it helps knowing he's here with me, it doesn't get rid of the feeling completely. There are too many people. Too many people who are assholes. Even with all the struggles of the last week and a half since school ended, I've been lucky to at least not have *that* to deal with, too—the bullying, the pressure of having to be around so many other people I don't trust.

I'm walking slower now, and Alex adjusts his speed next to me. His hand is no longer on my back, but he's close. I drop my eyes to the sidewalk just as we reach the end of the line. The couple in front of us turns around, and I'm surrounded by voices.

They know him, because everyone does. They say hi, and there are handshakes or fist bumps or whatever. More words, more voices. A few others come over. I shrink back just a step. If Alex notices, I can't tell. The conversation goes on, lively and loud. It's probably not even that loud. It's probably just me.

I hear every few words, especially if they're Alex's, but whatever everyone's talking about really doesn't register. The line moves forward, and I gravitate with it, as does the group surrounding us.

More handshakes. Something that sounds like an invitation to something in Omaha. For Friday night. Maybe.

Alex seems interested.

My stomach hurts.

Then, the others leave, and we're alone in line again. There's a group behind us now—a family with some young kids—and we shuffle forward as one of the children screeches at the top of their lungs. The mom gently reminds the child they have to wait until it's their turn.

I shove my hands into my pockets and take another step forward as the line moves.

Alex is talking now, and it takes me another moment to realize he's talking to me, his hand on my upper arm, giving me a soft squeeze.

"So, what do you think? I know it's not your thing, but it could be fun?" He sounds hopeful as fuck, and I clench my jaw.

"S-sorry, what do I think about what?" I stammer, shifting just slightly so he has to drop his hand from my arm.

We're at the doorway to the ice cream place now, and we both squish to one side to let the people exiting get by. Then we step all the way in. The chill of the building's air conditioning cools some of the heat simmering below my skin, but I'm still not okay, especially when the child behind us screams again and the mom isn't quite as gentle with her words this time.

Alex scoots closer to me, and his hand finds my back. "Everyone from school is getting together on Friday night, heading into Omaha to go to Dave and Buster's."

"Oh, right. Um. Cool." There's no sincerity in my voice at all, and I'm sure Alex hears it.

He laughs, and his hand presses into my back, guiding me forward a step. We're finally almost at the front of the line. I'm not even sure if I want ice cream now.

"We don't have to go," Alex says, and even though my mind wants to invent things, I can't hear any disappointment or negativity in his voice at all. "It sounded kinda fun, but I wouldn't want you to be uncomfortable."

I'm actually not sure how to respond, especially right now when I'm starting to feel lightheaded and everything seems to be closing in around me. Fucking anxiety. "C-can we talk about this later, maybe?"

"Yeah, sure. Of course." Alex's hand drops from my back, and a moment later, he steps up around me to the counter and orders. A double scoop of mint chip in a cake cone for himself and then chocolate peanut butter brownie in a cake cone for me. He gives me a look to confirm, and I manage a tight nod.

A few minutes later, we're stepping back outside in the early evening heat, ice cream cones in hand. Alex walks just behind me, and my stupid ass is imagining he's doing it to make me feel safer. His free hand finds my back, and he leans in and says, "How about we head out to the river? We can eat the ice cream on the way, and it should be quieter there, so we can just relax and talk."

"Yeah, okay," I agree, my voice low and shaky. And though he doesn't respond, I can almost feel his apology in the way his hand brushes my back lightly, guiding me in the direction of his mom's truck.

"Ugh, this is so good," he says, and when I glance sideways at him, I'm immediately distracted. He's licking around the base of the ice cream scoop, catching the melting drops before they can slide down the cone.

It's a fucking good distraction, really.

His eyes meet mine as he starts around the ice cream again, and he slows his tongue just enough that I'm sure he knows I can't have missed it.

Fuck. How is eating ice cream sexy now?

My eyes dart down to the cone, and I watch, my dick stirring with interest, as he licks up another drop of ice cream about to fall.

"Yours is melting too," he says with a smirk. We stop at his

mom's truck, and he glances back over his shoulder in the direction
we came before turning to face me again. His eyes are hungry as
they drop to my ice cream cone. "Don't want to make a mess."

"Mm-hmm, yeah." I give him just as good a show as he gave
me, slowly tracing a path with my tongue around the edge where
the ice cream meets the cone. I even close my eyes and moan a
little—because chocolate peanut butter brownie is fucking good.
My eyes flutter back open in time to see his cheeks flush and his
gaze darken. I recognize the look. It's the same one he had in the
hallway last week when he was watching my ass as I walked away.

I lean back against the truck, holding his heated gaze, and he
steps closer, licking the ice cream from his lips. He stops just a few
inches away, now biting his lip, his eyes drawn to my mouth. The
tension in the air is sharp, and he swallows hard and drags his eyes
up to meet mine.

"We should go," I whisper, and he nods eagerly, which makes
me laugh. Before he has a chance to move away, I tease him one
more time, running my tongue around the outside of the cone
again.

He groans, and I laugh as he opens up the passenger side door
for me. "Get in before I kiss you right here in front of everyone,"
he says, his voice almost a low growl.

Fuck, that's hot, too.

"Maybe I want you to," I tease, taking a lick off the top of my
cone this time. Slowly and deliberately.

"Maybe you want . . ." His eyes darken as he trails off.

I laugh, then wink at him, turn, and jump into the front seat of
the truck. "Come on, hurry up, let's go!"

With a sigh and a dramatic eye roll, Alex closes the truck door.
Then he shakes his head as he jogs around the front of the truck to
the driver's side.

The river.

We usually come here a few times every summer and then sometimes in the fall, too, when the summer heat lingers into late September and early October. There's this one spot that's secluded, off a short trail through the trees, and we're lucky that no one else ever seems to come to this specific spot, even in the summer when there are a bunch of people on the river.

It's quiet and calm and exactly what I need after a day like today.

I've been hiding, pretending. The whole last hour or so since I got home from work, changed my clothes, went to Harley's with Alex, flirted and teased him with the ice cream—I've been hiding how fucking awful my afternoon actually was.

God, I'm lucky I didn't get fired. Yet.

I should have told him already—because honesty and communication and all that. But we were having such a good time, and I didn't want to ruin it. Plus we've got plenty of other stuff we're supposed to talk about.

I'm tired, though, and I can feel my resolve crumbling as all the energy it's taken to keep pretending all day drains from me.

From his spot in the sand next to me, Alex shifts a little so his shoulder bumps mine. "You're quiet. Everything okay?"

I close my eyes and laugh without humor. "You're reading my mind now."

"Huh?"

"I was just thinking about how I'm really *not* okay."

He's quiet for a moment, then he says, "Do you want to talk about it?" He sounds hesitant, though, as if he's not entirely sure he wants my answer to be yes.

It's a bit jarring.

I lean forward so my elbows are resting on my knees, and I stare out at the shallow water in front of us, flowing slowly at the edge of the sandbar. When I've finally worked up the courage to talk, I drop my eyes to my hands.

"My mom came to the library today, after you left," I say, and my jaw clenches as I remember the conversation. The anger in her eyes. The resentment in her tone. The way she didn't really let me speak while she berated me, loudly, in front of my colleagues.

The way Caitlin had to step in and ask her to leave when she started to raise her voice.

The way Sharon scowled disapprovingly at me and told me to get back to work.

Without meaning to, I ball my hands into fists and shove them down into the sand. It's warm and dry, and maybe that should help me a little. But it doesn't, really. The pain's been gnawing at me for hours, and rather than go away, it worsens, knotting up my stomach and stabbing into my chest.

Alex clears his throat and scoots closer, his shoulder now touching mine. "What did she want?"

"Money."

"The money for your car?" he asks softly.

I nod and force a couple of breaths. "She said she wanted it right then, like I just had five hundred dollars burning a hole in my fucking wallet and could just hand it over, there at the library."

"What the hell?"

It was actually worse than that, and I clench my jaw again and let myself lean against him as I continue. "I told her I wouldn't have it until Friday, and she said no, that's not good enough any-more. She yelled at me in front of everyone and then threatened to report the car as stolen. And then she threatened to—fuck—" I'm shaking now, and I only manage to not panic more when his arm wraps around my shoulders. Tears slide down my cheeks, though, and I screw my eyes shut. "Sh-she threatened to send Patrick over to pick it up," I force out, "because she said Patrick would know 'how to convince me.'"

"Jesus." I feel him shake his head, and then he presses a kiss to my temple and tightens his arm around me. "That's horrible. What . . . or like, why? *Why?*"

"I don't know," I admit, and I turn and lean into him more, burying my head in his shoulder. "She sounded mad, like *I* was the one who betrayed *her*. And I . . . I just . . ." I blow out a sharp breath, unable to continue. I have no fucking clue why she's acting like this.

"She didn't report it stolen, right?"

I shake my head. "Not that I know of. But she didn't really say she wasn't going to, either."

"She shouldn't be allowed to do that," Alex spits out, and there's a venom to his voice that I've never heard from him before.

"Do what?"

"Threaten you with that asshole," he says. "Isn't there a restraining order or something?"

My chest hurts, and I close my eyes, still leaning into him. "No. It expired or whatever when I turned eighteen."

"Dammit."

"Yeah."

He's quiet for a minute, though he keeps holding me tight, and then he says, "We can stop by the ATM now. I have the money. We can pay for the car and be done with her. Then she'll have no more hold over you. You can pay me back whenever. It's not a big deal to me."

"No. No, I can't—"

"That's actually one of the things I wanted to talk to you about tonight," he cuts in, and that feeling that my stomach is knotting up intensifies.

I pull away and wrap my arms around my midsection, shaking my head. "I'm not taking your money, Alex."

"It's really not a big deal—"

"It is to me!" I don't yell, but I do raise my voice. And I hate myself for it. He's just trying to help. I sigh deeply. "I'm not taking your money," I repeat, and I look up to the water again. "She'll just have to wait until Friday, like we agreed."

Alex is silent, and my stomach aches with the thought that I've pushed him away when all he was trying to do was make me feel better and find a solution. Hell, I don't even know *why* it's a big deal to me. My jaw trembles, and I bite my lower lip as I glance over at him. His shoulders are tense, and he's staring off across the river, one hand rubbing at the back of his neck.

He must sense that I'm looking at him, because he turns his head toward me and gives me a tight smile. "I want to help." He blinks, and his smile turns into a frown just as I look away, back to my hands. "And I want you to know we're in this together, Nico. You don't have to do this alone. I have the money. It's just sitting there in my account. If it'll save you from worrying all week long, or—or from having to see that asshole again, I don't understand why you won't let me help."

It's logical, like he usually is. So I'm not sure why I can't just nod and accept it.

I got thrown into this—this life I didn't expect. Before all the shit hit the fan with my mom, I planned to stay there through the summer, save my money, use the experience I gained at the library to get a permanent job. Then maybe I'd have enough saved to move out, rent my own apartment, be on my own.

Instead, I'm living off the generosity of Alex and his mom. Still only forty dollars to my name. Still rewashing the same set of work clothes every night. Driving an uninsured car and relying on Wi-Fi signals to connect my cell phone.

"You're already helping me so much," I say through gritted teeth.

He moves closer, and his hand finds my back. I close my eyes at the gentle touch. It feels good.

"I want to help. Besides, you didn't ask for any of this. None of it is your fault. You shouldn't have to shoulder it all alone." He rubs up and down my back with smooth strokes, and I shudder as I shake my head.

"I just want her to honor her word," I admit, and my voice breaks as the tears start to fall. "She said Friday. I-I shouldn't have to—I shouldn't have to pay her now. It's not right."

"I know," he says softly. "I know. It doesn't make sense. But, Nico, she's not doing things that make sense right now. Whatever her reason, she's not being honest or predictable or caring. What if she . . ." He trails off, and I feel him move even closer until his arm is around my shoulders.

*What if she actually sends Patrick this time?*

Is that what he was about to say?

I let him pull me up against him, but I'm trembling. My hands close into tight fists as a scene suddenly plays out in my head.

Patrick showing up at the library, demanding to see me. His beady little eyes dark with rage as he pushes past Caitlin, back into the office where I work. Hate-filled words leaving his mouth as he knocks down a pile of books on his way over to me. Then pain as he grabs my shoulder and throws me back against the wall. His fist slamming into my face, just like—

"Fuck," I hiss, covering my face with my hands. I can barely breathe, and my heart feels like it's about to leap right out of my chest. "She wouldn't . . ."

Alex squeezes my shoulder. "I hope not. But that's why you should let me—"

"No. I'm not taking your money."

"Okay, okay. That's okay. I understand," he says, and the silence returns.

Which is bad.

I hold my breath as it happens again—the scene playing out in my head. Except this time, it's not an imagined scene. It's what actually happened four years ago. Patrick actually screamed at me, grabbed me, yanked me back so hard I had bruises on my shoulder. Then he actually hit me, his fist breaking my nose.

There was so much blood, and I couldn't breathe. And he kept screaming at me to shut the fuck up, threatening to do it again.

My mom heard the noise from the other room and came in to see what happened. She pushed him away, called 9-1-1, had him arrested for hurting me. I spent the night in the hospital, had surgery a week later to fix my busted nose, spent two weeks home from school because I had a concussion.

"She wouldn't," I repeat, and this time, it's a complete statement. Because I can't believe, not for one second, that she'd allow him—*encourage* him, even—to hurt me again. She's changed, and she's angry and awful now, and I have no idea why. But she's still my mom, and she still went through that shit with me. "She wouldn't."

Alex doesn't say anything, but he nods and holds me to him. Then he turns his head and kisses my hair.

Across the river, a deer peeks out from the trees and looks around cautiously before stepping up to the water to drink. Alex hums quietly and kisses me again, and some semblance of calm starts to wash over me. The deer stays there for several minutes, drinking and then grazing on the grass along the edge of the sandbar, and we both watch silently. It's relaxing this time, the quiet. It's maybe what I needed. When the deer finally wanders back into the trees after a bit longer, I close my eyes and rest my head up against Alex's shoulder.

My breathing is back to normal, and my heart is no longer racing so fast it hurts.

The sun's going down behind us, though, the distinct flickers of fireflies becoming visible among the trees and brush.

"We should probably head back home soon," Alex says, echoing my own thoughts. Then he laughs once and shakes his head. "God, we were supposed to talk about California and stuff."

"Yeah. Fuck, I'm sorry."

"I, uh, made a budget. You know, to show you that it's, um, doable, I guess."

There's that hesitation in his voice again. I focus back across the river, letting my eyes follow the bright, brief streaks of light from the fireflies as I try to keep my anxiety from returning. "And is it?" I ask.

He inhales a long breath and then lets it out slowly. "Yeah, I think so. I mean . . . kinda."

"Kinda?"

"It's complicated."

It would be. Of course it would be. I just nod and keep staring off at the fireflies. It's not more than a few seconds later, though, when his fingers brush against my cheek.

"Nico . . ."

He applies a gentle but firm pressure, tilting my chin toward him, and when our eyes meet, a rush of shame courses through me. I try to pull away, but he shakes his head and lowers his mouth to mine in a kiss that's not so gentle or chaste. His tongue traces my lower lip, and when I open my mouth for him, he eagerly explores. I groan when his hand slips down my neck, his fingertips grazing along the bare skin of my throat. He doesn't stop, and I don't try to pull away again. He deepens the kiss more, and he seems to be playing with things—the angle, the pressure, the way his tongue caresses me. And his hands aren't idle, either. His fingers find the hem of my shirt and tease along my skin, hot and intense.

"Oh, fuck," I grunt, and I finally break away, lowering my head as I breathe heavily. He keeps caressing along my waist, and his lips flutter light kisses along my jaw.

"Sorry," he apologizes, though I can tell he's not actually sorry at all. He does, however, slow down and—reluctantly—straighten up. His hand lingers on my hip, underneath my shirt, his fingers flexing into my side, and he lets out a shuddering breath as his eyes fall to my lips.

It's my turn to laugh, and I shake my head and set a hand on his chest, pushing him away. "Can you show me the budget you made? Back at the house, maybe."

His eyes are dark and unfocused as they dart up to mine, but he nods right away. "Yeah, of course. Yeah." He blinks a few times, then his face lights up. "You mean it? You want to see it?"

"If only to see how bad it is," I say. He frowns, but I roll my eyes. "I'm kidding. Yes, I want to see it. Though I don't . . . think . . ."

He hops up and dusts the sand off his shorts, shaking his head. "I'll show you, and we'll figure it out. Okay?"

With a tentative smile, he reaches down to offer me his hand. I stare at him for a few long seconds, and then I nod, take his hand, and let him help me up. His arm immediately loops around my waist, supporting and protective, and my heart flutters in my chest.

Is it possible—this dream of his where I follow him across the country and we start a new life together in California?

I have no fucking clue, and apparently, it's "complicated." But as we start back to his mom's truck, his arm holding me close, I find myself hoping, maybe for the first time, that "complicated" doesn't mean "impossible" and that we might actually have a chance to figure it out.

# chapter twenty-eight

## *alex*

THE VIEW FROM THE top of the stairs down frightens me tonight. The lights are on this time, and I can see Nico sitting on the couch in the living room, even from my vantage point. But something about it rattles me.

He's got his back to me, his shoulders hunched, and he's tense—I can tell that even from here. Still, that shouldn't be enough to have my heart racing unevenly, my stomach in knots.

I grip my laptop in my hand, pressing it against my side, and I let my other hand slide along the railing as I start down the stairs one at a time. The third step from the top creaks, even though I'm trying to walk silently, and my eyes dart back to Nico as he twists around toward me.

He's scared too. I can see it in the tightness in his jaw and the stiffness of his movement.

I force a smile and try to loosen myself up a bit, releasing my hold on the railing so I can jog down the rest of the steps.

"Ready to do this?" I say, as upbeat and positive as I can.

But his gaze darkens, and he frowns. "No." He turns so he's facing forward, away from me, and my fake smile fades.

I don't know what to say, so I say nothing.

He pulls his feet up from the floor to sit cross-legged as I come around the side of the couch to join him, and he seems to scoot away a few inches to give me more room, which doesn't help the knots in my stomach much. I settle into my spot with a sigh and set the laptop on my lap, but I don't open it. He's fidgeting next to me, his hands tucked under his arms and his body rocking ever so slightly forward and back. I wonder if he knows he's doing it.

When I glance sideways at him, he's staring down at the coffee table in front of him, his teeth clenched and his eyes unfocused.

We're both nervous, and I wish I could just ease that anxiety of his and tell him it'll all work out.

I reach over and set my hand on his knee, and he stops his rocking and turns his head to look at me. His eyes are almost pleading, and it makes my heart ache.

I force that small smile back on my face. "We can make this happen. Okay?"

"You're not exactly screaming confidence here, Alex." He drags his gaze away and closes his eyes.

"I know. I'm sorry. I'm—"

"Don't apologize. Please."

"Right, um . . ." With a sharp exhale, I open up my computer and click a few buttons. The numbers I'd worked so hard on earlier pop up on the screen, and I scan them quickly. It's a bit of a mess. Not the spreadsheet, I mean; the spreadsheet is clearly organized and easy to follow, I think. But the numbers. They're tight, and everything hinges on him finding a good enough job and a place to live that doesn't cost an arm and a leg. I take a deep breath and then shove the computer over to him. "Here."

I should probably explain. Go through line by line. Tell him how I came to the numbers I did. But I'm not sure whether he'll appreciate knowing how much my mom was involved or my thought process to get the numbers to "work."

He untucks his hands and adjusts the laptop, and I watch nervously as his eyes scan down the lines. His jaw is still tight, and he seems to be trying to hide the fact that he's shaking as he scrolls down the page. He blinks in confusion but doesn't say anything, and he keeps scrolling.

"What's . . . what's minimum wage there? It's not that much, is it . . . ?" The hopelessness in his tone pierces right through my heart, and I drop my eyes back to my lap as I shake my head.

"No, it, um, just went up to eighteen twenty an hour at the beginning of the year in Palo Alto. But twenty-five isn't *that* much higher. And if you can find a job that pays that much, and we get lucky with finding a place for you to rent, then—"

"A place to rent that's less than two thousand a month, including *all* utilities," he cuts in. "And, that's assuming they'll even rent to me, since I don't have an employment history. And that's assuming I can put down a deposit. And—"

"I can help with the deposit."

He's scowling at me when I look up at him, and I hesitate, feeling myself almost wanting to shrink away. It's an odd feeling for me, and I don't like it much. But I hold his gaze and watch as his scowl turns into pain and hurt and sadness.

"Even if—even if you did . . ." He shakes his head and looks back at the computer. "Twenty-five an hour? What if I can't get a job? What if I can't *keep* a job? And the—" He sucks in a breath and motions to the computer, though he doesn't say anything more.

His desperation is so clear and palpable, and I just want to take it all away. But this is the reality of the challenge we're facing if we want what we want—or at least, it's certainly what *I* want. With a deep breath, I scoot over closer, and I reach over and scroll back up to the top of the spreadsheet.

The first few lines are in bold, and I point to the top one.

"Barring any crazy shit, you'll have about this much saved by the end of the summer, yeah?" I say, doing my best to keep the uncertainty out of my voice.

"Um, I don't . . ." He closes his eyes for a minute, and his mouth moves silently, as though he's doing some mental math. "I think so?" he says after a few more seconds. "Each of my paychecks will be about four hundred fifty bucks, maybe. I get paid weekly. So, um, does that math work?"

"Yeah, for three months. That's a pretty decent chunk, yeah? I mean, you'll have some expenses here and there over the summer, but we can keep those down as much as possible, with you living here and everything. So you'll have enough for a deposit and at least a month or more of expenses, and I've got—"

"Alex." He shakes his head again, and he opens his mouth to argue, but I reach over and close the laptop, cutting him off.

"I've got about that much money saved too."

"That's your money."

I move the laptop to the coffee table and then turn so I'm facing him on the couch. "Nico," I start, my voice breaking on the single word. When he turns his head to look at me, his eyes are dark, sunken almost, and an urgency bubbles up in my chest.

I want to see him smile.

I *need* to see him smile.

I hate this hurt and pain. The stress and uncertainty. The anxiety.

Softly, I lift my hand to his cheek, holding his gaze as my fingers brush along his jaw. "Nico," I say gently, "I care about you."

"I care about you too," he counters. "But that doesn't mean you should waste your savings on me. You'll need that money. If not right away, then you'll need it eventually. I can't take it."

For a moment, all I hear is his first few words. My brain stutters to a halt on his *"I care about you too,"* and I just stare at him, the tension in my shoulders fading into hope. My hand is still on his cheek, and I slowly draw him toward me, relieved when he comes willingly. Our lips meet, and a burst of warmth and love and joy rushes through me. It's a short kiss, because he pulls back after just a second or so, but there's a hint of a smile on his face now, and I let my thumb brush along his lips as I revel in it. It's small but beautiful. I love it.

He rolls his eyes at me and sighs. "Did you hear *any* of my words after I said I care about you too?" he teases.

I laugh, which feels pretty good, and then I nod and tug him back in for another brief kiss before straightening up again. "Actually, I did."

"So . . . ?"

I let my hand drop back down to my lap, but I hold his gaze. "So, didn't you hear what *I* said too? I care about you. A lot. And I *want* to help you. We can do this together. You don't have to do it alone, Nico. That's what I want *you* to hear."

He doesn't respond this time, but his whole body tenses, and he shrinks in on himself, his arms gripping his stomach like it hurts, as he shakes his head.

I want to gather him up in my arms and hold him. And I want to kiss him and cuddle with him. Whisper all the wonderful things he is to me as I hug him close. I want him to really know what he means to me. And I want him to believe that he's worthy of that love.

Is that the problem? He doesn't think he's worth it?

Or is it something else? Like maybe he doesn't believe how much I care?

My heart breaks at the thought as I watch him curl in on himself more and screw his eyes shut. It would make sense. After all, the one person in the whole world who was supposed to love him unconditionally, no matter what, with all her heart—his mom—she abandoned him. Worse than that, actually. She be-

BECCA NEIL

trayed him, kicked him out, sided with his abuser. Lied to him and manipulated him.

She hurt him so deeply, it's no wonder he's having a hard time trusting that this is real.

"Why, um, why don't you . . . want me to help you?" I ask, though I'm not sure what type of answer I expect.

And he doesn't answer right away anyway. His arms tighten around his stomach again, and he shakes his head. "I-I don't know," he says, his voice small and uncertain. But then he inhales a slow breath and looks up at me, a battle raging in his eyes. I see it. I see him. He's fighting for it. For us. Even just being here is hard for him. Not running away, retreating. Not letting his anxiety take over. "I . . . do want what you do," he mumbles, every quiet word a struggle. "But I . . . don't feel comfortable knowing I might have to rely on your money."

I nod slowly, and I scoot closer. "It would just be a safety net," I say softly, reaching out to touch his back. His body shudders as I rub my hand up and down lightly. "Just in case, while you work out your budget and stuff. And we have three months to find you a job. Three months is a long time."

"I'm not qualified for—"

"You *are*, though. You're smart and resourceful and organized. And you're a hard worker, too, and a fast learner. And you're motivated."

He shakes his head, but I keep going, fueled by the fact that he's still here and listening.

"You're honest, reliable. Punctual."

"*Punctual*?" He's rolling his eyes now, and I smirk at him, shift my hands to his shoulders to push him back against the couch cushions, and swing a leg up and over to straddle his thighs.

"Mmm. You're also gorgeous. Sexy as hell."

He narrows his eyes at me as his hands find my hips. "I fail to see how being 'gorgeous' and 'sexy as hell' would make me a good employee."

"Ah, but you're not denying that you are in fact gorgeous," I counter.

"And sexy."

"Definitely sexy."

He huffs a small laugh, but then closes his eyes again and dips his chin, even as his fingers flex into my hips. "Alex, what if . . ." He trails off as I slip my hands around to the nape of his neck, my fingers teasing in his hair.

"What if we *are* able to find something for you? A good job, with benefits. One that pays well and works around or even *with* your limitations? What if . . ." I graze my fingertips along the smooth skin of his jawline and then tilt his chin up so I can see his beautiful green eyes. "What if we *are* able to find you a small studio apartment to rent that's reasonably priced? Maybe even close to wherever you're working so you don't have to spend so much on gas?" I pause again and then brush my thumb along his cheek and murmur, "What if . . . everything works out?"

His expression is pinched. Tense. Unsure. And he studies me for a few seconds, his uncertainty morphing into something rougher. I can almost hear the negative thoughts that must be running through his head.

*What if I can't? What if it doesn't? What then?*

I shake my head just once, then bend down and kiss his lips softly but with purpose.

"What if everything works out?" I repeat. This time, he shudders, and his arms wrap around my waist as he pulls me into him. I find his mouth again, and I hope this kiss conveys everything I need it to—my conviction, my support. My love.

He clings to me as he kisses me back, his lips needy and insistent, and when I pull back after a few deeper kisses, he makes a small sound that rips through me. It's full of uncertainty and need. He leans his head forward into my chest, shaking, and I bury my face in his hair and kiss the top of his head.

"We can make it work. We can figure out a way," I tell him, and I kiss his hair again. "We can have this. Us."

"I want it."

"Me too." I shift back a few inches, and he takes a deep breath and then lifts his chin. His eyes are intense now, stormy, and he shakes his head almost imperceptibly. "We can make it work, Nico," I promise.

He stares at me, still fighting that battle in his mind. I give him what I can—a gentle smile, a touch of my fingers to his jaw—and then I press my lips to his forehead and whisper, "Please, just say you'll give it a chance."

After what feels like a long hesitation, he swallows and nods. "Yeah. Yeah, okay."

Warmth bursts to life in my chest, and I'm pretty sure I'm smiling like an idiot as my hands frame his face. "You're sure? Really?"

He rolls his eyes at me, though there's a barely contained smile tugging at his lips. "I said yes, didn't I? Don't push your luck—"

I cut him off with another kiss, and he laughs against my lips before kissing me back. It's long and deep and slow, and his arms wrap around me tightly, holding me to him.

It's perfect, just like this, and as we kiss over and over, all I can think is how I never want this to end.

Mom (10:13 p.m.): Tammy and I are heading north for a couple of days to hike some trails in Preparation Canyon State Park. I'll send you the location. Might not have cell reception some of the time. We leave tomorrow morning. You two doing okay there? Did you talk? ;)

Alex (10:15 p.m.): yeah, some

Alex (10.15 p.m.): we're ok not sure the leftovers will be gone before you get back tho

Mom (10:20 p.m.): Glad to hear you talked. Keep talking, keep working on things, keep communicating. That's really important.

Alex (10:21 p.m.): i know mom

Mom (10:22 p.m.): =P I love you!

Alex (10:23 p.m.): luv u too

Alex (10:23 p.m.): when will u be home

Mom (10:25 p.m.): Friday or maybe Saturday. That okay?

Alex (10:25 p.m.): yep! have fun and tell tammy i said hi

Alex (10:26 p.m.): goodnight <3

My mom texted me earlier, too, and I know she was fishing for information, wanting to know how Nico reacted to our talk. I didn't really give her any details, and I can tell she's curious but giving me space.

I set my phone face down on the nightstand just as the door creaks open and Nico steps into the bedroom. My eyes dart over, and my breath catches in my throat.

He's wearing a towel around his waist. Nothing else. And his cheeks are some adorable shade of pink, tinged with embarrassment. He gives me a quick, tight smile and then turns away and heads over to the laundry basket in the corner, where he's been keeping his clean clothes. I shouldn't be watching him since he's obviously feeling self-conscious, but when he bends over slightly to sort through the clothes, the towel stretches over his ass and I have to tear my eyes away, forcing myself to look down at my hands instead.

That doesn't help much. I've got too active an imagination, and I can still see it. His perfect, pale skin and lean muscles. The thin trail of hair leading down from his belly button and disappearing under the towel. The water droplets sliding down his back.

I swallow back a groan and reach down to adjust myself in my pants.

Across the room, Nico straightens back up, and I lift my eyes to see him glance over at me, his cheeks still pink but his lips twisted up in a teasing half smile. He holds up a change of clothes. "Forgot these. Be right back. That is, unless you want me to just sleep naked tonight."

My face heats up, and I suck in a sharp breath as I stare at him openly now. God, his abs and that happy trail, just the faint hint of dark hair. I want to—

He takes a step toward me, his free hand moving to where the towel is tucked in to secure it at his waist. He tugs at the edge lightly, loosening it, and my heart stops.

Fuck. Fuck, is he serious?

"Wha—what are you—?" I stammer, but Nico doesn't answer. He just chuckles and then winks at me before disappearing back into the hallway and heading toward the bathroom.

And I let out a long breath and fall back onto the bed, groaning loudly this time as I bring a hand up to cover my eyes. My body continues to betray me, my dick reacting as though Nico were still in the room with me. Stepping closer. Tugging off the towel and letting it drop to the floor. Pushing me back onto the bed as he straddles me, then—

"So, Friday, you know if you want to go to that thing in Omaha—"

Nico's voice stops abruptly, and my eyes fly open to see him standing in the doorway. He's dressed now—just in a pair of navy sleep shorts and an old gray T-shirt that might actually be mine. And that should probably help me, but it doesn't. Not at all. I watch as his tongue wets his lips and his eyes drink me in, stopping at where my hand rests impatiently against my thigh, only inches from my cock. My sweatpants definitely don't hide how aroused I am, and I hear him hiss out a quiet "ah, fuck" as he steps all the way into the room and closes the door behind him, not taking his eyes off me the whole time.

I should probably feel embarrassed, like I was when he interrupted me jerking off last week. But his eyes just look hungry, and that sends a new pulse of heat through me. I prop myself up on my elbows, and he takes another step closer as he drags his eyes up my body to my face, his teeth now biting at his bottom lip.

*Ah, fuck* is right.

"I-I wasn't going to go," I stammer.

"Go?" He's closer now, his smile teasing and sexy at the same time.

I swallow hard as he stops in front of me. "T-to Omaha."

My heart hammers in my chest and heat floods my cheeks as he leans over, climbing on top of me onto the bed. His knees cage my thighs, and I drop down onto my back as he lowers himself to his elbows over me. His mouth pauses, his lips nearly brushing mine, and holy god, he smells good. All fresh soap and vanilla.

In a raspy whisper, he says, "Mmm. But you can. If you want."

"If I . . . Oh, fuuuuck." I screw my eyes shut and push my head back into the bed as he relaxes his hips down into me. He's as hard as I am, and his thick cock throbs against mine as his mouth skims down my skin, stopping at the base of my neck.

He stays there for several seconds, breathing hard, and I start to feel it. He's trembling, the muscles in his arms and legs shaking, and even his breath shudders on each exhale. I'm not sure what to do about it or whether it's just muscle fatigue and exhaustion or something else. So I give him a few more seconds.

Gently, I lift one hand to his waist, and at the contact, a small sound escapes him. It's not quite a groan or a whimper, but it tears through my heart with its pain and sadness.

"Nico?"

He immediately shakes his head and starts to push himself back up to his elbows. "Sorry. I—fuck, I'm sorry. I'll just . . ." He shifts slightly, and his lips capture mine, and he starts rocking his hips against me with a rhythm that doesn't quite work. His kiss, too, it's forced, detached. Or something.

Something's wrong.

I bring my hand up to his chest and push lightly. "Mmm, Nico, wait. What's . . . what's . . ."

His head drops to my chest, and his whole body shudders and jerks as he holds in a sob. At least, that's what I think he's doing. He rolls off of me onto the bed and immediately covers his eyes with his elbow.

"Sorry," he repeats, his tone full of what I can only interpret as anguish.

I don't know what's wrong, and it might not even be anything specific, I realize as I slowly turn onto my side to face him. He's pale, even his lips, and he looks exhausted and cold, even though it's quite warm in my room.

My heart aches. Whatever's going on in his head can't be good.

Slowly, I reach out and set my hand on his stomach, and I scoot myself closer to him. He doesn't pull away, but he also doesn't move at all, not even to lower his arm. I prop myself up onto my elbow, and then I lean in and brush a kiss against his temple.

"I'm here for you," I say, even though I have no idea if that's what he needs. I kiss him again, lingering close with my lips this time. Quietly, I suggest, "How about I just hold you? And we go to sleep?"

There's a moment of hesitation that I *feel*, a tension in the air. But then he nods once.

"Good, okay." I push myself up, and he follows, lowering his arm from his eyes and then sitting up. He's still shaking, but he's doing a better job of hiding it now.

I wish he knew he didn't have to hide anything from me. He doesn't have to pretend if he's not feeling well. But that's another conversation for another day.

I stand up and cross the room to turn the light off, and when I turn back around, enough weak moonlight peeks through the shutters for me to just make out his still figure now buried under the covers, the blanket pulled all the way up to his chin, his back to me. I pad quietly back to the bed and climb in behind him, and before I even get settled, he pushes back against me, nearly begging me to hold him.

So I do. I lower my head onto the pillow, slip my arm around his waist, and let my hand slide up his chest. His hand joins mine, and he sighs, deeply and fully. I kiss the side of his neck and tighten my arm around him. And he sighs again.

"Thank you. I-I'm okay," he mumbles. "I'm okay."

"Okay. Are you sure?"

"Yeah." He shivers, but it seems to just be a quick chill or something. "It's just been a long day. A lot of stuff to think about. And m-my mom. And . . . yeah."

I nod against him, hoping he feels it, and then I breathe him in and brush my lips against his skin. "Let's get some rest?"

"Yeah." He's silent for a moment, then he says, "Good night, Alex."

I hug him to me. "Good night, Nico."

# chapter twenty-nine

## *nico*

ALL DAY ON FRIDAY, the library is about as quiet as it's been in the two weeks since I started working there, and the last few hours of my shift are blissfully uneventful, just like the rest of the week after that fucking awful day on Tuesday.

Caitlin is still working on something at the circulation desk when it's time for me to go, and I force a smile and an awkward wave as I leave.

"Have a great weekend. See you Monday!" she says, grinning up at me.

I manage a nod in response and then make the words come. "You too. See you Monday."

A moment later, I'm out the door, walking across the parking lot, staring at my car as my hand slips down into my pocket to grasp my wallet. I've got exactly five hundred dollars in it, the wad of twenty-dollar bills barely fitting. I had to borrow forty bucks from Alex, since my paycheck was a little less than I expected.

But I'm okay with that. I think.

He didn't bat an eye when I asked earlier on my lunch break. He just pulled his wallet out, fished out the two twenties, and handed them to me with a smile. Then he went back to scarfing down his sandwich as though it weren't a big deal.

And maybe he's right. Maybe it's not a big deal. I'll pay him back next Friday, and after that, I'll save every penny I can so this whole moving-to-California thing can have some chance to work.

I unlock the door and slip into the driver's seat, pushing thoughts of California out of my mind. I'm still scared to think about it much. There are too many what-ifs, too many chances for everything to fail, and I have enough on my plate tonight. Or at least, one really big thing that I'm terrified of.

I can already feel my chest tightening as I start up my car and back out of the parking spot, and by the time I'm on the road, headed to my mom's house, my fingers are starting to go numb. Maybe I shouldn't have convinced Alex to go to Omaha after all. He was reluctant, kept insisting he should go to my mom's with me. But I didn't want that—both because I didn't want him to see her awful side, especially if she decides to be awful *to him*, and because I didn't want him to miss out on something I knew he wanted to do. Being my best friend or my boyfriend, if that's what he is, shouldn't mean he has to give up doing things he loves because of my anxiety.

So I'm by myself. And I'm fucking terrified.

It's a short drive, but it feels long—every second drawn out to its fullest. By the time I'm close, I'm uncomfortably cold and I can't feel my fingertips anymore.

And when I turn down the long driveway and the house comes into view, my heart fucking stops in my chest. I slam the brakes on, and the car grinds to a halt, dust billowing up around me.

Fucking hell.

A light-blue pickup truck sits in front of the house. *Patrick's* light-blue pickup truck.

My mom's car isn't there.

A pain rips through my head, and I close my eyes and force myself to breathe.

I was scared enough coming here knowing I was going to have to face *her*. The prospect of facing *him*, though . . .

My throat feels so tight, like it's closing on me, and I choke out a sob as I force my eyes back open and stare toward the house.

Maybe she's on her way home now. Maybe she just got held up at work for a bit—that used to happen all the time, after all. That's it. It has to be.

Any minute, she'll come down the driveway behind me. Then we can just exchange money for car title in the driveway, even. I won't have to step foot in the house with *him*.

I sit there, my foot still pressed hard into the brake pedal, my car shuddering as the engine adjusts and idles. Several minutes pass. Then several more. And I know she's not coming. Something deep down inside tells me that.

It's intentional, too. I'm not sure how I know, but I know.

My hands regrip the steering wheel, and I lift my eyes back to the house. With a nauseating swoop of my stomach, I see the curtains covering the front windows move. I can't see inside. I can't see him. But I can *feel* that he's watching me.

I'm going to vomit.

Holding tightly to the steering wheel, I jerk my foot off the brake, and the car lurches forward. I look ahead now, straight to the end of the driveway, and I force a breath and then another. I'm nearly hyperventilating by the time I park, and I shut off the engine, shove my keys into my pocket, and thrust the door open, desperate for fresh air.

But the heat outside doesn't feel fresh, and so I'm left gasping for breath as I stumble to my feet and close the car door behind me.

Fuck.

I move, though I'm not sure how. The numbness in my fingers is starting to work its way up my arms, and the stabbing pain in my head is shooting down my neck and back now.

This isn't right.

I shouldn't be here.

My feet keep moving until I reach the porch, then my hand lifts up to knock, even though I'm screaming silently at myself to *not* fucking knock. I should turn around and leave. I should meet my mom in some public place. Not meet Patrick here. Alone.

This is a fucking bad idea.

I knock anyway, and there's an immediate noise from inside the house. Something slamming. Then footsteps. Heavy, angry footsteps coming toward me. I shiver and pitch backward, almost tripping over my own feet.

Then he's there, standing in the open doorway, a furious scowl on his face, his eyes glaring at me. There's rage in them. Rage I can feel. And it's all directed *at* me.

A ghost pain jolts through me, my shoulder feels like I'm being ripped backwards, and all the air leaves my lungs as though he's slammed me back into a wall.

He hasn't moved, but his scowl turns into a sneer, and the numbness returns to my fingers.

"You little shit. I can't believe you came. Cind said you'd be by."

He's obviously been drinking. The smell of alcohol wafts off of him, sour as it hits my nose. I stumble back another step, and he just laughs cruelly as I grasp the porch railing.

"What's the matter, you scared of me or somethin'?" he taunts, shaking his head, and then lets out a malicious laugh. "Don't worry, I'm not fucking stupid enough to make the same mistake twice." I'm not entirely sure what he means, but then he turns and motions for me to follow him into the house. "Let's get this over with."

I try, but I can't move from my spot. My brain is screaming *absolutely fucking not*, and I'm shaking and lightheaded. I only barely manage to push myself away from the railing and take a step toward the front door after another few seconds.

Each shaky step is even harder than the last, and when I'm finally inside the doorway, Patrick is all the way in the kitchen already, sitting at the table. Several empty beer bottles and one that looks about half empty are scattered on the table's surface, and the place smells stale, like the same waft of air I got earlier.

"You got all the money?"

I force an exhale and nod, stuffing my hand into my pocket to pull out my wallet. Then I make myself move again as I take out the stack of twenties. The unfamiliar feel of the wad of cash helps distract me just enough that I'm able to keep my feet going all the way to the kitchen. I stop when I'm a few feet away.

My heart's hammering, and I clench my jaw to keep it from shaking as I reach out with the money. Somehow, I make words happen. "Here. It's f-five hundred."

Patrick's eyes narrow, and the sneer on his face sharpens as he glances at me, then at the money in my hand. "The car's twelve hundred now. Cind said she told you earlier this week."

"N-no. No, it's only five—"

The chair scrapes dangerously fast along the floor as Patrick pushes back and stands up, glaring at me.

"The fuck you trying to pull, you little shit? You sayin' your mom's lying?"

"N-no, I just—"

He turns and takes a step toward me, and my stomach drops. I back up, still clutching the cash in one hand and my wallet in the other.

"You little fucking shit. I can't fucking believe this. Coming here, wastin' my time." He's stalking toward me, hot fury making his face red, and I can't move or speak or even breathe.

The front door feels impossibly far away, and everything

around me is buzzing with a painful haze. It's suddenly dark, and I don't even realize I've screwed my eyes shut until I feel a hot breath near my ear.

"You broke into my house, refused to leave, threatened me," he hisses. "It's self-defense. And your momma's not here to save your skinny little ass this time."

*Fuck. Fuck. Fuck.*

"No, please. I-I'll leave. I'll—"

A rough hand slams right into the middle of my chest and shoves me backward hard, and I stumble and trip and fall, the money dropping from my hand and scattering all over the floor. I try to catch myself, but my back smacks into the solid corner of the entryway to the kitchen, pain lancing through my chest and all the way down into my toes. I'm suddenly on the ground, curled up on my side, unable to breathe. I try pushing myself away, but the wall behind me stops me.

And he's right there, bearing down on me. Laughing. An angry, disgusted, drunken laugh that sends a shock of icy fear through me.

He grabs my arm and yanks me up to my feet, pain ripping through my shoulder. His voice spits with anger and resentment. "You've got thirty seconds to pick this shit up and get the fuck out," he says, squeezing my arm harder before releasing me. "And leave the car key."

I scramble as soon as I'm free, dropping back to my knees to start gathering up my money and wallet. The pain in my shoulder comes in nauseating waves every time I move, but I ignore it as I rush to stuff the money into the pockets of my slacks. My fingers have gone numb again, and I'm clumsy and keep dropping the bills. I'm not even sure I get them all before Patrick's voice cuts in, cold and menacing.

"Time's up. Give me the key and get out."

I want to scream at him that it's my car, but any flicker of defiance I might have is snuffed out the second he steps toward me. I flinch back, pushing myself away from him with one hand while I fish for my keys through a messy wad of twenty-dollar bills with the other. Several of the bills fall back out of my pocket to the floor, and I hastily scoop them up, then stand, still backing away from him.

"H-here," I stammer, fumbling with the key ring. My vision's so blurry I can't see for fuck, so I struggle for too many goddamn seconds to free the car's key from my key ring. It falls to the ground, and I don't bother picking it up to hand to him. I fucking can't.

I need out.

Shaking, I spin around and force my feet to move, Patrick's awful laughter chasing me out the front door.

# chapter thirty

## *alex*

"LET'S GOOOOOOOO! BRO, THAT was sweet!"

Shane claps me on the back as the game in front of me flashes, the bright lights accompanied by some garbled electronic cheering. The jackpot number lights up at the top—apparently, my amazing expertise at being stupidly lucky at arcade games has won me two thousand "tickets," which is possibly the biggest single haul of anyone in our group so far tonight.

I grin and shake my head as Shane steps up to take a turn spinning the monster-sized wheel. Jenna stands on the other side of him, her arms crossed over her chest, and Leela hangs off of her, giggling at something on her phone. It's busy and loud, and everything's bright and obnoxious. But it's fun, and everyone seems to be having a great time. A bunch of others are back at the three tables our large group commandeered, sharing nachos and pizza and wings, and across the arcade, there's another round of loud, overzealous shouting from the basketball shooting game.

"Guess Cooper did it again," Leela says on a laugh.

"Show-off," Jenna adds, though she's laughing now too.

"The one-arm backwards no-net shot?" Shane reaches up as high as he can on the wheel and grasps one of the pegs. "I'd be showing off, too, if I could do that."

He sends the wheel spinning as hard as he can, and it speeds up, electronic beeps sounding when each slot passes the marker at the top.

I pull my phone out of my pocket as the beeps start slowing.

"Come on, come on, come on . . ." Shane grabs my shoulder again, and I glance back up at the wheel, which slows more as it approaches the jackpot slot.

"Not a chance," Jenna taunts, though she leans in closer.

Shane's hand tightens on my shoulder, and we all watch in disbelief as the wheel stops in the same spot it had the turn before. The lights flash, the cheering sounds, and Shane jumps up in the air, pumping his fist.

"No way! Awesome! Yessssss!"

There's much more cheering and much more laughing, and when the group starts to move away to join the others at the basketball shooting game, I excuse myself to head back to the table, tapping the screen on my phone to check the time.

It's after seven thirty.

Nico should have gotten home a while ago. And he said he'd message me when he did.

But I haven't gotten any notifications. No Discord messages, no texts, no calls. Nothing at all.

My stomach drops, and I glance up so I can navigate faster through the arcade into the dining area. When I reach our tables, they're mostly empty except for two guys I recognize but don't really know. I nod at them, and they go back to their pizza and conversation as I slip into one of the end chairs and open my phone again, tapping on the icon for my Discord app.

**Alex**  4:50 PM
im leaving for Omaha
be home late
call if u need to


**Alex**  5:39 PM
everything go ok?
how does it feel to officially own ur car? lol


**Alex**  6:23 PM
nico
bro ur making me worry lol
text me back


I stare at my messages, frowning, and an uncomfortable heaviness settles on my chest. He was supposed to head straight to his mom's from work. Give her the money and leave. He should have been home by five thirty or six at the latest.

It's not unlike him to ignore his phone, especially if he's upset or having a bad day. And I know he hates having to use Discord, since he hasn't had a chance—or the money—to reactivate his phone with a new number.

So maybe I shouldn't be as worried as I am.

But something about this just doesn't feel right.

I glance up at the arcade and see Jenna watching me. She gives me a thumbs-up, but from her expression, I can tell it's a question. I frown and shake my head, and she purses her lips and narrows her eyes. Then she leans over and says something to Leela before starting on her way over to me.

With another glance back down at my phone, I push myself slowly to my feet, willing those three little dots to appear by his name. But still, nothing happens.

"Hey, what is it? What's wrong?" Jenna's hand settles lightly on my arm.

I lift my eyes and try to force away my unease long enough to give her a small smile. "It's probably nothing. Nico was supposed to text me, and he hasn't. I think I'm gonna head home, uh, you know, just in case."

She narrows her eyes at me, and I get the sense she's reading every word I *didn't* say from whatever expression is on my face. With a soft nod, she says, "I'll tell everyone you had to take off."

"Thanks."

"Of course." She smiles tightly and adds, "I hope everything's okay. I mean, with Nico and all."

"It's probably fine."

She nods in agreement and then tilts her head back toward the arcade. "I'm gonna get back."

As soon as she leaves, I pull out my wallet, drop a ten-dollar bill on the table as my portion of the server's tip, and then spin around and start jogging through the maze of tables toward the entrance. Outside, the air is warm and humid, the sun still shining as it dips down toward the horizon. I stop for only a few seconds to send Nico another message (*im on my way home plz call me!*), then I stuff my phone back into my pocket and hurry the rest of the way to my mom's truck, which is parked near the back of the huge parking lot. A minute later, I'm pulling onto the highway, headed south, my phone sitting on the passenger seat.

I crank up the air conditioner and turn on the radio to distract myself. Still, the thirty-something-minute drive home seems much longer than it is, giving me too much time to imagine all the worst-case scenarios.

They cling to me, burrowing into my thoughts even as I tell myself over and over that he's fine. He's probably just hiding out in my room, playing video games or something. That would make much more logical sense.

If only my brain was listening to logic right now.

I glance over at my phone just before my house comes into view, expecting to finally see the screen light up with his name and the little Discord icon. But it's blank. Frowning, I look back up and put my blinker on as I start to slow down to turn onto my street. And my stomach twists into a tight, painful knot.

The lights inside the house are all off.

And the driveway is empty.

And there's no little silver sedan parked along the curb in front of the house.

And so all of those worst-case scenarios start blasting through my mind again, playing in full-color, HD on repeat.

I park and hop out of the truck, and a few seconds later, I push open the front door to a heavy silence. The living room is empty, the TV is off, and everything's so still and quiet that it almost feels cold despite the oppressive heat outside. I shut the door behind me and slip my shoes off, and I pause as I glance around again. Nothing is different from when I left earlier, and there's no sign that Nico was ever home, not even a note sitting on the kitchen table or stuck under one of the magnets on the fridge.

I'm not sure what I expected. His car's not here, so he must not be here. I'm not sure where he could have possibly gone, though, and really, I can't see him going anywhere, especially not after the long, stressful week he had.

He'd have come right home. I'm sure of it.

I check my phone *again*, but again, there's nothing.

And I'm suddenly terrified. Because all of those worst-cases don't seem so hypothetical anymore. Shoving my phone back into my pocket, I turn and jog up the stairs, taking them two at a time. I stop right in front of my bedroom door, my breath catching and my hand hovering just over the door handle.

It was open when I left earlier.

I'm certain of it.

I hadn't shut the door all the way. And yet, the door's shut now.

Slowly, I close my hand over the handle and turn the knob, then I push the door inward.

And there he is.

The relief is instant and strong, hitting me like a wave, and I grasp the doorjamb to keep myself steady. Nico's curled up on the far side of my bed, his back to me, the comforter tugged up to his chin. His shoes and socks are strewn across the floor, like he shucked them off as he came in, and his slacks and work polo lie in a heap in the corner, just next to the dirty laundry hamper.

His cell phone sits on the nightstand, face down. And next to it is a huge pile of cash, the bills crumpled and disorganized.

I suck in a breath as my stomach lurches. He's got the cash but no car. Something went wrong.

"Nico?" I ask softly, stepping into the room.

There's no movement or noise or response, and I can't tell from over here if he's asleep or not. I turn around and close the door behind me, making sure it's as quiet as possible. Then I cross the room slowly, stepping over his shoes and socks, and I lower myself to the bed.

The second the bed creaks, Nico flinches, and he turns over and hastily pushes himself back against the wall, his eyes wide.

He looks . . . terrified.

Of me.

That's not something I've seen in a very, very long time. I'm usually the *one* person he's not terrified of. I'm usually the only person he seems to be able to even tolerate being close to him. I fight the urge to back off and give him space, because I'm not sure that's what he needs right now.

Not that I know what he needs.

"Hey," I murmur, trying to keep my voice level, even as my heart breaks. I don't know what else to say or do or how to act or what to think. So I just shift a little, slowly, and ask, "Would it be okay if I lie down with you?"

His eyes close, but the tension doesn't leave him. "Yeah."

I blow out a quiet breath and nod, even though he can't see me. Then, moving carefully, I take my phone, wallet, and keys out of my pocket, set them on the nightstand, and turn to crawl under the covers with him. Maybe I should take a few minutes and get ready for bed, but honestly, I don't want to leave him right now. Not before I know what's going on.

He turns back onto his other side, facing away from me, but there's still so much tension in him I can feel it, sharp in the air between us. Then he inches away even more until he's scrunched up against the wall, like he really doesn't want me here.

I lie there and watch the blanket shift slightly with each of his stilted breaths, and it's several minutes before I work up the courage to scoot closer.

He flinches again as soon as I move.

And god, that makes my heart hurt even more. I freeze and close my eyes. "I can leave . . . go to the downstairs room . . . if you need me to."

"No."

Desperation. That's what I hear in his single-word answer. Desperation and panic. I don't even want to think about what it all means.

I swallow tightly and nod. "Okay. I'll stay. I'll stay."

"Thank you," he says on a breath.

But he makes no move to scoot closer, no request for me to hold him. He gives no reassurance that he's okay or that he'll be okay.

So I just lie there on my back, staring up at the ceiling, not daring to make any other moves myself. Instead, I listen quietly as his breathing first slows and then becomes steadier, and finally, by the time the sun is down outside and the bedroom is dark with night, he starts snoring softly.

I close my eyes and will my heart to stop aching long enough for me to fall asleep as well.

# chapter thirty-one

## *nico*

THE NIGHTMARES COME AND go. Darkness pulling at me. Memories roaring to life in my head. For hours, I'm tugged in and out of sleep, fear waking me and exhaustion drowning me again, sending me back into my mind, where nothing is safe or soft or quiet.

I want to go to him. I want to wake him up, beg him to hold me. But then the fear comes back, and I know I need to keep that space between us, minimal as it is.

I fucking hurt, too. My chest is sore right in the middle, where that asshole shoved me, and my back aches where I hit the wall. When I move my shoulder wrong, or actually, when I move it at all, jolts of deep pain shoot down into my fingers and up into my neck.

And I really don't want Alex to know about any of that.

So I try to deal with my shit alone, lying as still as I can, huddled up at the edge of the bed. Holding in the cries that want to rip from my throat every time I yank myself out of a dream where Patrick has me pinned against the wall, about to hit me again.

At one point, I hear noises downstairs—quiet voices, a door shutting, then footsteps up the stairs and heading off down the hallway. Alex's mom is home. Then Alex's phone vibrates with a series of what are probably text messages.

He doesn't wake up next to me, and shortly after that, I'm pulled back in, deeper this time. A dark room. Glass shatters next to me. Mom's there, hanging off of Patrick, and they're sharing a cigarette. Then she's in my face, blowing hot, rotten smoke at me.

"It's twelve hundred. Where's my money?" she hisses, her eyes turning red with fury.

Laughing turns into cackling behind her, and her form morphs into his. Then he's got me by the throat, and his other hand grabs my arm, yanking me up, twisting my shoulder. Everything explodes in a burst of pain, and I inhale a sharp breath as I wake up. *Again.*

I'm sweating this time, panting, and staring up at the ceiling, my right arm pushed up against the wall. Every breath reminds me of the ache in my back and chest, and I screw my eyes shut and groan as I turn gingerly onto my side, facing away from Alex. I lie there for a few minutes until I feel myself slipping back into that awful dream. Then I force my eyes open partway, hoping that might keep me awake.

If I tilt my head just right, I can see out through the slats covering the window above me. The blackness of night has started to give way to morning, weak light filtering in from the rising sun.

I've never watched a sunrise.

Not that I'm going to drag myself out of bed right now to do it. But maybe . . . someday.

I let my eyes close, imagining it. The sunrise. I'm sitting at the river, at our spot. Alex sits behind me, his arms wrapped around me and his chin resting on my shoulder as I lean back into him. Out across the water to the east, over the tops of the trees, the sky turns lighter—first a deep orange that grows more vibrant as the sun inches over the horizon, then pinks and yellows that slowly melt away into bright blue.

I wish I could dream about *this* when I sleep.

"Alex?" My voice sounds hoarse, and it's too quiet; there's no way he heard me. I clear my throat and scoot away from the wall a few inches. "Alex?" I say again, a little louder.

There's a gentle shift behind me, and I hold my breath, trying to keep my heart from jumping.

"Hmm? Yeah? Yeah, what is it?"

"Hold me?" I swallow hard. "Please."

It's just a couple of seconds, just long enough probably for him to process what I said, and then the bed moves again. A cold shiver courses through me, but I fight against the unwelcome warning, reminding myself where I am and who's here with me. Even still, when his fingertips graze lightly along my upper arm under the comforter, I can't stop myself from flinching.

He pulls his hand back.

"Please," I beg again. If I could move, I'd scoot back into him. I'd turn and grab his hand and pull it back around me. But I can't do that.

"You're sure?" he asks.

"Yes."

"Okay."

He tries again, and I react in the same way, my body jerking away involuntarily at his touch. He doesn't pull back this time, though, and he slowly inches up behind me, his hand caressing down my forearm now with the most gentle touch.

I muffle a sob into my pillow, and as my body starts shaking, Alex's warmth surrounds me, his chest pressing up against my back and his arm wrapping around my midsection, holding me to him carefully but tightly.

It's exactly what I need.

"I'm here," he whispers. "I'm here."

His lips press into my bare shoulder, and I sob again. It doesn't hurt—his kiss on my shoulder. I just feel so fucking lost. And exhausted. And I'm still terrified, even though I know I'm safe now.

Patrick's angry, cold words from yesterday echo in my head, and my heart slams to a stop as I see him coming toward me, threatening and intentional and vengeful.

*Fuck.*

I move my hand to cover Alex's on my stomach. *That* hurts—the movement sending another of those sharp pains outward from my shoulder. But I *need* to touch him, because I need that to remind me. To ground me. To anchor me in the here and now.

"Please," I choke out.

I don't even know what I'm asking for.

He probably doesn't either, but his lips stay touching my shoulder, and his hand drifts lightly back and forth across my stomach, soothing me.

"I'm here. Breathe," he says softly, and I shudder and do as he says, taking a long, slow, deep breath. "Good. Again."

Minutes pass. He holds me and talks to me and touches me, everything careful, gentle, and tender.

Maybe that's what I needed.

It feels good. Or at least it does after my heart stops hammering in my chest.

Eventually, the shaking and crying also stop. Yet he still doesn't let me go. His kisses flutter along my shoulder and neck, and, when he settles down onto the pillow more after a few minutes, he buries his face in my hair as his arms tightens around me just enough.

I hold my breath, waiting for the questions I know are coming. But they don't come. He doesn't ask them.

He doesn't ask me where my car is, or why I'm breaking down in his arms, or why I flinched away from him. He doesn't ask why I didn't return any of his messages yesterday, or even if I'm okay.

And I know it's not because he doesn't care or doesn't want to know.

It's because he knows I'm not ready to talk about it.

I take another of those long, deep breaths, letting myself relax back into him, and when he whispers "good, that's it" into my hair this time, I feel warmth in my chest and a flicker of something not so awful.

The sun slowly grows brighter outside, and after a while, quiet noises from the rest of the house remind me that we're no longer alone; his mom is home. Alex doesn't seem to react, but after a few more minutes, he props himself up slightly, kisses my shoulder, and then pulls away to grab his cell phone from the nightstand.

The air from the ceiling fan overhead feels cool against my back as the comforter is pushed down, and I try not to wince as I lift my hand to tug it back up to my chin.

"Ah, Mom texted last night when she got home. She wants to take us—" Alex's voice cuts off abruptly as the bed shifts, and then he sucks in a breath. "God, Nico . . ."

Before I can register what his tone probably means, I hear the phone set back down on the nightstand with a haphazard clunk, and then he's lying behind me again, a cold space between us. I can feel his hand hovering just next to me, but he doesn't touch me, and instead, the blanket pushes back off my shoulder a few inches. His breath hitches.

Then his fingers graze along the middle of my back, barely a whisper of contact.

"Nico, what . . . what the hell happened? Jesus."

There's alarm in his voice, and I screw my eyes shut, trying desperately to keep myself from panicking. I'm not even sure what he saw, but I shake my head.

"Nothing," I say, and I twist onto my back as I pull the blanket back up over me. I can't look up at him, but I hear him let out a sharp breath. His hand falls away from me, and the bed shifts.

"No, that's not nothing . . . Nico, your back . . . the bruises . . ."

I shake my head again, as much in response to him as in a poor attempt to keep myself from remembering. It doesn't work. I feel everything, just as I did when it happened last night. The rough shove as Patrick pushed me, all the air crushed from my lungs as I hit the corner wall, the jolt of pain in my spine. My heart racing, my chest tight. The panic and fear and there he was, coming toward me again—

"It's nothing. I'm fine," I insist. Because I am. Hell, I had no idea I even hit the wall hard enough to bruise. Yeah, it hurts, and yeah, it's sore, but the pain's not anywhere near as bad as the pain in my shoulder. I force a breath and then ask, "Can you grab me a shirt?"

He hesitates but then mumbles, "Yeah."

I risk opening my eyes as he stands and moves across the room to hunt through my laundry. When he returns a moment later and hands me a plain blue T-shirt, I still can't look at him.

"Thanks," I say. Then I clench my teeth as I sit up and pull the shirt on, barely holding back a hiss of pain when I slip my left arm through the sleeve.

Alex is sitting very still at the edge of the bed, like he's not sure what to do. I don't know what to tell him, either, and I don't really want to talk. So I just lie back down, facing the wall with my back to him, and I close my eyes.

It's probably several minutes later when he finally speaks.

"I'll be right back," he says quietly. Then I hear him stand up, followed by the door opening and closing.

I can just make out him greeting his mom downstairs, and they talk for a moment, though I can't quite hear what they're saying. Which is probably good. I don't really want to know what he's telling her.

Just as my breathing starts to settle, the stairs creak, and then the door opens and closes.

"I'm back. Sorry to take so long. Um, I mean . . ." Alex exhales a breath that sounds frustrated. Behind me, the bed compresses. "Here, take this."

I force myself to turn over onto my back again, which isn't super comfortable after all. Although maybe that's just because I'm aware of the bruises now. Alex is sitting with one leg hitched up on the bed, his face tight with worry. He's holding a glass of water in one hand and a couple of white pills in the other, and then he's got an ice pack wrapped in a paper towel tucked under his arm.

Dammit. "I don't need anything. I said I'm fine."

His eyebrows pinch together, and he shakes his head. "O-okay, um . . ." Moving carefully, he sets the glass and pills on the nightstand next to his phone and then pulls the ice pack out from under his arm and offers it to me, frowning. "At least ice it? That should help."

I clench my jaw and turn back over onto my side. "I said I'm fine," I repeat.

"Nico—"

"I don't need to ice it, and I don't need any medicine. I just need to sleep. And be alone."

Fuck, I hate myself. He doesn't deserve that. And I don't mean it anyway. I don't actually want to be alone. I want him to come back to bed, to keep holding me and helping me breathe, to chase the nightmares away. And the words are right there, trying to come out. But something's keeping my mouth glued shut, and there's that awful irritation and anger simmering under my skin.

I hate it. I'm sorry, Alex.

Fuck.

"Okay," he says after a long pause. The bed shifts, and I know he's gotten up. "I'll leave the water and Tylenol here, um, in case you want them. And the ice pack, too. And I'll just be downstairs, I guess. My mom probably needs help with something."

Please don't leave. I'm sorry. Goddammit.

"Alex . . ." He doesn't hear me, because by the time I finally force out the word, he's already gone.

# chapter thirty-two

## alex

"So, here's what I need." My mom hefts a large box up onto the desk in the garage. She takes the top off and pulls out a folder. "Each of these is a client file. I want the basic data for each client input into a spreadsheet so I have a digital record to go with my physical records."

"I can do that," I say, reaching into the box and grabbing one of the folders. I open it up and start scanning the invoice—this one for a landscape painting my mom created for a man in New York last year.

I make the mistake of glancing up, and my mom's watching me with the same expression she's had since I came back downstairs about an hour ago. I quickly look away as I slip into the office chair and adjust the keyboard. "How much information do you need? Name, date of sale . . ."

"Yeah, and transaction amount and date. Invoice number. A description of the piece, and . . . Alex . . ."

Her hand settles on my shoulder, and I shake my head. "I can, um, include a link to the digital images you have of each of the paintings, too, if you want."

"Sure. But, Alex—"

I shake my head again, cutting her off. I know what she wants.

She wants to talk . . . because "everything can be fixed by talking it out." That's what she believes, and I guess I usually believe that too. But right now, I just don't think that'll be enough. After all, how can I fix things if Nico *won't* talk to me and is actively pushing me away?

I still don't know what happened. And the fact that he doesn't want me to be there with him right now hurts a lot, especially when I think about how much *he* must be hurting, emotionally *and* physically.

Too many horrible scenarios are running through my head and have been since earlier this morning. I can still see his back—the ugly purple-and-black bruises forming right along his spine. I can still see the shame in his eyes and the grimace he tried to hide when he turned over.

He said he was fine. But it *has* to hurt. There's no way it doesn't.

I clear my throat to keep the tremor out of my voice. "I think the, uh, digital images are in your Google Drive folder here, right?"

"Alex," she says again, squeezing my shoulder.

I close my eyes and sigh, letting my hand fall down to my lap. "I know what you're going to say, but I already told you, I can't talk about it."

"I understand that." She moves so she's leaning against the desk, and I force my eyes up to meet hers. She gives me a small, knowing smile. "But even if you can't tell me what happened or what's going on, you can tell me how you're feeling about it."

A buzz of something uncomfortable and uncertain flutters in my chest, and I drop my chin down, clenching my jaw. "I feel like shit, okay?" I blurt out, and I immediately grimace. "Sorry. I meant awful. I feel awful."

Her arm comes around my shoulders, and I let myself lean into her hug. She doesn't say anything, which I know means she's waiting for me to say more. I'm not even sure how much I *can* say, and I honestly don't know what happened anyway. All I have is what's been floating around in my head, my dumb imagination going wild.

"He won't talk to me," I mumble, finally. Then the dam breaks open, and I'm just trying not to cry as I walk the careful line of telling her but not telling her . . . "Something's wrong, and I don't even know what it is, and he won't talk to me about it. And I'm worried about him because . . . because I have reason to worry. But he doesn't want to talk and he doesn't want my help. And I'm scared and I don't know what to do."

She saw me get the Tylenol and the ice pack earlier this morning. And she's smart. I'll bet she can guess something at least close to the truth. But if she has, she doesn't say.

"Oh, sweetie." She pulls me out of the chair and to my feet, and she wraps me up in a tight hug like she knows just how much I'm hurting. She holds me for a few long seconds. Then she says, quietly, "Nico's always had trouble communicating about difficult things, right? Even with you?"

"Well, yeah."

"Does this seem different than that?" She straightens up a little and moves her hands to my arms. Her eyes are a little glossy, like she's holding back her own tears. "By that I mean, is there anything different about it now—how he's told you he doesn't want to talk or doesn't want your help? If you think about it, is this how you'd expect him to behave, normally? Or, normal for him, I mean."

I sniffle and look down at the space between us, and even though I don't want to, I think back on earlier this morning and even back to last night. How I got home to see him in my bed, scrunched up against the wall. How I lay in bed with him. How, early in the morning before the sun was really up, he woke me up, asked me to hold him. How he flinched away from my touch, not once, but twice. Then, how his tone changed—scared and angry and irritated. Anxious . . . just like . . . "normal" for him, when he gets anxious.

"I thought . . . we've been getting closer," I stammer, "and he's been more open with me, and . . ."

"It's hard to change habits, especially ones rooted in the type of trauma his is."

My heart misses a beat, and I inhale a rough breath as I shake my head. She's right. Of course.

I remember how he changed before—gradually but obviously. His slow withdrawal into himself after Patrick started coming around. His reluctance to want to spend time at home. The bruises he tried to hide, even from me. The whole terrible week freshman year when he stayed home from school and didn't return any of my calls. I found out what happened later, after he had surgery to repair his broken nose. He told me. Eventually. Reluctantly.

"He was always quiet and stuff, but when the, uh"—I swallow hard and look up to meet my mom's eyes—"when the abuse started, it got worse."

She knows already. But my stomach churns, and I find myself wishing I could take back the words. Nico hasn't said I can talk to my mom about any of this. But what happened in the past—yeah, she knows about all of that. We had to talk about it then. She and I talked *a lot* about it then, actually, which I desperately needed at the time.

"He's had nearly a decade of this now," she adds quietly, and I nod, the lump in my throat painful. "And I don't know what's going on now—"

"Neither do I," I cut in.

"Right. So whatever it is, if you care about him—"

"I do. Very much."

She pulls me back into her and holds me tightly. "I know, sweetie. I know."

I'm crying now, and I bend down and bury my head in her shoulder.

"So whatever's going on," she continues, "the best thing you can do is just be there for him as much as possible. Be there *when* he's ready to talk. Remind him how much you care. And be patient with him. Accept where he is, meet him there, and know that even if he doesn't open up right now, if it takes him time, if he seems to be pushing you away, it's only because that's what he's had to do for years now to protect himself."

I nod into her. "I can do that."

"I know you can." She steps back, letting her hands drop away. Then she reaches up and touches my cheek. Something like pain flickers through her expression as she studies me, and she purses her lips and says, "Don't . . . don't give up on him. I . . . don't think you will, but I worry about him, too. I worry . . ." She hesitates and lowers her eyes, frowning. "I worry that he doesn't see his own worth. Especially now, with everything happening with his mom and that awful man coming back into his life."

Fear seizes me, just like it had that moment on the stairs the other night, and I nod again. "I worry about that, too. More than you know." When I look up at her, the pain is back in her expression. "I . . . want to be there for him," I add. "I'm just not sure what to do when he pushes me away. Do I stay anyway? Do I give him space? Do I insist, or do I leave him alone and hope he comes back to me? What . . . what do I do?"

I know there's no right answer. There's no answer she can give me that's definitive. And her brief smile as she shakes her head tells me that.

Letting out a sigh, I turn back to the computer and slip into the chair. "I should be able to get this done in a few hours."

Her hand sets on my shoulder, and she squeezes me gently. "Perfect. I've gotta run to Omaha and pick up some paints and supplies. I got a new commission just this morning. I should be back around noon, maybe a bit later. Although I think I need to stop at the grocery store too. Anything you need that's not on the list on the fridge?"

I start to shake my head, then stop and smile. "Syrup?" I turn in the chair to face her. "We ran out a few days ago."

With a laugh, she nods. "No problem." She leans over and kisses the top of my head. "I'll grab eggs and potatoes, too, and we'll have breakfast for dinner."

"Sounds great, Mom. And thank you."

"Everything'll be okay, sweetie."

"I know."

She gives me one more smile, and even though it's a small gesture, it makes me feel a little better. "Be back soon," she says.

And I smile and nod and then get to work, trying to keep my thoughts from straying back upstairs.

It's just after twelve thirty when I finish with the work my mom wanted me to do. I log my hours in a notebook she keeps in the top drawer of her desk and then pull my phone out of my pocket. I've got three messages—two from my mom and one from Jenna.

My mom's messages are both just to let me know she's going to be gone a bit later than she expected—the art supply store she went to was out of the specific type of canvas she needed, and so she had to head across town to another store. That, and she decided to run a few more errands while she was out.

I send a quick text back with a thumbs-up. Then I stand as I click on Jenna's text.

*Jenna (10:14 a.m.):* Hey. Everything okay
with Nico? Text me back :)

I'm not sure what to say, so I stuff my phone back in my pocket, pick up the box filled with my mom's client paperwork, and put it away on its shelf. Then I head inside.

It's quiet, which I expected, I guess. And when I glance toward the stairs, wishing I'd see him coming down to meet me, all that's there is more quiet and an emptiness.

*Accept where he is, meet him there . . .*

He's hurting. And probably lost. And maybe scared.

And I'm *sure* he's hungry.

With as much certainty as I can muster, I turn and head to the kitchen. If nothing else, I can make him something to eat, spend a few minutes up there checking on him, and remind him that I'm here for him.

Maybe that'll be enough. Or at least a start.

A quick search of the kitchen tells me that all the leftovers are gone, and we're down to just a few essentials, which is why my mom is going shopping, I suppose. But we do have bread and cheese and some oranges that a neighbor brought over a few days ago. So I cook up a couple of grilled cheese sandwiches and slice up two of the oranges.

A few minutes later, I knock lightly on the bedroom door with my free hand, balancing a tray with the food in the other. There's no answer, and I swallow back my unease and worry and slowly open the door.

"Nico?"

My eyes immediately land on the bed, and my heart sinks. He's lying in the same position he was in when I left the room hours

ago—curled up on his right side, facing the wall, with the comforter pulled all the way up to cover his shoulders. A quick glance
at the nightstand tells me he hasn't touched the glass of water and
he didn't take the Tylenol. The ice pack also sits in the same spot
where I set it.

He really hasn't moved.

I can't tell from here whether he's awake or not, so I shut the
door behind me and then step closer to the bed.

"Hey, Nico. I, um, made some lunch, if you're hungry."

He reacts this time—a tiny movement that's actually just him
curling up into himself more. I stop near the end of the bed and
hold my breath, waiting for any real response. His mess of black
curls covers his face, and he turns his head slightly until our eyes
meet.

My heart hurts even more.

He's been crying, and the dark circles under his eyes suggest that
he maybe hasn't been sleeping this last four or five hours since I
left. I hate that. I hate that I left, that he's hurting so much himself,
that he's spent all this time alone. I hate that I wasn't here for him.

I should have been here for him.

I purse my lips and then force a small smile. "Grilled cheese. If
you want."

His eyes flicker down to the tray in my hands, and I watch as he
swallows and then shifts gingerly onto his back, obviously trying
not to grimace. He must see the worry in my face, because he drops
his chin and pushes himself up first to his elbows and then to a
seated position, carefully avoiding my gaze.

"That's a yes, then?" I ask when he pulls his knees in to sit
cross-legged and scoots back against the wall.

He doesn't say anything, but he does nod, and to me, that feels
like the biggest win of the day so far. It's even better when he lifts
his eyes and tries for a smile, then pats the bed next to him.

"You sure?"

"Yeah. Um, I mean, assuming you made yourself lunch too?"

I'm the one nodding this time, and my smile grows. "I did."

There's still pain in his expression, but he holds my gaze, and the corner of his mouth twitches up ever so slightly. "And did you cut the sandwiches into triangles like your mom always does?"

"Of course," I say with a fake scoff, setting the tray down on the bed. "Any other way would be completely wrong and affect the whole sandwich-eating experience."

"Right."

I'm grinning now, and he is, too, and for a brief moment, everything feels kind of okay again. I climb onto the bed, careful not to make the mattress shift too much, and I settle next to him with my back against the wall. Then I slide the tray over between us, turning it so his plate is closer to him.

"See? Perfect triangles," I say, motioning to his plate.

He squints and leans over. "I dunno. This one here—slightly smaller than the others. Might need to send it back to the kitchen." With a smirk, he glances up at me.

"Guess you'll have to taste it and see."

We start eating, and I'm glad to see he actually does have an appetite. He eats slowly, though, and I try not to show that I'm noticing every stiff movement he makes, every wince or flinch, every sharp breath. He *is* hurting, even if he doesn't want to admit it to me.

That's okay, I tell myself. And I close my eyes and lean my head back against the wall. He'll tell me when he's ready to.

"Thank you," he says quietly after a few more minutes.

I turn my head toward him as he awkwardly pushes the now-empty tray out of the way and then scoots himself over closer to me. He doesn't look at me, his gaze focused somewhere between us on the bed, but he moves closer all the same. My heart aches and soars simultaneously, and I want nothing more than to hold him in my arms. Cautiously, I lift my arm up in invitation, giving him a spot to cuddle against me. He pauses, but only briefly, and then he lets out a shuddering breath and scoots over the rest of the way. I feel all the tension in him, even as he leans into me and rests his head in the crook of my shoulder, his hand coming to settle on my stomach.

I wish I could just chase it all away.

Gently, I settle my arm across his shoulders, and then I tilt my head and press a kiss into his hair. "I'm glad the triangles were cut to your satisfaction," I tease.

His body shakes with a weak laugh. "They were perfect."

"Good." I kiss him again, then let my head fall against his, closing my eyes.

We stay like that for a few long minutes, and eventually, his shoulders relax, his breathing deepens, and his hand slides lower until it's quietly resting on my thigh.

He's asleep.

I hold back a smile, but I feel it in my heart—how much I love him. If this is what he needs from me—to just be here, to hold him, to take care of him, to let him open up in his own time, when he's ready—then I'm here for it.

I'm here for all of it.

# chapter thirty-three

*nico*

WHEN I WAKE UP, it's warm. And I'm comfortable in a way I can't explain. It's calm—around me and in my head. Nothing's screaming. My heart's not racing. The dreadful, cold numbness isn't spreading from my hands.

Alex's arm tightens around my shoulders. "Good afternoon, sleepyhead," he murmurs into my hair with a light laugh.

I just sigh into him. I don't want to move from this spot, snuggled up against his chest. And he doesn't seem to want to, either. His free hand covers mine, which rests about midway up his thigh, and he caresses softly just past my wrist and then back to my knuckles.

I'm not sure what feels better—how he's holding me or how he's touching me.

Both make me feel loved.

I sniffle and squeeze my eyes shut, cursing inwardly as I try desperately not to cry. It's overwhelming—this feeling. It's overwhelming and depressing at the same time, because I'm immediately reminded of yesterday and how little my mom must think of me. How little she must love me.

She had to have set me up; she had to have known how terrifying it would be for me to face Patrick, and yet, that was what she forced me into. That and not fucking caring enough to even give me a warning about changing the price of the car. I've told her how much money I'm making and how little I have. She knows I'm struggling.

But she doesn't seem to give a damn.

She doesn't seem to love me at all.

Alex's hand caresses a little higher up my forearm this time, his fingers pausing just below my elbow, and at the same time, he presses another kiss into my hair. It's gentle and caring, and I feel his intention in it.

He *wants* to make me feel loved.

The contrast between him and my mom is sharp, like a knife in my gut . . . or a closed fist to my face.

I inhale another shaky breath, still trying to hold back tears, and I shift in his arms so that I'm hugging him, not bothering to hide my hiss of pain as I move my left arm—god, my shoulder is fucked up. I bury my head into the crook of his neck, and I cling to him.

I can't hold back anymore. The tears fall. I should be embarrassed by it, but I'm not. I'm just thankful he holds me, still—his arms slowly, carefully wrapping around me. Keeping me warm. Taking care to not hurt me because apparently my back is covered in bruises that *are* actually painful too.

"Shh, shh. I'm here. I'm here," he whispers, ever so lightly rubbing my upper back. "I'm here. You're . . . you're okay, Nico. I've got you."

And those words are too much, pushing me over an edge I hadn't even known was there.

"I need you," I choke out, and he somehow holds me tighter without hurting me.

"You have me." His lips brush my temple, soft but promising. "I'm here. You have me."

Something inside me rattles and breaks loose, and I tilt my head back, aware that my cheeks are wet with tears. He doesn't care about that. He doesn't let me go. He just lowers his mouth to mine and kisses me. Slowly. Softly. Surely.

Fuck.

I feel it in his kiss. I feel it.

He loves me.

*He loves me.*

His lips continue to caress mine, still just as gently, again and again until he breaks away to flutter tiny, light kisses all along my skin. He kisses my jaw and cheeks and nose, and then he pulls back slightly, tilts his head, and, as I close my eyes, he kisses my forehead, lingering there, breathing deeply.

My jaw trembles, and I know I should say something. Another thank you, at least. Or an apology for being an asshole to him earlier. But my voice won't work, and I feel shaky and weak and tired, even though I just had the world's best nap on the world's most comfortable pillow.

So instead, I relax against him again and let him hold me.

We stay there for another long few minutes, his hand caressing my arm and his lips occasionally dropping kisses in my hair. I feel like I might fall asleep again.

"Mmm, you're so comfortable." I smooth my hand across his stomach and hook my fingers around his hip.

A laugh rumbles through his chest, and his arm tightens around my shoulders. "I'm glad," he says. His voice becomes softer as he adds, "You seem like you need the rest."

I nod. "I didn't sleep well. Nightmares." Nausea rises up in my chest, and I know I've opened the door for his questions. Part of me wants him to ask so I have that extra push to tell him the truth. Another part of me is already pulling away, seeking the safety of solitude under the blanket. Alone.

He hesitates—I feel it in the way he stiffens and holds his breath, the way his cheek presses into the top of my head. Then everything around me seems to soften, and I'm surrounded by a comfortable warmth again. Quietly, he says, "You can sleep more now. I'll stay. If you want."

It doesn't seem fair or right or honest of me. But I nod. "Please."

"Mm-hmm, of course. Did you want to lie down?"

I nod again, and he pauses for only a moment to pull back and kiss my forehead. Then he says he'll be right back, and he takes the tray and leaves the room for a moment. I sit up, blink my eyes open, and look over at the nightstand. The Tylenol and glass of water still sit there from this morning.

Maybe it'll help. I'm not sure why I'm at all opposed to it.

Slowly, I push myself away from the wall and scoot over to the edge of the bed. Then I pick up the glass and the pills, pop the pills into my mouth, and wash them down with a small sip. I take a few extra sips for good measure—I'm actually not sure I've had anything to drink since sometime midday yesterday, at lunch, maybe, though I don't feel thirsty.

There's a light knock on the door as Alex returns. I quickly set the glass back down and climb under the covers again as he shuts the door. Silently, he slips off his pants, leaving only his boxer briefs on, and then he takes a moment to close the shutters all the way and turn on the ceiling fan. By the time he joins me in bed, I'm settled in my spot on my right side, facing the wall. The bed compresses behind me, and I close my eyes, willing my body not to react as he scoots closer.

"Can I hold you?" he asks softly, and I nod.

"Please."

He finds my arm under the blanket, and his fingers trace lightly down past my elbow. Then he slips his hand under mine and presses his body up against me. His lips brush along my neck.

"Is this okay?"

"Yeah."

"Good." He kisses me again and then settles down, still holding me. "I'll be here as long as you need. Okay?"

I can't respond this time, even though that's exactly what I needed to hear. Instead, I press my hand against his and snuggle back into him. He hums contentedly. I love that sound.

I fall asleep not long after, comfortable and warm.

I sleep for a few more hours, and after I wake up, Alex coaxes me out of the bedroom to play some video games downstairs. His mom makes breakfast for dinner, complete with pancakes, scrambled eggs, hash browns, biscuits and gravy, and a bunch of fruit. It's way too much food for the three of us, but, as she cheerfully reminds us, that means leftovers for tomorrow.

After dinner, Alex and I settle back on the couch to watch a movie, and his mom disappears into the garage to get started on a new commission.

As usual, Alex picks some bloody, violent horror film—this time one that came out earlier in the year, a sequel to a movie he made me watch last year. I don't object. It's almost funny to me, actually, since his odd love of horror films is pretty much opposite his personality. And anytime whatever's on the TV is too much, I get to bury my head against his chest, and he holds me. So it's all worth it anyway.

When the movie's over, it's almost midnight. His mom is still working in the garage, and he goes out to check on her while I head upstairs to shower and get ready for bed.

I'm surprised at how stiff I am as I undress in the bathroom, and the water's just hot enough to start fogging up the mirror by the time I've carefully peeled off my T-shirt, so I can't see how bad my back looks. I can, however, see the redness and swelling in my left shoulder. And it doesn't look good.

My stomach sinks as I touch the tender skin, testing out where it's sore. The answer is all over, and when I hit a particularly bad spot, pain shoots down into my fingers and across my chest. It's gotten worse since last night, which isn't good. What bothers me more, though, is that I don't know what to do about it. Should I go to the doctor or wait it out? And, if I do end up needing to go to the doctor, how the hell will I pay for it?

"Fuck," I hiss, both at the pain as I find another tender spot and at the fact that I don't know if I have health insurance right now. I don't know how any of that shit works. And I should be finding out. Another thing to add to my long list of to-dos.

I shake my head and step into the shower, adjusting the water temperature down a little. I wash as quickly as I can, given that using my arm at all hurts like hell, and when I'm done, I dry myself off, get dressed in sleep shorts and a clean, loose T-shirt, and brush my teeth. Then I pause, staring at the hazy figure in the fogged-up mirror.

I should probably see how bad it is. Even if it's just so that I know how it'll look to Alex.

Frowning, I reach forward with my good arm and wipe away the condensation on the mirror. Then I pull my shirt off again, turn around, and look back at myself over my shoulder. Large black-and-purple splotches cover much of my mid-back, right where I remember hitting the wall. Hell. It does look bad. No wonder Alex was upset when he saw it.

He was right to suggest I take medicine and ice it. And if he knew about my shoulder, I'm sure he'd have insisted even more.

With a shudder, I wonder what my mom would say if I told her—or if I *showed* her. Maybe she'd believe me . . . until Patrick comes in with his fucking lies and tells her some awful alternate-reality version where I somehow attacked him first.

The thought makes me sick, and I quickly slip my shirt back on and push open the bathroom door. The hallway is mostly dark, but the lights from downstairs give me plenty to see by. I cross over to Alex's bedroom and push open the door about halfway. Alex is working on his computer at his desk, and he looks up at me, grinning, as I step inside.

"What?" I ask, closing the door behind me. His eyes are bright and curious, and he starts to open his mouth to talk when I hold up my hand. "Hang on. This is about space or gravity or black holes or something nerdy, right?"

He snorts a laugh. "Yeah, I just checked my email, and Dr. Ellis sent me this article—"

I try not to groan out loud, but I fail miserably. He laughs again as I reach over and take his hand, tugging gently. "Can you tell me about it while we cuddle in bed? I'm tired."

His grin softens. "Yeah, of course." He shuts his laptop as he stands up, then he squeezes my hand. "Let me just go brush my teeth and stuff. Five minutes, 'kay?"

At my nod, he leans in and kisses my cheek. Then he grabs a change of clothes and takes off out of the room, leaving me alone. I glance at his computer and then up at his corkboard, where his Stanford acceptance letter hangs proudly.

There's a tightness in my chest, and I realize I'm holding my breath. I turn away and head over to the bed, forcing a long exhale. And I sit and wait for him. My heart's now racing, and I'm not sure why.

Maybe the reminder that he's leaving. Or . . . or *we're* leaving. *We're* leaving, and I still don't have a plan for how I'm going to make that work. A job. A budget. A . . . vehicle.

Fuck.

Alex pushes the door open then, smiling, and he turns around, closing it softly. "My mom's still working, but I think she'll be up soon, so, uh, you know, we'll need to be quiet if—" He faces me and pauses. "What's wrong?"

I almost laugh at how easily he can read me. And I love his assumption that we'll need to be careful to stay quiet. But instead of laughing, I blurt out, "What's the public transportation like in Palo Alto? A-and nearby?" Then I drop my eyes to my hands and shake my head. "Do they have buses or trains or something?"

"Um, I . . . think so?" He pads across the room toward me and sits next to me, then rests his hands on top of mine in my lap. "Why?"

I shouldn't have started this. It's late. I'm tired. He was going to tell me happy stuff about some article he read, and we were going to cuddle. Maybe even more than cuddle. But I can't just wave it off now.

"I need to know. For my budget. If—if I'm going to California with you. I . . . don't have a car anymore. My mom . . ." I shake my head, deciding I can't go into detail tonight. "I don't have a car. Can we find out?"

"Right now?" he asks, rubbing his thumb along the back of my hand.

I nod quickly.

"Okay, yeah. Let's take a look." He gets up and returns a moment later with his laptop. Together, we scoot back on the bed until our backs are against the wall, and then he opens up the computer and types in a quick search. "Okay, so . . . here's the public transit info . . ."

He clicks through the websites for both the Santa Clara Valley Transportation Authority and Caltrain, stopping to read to me every once in a while. He finds maps and schedules of the bus and light-rail routes, and we look through those for a few minutes.

He even opens up the local subreddit for the area, finding general praise for the public transit systems before hopping back to the Transportation Authority website and looking up options for bus fares.

"Ah, look, they have a monthly pass," he says, pointing to the screen. He lowers his voice and adds, "And it's actually much less than the cost of car insurance in California. So, that's good then, yeah?"

I close my eyes and nod. It *is* good. Maybe even better, actually, budget-wise. I'll ignore the fact that my anxiety is going to be through the roof if I have to ride a crowded bus or train, but at least I'll have options.

"Yeah. Yeah. Um, thanks. Thank you. Sorry, I just . . . I kinda freaked out for a second there."

"It's okay." I hear his laptop close, and his lips brush my forehead. "Ready for bed now? Are you okay? Or, um, did you want to talk more?"

I shake my head immediately. "No more talking. Or, I mean"—I open my eyes and tilt my head back to look up at him—"you can still talk. But I'm done. For now."

He holds my gaze for a moment, like he's studying me to make sure I'm actually okay. When he's maybe found what he's looking for, he smiles, bends down, and captures my lips in a soft kiss. "Okay, yeah. One sec. I still need to tell you about this article from Dr. Ellis. You won't believe it."

This time, when he gets up, I crawl underneath the covers and settle on my back on my side of the bed near the wall. He climbs into the bed next to me just a few seconds later, after he puts his computer away and switches off the light. Then he's on his side, his hand caressing my forearm as he kisses my shoulder over the top of my T-shirt. His touch is so gentle and caring, and I just close my eyes with a quiet hum as his hand moves to my stomach, slips under my shirt, and starts stroking slowly across my abdomen.

"So, this article," he begins, pausing to kiss my shoulder again.

"Hmm?"

"It was just published last week in *Nature Astronomy*—that's one of the top journals for astrophysics research in the world—and it's by a research group working in The Netherlands. They were studying giant elliptical galaxies that had become dormant, and what they found was . . ."

He says a bunch of words I don't understand, but I try to listen anyway, even as I'm very, very distracted by the searing touch of his fingers on my skin and the occasional light kisses he places on my shoulder. He's obviously excited by the conclusions of the research, and he says something about how Dr. Ellis wants to hear his opinion on it. That makes me smile, and I turn my head sideways and open my eyes. It's dark, but I can still see him smiling back at me. He scoots a bit closer, props himself up on one elbow, and then leans down and kisses me, his lips soft and warm.

"Mmm," he hums into the kiss, and I smile against him. When he pulls back, he's grinning again. "Thanks for listening. I know you were tired."

He's adorable and so sweet to me, and it's taking all I have to not pull him back in for another kiss. The way he was touching me was arousing as hell, and I wish I wasn't still exhausted and anxious and hurting, because even with all of that, I want him.

His fingers flex against my hip, and he lowers himself to kiss my lips again. It's the same gentle, loving kiss with no expectations—just his lips caressing mine in a slow, careful exploration. I lift my hand to cup his cheek, then let my hand slip back to play with the hair at the nape of his neck. And he moans softly, breaks the kiss, and lowers his head to my chest.

He rests there for a moment, then asks quietly, "Ready for sleep?" He lifts his head and starts to flutter tiny, light kisses along my jaw, and his hand caresses low along my stomach, just above the waistband of my sleep shorts. A low groan escapes me, and Alex laughs, the huff of air warm against my neck. "Is that a yes? Or something else?"

I want to whisper roughly in his ear that it's *definitely* something else. That he should keep doing what he's doing. That I'm very much *not* ready for sleep. I want to reach down and push his hand lower. I want to beg him to touch me. And I almost do it. But my hesitation alone seems to be enough to tell him the answer because he hums softly, kisses my jaw, and then lowers himself back onto the bed next to me, moving his hand to rest on top of my shirt.

"It's late." There's no disappointment in his voice. Just understanding.

I close my eyes, fighting to keep myself from apologizing, and that struggle turns into a buzz of anxiety, which is even worse. "I slept so much today, but I'm still tired," I admit, if for no other reason than to try to distract myself from the feeling.

"Mmm. That's understandable."

"Is it?"

He nods. "Yeah. I mean, I think so."

He's guessing, since he doesn't really know what happened. And I appreciate that he's still not demanding I tell him. I owe him more, though. I owe him the truth, and another honest talk about everything.

I turn onto my right side, facing away from him, and pull the blanket up to my chin. Before I even ask, his arm slips around my waist, and he snuggles up behind me, holding me close. His knee pushes between mine, and his lips brush against my neck. Then he settles against me and breathes in deeply.

"Mmm, you're warm," he murmurs, nuzzling my neck. "Is this okay?"

"Yeah. It's good," I say, managing to keep my voice level.

It's more than okay, though—it's exactly what I need right now. I wish I could just tell him that. I wish I could just tell him a lot of other things, too, like what happened with Patrick, the car, my mom. Like how much I appreciate him taking care of me, even if I don't always show it. Like how much I care about him.

Like how nothing else in the world is more important to me than he is.

*I love you.*

That's what I wish I could tell him.

"Tomorrow," I blurt out, the single word breaking through the jumble of thoughts in my head. I cover his hand with mine on my stomach and hold him to me. "Tomorrow, can we talk?"

"Yeah. Of course," he answers immediately. His arm tightens around me, and his breath warms the back of my neck, chasing away the little buzz of anxiety underneath my skin. "I'm here. I'll be here. Just rest now, okay?"

My whole body shudders as though releasing more of that deep pain that's constantly suffocating me. I nod and close my eyes and wriggle backwards to settle into him. It *is* warm. And comfortable.

A tear slips down my cheek, and I sniffle and wipe it away.

"Good night, Nico."

"Good night, Alex."

# chapter thirty-four

## alex

I WAKE UP TO a face full of dark hair, a hot breath on my neck, and a heavy weight sprawled on top of me. One of my hands is already under his shirt, my palm resting on his low back, and he's got his fingers threaded through my hair. He sighs, mumbles in his sleep—something quiet that I can't understand—and shifts slightly. And the sweetest sear of arousal burns through me as his thigh slips between my legs, my semi-hard dick pressing against his hip.

I have no idea how or when he ended up in this position on top of me, but I love it. It's perfect. He's perfect. This is perfect.

I muffle a groan into his hair and open my eyes halfway. The room is dimly lit—the first light of morning just barely peeking around the edges of the closed shutters—and the comforter is mostly pushed off of us, bunched up down past Nico's ass.

Even my view is perfect.

With a sleepy grin, I smooth my hand low along his back, gentle and light. His shirt tugs up slightly, exposing pale skin and a tease of his light-gray briefs just under the top of his sleep shorts. I close my eyes again and breathe him in, letting my hand rub back and forth slowly.

"Mmm . . ." Nico inhales deeply as he wakes up, turning his

head so his lips brush my neck.

Heat pulses through me—a throb of want that rushes straight to my cock—and he hums again as one of his hands slides down my side to my hip.

"Good morning," I murmur, failing to keep my voice level as he shifts his position just enough for me to feel his erection rub against mine. "Holy fuck." The words slip out of my mouth with a rough groan, and Nico laughs quietly.

"Mmm, I love it when you curse like that," he says sleepily. His lips press into my neck again, and his hand sneaks just barely under my shirt so he's skimming his fingers along my bare skin. "You sound so fucking needy."

"I *feel* needy," I admit with another groan.

He lets out another laugh, just a puff of hot air warming my throat, and then his other hand lowers from my hair, his fingers tracing down along my throat to my side, under my shirt, settling just below my waist.

"Is there something you need?" he teases, both of his hands gripping my hips. He grinds into me with a slow, deliberate motion, his quiet moan sending a shudder through me.

"You," I force out, my heart pounding in my chest. "Need you. Want you."

"Mmm." He rolls his hips into me again with a delicious slowness, his hands countering the motion and holding me down.

I shudder and whine and writhe under him, my whole body now awake and buzzing, aching for more. I remember last time, how his hard cock felt in my hand, how he'd nearly begged for me to touch him, the sweet pressure and the overwhelming relief as I came. Another surge of desire pulses through me, and I moan.

Fuck, I *am* needy.

"Nico," I breathe, my voice rough. I let my hand slip down under his sleep shorts and briefs to cup his ass, and when he grinds into me this time, I squeeze encouragingly as I tilt my hips to meet him.

With a groan of approval, he kisses my neck again and then shifts one hand from my hip to the bed to prop himself up. But he suddenly pauses with a sharp grunt and drops his forehead to my chest, his shoulders tight. "Goddammit," he hisses.

My hand stops on his back, my arousal immediately melting away into concern. I lift my other hand from the bed to his shoulder, but as soon as I touch him, he flinches, hissing again in pain. I pull my hand away.

"Shit, sorry," I say, worry twisting my gut. I don't know what to do, so I stay as still as I can and lower my voice. "Wh-what . . . I-I mean, um, are you okay? Please tell me you're okay."

He shakes his head, although I'm not sure exactly what he means. He seems to try to move again, to push himself sideways off of me, maybe, but he immediately freezes, sucking in a breath through clenched teeth.

"Can I help? What hurts?" When he doesn't say anything, I bend forward to kiss the top of his head. "Here, lower back down onto me. Is it your shoulder?"

This time, he nods, and then he does as I suggested, taking the weight slowly off his arm and allowing himself to settle back on top of me. "S-sorry," he says quietly. "I wanted . . . to make you feel good. I didn't think . . ."

"It's okay," I reassure him. I wrap both my arms around him—very carefully—and kiss the top of his head again. "Are you okay now? It doesn't hurt anymore?"

"Yeah. Kinda."

I close my eyes and just hold him there for a moment, letting my heart slow back down from the double rush—first from arousal and then from worry. "Your left shoulder?"

He nods again.

"Alright." I'm not entirely sure what I'm doing, but I keep holding him on top of me as I start shimmying over toward the wall, figuring that maybe I can shift him onto his right side next to me if I make space on the bed. Or something like that.

"Alex, what the hell are you—"

"Shh. Just . . . trust me," I cut in. When I'm far enough over, I tighten my hold on him slightly—mindful of the bruises on his back, too—and I pause. "Tell me if I need to stop."

He swallows hard, but then keeps his head buried against my chest as I turn us and lower him to the bed on his right side. I slip my arm out from under him, keeping my other hand securely on his lower back.

His breathing is still strained, and I lean in and kiss his forehead as I give him a moment. Then, softly, I ask, "Better?"

"No."

"No?"

"Well, yes. But . . . but also no."

His tone sounds almost pouty, and when I pull back to look at him, he's frowning, staring unfocused at my chest. His dark hair falls across his forehead, messy and also begging for me to brush it out of the way. So I do, letting my fingers comb back through his soft, loose curls. He closes his eyes.

"That feels good, though."

"Yeah?"

"Yeah." He pauses, then tenses a little as he shifts over slowly, grimacing, until he's lying flat on his back, his left arm resting at his side. He brings his right forearm up to cover his eyes. "I'm sorry," he mumbles, all the teasing and happiness gone from his voice.

I don't have to ask him what he thinks he needs to apologize for. But I hate that he thinks it's his fault at all that we were interrupted.

I scoot as close to him as I can, settling my hand on his stomach, and I lightly kiss his shoulder. It's his good shoulder, but I'm still glad when he doesn't flinch or move away. "Can I get you Tylenol?"

He hesitates, then lowers his arm and turns to look at me. His eyes are beautiful in the soft light of early morning, though there's something in them that worries me, and I'm not sure why. I smile gently, bring my hand up to touch his cheek, and then lean over and kiss him—a slow, deep kiss that I hope shows him how much I care.

When we part, he takes a breath and then nods. "I'll take the Tylenol."

He doesn't say anything more, so I steal another kiss—a shorter one this time—and carefully crawl over him off the bed to head downstairs. It's early enough that my mom's not up yet, and so, less than a minute later, I'm back with two tablets of extra-strength Tylenol and a glass of water.

With a grimace, he sits up, and I hand him the glass and then the pills, which he pops into his mouth. He takes a long sip or water, swallows, and places the glass on the nightstand.

"Thanks," he says. He glances up at me and tries for a smile, but it's strained and brief. Tentatively, maybe as though he's trying to convince himself it's okay, he reaches out and brushes his fingers up my forearm to my elbow in invitation. "Come back to bed? I . . . um, I think I'll be okay if we're just careful."

I hesitate. The last thing I want to do is hurt him, of course. But when he lets his fingers continue up higher on my arm and then flattens his palm along my bicep, there's a renewed rush of heat and arousal to my groin.

"You're sure?" I ask, my voice rough.

"Yeah," he says with a small nod. His hand drops from my arm as he slowly shifts over on the bed and starts to lie down on his back again.

"Okay, uh, but wait," I say softly. When he stops, I lower myself onto my knees on the bed, crawl over toward him, and push the comforter all the way back off his legs. My hands find his hips and slide under his shirt and up a little. "Before you lie down . . . ?"

I hope he understands my question, but he doesn't answer. Instead, he dips his chin, and his cheeks turn pink. Without a word, he reaches back to remove his shirt, pulling it off over his head with just his right hand.

He's all lean muscle and smooth skin, and my dick throbs as though waking back up after our sudden interruption. I swallow hard, watching his muscles shift as he tosses the shirt onto the bed next to us. I have seen him shirtless before, a bunch of times, actually. But this feels different. Maybe it's because this time, I don't have to hold back. This time, I get to worship his body like I've always wanted to. This time, I get to touch him, kiss him, taste him.

"Nico," I whisper, which is enough for him to glance up through his thick lashes. I slowly lean in as my hands graze up his sides, and my lips find his. We kiss—deep, tender, loving. Somehow, I find myself kneeling between his legs, my mouth still on his, my tongue tasting him. One arm wraps low around his waist, and I help him slowly lower himself back onto the bed. Then I drag my lips away to flutter tiny kisses along his jaw. I pause just under his ear. "You're gorgeous. Perfect," I murmur against his skin. His hand lifts up, and he runs his fingers through my hair, which feels incredible. I groan and continue on a lazy path with my kisses—down his neck, back up, alternating kissing and licking and sucking.

He's quiet, but it's a restrained quiet. His hands and body are plenty loud, his heavy, stilted breathing and the straining bulge in his shorts betraying how he really feels.

I sit back on my heels and stare down at him, letting both of my hands come to rest low on his stomach. His eyes are half open, looking up at me lazily, and his cheeks are still flushed and hot.

"You're okay, right?" I ask, needing to be sure. "Not hurting too much?"

He gives a small nod and says, "Yeah, I'm okay."

"So, I can touch you?"

He nods again.

"Anywhere?"

He huffs a weak laugh and nods again.

"And can I—"

"Yes. Fuck, please, yes."

I crack a smile, but then I sober up pretty quickly as my fingers drift outward toward his hips and inch under his sleep shorts and briefs. I pause, letting my eyes drop to where his cock twitches with arousal under the double layer of cotton.

God, I want to see him—*all of him*—for the first time.

A rush of need hits me, my own cock throbbing with want in my shorts. I reach down and adjust myself with a groan, and Nico laughs quietly, then lifts a hand and rubs it up along my forearm.

"What do you want to do?" he asks, his voice low but rough.

I tear my gaze away and meet his eyes. "I want to see you. And I want to kiss you everywhere," I admit. My cheeks feel hot with embarrassment and arousal, but I don't look away as I add, "And then . . . then I want to make you come."

He closes his eyes and groans. "How?"

"With my mouth."

His hand pauses over the top of mine, and he lets out a short, sharp breath. "You want to . . . with your . . ."

I hook my fingers under the edges of his shorts and briefs and lower them just an inch or so, and I lean over and kiss his newly exposed skin. "With my mouth," I repeat.

"Fuck."

I laugh and shake my head. Then I start kissing a slow path

upward, taking my time with each kiss.

He's sort of quiet again, like he was earlier, but he's breathing hard and he's restless. Little whines escape him, especially when I pause just below his nipple. His hand leaves my arm and threads up into my hair, gently encouraging me.

*He wants this as much as I want to give him this.*

Something in that thought is arousing as hell, and I pull back just enough to look up at him before lowering my mouth to his nipple. It stiffens at my touch, and I flick my tongue across the hard nub and then suck.

"God, Alex." He lets out another sharp breath. "Jesus."

I absolutely love his reaction, and I love knowing that he's reacting to *me*. So I continue, slowly pleasuring him, teasing out more breathless moans, more muffled pleas to keep going, to do that again, to—god, please, please, fuuuuuuck . . . He's still holding back, but with each slow, deliberate touch of my lips to his skin, he seems to lose control a little bit more.

I'm aching with arousal when I've finally worked my way back down his body, my hands finding his hips again, fingers slipping under the two layers of cotton. I linger with my mouth just below his belly button, and his hand threads into my hair, then down my neck and under my shirt to my upper back.

I pause to breathe him in, and before I undress him the rest of the way, I shift down even lower, nuzzle my face into the junction at the top of his thigh. His dick throbs against my cheek, heat radiating from him, and he gasps as his hand squeezes my shoulder.

"Please, Alex."

At his hushed, strained words, the fire in my belly surges. I want him so badly. But I force myself to keep moving slowly, to prolong the pleasure for both of us. I smile and hum as I turn my head and kiss his hard cock through the fabric of his shorts. He hisses another plea and bends one knee up and out, giving me more room.

I shift my hand from his hip to his knee, and I kiss him again, lingering with a good amount of pressure, as my hand caresses up his inner thigh with a deliberate, teasing stroke. "Mmm," I breathe, my fingers inching under the bottom hem of his briefs and stopping just as I feel the roughness of his pubic hair. His hand leaves my shoulder, and I hear a muffled whine.

"Mmm, you want to be in my mouth now, don't you?" I ask, my breath hot as I rub my cheek up along his throbbing erection. I've only ever imagined saying words like these in my fantasies—taunting him, pushing him to the edge. But he must like it, because he groans, and his hand presses against my shoulder again, insistently.

He chokes out a rough, "Yes. Yes. Fuck, please."

I'm not sure I could make him wait anymore, even if I wanted to. I sit up, and he helps me tug off his shorts and briefs by lifting his hips off the bed. I toss them over with his shirt and then pause for a second, taking him in—all of him.

He's beautiful. There's no other way to describe him. His gorgeous eyes, lean muscles, pale skin, the tantalizing line of dark hair leading to his hard, rigid cock. Beautiful and perfect.

And he's mine.

I swallow in anticipation as I reach out and run both of my hands up his inner thighs, still staring. His cock lies flat against his stomach, leaking precum from the tip. It twitches with need as my fingers stop just inches away, and Nico's breath hitches.

Maybe I should feel nervous. After all, I've never done this. Hell, his is the first dick I've seen other than my own. And he's putting so much trust in me. *That* alone should be scary enough. But I don't feel nervous at all. I just feel eager—eager to pleasure him, to find out what makes him feel good.

So I only hesitate one more moment—just long enough to

stretch up and kiss his lips—before I let my hand finally close around the base of his swollen shaft. I settle back between his legs, ignoring the ache of my own cock, and I stroke him lightly just once, then lower my head and place a slow, wet kiss on his tip.

He lets out a rough moan and turns his head to muffle several curse words into his pillow. And I touch my lips to him again, this time letting my tongue peek out to taste him before I take just the tip into my mouth.

"Alex . . . Alex, I . . . Holy fuck," he mumbles, his hand finding my hair as my tongue first slides along his slit and then swirls around him.

It's fucking incredible—the taste, the heat, the sounds he's making, how his hips jerk and his body writhes with pleasure. I groan, reach down to stroke myself through my shorts, and then give in to what I really want to do. I take him in my mouth deeper—an inch, then another and another until I feel him at the back of my throat. I pull back, my hand still holding him steady at the base of his cock, and then plunge down again, working him with my tongue as I do.

And I guess I'm doing something right, because he pushes his hand through my hair with an intensity that says he's on the very edge of his control. I try to find a rhythm, bobbing my head up and down and letting my hand follow as I take him in again and again, his little sounds guiding me. Without really meaning to, I find myself stroking my cock with the same rhythm, my briefs pushed down below my balls so they're out of the way. I'm close, and there's an urgency to his breathing now as well.

I pop off and look up at him, and god, I didn't think it was possible, but he's even more beautiful—his eyes half open, watching me. So vulnerable, so trusting.

I hold his gaze as I lower and take him in again, all the way to the back of my throat. He sucks in a sharp breath and screws his eyes shut, his hips jerking up slightly. I nearly gag but manage not to as I slide my mouth back up his shaft. After a breath, I go down again, working back up to the rhythm we had. He groans, and his hand grasps my shoulder.

"Ah . . . Alex . . ."

"Give it to me," I say, coming off him just long enough. I plunge back down, and his hand squeezes me again. With a moan, I let go of my cock—because if I don't, I'm done for—and I gently rub my hand up his thigh and then to his stomach.

He finds me there, pressing his hand on top of mine, our fingers intertwining.

"Mmm, ah fucking god, I'm—" His hand grips mine harder as his cock stiffens even more, and then he's grunting, his face turned to muffle whatever sounds he's making into his pillow, as his release spills into the back of my throat with each strong pulse of his cock. It's salty and warm, and I swallow everything I can before sliding back up his length and letting him slip out.

I'm breathing hard, my heart pounding, and I rest my forehead against his hip. His hand releases mine and threads into my hair, gently this time, his fingers massaging my scalp.

"That was . . . incredible," he murmurs between breaths.

"Mm-hmm," I agree. I'm not sure I can form any real words right now, and although I'm still achingly hard myself, I don't think I can move to take care of it. "Perfect," I manage to say. I turn my head just enough to kiss his hip. "You're perfect. That was amazing."

He takes a long, deep breath and then asks quietly, "Did you come?" His fingers are still running slowly through my hair, and it's distracting and feels so good.

I manage to shake my head, and then I tilt my chin up so I can see him. He looks soft, relaxed, like maybe he wants to just cuddle up and go back to sleep. He smiles down at me.

"Do you want to?" he says.

I close my eyes. "Mmm."

"That's not an answer."

A huff of a laugh escapes me. He's right, though.

My hand finds my sensitive cock, still hard and ready, and now leaking precum. The moment I touch myself, my whole body jerks, and I hiss. "Fuck. Yeah. Yeah, I want to come."

"Good," he says. His hand slides down to my shoulder. "Sit up so I can watch."

I do as he says, pushing myself up off him. I rest my free hand on his thigh and kneel, leaning over him slightly as I start stroking myself. It's perfect—the buildup of pleasure and heat and pressure, ready to burst as I keep working myself toward that edge. His hand covers mine on his leg, and I groan and close my eyes again.

I'm so fucking close now.

"Can I come on you?" My voice is rough, and the words sound stilted, but Nico answers immediately with what seems like a greedy *hell, yes*, and that's all the permission I need.

I stroke myself just another couple of times, and then I'm there, falling apart over him. I come hard and fast, everything bright and hot and buzzing as my release shoots out onto his stomach.

I'm not sure if I manage to keep my voice down, but I don't really care much at this point. As the last pulse throbs through me, I fall forward, breathing hard, barely managing to catch myself with one hand. "God. God, wow."

Nico laughs quietly, and his hand comes up to rub along my forearm. "That good, huh?"

I can only nod this time. My heart's thrumming in my chest, and I'm trembling slightly, as though my body's weak from the exertion. Weak but yet completely, utterly, totally sated. And happy.

"God," I say again. I want to kiss him, and I think he wants the same, because his hands—both of them this time—reach up to frame my face.

His thumbs brush along my cheeks, and he tugs me forward. "Come up here and kiss me," he begs.

I lift my eyes to his, and a warm rush hits me.

God, I love him so much.

And his eyes, his expression, how he's looking at me right now—I think . . . I think he loves me, too. And more than that . . . I think he's happy.

I move, pushing myself over and up along his side, and then I touch his cheek and lower my mouth to his. I kiss him sweetly, tenderly, and with every bit of love I've got for him. And my heart nearly bursts with joy as he kisses me back the same way.

We clean up, and Nico puts his briefs back on but forgoes his shirt, which is just fine with me, especially when he frowns and tugs *my* shirt off as well, complaining that it's not fair if he doesn't get to see me too. I don't argue—I just laugh and gather him up in my arms and kiss his forehead, and I hold him as he closes his eyes with a deep, contented sigh.

He's asleep within a few minutes, but I lie there awake, listening to the birds chirping outside and letting myself be distracted by thoughts of the future.

*Our* future. Together. In California.

Far, far away from—

I screw my eyes shut, but not before they dart to his left shoulder and see the hint of redness and swelling I hadn't let myself notice earlier.

Had Patrick hurt him?

The thought makes my stomach churn and my blood run hot,

and I take a slow breath to keep myself from tensing up too much. Then I turn and press my lips into his hair.

"Never again," I murmur against him.

I'll never let that asshole touch him again.

I should have been there on Friday; I shouldn't have been in Omaha. This shouldn't have happened.

I know I'm jumping to conclusions and that none of this is my fault, but given everything, it doesn't seem like too much of a stretch. It could also explain why he doesn't have a car anymore and why there's a large stack of twenty-dollar bills on my nightstand. And it would explain, almost too well, why he reacted like he did to my touch on Saturday morning—why he flinched away from me, why he had such a difficult time letting me hold him.

Over on the nightstand, my phone chimes quietly. I hesitate, not wanting to wake him, but he must not have been sleeping too deeply anyway, because he groans and burrows into my chest, mumbling something about it being too early to get up.

I laugh lightly. "It's eight thirty."

"Too early for a Sunday."

"I don't disagree with you."

"Then why are you still awake?" He slides his leg between mine as though he just needs to be even closer to me. The phone chimes again. "Are you going to check it?"

I sigh. "Well, that depends."

"On what?"

"On whether me moving is going to hurt you . . ." I say softly.

He tilts his head back to look up at me. His expression is hard to read, but his eyes are dark with shame, and he doesn't hold my gaze long.

"It won't," he says, his voice flat. He rests his head back on my chest and sets his left hand low on my stomach.

I swallow hard, and even though I want to, just to be sure,

ALL OF MY HEART                                    331

I manage to keep myself from asking him again. Instead, I bend down, kiss the top of his head, and then reach over him, as carefully as I can, to get my phone. When I settle back down, he just snuggles back into his place and closes his eyes.

I kiss his forehead and then unlock my phone to check my messages. Jenna's is first, and I grimace as I read it.

> *Jenna (8:32 a.m.):* It's been two days. Should I be worrying? Everything ok? Plz let me know

"What is it?" Nico asks quietly.

I turn the phone to show him, explaining, "I was worried about you on Friday night. Jenna was, too, when I told her you weren't answering my texts."

"Oh."

I tilt my head to rest against the top of his. "Can I tell her that, um, everything's fine?"

He nods, and so I type a quick response, apologizing for not replying earlier and telling her Nico's okay. Then I click back to the other text, which is from my mom.

> *Mom (8:34 a.m.):* Are you free to pick up a few things for me later today?

That one's easy.

> *Alex (8:40 a.m.):* yep!

Her response pops up immediately, like she already had it typed and was waiting for me to respond so she could send it.

> *Mom (8:40 a.m.):* Thanks! I'm going to be working all morning, but I'll write a list and leave it on the table. I need a new apron and a tarp for the floor. Both things are available at the art supply place in Omaha. No rush, but they close at 3 today.

> *Alex (8:41 a.m.):* got it!

"You up for a shopping trip with me today?" I ask Nico as I shut off my phone and toss it on the bed behind me.

"Where to?"

"Omaha, for my mom."

He doesn't answer right away, and I'm about to tell him he doesn't have to come when he tilts his head back again and mumbles, "Can we stop at the T-Mobile store also? And then maybe, um, if there's a secondhand clothing place? Or something. I, um . . ." He drops his chin and settles his cheek on my chest. "I need to get my phone working and buy some new clothes for work since I, um, have money now."

"Of course, yeah," I answer quickly. I lift my hand to his cheek and brush along his jaw with the back of my knuckles. "Actually, I know just the place. My mom took me a few weeks ago to get clothes for graduation. They have a bunch of nice clothes, and everything's pretty cheap."

"Cool. Thanks." He seems to shudder a little, and then his shoulders tense. "I . . . I should tell you what happened on Friday."

"Only if you want to," I say as my hand settles on the middle of his chest.

He looks up at me, and he's frowning, though he seems to be trying to hide it. "I don't *want* to."

"Then you don't—"

"You're telling me you don't want to know?" This time, he does manage a snarky expression, though it fades almost immediately into something much more serious, and he looks away again. "You . . . you should know. I definitely *don't* want to talk about it, but I do want to be honest with you. I-I'm sorry it's taken me so long. It's . . . hard, this, um, communication thing."

My chest feels tight, so I just hold him, lower my head to rest on top of his, and listen. He doesn't go into much detail, but what he does tell me is chilling. How he showed up, expecting to meet with his mom. How his mom wasn't there. How Patrick was waiting instead. His voice wavers as he tells me how Patrick turned on him, how his mom had apparently more than doubled the price of the car without even letting him know, and then how that asshole threatened him, shoved him into a wall, and yanked him up by his arm, injuring his shoulder.

He was forced to leave the keys to the car; something that had been his birthday gift when he turned sixteen had been weaponized and used against him.

It's awful. It's wrong and awful and manipulative. And it must have been worse than terrifying for him.

I bury my face into his hair and wrap my arms around him gently, carefully pulling him up against me. "That's horrible. I hate that you went through that." I stop myself from apologizing, because he wouldn't want me to, and instead, I just hold him.

He doesn't cry, and he doesn't pull away or try to retreat, though I'm not sure how. He's shaking, however, and he stops talking altogether for several minutes.

Finally, he takes a long, slow breath, and he says, "I keep trying to figure out where I fucked up so badly that she . . . that she would do this to me."

"No." I shake my head. "No, this isn't on you. You didn't do anything wrong. This is her. This is—"

"But *why*, Alex? Why the fuck doesn't she—" He stops himself, and then, very quietly, he says, "Why doesn't she love me anymore?"

My heart crumbles as I hold him tighter. I don't know what the answer is. I don't know what to say or what to do. All I know is that it's not right or fair, and he deserves much better.

He deserves it all.

I pull back just enough to kiss his forehead. And then I hold him as his body starts to shake with quiet sobs.

# chapter thirty-five

*nico*

"MOM'S MAKING BLUEBERRY WAFFLES." Alex slips his arms gently around my waist, holding me from behind. Our eyes meet in the bathroom mirror as he dips his head down to kiss my cheek. "And then, after breakfast, I'll drive you to work, 'kay?"

We already talked about it—or argued about it, really—last night after getting home from our errands and shopping in Omaha. I stubbornly insisted I could walk the two miles to the library. He stubbornly insisted I would not.

He won the argument after much negotiating, kissing, and another round in bed where I discovered that giving oral is just as fucking incredible as receiving it.

"Yeah, thanks." I give him a half smile and then finish running a brush through my hair. "Um, we should leave by eight fifteen. Is that okay?"

He straightens up, and, keeping one arm around my waist, he pulls my phone out of the pocket of my new slacks and holds it up so we can both see the time. "A half hour? Yeah, no problem."

He slips the phone back in my pocket, kisses my neck again, and then steps away, tugs off his shirt, and reaches into the shower to turn on the water.

I'm allowed to stare now. So I let my eyes linger on him, admiring parts of his body I'm becoming intimately familiar with—his strong forearms, well-defined abs, smooth skin, perfect ass.

"I'm gonna take a quick shower, and then I'll meet you down-stairs," he says, turning back to me. He pauses, his eyes glinting as he sees me watching him. "Unless you want to join me?"

A flood of possibilities hits me, and I can imagine it—water dripping down his chest, over his nipples and stomach and down to his hard, stiff cock; my hands following the same path, his skin smooth and wet and warm; getting down on my knees and taking him into my mouth as he stands there under the stream of water from the showerhead, my hands massaging his ass cheeks.

I've got some crooked grin on my face, I'm sure, because the teasing glint in his eyes darkens to want, and he steps up to me, hooks an arm around my lower back, and tows my hips to his.

"Maybe that's something for later, when we've got more time?" he whispers. Without waiting for my response, he lowers his mouth to mine and claims a hungry kiss that contradicts his words. His tongue finds mine, and his hands slip down to grasp my ass.

He's bold. Confident. Sure.

And that fucking turns me on.

It's over much too soon, although I'm breathless and panting when he pulls back, grinning at me. I want to swat him on the arm and make some joke about how he's a tease. I also want to tug him back in for another kiss, just as hot as that last one.

But instead, I just stare at him as an incredible warmth builds up in my chest. Slowly, I reach up and touch his cheek, watching as the tips of my fingers graze along the light stubble on his jawline. Then I take a deep breath and lift my eyes to his.

"Definitely later," I say, and my lips twist up into a smile that matches his.

He huffs a small laugh, his cheeks turning pink, and he ducks his chin. "I'll just be a few minutes."

"'Kay."

With obvious reluctance, he steps away from me, and as he finishes undressing, I slip out of the bathroom, take a moment to steady myself, and then jog down the stairs.

Just as he said, his mom is making blueberry waffles. She's got a platter of them already cooked, sitting next to a plate heaped with scrambled eggs, and she's pouring what looks like the last cupful of batter into her waffle iron. She glances up at me as I reach the bottom of the stairs, her smile as welcoming as always.

"Good morning! Hope you're hungry," she says in greeting, motioning to the platter on the counter. "Waffles, eggs, and I think we've got OJ in the fridge still, unless Alex drank the last of it yesterday."

"Ah, um, I did, actually," I admit, frowning. "Sorry, I—"

"No worries," she interrupts, closing the lid on the waffle iron. "We do have milk, and I made some coffee too."

"Coffee sounds great."

She smiles. "Help yourself."

I do—pouring myself a cup of coffee, then helping her move the food from the counter to the kitchen table, careful to carry things only in my right hand since the injury to my shoulder has my whole arm feeling weak. Not more than a few minutes later, she sits down next to me, giving me a silly look as I smother all of my food in an excessive amount of syrup. I just grin back, and she laughs.

The waffles are delicious, and I make sure to tell her that. She thanks me and then asks what my week looks like and whether I have any plans outside of work. It's small talk, which I usually hate. But somehow, she makes it easy.

I've never been able to say that before.

We chat for a few more minutes, and then there's a brief silence as I finish the last bites of my syrup-covered eggs. From upstairs, I hear the water shut off in the shower, and I pull out my phone to glance at the time. We've still got fifteen minutes before we have to leave, which should hopefully give Alex enough time to eat.

His mom must be thinking the same thing, because she says, "He's driving you in, right?"

I stuff my phone into my pocket and look back up at her. Does she know? Or rather, *how much* does she know?

Her eyes are soft with understanding, but they're sort of always like that.

Alex probably hasn't told her. In fact, I'm not even sure he's told her about *us*. I blink and look down. Does she know about *him*?

"Um, yeah. I hope . . . I hope that's not a problem?" I can't look back up to see, though I'm not really sure why. But she answers right away.

"No problem at all."

I can hear the same soft understanding in her voice, and I purse my lips and nod slightly. "Thank you."

"Anytime. Really."

My chest tightens. "I appreciate it. Everything, actually. I appreciate it all so much," I say, my voice catching. "Did . . . did Alex tell you why I don't have my car anymore?"

"No, he didn't," she replies softly, and I almost hear her unspoken words as well. She doesn't need me to tell her. She doesn't need a reason to want to help me.

That's both a relief and painful at the same time—to know that I have her support and yet to be reminded again of my mom's abandonment.

I glance up at her, meeting her eyes for the briefest of seconds. Then I stare at my half-empty coffee mug, and my heart cracks. I hold back the tears I let Alex see yesterday morning. But I tell her the truth.

"When I showed up to pay my mom for the car on Friday after

work, she wasn't there," I start, doing the best I can to keep my voice steady. "Patrick was. Her . . . her ex-husband. He told me she increased the price of the car to twelve hundred dollars. A-and since I didn't have the money, he took the keys. She . . ." I close my eyes and shake my head. "She never told me the price changed. And she knew I didn't have that kind of money."

"Oh, Nico . . ."

There's more, of course. The constant ache in my shoulder and tenderness of the muscles in my back are proof of that. But I can't get myself to tell her what Patrick did to me. Instead, I try to force a smile, and I make myself look up at her. "Alex and I looked up the cost of public transportation near Palo Alto, and it's cheaper than the car insurance I was going to have to buy, so I guess at least there's that."

She gives me a sad smile, but nods. "They have a pretty good bus and train system there, from what I understand."

"Yeah."

She's studying me with a gentle but knowing look, and I try for another smile, then take a small sip of my coffee.

"Have you thought about what kind of job you'd like?" she asks, and I frown and shake my head.

"I don't know what . . ." I swallow hard and glance toward the stairs, wishing Alex was here to help me talk. Or something. "I really don't know what I'd be any good at. And it'll have to be something where I can make at least twenty-five bucks an hour."

There's defeat in my voice, and I know she hears it. Her expression changes to one I've seen from her before—that sort of *motherly-advice-incoming* expression she always has when she talks to Alex about certain things.

"It feels pretty impossible, doesn't it?" When I nod, she continues. "I won't sugarcoat things. It's not going to be easy. *But*, Nico, I've known you for a long time, and I've watched you grow up, and

I honestly believe that you'll figure it out. I know how hardworking you are, how determined. You're smart and thoughtful. And organized."

"And punctual!" Alex pipes in, jogging down the last of the stairs. His mom arches her eyebrows at him, but he shrugs and winks at me. "He is. Always on time."

I roll my eyes and turn back to his mom. She's smiling softly still, her head tilted ever so slightly to the right as she regards me. "I do have a suggestion that might help, if you're interested."

Alex slides into the chair right next to mine and starts piling up waffles and eggs on his plate. I ignore how good he smells—clean and fresh and with just a hint of that aftershave he uses—and I nod slowly to his mom.

Her smile grows, and she scoots her chair in a little. "Okay, so I have a friend in San Jose—do you know where that is?"

I try to picture the maps Alex and I looked at the other day when we were checking out the public transit stuff. "South of Palo Alto, I think?"

Alex's mom nods with enthusiasm. "Yep! So my friend Vera lives there. I've known her for ages. We met through a professor of mine back when I was in college. She was here in Nebraska, setting up an exhibition at a small gallery in Omaha. It was the very first exhibition that featured any of my paintings. She and I kept in touch after, though she's been on the West Coast for the last fifteen years or so. She runs a huge art collective, manages multiple galleries, puts on events all year round. And she's always looking for good, reliable employees. She's demanding but fair. I don't know for sure, but I'd venture that she pays quite well."

She glances at Alex, who's now shoving a huge bite of eggs in his mouth, and he nods, chews quickly, and swallows. "Sounds perfect for you," he says, nudging me with his elbow.

I frown. Did he already know about this? "I don't have any

experience working with art or art galleries or exhibitions," I say quietly, but again, his mom just smiles, shaking her head lightly.

"Your job at the library right now—what is it that you do?" she asks.

"Um, I've mostly been working on the library's annual fundraiser. Sorting through donated books, cataloging them. Inputting the details into a spreadsheet, assessing damage." I pause, and Alex's mom is nodding gently at me now. "Filing and organization." She nods more, and her smile brightens. "I've also helped set up for some of the summer events the library runs, and I did some work on a new display for the children's books section."

"Nico, that is exactly the type of work experience I bet she'd be looking for," she says. "I mean, I don't know for sure whether she's hiring right now, but even if she's not, she's got a huge network of artists and other professionals she works with, and I bet she'll know someone."

It's hard to believe it might actually be possible, but I *want* to believe it. I glance at Alex, and he's got this incredible smile on his face, his blue eyes lighting up with that same sort of excitement he has when he's talking about astrophysics and stuff.

"Sounds like a good place to start, right?" he says, and I nod.

This sense of hope inside me is an odd feeling that I'm not entirely used to. But it's immediately at war with another, not-so-nice feeling—something telling me there's not a chance in the world for this to work out, but all the chance in the world for me to fail at it and let Alex down.

"If you want, I can give Vera a call," Alex's mom suggests.

I blink and look down for a few seconds, trying to get myself to fight against that not-so-nice feeling and agree. "Um . . ."

Alex's hand settles gently on my upper back, and when I force myself to look up and over at him, he's got the same encouraging, hopeful expression in his eyes.

"Maybe it'll work out," he says softly. There's a flicker in his eyes of some other emotion, almost pleading. "You can't know if you don't give it a chance."

He's right. Of course.

His hand slides along my upper back and stops at my shoulder, giving me a light squeeze, and I reach up until my fingers find his. The corners of his lips twitch up into a fuller smile when I nod slightly, and that grin—his gorgeous, kind, heart-stopping grin—brightens up the whole room.

I can't help but feel his excitement and just enough of his confidence that I nod again and turn back to look at his mom. "Okay, um, yeah. I would really appreciate that, Ms. Hayes."

She pauses to glance from me to Alex and back, and then she nods and says, "I'll give her a call later today."

"Thank you."

"I'm happy to help. Really." With another understanding smile and another glance from me to Alex, she stands up and starts clearing the table. "Finish eating, sweetie. You don't want Nico to be late."

"Oh, right," Alex says. He squeezes my shoulder again before letting his hand drop, and then he shoves the last of his waffles into his mouth and swallows as he pushes back his chair. "Ready to go?"

I am. But there's a lump in my throat now. Because if his mom didn't know about us before, I'm pretty sure she does now. Like, ninety-five percent sure.

I push my chair back and stand up, and Alex's hand finds my back as he stands as well. "I'll clear our dishes and meet you out at the truck?"

"Sure, yeah, thanks," I reply.

He steps closer and lowers his head slowly, giving me time to back away if I'm not *really* comfortable kissing him in front of his mom. My cheeks flush with heat, but I nod my consent, and his eyes brighten before he leans in the rest of the way and kisses me softly on the lips.

It's a brief kiss, and I feel him smile against me as he kisses me a second time. Then he pulls back, grinning. "I'll just be a minute."

"'Kay." I manage to hold myself together, and as Alex gathers our dishes and steps away, I take a breath and head toward the front door. "Thank you for breakfast, Ms. Hayes," I say when I reach the door.

I glance back over my shoulder and see Alex standing next to her, setting the dishes in the sink. She's got her arm around his waist in a half hug, and she releases him and turns around, her eyes glinting with amusement. "You're welcome, sweetie," she says. "Have a great day, and I'll see you after work."

I nod, hold her gaze for another second, and then head out the door to wait for Alex.

# chapter thirty-six

## *alex*

NICO JOGS UP THE stairs ahead of me, his right hand on the railing and the other holding his cell phone. "I have the resumé I wrote when I applied for the job at the library. It's in my email," he says. "We could use that and update it?"

I nod. "Yeah, good plan."

He reaches the top step and pauses to wait for me, and my heart skips a beat when my eyes meet his. He's happy. He's smiling and happy, and for the first time in a very long time, he looks hopeful. It's beautiful.

"I talked with Caitlin and Sharon today. They both said I could list them as references if I need it. I knew Caitlin would agree, but I was surprised Sharon said yes. I mean, I've only been there a couple of weeks, so they don't really know me that well. But they both said I'm doing a great job with the project and the other work they have me doing. Hopefully that helps if Vera contacts them."

He's talkative, too, which is new for him. He stuffs his phone into his pocket and takes my hand as I reach the top step. Our fingers intertwine, and he tugs me along with him on the way to the bedroom as he continues to go on about all the things, including the new information my mom gave him at dinner.

"So do you know exactly how far San Jose is from Palo Alto?

If I get this job, should I look for an apartment there or closer to Stanford? It's probably more expensive near Stanford, right?"

I laugh and shake my head. "Bro, I have no idea. But we can check it out, maybe after you send the email, yeah?"

He lets go of my hand and pushes the bedroom door open ahead of us. "You're right, yeah. Resumé and send the email, and then we can—" He stops rather abruptly right at my desk and turns to me. I half expect to see him shutting down, like he remembered how hard this is all going to be and that the interview he *might* have, if the woman my mom knows likes Nico's resumé enough, is just the very first step in a long, challenging process. But the light in his eyes hasn't disappeared. In fact, it's gotten brighter. Mischievous, even.

I smile crookedly at him. "We can what?"

"Nothin'," he says with a smirk. He stretches up and kisses me quickly on the lips. "I can use your laptop, right?"

He's already slipping into the chair at my desk and opening the laptop before I manage to mumble a quick "yeah" in response. My computer boots up quickly, and within just a couple of minutes, he's sifted through his emails, downloaded his old resumé, and opened it up to edit it. We work together to add his high school graduation date, recent work experience, and references. Then he tabs back to his email and pulls out his cell phone.

"Vera Kotovskaya, Bay Area Arts Collective," he reads from the text my mom sent him. He sets the phone next to him on the desk and carefully types out Vera's email address on the computer. Then he freezes, his fingers hovering just above the keyboard. "I should be formal, right? Start with something like 'Dear Ms. Kotovskaya'?"

"Yeah, I think so. I've sent a few emails for my mom, and she's always told me to write formally like that," I say.

Nico laughs and tilts his head back to look at me. "She had

to tell you that so you'd actually take the time to use complete sentences and type out full words."

"She did not."

He rolls his eyes and laughs again. "Whatever you need to tell yourself." Then he shifts his focus back to the computer. "Alright, so . . . Dear Ms. Kotovskaya . . ."

He types; I watch. He thought he was going to need my help, but by the time he's at the end of the short email introducing himself and asking to connect with her for a phone interview, the only things I contributed were to suggest rewording part of one sentence and to remind him to attach the resumé.

He pauses after he writes his name and new phone number at the bottom of the email, then he looks up at me. "Good to send?"

Hope and love threaten to burst right out of my chest, and for a second, I can't respond.

This is it.

This is real.

This is him, overcoming everything he's been through and taking this impossible leap, to be with me.

He arches his eyebrows. "Yo, Alex? It's good, right?"

I nod, and he grins, turns back to the computer, and clicks send.

"How long do you think until she gets back to me?" he asks, swiveling in the chair to face me. He scoots a little closer and spreads his legs until I'm standing right between his knees. Then he leans forward and rests his head on my stomach.

I let my fingers run through his hair as I think about the answer. My mom called Vera a few hours ago—early afternoon here, but late morning in California—and I remember very casually eavesdropping on the half of the conversation I could hear through the open door to the garage. They talked for a while, and not everything was about Nico. In fact, they talked at length about some art exhibition Vera is planning for next year. The conversation wasn't hurried or rushed in any way, which could mean she wasn't busy. Or any other number of things.

"Maybe not long? Or hopefully not, anyway. I really don't know, though." I trail my fingers down his neck, and Nico hums contentedly, which makes me smile.

"Thanks for helping me," he says, turning to kiss my stomach. He tilts his head up to look at me, a soft expression in his eyes.

A million little moments flutter around me, reminding me of all the times I've wished to see him look like this—comfortable, happy, hopeful, content. It's overwhelming again, and my heart feels so full.

Carefully, I bring my hand up to touch his cheek, my fingertips grazing his skin. He smiles.

"I'm so proud of you," I say softly. My hand cups his cheek, and I get lost in his beautiful eyes—lost in possibility and hope and joy, because that's what I see in them now. I lean down and tilt his chin up, and I kiss him with a slow tenderness. A promise.

And when I pull back and straighten up, he's still smiling, blissful and gorgeous. My thumb traces his cheekbone as his eyes open partway, and I'm struck with that feeling again—how incredible it is to see him like this.

"I love you, Nico," I murmur. There's a slight roughness to my voice as I say the words out loud for the first time. They're true. I've known them to be true for a while now. But that doesn't stop my chest from tightening and my heart from leaping up into my throat.

I stroke his cheek gently and watch his eyes grow wide and his mouth open. His lower lip trembles, and then he stands, one hand coming to rest on my hip, the other settling right in the middle of my chest.

"You mean that?" he asks quietly.

I lower my forehead to rest against his and whisper, "With all of my heart."

He leans into me, his hand pressing into my chest. "I love you, too," he says on a breath, and then his lips are on mine, his kiss passionate, tender, and needy all at once.

I wrap my arms low around his waist and hold him tightly as I kiss him back. Something inside me is bursting with joy, and suddenly I'm laughing as we kiss. I bring both of my hands up to his cheeks, pull back just enough to see his gorgeous eyes and his smile, and then I kiss him again.

"I love you," I repeat between kisses, and he breaks away and drops his chin, shaking his head. His cheeks are wet with tears, and he blinks and reaches up with his right hand to wipe the tears away.

"It almost doesn't feel real," he admits, though he quickly corrects himself. "I mean, it's just . . . it's hard for me to believe that you could . . . love me."

I shake my head. "I do. It's real. This"—my hand finds his, and I bring it up to my lips and kiss the back of his knuckles—"is real. I promise."

He sniffles and lowers his eyes, then he slips his arms around my waist and rests his head on my chest. He's quiet for a few minutes as we stand there, holding each other. Then, he presses his cheek against me and breathes in deeply. "You make me feel good . . . and loved." His arms tighten around me. "You always have."

He smiles into me, and it's the best feeling. I straighten slightly, bring one hand up to his chin, and tilt it back so he's looking up at me. Then I lean down and touch my lips to his in another gentle kiss.

I'm about to say something more, to tell him I always want to make him feel that way, when his phone chimes from where it sits on the desk next to my computer. He pulls back, grinning, and kisses me again before turning to grab his phone. His shoulders tense almost immediately.

"What is it?"

"She emailed me back already," he says, all of the blissfulness gone from his tone. "That was too fast. That can't be good. Can it?"

He hasn't clicked on the email notification yet, and he closes his eyes and shoves the phone at me.

"What? You want me to read it?"

He nods. "Please. I can't."

"Okay, yeah, sure. Um . . ." I take the phone from him and click the notification. And I quickly skim the message, a smile working its way onto my face. I clear my throat. "'Nico, thank you for your email,'" I read, letting my free hand find his lower back. "'After speaking with Laina earlier and reviewing your resumé now, I'm hoping we can set up a time for a phone interview, preferably this week. Will Friday afternoon at six your time work? Sincerely, Ms. Vera Kotovskaya.'"

"It doesn't really say that," he blurts out, but at the same time, he grabs the phone from me, his eyes immediately scanning the email. "She . . . she really wants a phone interview? I—I can't . . . I can't believe it."

He shakes his head as he looks up at me, and I just smile back.

"Believe it," I say gently. I motion to the desk. "Write her back. Six on Friday—that works, yeah?"

He nods, and then he swallows hard, like he's still having trouble processing. I lean over and open the laptop back up.

"Write back to her."

"Oh, yeah. Right. Right." He turns slowly, but then stops and spins back around to face me, his eyes now lit up. "She wants an interview!"

"Yes."

"With me!"

"Yes." I'm laughing at him now, and he's grinning, too—his

eyes filled with excitement and a sort of cautious hope.

He swats at me and rolls his eyes, then he sits down and composes a very short response confirming that yes, he's available for an interview on Friday at six. When he's done, he swivels the chair back to me and reaches out to take my hand again, threading his fingers through mine. His cheeks flush the most perfect pink, and he tugs me gently back to him.

"I wasn't expecting that," he admits.

I shake my head. I'm not really sure what I was expecting, but this is about the best outcome either of us could have hoped for.

He stares at our hands for a few seconds, then lifts my hand to his lips and kisses it lightly, like I had with his hand earlier. When he glances back up at me, my chest aches. He's so beautiful. Beautiful and happy. And mine.

I squeeze his hand. "So . . . what do you want to do now? We've got the whole evening," I say.

His eyes flash playfully. "I have a couple ideas."

He stands up, releasing my hand and hooking his fingers under the waistband of my shorts. He tugs me closer to him so our hips meet, and his hand sneaks up under my shirt.

I suck in a breath. "I'm listening."

The corner of his mouth quirks up in a crooked grin, and he turns us around, his fingers still hooked into my shorts, and starts backing toward the bedroom door, stopping to glance out into the hallway as though to check that we're alone. He knows as well as I do that my mom's working in the garage, but he's adorable and silly, and I go along with it.

He faces me again, still grinning, and his hands slip around to my back and then lower, until he's cupping my ass, squeezing, pressing his groin into mine. He's already hard—I can feel the bulge of his erection through his slacks. I close my eyes and groan.

"Nico . . ."

"We should celebrate, right?"

"Mm-hmm. Yeah. Definitely," I mumble, letting my fingers inch under his shirt.

He stretches up and kisses just under my ear, and when I moan, he huffs a quiet laugh. His voice rough, he whispers, "Follow me."

And he takes my hand and leads me toward the bathroom.

# chapter thirty-seven

## nico

"THANKS FOR COMING." I lean against Alex's shoulder and close my eyes, ignoring the rest of my half-eaten lunch sitting on the other side of me. He carefully slips his arm up and around my shoulders, resting it on the back of the bench.

"I hope you're feeling better now?"

"Mm-hmm."

I can tell he wants to kiss me by the way he settles his cheek against the top of my head and the way he takes a long, slow breath in. But he holds back, as he's been doing since he arrived. The little courtyard at the library isn't exactly crowded—the students in the summer group finished their lunches and headed back inside maybe about ten minutes ago—but there are several others sitting on the grass reading books, including a couple of families with small children.

It's quiet and peaceful. And that, along with Alex being here, has really helped curb the anxiety I've been feeling all morning.

It's Friday.

The week passed quicker than I expected, and my interview with Vera is only a few short hours away. I *know* I can't afford to mess it up. I need to be everything Alex and his mom have been assuring me I am, and somehow, I need to convince Vera of that as well. And that's fucking terrifying, really. I've been going back and forth between hopeful excitement and an anxious near-panic most of the day, which is why I'm glad Alex was able to come meet me for lunch.

We sit there in silence for a few more minutes, and it's comfortable and relaxing. My lunch hour is probably almost up, although I don't want to move to check my phone. So I shrug my shoulder a bit into Alex.

"What time is it?"

He mock-grumbles and reaches into his pocket to pull out his phone. "Twelve fifty-five."

"Ugh."

With a quiet laugh, he straightens up, and I sigh and copy him. His hand finds my thigh, and he lets his fingers linger there for a moment before he gives me a light squeeze. "Walk with me out to the truck?" He leans in closer and adds, "So we can say goodbye properly."

I nearly groan, remembering how we "said goodbye" this morning when he dropped me off—his tongue exploring my mouth as his hand slid up my thigh, his fingertips stretching out to barely brush against the base of my semi-hard cock. Completely inappropriate. I fucking loved it.

"You can't touch me like that again," I whisper back hoarsely. "Not when I've gotta work and—"

"*There* you are, you little shit."

I barely have time to register the pure hatred in the voice or the dank, rotten waft of alcohol before a hand grabs my shoulder and wrenches me away from Alex, slamming me back into the bench. A sharp pain lances through my arm and shoulder, and my heart slams to a stop. I can't breathe. I try to scream in pain, but no sound comes out.

Patrick stands there, leaning over me, one hand still on my bad shoulder, pushing me back harder into the bench. His other hand is balled into a fist, lifting up from his side with clear intention. His eyes look wild and angry. Violent. Rageful.

Holy fuck, I'm going to die.

Next to me, Alex jumps to his feet, yelling something. I can't understand the words. And Patrick, too, he's screaming at me—but all I get are bits and pieces. Something about it being all my fault. Him getting fired. My mom kicking him out. I can't hear it all, not with how hard my heart is hammering in my chest and with the pain slicing through my shoulder.

Alex tries to put himself between me and Patrick, but Patrick is larger than both of us. He easily shoves Alex out of the way with some nasty curse and lifts his fist again.

*Holy fuck. Holy fuck. Holy fuck.*

I try to move—to struggle or something—but my body won't respond. And the pain as he puts more of his weight into my shoulder is nearly unbearable.

Caitlin is running over to us, yelling something, her phone in her hand. Our eyes meet, and she looks as terrified as I feel.

"Call 9-1-1!" Alex shouts, and he tries again, stepping in between me and Patrick. "Get away from him, you asshole! Someone help!"

Alex turns to shield me, then grabs my free arm and starts pulling me away. At the same time, someone else grabs Patrick. Or maybe it's more than one person, I'm not sure. Sharon's suddenly there, too, standing between me and Patrick, telling him to back the fuck off, and Caitlin's talking on the phone, her voice frantic and loud.

It's chaotic and terrifying, and I'm trembling and lightheaded, clinging to Alex so I don't collapse. Patrick shrugs off the men who pulled him away from me. He yells another couple of curses, spits on the ground, and then turns and storms off around the side entrance to the courtyard, his fists still clenched.

I can't breathe. The air is too thick and hot, and my chest is too tight. Pain rips through my shoulder and arm as my trembling turns into full-blown shaking.

Alex's hand rubs along my lower back. "God, Nico, are you okay?" he asks, hugging me to him.

I don't get to answer before Caitlin pipes in. "The police are on the way. Sharon, I've gotta—"

"Get back inside with the children," Sharon cuts in. "Actually, everyone. Let's all get inside and lock the doors until the police get here."

They keep talking around me as Alex guides me inside, Sharon staying right next to us the whole time. She directs the other library patrons to stay and wait for the police and then tells Alex to help me to the back office where I've been working. It's quiet there, she says. That'll be best.

A moment later, Alex kneels in front of me as I slump into one of the chairs in the office. His hands hold mine, and he's talking again, asking me if I'm okay. I lean forward, trying to catch my breath, but my chest hurts and my shoulder throbs, and no matter how slowly I breathe, I can't seem to fill my lungs.

"I . . . can't . . . breathe . . ." I force out, and I'm suddenly dizzy and lightheaded. I start to fall forward, unable to hold myself up. He catches me with a hand on my chest.

"I've got you, I've got you. You're okay. Breathe with me, okay? Breathe in . . . there you go, and out . . . Good. Again. In . . . and out . . ."

He talks me through each breath for what seems like several long minutes, until I'm finally feeling a bit more steady, like I'm not actually going to pass out.

"Thank you," I say. My voice is still shaking, even though my heart is beating at much closer to normal speed. "Thank you. God,

I-I thought I was going to die. Th-that was . . ."

"It was awful. And scary," Alex finishes for me when my words fail. I nod and lift my eyes to meet his, fighting against nausea and a growing headache. His expression is tight with concern. "*Are* you okay?"

"I-I . . . don't know." I drop my eyes to where our hands are clasped together in my lap. "I mean . . . my shoulder's pretty fucked up."

Alex's frown deepens, and he lets go of my left hand and grazes his fingers lightly up my forearm, stopping below my elbow. "I'm so sorry. I—"

"No," I cut in, shaking my head. "Don't." I bite my lower lip and hold Alex's gaze. His whole expression softens, and he's about to say something when there's a light knock on the door.

"Nico, the police are here." I recognize Caitlin's voice, and I try to look up at her, which is a bad idea. The room seems to tilt sideways, and I groan and close my eyes. Alex's hand finds my chest again, steadying me. "Is he okay?" Caitlin asks quietly.

"He was having trouble breathing, and his shoulder isn't . . . good," Alex answers from where he still kneels in front of me.

Two sets of heavy footsteps enter the room, and even though I know I'm safe and Patrick's not here, I can't stop the tension from growing in my shoulders as I screw my eyes shut tighter and curl in on myself.

"Alex—" My voice comes out as a rough whisper, like I really didn't have the air in my lungs for even the one pitiful word. I grab his hand with my good one, the sudden movement sending a fresh jolt of pain through my arm and into my chest.

"I'm here, Nico. I'm here. You're okay. You're safe." He gives my hand a gentle squeeze, and when I manage to open my eyes partway, I see him, his soft smile as reassuring as it always is. He nods slightly, squeezes my hand again, and then turns to address whoever's standing in the doorway. "He's got severe social anxiety, and he was just attacked," Alex explains. "Please just, um, move slowly when you come in."

"Of course. Alex, right? And Nico?" The woman's voice sounds familiar, but I can't remember where I've heard it before.

"Yes, ma'am," Alex answers.

"I'm Officer Morris, and my partner here is Officer Pulman. Can either of you tell us what happened?"

I know there's no way I can talk about it right now, so I'm relieved when Alex nods.

"Yeah, sure, um . . ." He holds my hands tighter as he explains to the police officers everything that just happened. He's thorough, and he goes into much more detail than I'd have been able to. Apparently, Patrick *was* screaming at me that he lost his job and that my mom kicked him out and that I was the reason for both. He said more than that, too, words Alex has a hard time repeating. "He said, um, he said he should have 'beaten the shit out of Nico when he had the chance.'" Alex pauses. "And he . . . he looked like he meant it."

Officer Morris nods and turns to her partner. "It's consistent with Anderson's statement last night." She turns back to us.

My head's pounding now, and my shoulder throbs, but I manage to look up at her and listen as she explains how one of Patrick's coworkers came in to the police station the night before and filed a report alleging that Patrick had been bragging while on the job about "scaring the shit out of his ex's son" and "wanting to do a fuck of a lot more than just scare him." The report was serious enough that the police followed up on it this morning. They went out to the construction site where Patrick worked and questioned him and his other coworkers.

"It wasn't pretty," Officer Morris admits. "His boss was pissed and let Patrick go on the spot."

It's so much to take in. I almost can't breathe again. I grip Alex's hands tighter and take several short, shallow breaths, and he lets his thumbs rub soothingly back and forth along my knuckles.

One of the officers steps closer. "Nico, I know this is difficult, but I need you to answer a few questions, too, just so we can be sure to have the whole story. Okay?"

I look up, and I finally remember where I recognize her voice from. She was one of the officers who responded to the 9-1-1 call my mom made four years ago, when that asshole broke my nose. I close my eyes again as the discomfort in my chest grows.

"Y-yeah, okay," I mumble, and I lean forward to be closer to Alex, ignoring the pain radiating from my shoulder.

"Something happened earlier this week?" the officer asks.

I suck in a sharp breath and nod. "Yes. Um, well, last week actually. L-last Friday."

"Tell me what happened, Nico."

# chapter thirty-eight

*alex*

"So, MY TENTATIVE DIAGNOSIS is a torn rotator cuff. Based on my exam, I'm suspecting it's only a partial tear, but we'll write you up a referral for an MRI—that'll tell us for sure whether it's a full or partial tear, and you can follow up with your PCP for a treatment plan from there. Until then, ice, ibuprofen, and rest. Alright, Nico?"

I watch as Nico nods stiffly at the physician's assistant standing in front of him, his jaw clenched tight. There's an older male nurse on Nico's left side, carefully adjusting the sling they fitted to him to keep his left arm supported and less mobile.

They've been friendly and helpful here at the urgent care clinic, where we came to have Nico's shoulder injury assessed. But that hasn't done much to mitigate Nico's anxiety. After everything that happened today, I don't blame him. All that shit at the library was more than terrifying—seeing the pure rage and hatred in Patrick's eyes, knowing it was directed at Nico, panicking myself as I tried to protect him, to put myself between him and that monster. Then the aftermath—talking to the police and Nico's colleagues at the library, filing a report with the police to document what happened, explaining to the medical team how his shoulder was injured. I did what I could to help, but I feel like I've been drowning right along with Nico, watching him struggle all afternoon.

And now, I wish I could be right there next to him, holding his
hand to keep him calm. The exam room is too small, however, and
I had to move away a few minutes ago to let the PA and nurse do
their jobs. I shift uneasily on my feet as the nurse finishes what he
was doing, says a few words to the PA, and gathers up the box the
arm sling came in and leaves. Then I quickly slip back into my spot
next to Nico and take his hand with a gentle squeeze.

"Almost done," I say softly, and he lets out a shuddering breath
and leans against me.

The PA tucks his tablet under his arm. "Take your time in here,
no rush. The paperwork and MRI referral will be at the front," he
says. Then he leaves the room as well, and it's just the two of us
again.

I turn and press a light kiss to Nico's temple. "Ready to go?" I
ask softly, and Nico nods without a word.

I slip my arm around his waist to help him stand, and together,
we head out of the exam room and down the hallway to the waiting
room. He's not super steady on his feet, but we make it through
the set of double doors into the waiting room. My mom is sitting
in one of the chairs close to the entrance, and she sees us almost
immediately and stands up to meet us at the reception desk.

Nico stiffens as my mom pulls out her credit card and hands it
to the receptionist to pay the bill. She glances at him with a kind
smile and reaches over to set her hand softly on his upper arm.

"Don't you even worry about it, sweetie. Okay?" she says.

I tighten my arm around him as I feel him tense up even more,
but he nods and says a feeble "Thank you, Ms. Hayes" in return.

My mom smiles again and then turns back to the receptionist,
who hands her several papers.

"The top page there is the receipt," the receptionist explains.
"Under that, there's the referral for the MRI and then a list of

imaging clinics. Unfortunately, you'll have to go to Omaha or Lincoln since we don't have one here in Redland, but they're usually able to get patients in within a couple of days."

My mom nods and then asks a few more questions as she looks over the papers. Next to me, Nico shrinks a little as the subject of cost comes up, and I hear him inhale a short breath when the receptionist mentions the MRI is "usually only three or four hundred dollars" if paying out of pocket. My mom nods again as though that's a good deal—and maybe it is, I have no frame of reference for these things—then hands me the papers to hold onto.

After my mom thanks the receptionist, we turn and head toward the exit. Nico's still quiet, but he seems to be walking steadier, and so I let my arm drop from around his waist and slip my hand into his instead as we make our way through the parking lot.

"We're still planning to stop at the police station on the way home, is that right?" my mom asks just before we reach her truck.

"Um . . ." Nico's hand grips mine, and I give him a gentle squeeze. "We—we should, right?" He can't seem to look at me or my mom, and I start to answer, but he cuts in. "But I can't be late for my interview. Do we have time? What time is it?"

Slightly ahead of us, my mom pulls out her phone, and her expression softens as she glances back at us. "We've got plenty of time. It's just after four thirty," she reassures, adding, "But also, sweetie, if you need to reschedule, I'm sure Vera will understand."

He immediately shakes his head as though rescheduling isn't even an option. "No, I don't want to do that."

"I understand, sweetie. And don't worry, we have plenty of time," my mom repeats, slipping her phone back into her pocket.

Nico gives another nod, though it's rushed and I can feel him swaying again. I move a little closer and wrap my arm back around his waist for more support, and together, we walk the rest of the way to the truck. I help him into the back seat, fasten his seat belt for him since the sling makes everything difficult and awkward, and then I settle into the middle seat to be close to him. He leans on me and closes his eyes as the truck starts moving.

I'm not entirely sure what's running through his head right now—whether he's in a daze or whether he's forcing himself to relive the last few hours, the terrifying moments at the library and after, all the heaviness and anxiety and stress. I am sure, however, that today has only shown how strong and resilient he really is, even if he can't see that yet.

Gently, so as not to hurt him, I lift my arm up around his shoulders and hug him to me, and I let my cheek rest on the top of his head.

My mom drives more carefully than usual, taking all the turns slowly, braking more gradually. Still, we're at the police station within about ten minutes. The next half hour or so after that is a blur. We head inside, drop off a copy of Nico's discharge papers to go with the report we filed earlier, and talk with Officer Morris for a few minutes. She gives us an update that sends Nico into another mini spiral—clinging tightly to me as he struggles to breathe again. Apparently, Patrick was arrested at a local bar and taken into custody about an hour ago, while we were still waiting at the urgent care center. He's being charged with assault and disorderly conduct, both based on the events of today at the library and on Nico's report of what happened last Friday at his mom's house. Officer Morris asks Nico a few more questions, which he somehow manages to answer more bravely than I think I'd ever be able to in his situation. Then we're back in the truck and on our way home, him leaning into me again, his eyes screwed shut as he takes shallow breaths.

My mom's eyes meet mine in the rearview mirror, and I give her a tight smile and then close my eyes and settle my cheek on the top of Nico's head.

"I know that wasn't easy. I'm so proud of you," I whisper to him. "I love you."

"I love you, too," he says on a breath, his voice clouded with shame and guilt and embarrassment. He makes a small sound and buries his head in the crook of my shoulder, and his good hand presses into my thigh for a few seconds, as though maybe whatever's running through his mind isn't all that great.

I wish I knew exactly what to say to take away all his pain and give him all the confidence he deserves to have. But if I've learned anything at all in the last few weeks, it's that I can still give him what he needs, even if I can't find the right words. I just have to be here for him.

So I squeeze his shoulders again, carefully, and then I kiss the top of his head and start talking quietly. I give him every reassurance I can think of to uplift him. I even dramatically pull out my phone to check the time and remind him how exceedingly *punctual* he is and that he'll be very on time for his interview. That earns me a snicker and a shake of his head and some mumbled "pfft, whatever."

And he sort of relaxes with a long sigh.

"You're going to do great," I murmur after he settles against me again.

I almost feel him smile, and then he nods like maybe he's at least trying to believe me.

The rest of the ride home is a more comfortable kind of quiet, and we pull up into the driveway at about five thirty, still plenty on time. My mom offers him a small snack to try to calm his nerves, but he refuses, saying he'll eat afterward. Instead, he and I head up to my room, and we just talk for a few minutes. Well, I talk; he leans against me as we sit together in my bed.

I talk about nothing consequential, really. He doesn't need that right now. All he really needs is to relax and breathe and maybe, hopefully, laugh a little. So I start telling him about this theory I read in a blog the other day—some weird concept about the relativity and reversibility of time. When I reach over to the nightstand to dig a piece of paper out of the drawer so I can explain to him exactly what I mean, I do get a laugh out of him, and he grabs my arm and pulls me back, shaking his head and telling me that's not necessary.

At five minutes to six, he sits up and scoots to the edge of the bed. Then he closes his eyes and takes several long breaths. When he turns to me, his eyes are uncertain but also not, and he smiles a little.

"Thank you for distracting me," he says, and he leans in and kisses me. It's a short, sweet kiss, but there's some hope in it too. He pulls back and then gives me a weak shove. "Now get out of here so I can do this thing."

I sit there staring at him for a few seconds, then I nod, steal another quick kiss, and hop to my feet. "You're ready, and you're going to be great," I say as he stands up next to me.

He swallows and nods, and I give him a light hug before disappearing out of the bedroom, shutting the door behind me.

My mom's in the kitchen downstairs, chopping veggies to add to a large pot on the stove, and she looks up at me when I pause at the bottom of the stairs. It's only when her eyes meet mine that I realize how much tension I'm carrying in my shoulders and how tired my brain feels—like I just took three AP exams in a row after staying up all night cramming. And as usual, my mom seems to know. She smiles gently at me and motions me over.

"I'm making taco soup. Come help? The meat's already cooking. I just need these cans opened while I finish the veggies."

I manage a nod, and when I finally get my feet to move a few seconds later, that exhaustion seems to have traveled all the way down into my limbs. I shake it off and join my mom on the other side of the island. She pushes a can opener toward me, then resumes chopping a bell pepper as I start silently in on the cans of beans, corn, and crushed tomatoes sitting on the counter.

After everything's added to the pot, along with a bunch of seasonings and some beef broth, my mom quickly washes her hands and then steps up to me and wraps me up in a huge, warm hug. My body trembles, and I find myself hugging her back, clinging tightly to her as the whole afternoon's events weigh me down.

"Shh, shh, sweetie," she says softly, and I shake my head into her. I'm not even sure what's so suddenly wrong, but it's all overwhelming and all too much.

"Mom . . ." My voice breaks, and then it all comes tumbling out, rushed and on a single breath. "God, Mom, it—it was so scary. He showed up out of nowhere and he was going to hit Nico and I-I tried to stop him but he was too strong and there was nothing I could do about it. I was so scared. I was so scared."

For once, it seems like my mom doesn't know what to say. She lets out a sharp breath and just hugs me to her tighter. "I'm so sorry, sweetie. I'm so sorry."

We stand there together for a few minutes, until finally, she pulls back. Her hands reach up to frame my face, and she wipes away the tears on my cheeks. Then she shakes her head.

"You were so strong all afternoon for Nico," she says.

I nod and step back so I can wipe my eyes. "I had to be. He needed me to be. But I . . . I . . ."

"He's okay, and you're okay," she reassures me when I can't find the words. "And whatever you did, it was the right thing, because Patrick is going to be heading back to prison, I'm sure of it. I'm sure of it, sweetie."

She's right, like she usually is. Nico is okay. His shoulder's injured, but it will heal with time. The rest of him will heal, too. He's got so much courage and strength, and now I know he sees all the love and support he has as well—both from me and from all the people who care about him.

He will. He'll be okay.

I'm too tired to say anything more, but I nod again, and my mom pulls me back in for another long hug.

# chapter thirty-nine

## *nico*

"WELL, THEN, I THINK that's it for now, unless you have any more questions for me?"

My heart's thrumming in my chest. I'm not sure it's stopped for the whole hour-long interview. I clear my throat. "No, nothing else, I think," I say. I already asked Vera the questions I had prepared earlier, although she was so thorough during the interview that I almost didn't even need to.

"Okay, then," she says. "It was great to talk with you, Nico. I just have a few things to think about, and I'll be in touch, probably within a few days."

That sounds oddly promising.

I close my eyes and try to hold back my smile. "I really appreciate you giving me the opportunity to speak with you."

"It was my pleasure," Vera says, and I swear I can hear a smile in her voice. "Have a good rest of your evening."

"Thank you. You, too." My hand tightens on my phone, and I hold my breath, waiting through the silence until the phone beeps to indicate the end of the call. Then I hit the power button to black out the screen and exhale sharply.

It's fucking over. Finally. And it went well. In fact, I think it went really, really well.

I close my eyes and breathe in and out slowly. Then I slip my phone into my pocket and stand. I don't sway on my feet, like I did earlier, and while I'm a little stiff, I don't feel shaky or weak. Even my shoulder feels okay, although that might just be the large dose of ibuprofen Alex's mom gave me after we left the urgent care center. I am exhausted, though, and for a second, I contemplate just collapsing into bed.

But then I hear a familiar laugh from downstairs, and feelings of warmth and love and acceptance fill me. Shifting my left arm to rest better in the sling, which I'm quickly learning to despise, I open Alex's bedroom door and then head for the stairs, needing to see him.

When I reach the bottom step, he's there, like he heard me coming, and he must be able to see it on my face—that the interview went well—because he grins brightly and immediately wraps both of his arms around my waist, pulling me to him. I think he's going to kiss me, but instead, he just dips his forehead down to rest against mine.

"It went well?" he asks.

"Yeah, I think so."

He smiles even wider and straightens up enough to place a light kiss on my forehead. My stomach swoops with the most wonderful warmth, and I close my eyes and let myself lean into him.

"Mom just took the cornbread out of the oven, and the soup's ready, if you're hungry."

I just hum a nonresponse and bury my head into his chest. He laughs quietly, kisses the top of my head, and then backs up a step so he can see me. He seems to study my face as though looking for something, and I guess he finds it, because he smiles again and then bends down and kisses my lips as his hand slips into mine.

"Come on," he says, squeezing my hand gently.

With a deep breath, I nod, and we start across the room toward the kitchen. Ahead of us, his mom is setting a small glass casserole dish on top of a pot holder on the table. Her eyes meet mine, and she smiles softly.

"Dinner's ready." She straightens up and takes off her oven mitts, pausing to look from me to Alex and back again. Then her eyes seem to get a little misty, and she shakes her head. "You two are adorable together, you know that?"

My cheeks heat up, and I drop my eyes to the floor.

Next to me, Alex coughs roughly. "Mom!"

"What? It's true," she argues, her grin turning teasing. "And anyway, I'm allowed to say that."

"Are you, now?"

"Yes, I am," she declares without any other explanation. "Now sit and eat before dinner gets cold."

Alex sighs. "That huge pot of soup will be scalding hot for at least another half hour, even if we don't touch it, Mom."

"Nonsense."

I let go of Alex's hand to muffle a laugh, and Alex groans and shakes his head. It all feels something close to normal—watching the two of them joke like this—and it helps. Alex steps ahead of me and pulls out my chair, and this time, it's his cheeks that are red when our eyes meet.

"Oh, see, she's right. You *are* adorable," I tease with a smirk. His cheeks redden even more, and from the other side of the table, his mom snorts a laugh. He flashes her a look, but she just laughs again, and when he glances back at me, there's amusement in his eyes. I shake my head, then stretch up and kiss his lips before slipping into my seat.

Dinner is amazing. I didn't think I was hungry, but the taco soup and cornbread are the perfect meal. I'm too tired to talk much, but they both seem to understand, and beyond a few brief questions about how the interview went, they don't push me. The conversation steers to other things instead, like the new painting Alex's mom is working on and some details about housing stuff Alex received in an email from Stanford this morning.

When we're all finished eating, Alex's mom stands up and starts to gather her dishes. Alex moves to join her, but she shakes her head.

"I've got it tonight," she says. "The two of you go relax. It's been quite a day, and I'm sure you're both tired."

Alex seems poised to argue, but I reach over and set my hand on his thigh to stop him. He glances at me, and I smile weakly and tilt my head toward the stairs, hoping he'll understand. I'm exhausted, and I need him tonight.

He hesitates only another second and then covers my hand with his and nods. "Okay, yeah. Thanks, Mom."

Together, we both stand up, and his hand finds my back as we start toward the stairs. I'm more tired with each step, and by the time we reach his bedroom, I'm ready to collapse.

Wordlessly, he guides me over to the bed, helps me sit, and then starts undressing me, every touch soft and tender. He kneels down in front of me and takes off my shoes and socks first. Then he unfastens and removes the sling, being extra careful not to hurt my shoulder. Still gentle and slow, he slips off my slacks and my polo shirt, and then he helps me lie down and get under the covers. He lingers there with me for a second before getting up to turn out the light and undress himself. By the time he joins me a few moments later, immediately scooting in behind me and gathering me up in his arms, I'm feeling more loved than maybe I ever have.

"Thank you," I murmur, snuggling back into him. And I hope he knows I mean I'm thankful for more than just what he's done for me over the last few minutes.

He hums in response, though he doesn't say anything right away. After a moment, his hand slides up to rest on the middle of my chest, and he lets out a short breath as he holds me a little tighter.

"I was scared today," he says quietly.

I don't have to ask him what he means. I already know.

I was scared too.

I tilt my head toward him, and his lips find mine in the darkness. He kisses me with that same softness and tenderness he showed while undressing me. There's an honesty and vulnerability to it that I'm not used to.

When we part, he trails his lips along my jawline, his warm breath on my skin, and then he settles back behind me again, his hand pressing gently into my chest to hold me to him.

"I'm also beyond proud of you," he whispers. "Whatever happens with the job, I'm proud of you. I hope you know that."

Warmth washes over me again, and I close my eyes and nod. "I'm actually . . . a little proud of myself too," I admit slowly. The words feel weird to say, but they're true. I bring my hand up to cover his on my chest. "And I'm also hopeful. I-I think . . . I think even with everything that happened today, I feel loved. And close to you. And that . . . that gives me strength. And hope."

He seems to smile into me, and then he kisses my hair. "God, I love that," he says, holding me to him tighter. "And I love you, Nico."

"I love you too."

We're quiet then. He just keeps holding me, occasionally letting his lips graze my neck, and I let myself relax into him, comfortable and warm. Not too long after, I drift off into sleep, feeling loved and safe in his arms.

# chapter forty

## alex

"PLEASE, PLEASE, *PLEASE* CALL me when you land. Oh, and don't forget sunscreen if you spend too much time outside. And water! Don't forget to drink enough water, too, okay? It's easy to forget when you're traveling. Nico, I put Alex's EpiPen in the outer pocket of his carry-on. You know how to administer it, right? Please be careful about what you eat. Oh gosh, I'm going to miss both of you so much."

My mom hastily wipes a tear from her cheek, and I shake my head, laughing.

"We're only going to be gone for a couple days, Mom."

"I know, I know, but I'm still going to miss you," she says, and then she quickly pulls me in for a hug, squeezing me tight for several long seconds before she lets me go. She turns to Nico, who's standing stiffly next to me, his backpack hanging from his good shoulder and his left arm still in the sling he got from the nurse at the urgent care clinic three weeks ago.

I can see him hesitate, but then he drops his chin and steps forward into her embrace. His eyes close, and his shoulders relax a little. And my heart stutters.

"You're going to do great, I know it," I hear my mom whisper to him, and he sucks in a breath and nods against her. My mom's holding back more tears when they part, and she smiles gently at him, one hand still on his upper arm. "Vera's a very nice woman, and she wouldn't have invited you for an in-person interview if she wasn't serious about you as a candidate for the position. Just remember that, okay?"

Nico nods again, more decisively this time, and then he steps back closer to me. I reach up and set my hand on his back.

My mom just stares at us for another few seconds, blinking away tears as she smiles.

I tilt my head toward the security line. "We should go."

She nods. "Yeah, yeah. Call me. Please?"

"I will, Mom," I assure her. I shoulder my duffle bag and give her a smile. "Love you."

"I love you, too. *Both* of you," she says, and then she purses her lips and wipes another tear from her cheek as Nico and I turn and start walking toward the short security line.

It's not busy for a Friday evening. Not that I have much experience at busy airports, or even airports in general, but there are only a couple of people in line ahead of us, and within just a few minutes, we're through the TSA check, slipping our feet back into our shoes on the other side of the scanners. I look up and find my mom again, and I give her a wave. She blows me a kiss and forms a heart with her hands, and I grin and send her a heart back.

Then I turn to Nico, who's just finished stuffing his boarding pass and wallet back into his pocket.

"Ready?" I ask.

"If I say no, will we have time to catch your mom before she leaves?" He lifts his eyes, and I can tell he's only half joking. "Also, I hate this stupid sling. *Why* are you making me wear it again?"

I shake my head and laugh, but he gives me a scathing look. He's getting anxious, which I really don't blame him for. He's never been to an airport, or on an airplane, or to California, or on an all-expenses-paid trip funded by a potential employer. And even if it's not busy by my standards as an inexperienced airport-goer, it's a lot for him just to be here.

I reach my hand out to him, and he frowns but takes it, our fingers intertwining. I bring his hand up to my lips and kiss his knuckles. "No, we won't have time to catch my mom, I'm sure she's already out at her truck." I'm really *not* sure, and I bet if I turn around, she'll still be there, watching us from the other side of the security lines. But I continue anyway. "And you're only wearing the sling while we travel—at the recommendation of Dr. Carlisle and your physical therapist—because having it in the sling will keep you from overusing it. They both said you can take it off when we're not traveling."

He scowls but doesn't argue, and then he looks up and around the airport. "We're flying out of the North Terminal?" he asks, tipping his chin to my left.

"Yeah. Gate B14."

He swallows hard and nods, and together, we make our way to the gate. Our flight doesn't leave for an hour and a half still, and we already ate an early dinner on the way here, so we just buy a couple of bottles of water and some snacks for on the plane, then find a place to sit that's not crowded.

"You okay?" I ask after we get settled. He shrugs but closes his eyes and leans against me.

"I'm nervous."

"About the flight?"

"Yeah, but also . . ." He takes a slow, deep breath, and when he exhales, his whole body seems to shudder. "Tomorrow's important," he says quietly. "I don't wanna fuck it up."

His interview with Vera is tomorrow morning. After his initial phone interview three weeks ago, on the same day that Patrick attacked him at the library, and another interview last week via a Zoom video call, Vera requested an in-person interview at her office in San Jose. She's paying all of his travel expenses—flight, transportation to the hotel, hotel for two nights, even a "per diem" for his meals. He couldn't believe it when she offered. And he's been bouncing back and forth between hopeful and anxious ever since.

I don't blame him. I'm actually a little anxious myself—not because I'm worried about him doing well at the interview but because of what it will mean *when* he gets offered the job.

Vera *does* in fact pay well, as my mom expected. The position is a full-time position *with benefits*, including health insurance, and starts at twenty-six dollars per hour. Nico would have a lot to learn, but my mom was also right that his experience at the library is giving him many of the skills he would need.

Tomorrow *is* important.

But I just *know* he's not going to fuck it up.

I slip my arm up around his shoulders and rest my cheek against the top of his head, even though what I really want to do is kiss him. "You're perfect for this job," I murmur, "and tomorrow's just going to prove that. You can do this. I know it."

He sets his hand on my thigh but doesn't say anything right away. It's pretty quiet around us, generally sort of low-key and calm, with only a few other passengers coming and going. Finally, he breathes deeply again and then asks, "What time is your meeting tomorrow?"

"Ten. Ten to about noon, Dr. Ellis said. Maybe a little later. He'll give me a tour of his lab, and then one of his grad students is giving a presentation to the department at eleven. It's going to be about how stars gain mass. Dr. Ellis said it'll be good for me to come and listen." I try to not sound too excited, but I know I've failed when Nico sits up and turns to me, grinning for what might be the first time today.

"You're going to be in fucking heaven there, all that nerdy space talk," he teases, nudging me with his shoulder.

His eyes are beautiful, gleaming with a hint of silliness that I just adore, and I can't help it. I give into the feeling I've been fighting since my mom and I picked him up from work about an hour ago, and I lean in and kiss him. It's a brief kiss—short, sweet, and soft—but he meets me in it, kissing me back with a quiet longing and need I can feel.

Warmth spreads from my chest down into my groin, and I pull back with a muffled groan before I do something I very much should not do in the middle of the airport. The look on Nico's face doesn't really help my predicament. He's smiling at me with a crooked, knowing grin as though he can read my mind, and when he gives my thigh a subtle but deliberate squeeze, I nearly groan again.

His smile turns into a smirk, and I shake my head. "You're awful, you know," I say.

He leans back in, his fingers sliding up my leg a little higher, and he whispers in my ear, "Yeah, but you love it." Then he straightens up as I inhale to hide the heat rushing to my cheeks.

I do love it. And I love him.

He's still grinning as he holds my gaze for a few more seconds, and then he winks at me and reaches down to his backpack.

"Wanna help me beat Absolute Radiance?" he asks, completely casual, pulling my Switch out.

It takes me a second to reset and steady myself. Then I shake my head. "Bro, you don't need my help."

"Yeah, you're right," he quips with a laugh. "Wanna watch me kick Absolute Radiance's ass?"

Several hours, one cross-country flight, and a short drive later, I hold open the door to our hotel room in downtown San Jose, California. Nico steps in ahead of me, his shoulders tight and hunched. He lets his backpack fall from his shoulder just inside the entryway, and then reaches out to flip the light switch on as I follow him inside. The door shuts with a decisive click just as the light flickers on, and Nico shakes his head and huffs a laugh.

"Wow. Wow. Holy shit, this place is nice," he says, stopping just at the edge of the large king-size bed.

It *is* nice, maybe even the nicest hotel room I've ever stayed in, and the room is huge—easily three or four times the size of my bedroom at home. In addition to the fancy kitchenette behind us, there's a cushy-looking sectional in one corner opposite a small dining table with two chairs and a full-size desk situated in the far corner. Hanging on the wall across from the bed is a massive TV positioned over a dark-wood dresser.

Wordlessly, I set my duffle bag down next to his backpack and step up behind him, slipping my arms around his waist. He's still stiff, but he leans back into me, closes his eyes, and takes a deep breath.

"This is so . . . much," he breathes, and then he turns around in my arms, letting his head drop to my shoulder. "I hope I don't screw up—"

"No," I cut in, and I let my hand rub up his back slowly. "No, you're not going to. You're amazing, and tomorrow is going to show Vera that."

He feels so tense and tight, even as he nods and at least pretends he hears what I'm saying. My hands find his hips, and he straightens up and lifts his eyes. I smile softly and lean in to kiss him, a brief touch at first.

He wants more; I can feel it as he presses himself up against me and opens his mouth and swipes his tongue along my lower lip. He wants more, and I do too. But I want to take care of him tonight. More than anything, I want to help him feel relaxed and comfortable and loved. So I flex my fingers into his hips and push him back slightly, breaking the kiss. He grumbles, but I shake my head and laugh lightly.

"Here, sit." I guide him back to sit on the bed, and then I kneel in front of him and reach up to touch the sling holding his left arm. "Let me help you take this off?"

When he nods, I help him, slowly undoing the Velcro of the strap that goes around his neck and then lowering the sling itself. He shrugs his shoulder with a grimace, as if testing out how it feels. I know it's not nearly as painful for him anymore—nothing like it was almost a month ago, when the injury first happened, or three weeks ago, when his asshole ex-stepfather attacked him at the library. And thankfully, the injury has responded well to the conservative treatment his doctor and physical therapist recommended. But I'm still careful nonetheless.

"Okay?" I ask.

"Yeah. Stiff, but I'm fine. Thank you . . ." He trails off, shaking his head like he wants to say something more. When he doesn't, I settle my hands on his thighs, squeeze gently, and then let my fingers trace upward until I reach the waistband of his slacks.

"How about a quick shower, and then we can go to bed?" I suggest. "Unless you needed something to eat or anything first?"

He shakes his head. "Nah, the snacks on the plane were enough. Um . . . a shower sounds good, though."

"It sounds *really* good, right?" I wiggle my eyebrows at him, trying to be silly, and it's enough to get me a semi-annoyed grin and a light shove.

"You're just horny," he says, and he rolls his eyes at me as I shift both of my hands back to his thighs to keep myself balanced. "Wasn't last night enough for you? All that getting up close and personal with my ass? You seemed to enjoy yourself, if I recall."

Blood rushes to my cock at the reminder. Last night . . . Fuck, last night was incredible—fingering him for the first time. Hearing him gasp and moan when I curled my fingers up and found that perfect spot. Then sucking him dry when he came.

"You seemed to enjoy yourself too," I counter, lifting my eyes.

He's smirking now, and he leans forward and runs his fingers up my arms. "I did. It was fucking amazing."

My skin tingles where he's touching me, and my heart's hammering. I groan again, letting my hands inch back up to his waistband. He stops me, his hands covering mine.

"Hmm, you know," he says, his fingers teasing along the backs of my hands and then up my forearms and back down again, "I *am* kinda tired. It's late. And tomorrow's a big day."

I'm still new to all of this, but he sure *seems* like he's deliberately taunting me. His touch is playful, and his eyes are shining. But the last thing I want is to read the situation incorrectly. So I quietly agree. "It is late, and tomorrow is important."

I hold his gaze, trying to figure out exactly what he wants. When his lips quirk up into a crooked, silly smile and his hands push mine down to the top of his thighs, I'm pretty sure I have my answer. I let my fingers brush along the length of the bulge in his slacks, and he groans, his cock throbbing in its confinement.

"Well, if you're too tired . . ." I trail off with a shrug and start to move my hand away, but he stops me, tightening his hands on mine. He pushes one hand inward more until I'm cupping his hard cock through his pants.

"Mm-hmm. Yeah. Too tired," he mumbles, and then he groans and screws his eyes shut. "Jesus fuck," he hisses, and with another groan, he adds, "I mean, oh, wow, yeah, I'm . . . just so tired."

I laugh, glad I know exactly how he's *really* feeling now, and then I bend down, because I just can't stand not to, and nuzzle my face into his groin. "We should sleep, then," I say, stroking his dick as I press my lips against him and inhale deeply. "So you can rest."

"Uh-huh. Yeah. God, holy . . . fuck," he breathes, both of his hands now threading through my hair.

"Mmm, although, if you're too tired"—I run my lips along his length, humming as I go—"maybe you need help getting ready for bed."

His dick throbs against my lips, and he chokes out, "Yeah. Yeah, I might."

I shift slightly, resume stroking him with my hand, and then press a kiss to his inner thigh, letting my other hand run up to tug lightly on his shirt. "I can do that. Undress you. Help you shower. Wash you. Thoroughly."

At my last word, he moans, a low, rough sound that makes my cock pulse, and then he says, "Th-thoroughly, huh?"

"Yep. Gotta be clean." I kiss his thigh again and tighten my grip on him through his pants. He mumbles another couple of curse words under his breath, and I chuckle against him. "How does that sound?"

He nods quickly, and I grin up at him, then start undressing him. I move slowly and carefully, teasing him with every touch while also making sure I don't hurt his shoulder. His polo shirt comes off, followed by his belt, his shoes and socks, and his slacks. My fingers trail all along his skin, up his calves, brushing the insides of his thighs. By the time I'm inching under the bottom hem of his boxer briefs, he's gone quiet, his eyes closed lightly and his breathing controlled and deep.

I pause and then lean down and kiss a slow path up his inner thigh, stopping in the same place as my fingers, just at the edge of his briefs. "I'll go turn on the water?" I ask softly, my breath warm against his skin.

He lets out a sigh that sounds content and relaxed, and he nods.

"Yeah."

"Perfect." I rub his leg gently as I stand up, and then I turn and head into the bathroom, grabbing my duffle bag on the way.

The bathroom is as impressive as the rest of our hotel room, though I'm much more interested in getting the shower going for my boyfriend than I am in admiring the size and elegance of the room. I do, however, take a few seconds while I'm adjusting the water temperature to appreciate just how much space we're going to have in the massive walk-in shower.

After I get the water turned on, I fish out the small bottle of lube I brought with us, just in case, and stick it on a shelf in the shower. I undress myself down to my briefs, and I'm about to head back out to the bedroom when Nico's hands smooth up along my back and then down around my waist. His lips brush my shoulder.

I groan. "I was just coming to get you."

"Mmm, you were taking too long."

I turn around, and he grins at me, then stretches up and captures my lips in a searing kiss. He doesn't waste any time. Both of his hands slip down under my briefs to grip my ass, and he tows our hips together. I groan as I feel him—his cock hard and hot.

"God, Nico . . ." I mumble against his mouth. My own arousal is straining in my briefs now, and he rocks against me with a moan. His hands push downward, taking my briefs with them, and then he's stroking my dick and exploring my mouth with his tongue.

It's all fast and hot. Heat and desire and—god, my heart's racing and my toes are curling.

I moan some other nonsense words as I tear my lips away from his, breathing hard. "I thought you were tired?" I rasp, trying desperately to hold myself together.

There's a puff of warmth on my neck as he laughs lightly. "Maybe I'm not *too* tired."

His hand pumps slowly up and down my cock, and his thumb

brushes over the head, sending a jolt through me.

"Fuck," I hiss, unable to stop the curse from slipping out. Some other pathetic sound leaves my lips as he repeats the motion with his thumb, and he laughs again.

"You like that?" His lips flutter kisses along my collarbone, the heat making my knees weak.

Rather than answer him, I let my hands shift to his hips and then hook my fingers under the waistband of his briefs. His hand slows on my dick, and he releases me as I inch his briefs down.

I lower my eyes to watch his cock spring free. He's rigid, his erection on full display before me, almost begging me to swallow him up. With a groan, I kneel, sliding his briefs down all the way to his ankles. He steps out as I grip the base of his shaft, and his hands settle on my shoulders, squeezing me insistently when I take his tip into my mouth.

It's divine. Perfect. And I lap him up, teasing my tongue along his slit. The moan he lets out is positively obscene, and he follows it with another few choice curses as his body shudders.

I wanted to take my time with him, teasing him while we showered together, touching him everywhere, maybe fingering him again before making him come. But when his fingers run through my hair and he moans my name, I'm too eager to make him feel good now.

One hand on his thigh to steady myself and the other slowly moving down to cup his balls, I take him in all the way to the back of my throat. My tongue plays along the underside of his cock, and I hold there for as long as I can stand it. He's writhing and moaning and panting my name by the time I slide my mouth up and then back down, and he groans as his hips buck forward, thrusting himself into my mouth. Again, I hold there, the head of his cock at the back of my throat.

"A-Alex, Alex, fuck, that's—" he whines, cutting himself off with another rough, raspy moan.

I can feel my own cock leaking, and I shift one hand to stroke myself as I move the other to his ass, gripping tightly. I bob my head and work my tongue around him as I jerk myself, slowly building the pace to exactly what I know he wants. And it's not long until he's got both hands on my shoulders again, and he's tugging me up.

"Wait, wait, wait," he pants. "Come up here. Please."

I pop off of him, which elicits another groan, but then he's tugging me up again. I release myself and wipe the spit off my mouth as I stand. His hand immediately takes mine, and he pulls me toward the shower.

"Nico, what are you—"

"Trust me," he says, and he opens up the glass door, releasing a warm puff of steam, and pulls me in with him.

Before I know what's happening, he pushes me up against the flat, warm tile, pressing his body against mine. The water's hitting his back, rivulets sluicing down his chest, and he grins, then leans in and kisses me, reaching out to the side at the same time. His shaft rubs against mine, and I close my eyes as I slip my hand between us. With a groan, he pulls back and shakes his head.

"Wait. Here." He's holding the bottle of lube, and he pops the top and then drizzles the liquid down between us. "There."

He rocks his hips so his cock rubs against mine, slicking it up with lube, and I moan and tilt my head back against the wall.

"God, that's perfect." I reach between us again as he sets the lube back on the shelf and then positions himself just right. Sliding my hand down his cock first, I spread the slippery liquid over him. His breath catches, and I grin.

"Both of us," he says, now breathless. "Take both of us."

A wave of desire and want courses through me. I nod wordlessly, slip one hand up to cup his cheek, and tug him in for a needy kiss as I stretch my fingers around both of us and stroke slowly up our lengths.

He shudders and breaks the kiss almost immediately, dropping his head to my shoulder and steadying himself with a hand on the wall. "Why—why haven't we done this before?" he asks. "Fuck. God, it's . . . God, yeah, just like that."

"Mm-hmm" is all I can manage, overcome by the tingling and buzzing and the intense, unrivaled coiling of pleasure deep in my groin. I bury my face in his hair, which is now slightly damp from the shower, and I continue stroking us. Both of us. Together. Slowly at first. Then a little faster, my fist tightening at the top, my thumb moving to brush over the head of his cock.

He moans and rocks his hips in time with each stroke, and then, just when I think I'm about to come undone, his body goes rigid and he clings to me, his wet hands gripping my hips. He muffles a cry into my chest, and his cock pulses, spilling his release over my fist.

It's enough to push me that last bit. I screw my eyes shut, slip my free hand around his back to hold him closer, and follow him over the wonderful, wonderful edge, coming hard. I keep stroking both of us until the very last throb of my orgasm. Then I release us, slide my hand around his waist, and pull him flush against me. We're both breathing heavy, panting, and he lets out the neediest little whine as he leans against me for support.

"Jesus," he huffs, still clinging to me.

I nod and nuzzle my face into his hair. "*Why* haven't we done that before?" I ask, repeating his question.

He just shrugs. "Dunno. And now I *am* really tired. God, my legs feel like fucking Jell-O."

I laugh lightly and rub his back. "Mmm, I've got you." I press a kiss against the top of his head. He hums with contentment, and then he takes another deep breath and relaxes into me. I smile.

"Here, let's get you cleaned up and into bed, hm?"

"Mm-hmm, yeah," he agrees, lazily nodding against my chest.

I absolutely love it.

One more kiss, this time to his forehead, and then I back him up a step so he's under the water and let my hands slick up and down his body, rinsing away the evidence of our lovemaking. He's quiet as I continue, helping him wash his body and shampoo his hair, and the whole time, there's this soft smile on his lips.

Like he's really content.

Like he's really, finally happy.

# chapter forty-one

## *nico*

SATURDAY MORNING, MY ALARM goes off at six thirty. Alex is snoring away next to me, one arm flung over my stomach and his face buried in his pillow. It's fucking adorable. I know we don't actually need to get up yet, so I just lie there for a few minutes, watching him sleep.

He's peaceful, lying there next to me, and I let myself reach out gently and run my fingers through his hair, brushing back the short strands. A deep sense of gratitude builds up in my chest, almost like an ache, right in the center. And with it, there's something else—a contentment that I've only really started feeling in the last few weeks.

It's him.

He's the reason.

*My* reason.

My reason for not letting all the shit with my mom and Patrick drown me.

My reason for being here, now, in California, about to get ready for a job interview.

My reason for having hope. For feeling loved.

He's the reason I suddenly know I'm going to get this job—because he's given me a confidence I've never, *ever* had before.

I can do this. For myself. And for him. So we can have our life together.

With a soft smile, I lean in and kiss the top of his head, and then I pull myself away and carefully scoot out from under his arm. Quietly, to avoid waking him, I cross the room, pick up my backpack, and then go sit on the sectional in the corner, pulling my knees up under me.

I brought my sketchbook, but only because I finally showed it to Alex a couple of weeks ago, on the day Patrick was arraigned and pleaded guilty to two counts of third-degree assault. My mom was at the courtroom that day. She came in just before Patrick's arraignment, took a seat in the far back corner, opposite where I was sitting with Alex and his mom, and left immediately when the proceedings were finished. She never spoke to me, never reached out to me, never offered up an apology or explanation or even asked me if I was okay. Afterward, back at Alex's house, we lay together in bed, and I cried into his chest while he held me. And then, when I had no more tears left to cry, I asked Alex to grab my backpack for me. I pulled out my sketchbook, curled back up in his arms, and drew for a while in silence, Alex watching.

I drew a rose bush. I didn't have to explain to him why. He knew.

I quietly unzip my backpack, take out my sketchbook and pencil, and set it on my lap. Then I let myself draw. I'm not sure what I'm drawing, even as I start to move the pencil across the paper. It feels different, too, because maybe for the first time ever, I'm not sketching out of some need to manage my unsettled anxiety.

A few minutes later, the drawing is taking shape, and I can see what began as just a feeling in my heart. It's his hand covering mine, his touch gentle, his thumb caressing along my skin with such love and care. It's him telling me *I've got you*. It's his reassurance and support.

I smile as I continue, slowly adding detail and texture and shading. And when I finish after another half hour or so, I take a moment to study it. It's really not that impressive—the drawing itself. It's simple at best. But that's not the point anyway. The point is what I feel when I look at it and how it made me feel when I drew it.

I glance up across the room. Alex is awake now, though I don't know how long he's been lying there in bed, his face turned my direction, his expression soft as he watches me with half-lidded eyes. I hold his gaze for a few seconds, then set my sketchbook and pencil on the couch next to me, stand up, and cross back over toward the bed.

As I near, he lifts the comforter, inviting me to climb back into bed with him, and I do, eagerly.

"Good morning," he murmurs against my lips. Then we kiss. And it's slow and loving and this incredible mix of sensual and sexy.

When we part, I snuggle up into his arms, and he holds me, quietly rubbing my back. It's perfect. I love it.

"Are you okay?" he asks after another few minutes. When I tilt my head back and look at him, he clarifies, "You were drawing. Don't you usually do that when you're not okay?"

"Oh, right." I shake my head, then I close the distance between us and kiss him—that same slow, tender kiss. My hand settles on his chest. "I'm okay, actually. Usually, yeah, I sketch when I'm anxious. But now, I just, um, wanted to draw."

His eyes shine as he looks at me, and his hand stops low on my back.

"That's great," he says softly.

We kiss again, and then I snuggle up against him more, my head in the crook of his shoulder.

"I mean, I *am* nervous," I say, "and I'm sure I'll be more anxious later, but I'm also ready, I think."

He hums, his cheek resting against the top of my head. Then, after a moment, he says, "You *are* ready. You're going to be great. I just love this for you, and I'm so proud of you."

Heat rushes to my cheeks, and I duck my head even more. "Thank you."

He huffs a small laugh and runs his hand up and down my back, his fingertips grazing teasingly along my skin. "This *is* an interesting choice of attire for a job interview, though. I thought you would've chosen something just slightly more formal."

I roll my eyes and then push him away and sit up, resisting the urge to stick my tongue out at him too.

He's grinning, and then he laughs again, like he knows what I'm thinking. "We should get up, yeah?"

I grin back. "Yeah."

By eight o'clock, we're both up, and I'm dressed in the nicest clothes I have—dark slacks and a light-gray dress shirt that thankfully didn't get wrinkled while folded up in my backpack. I borrowed a pair of black loafers from Alex, and I've spent too many annoying minutes in the bathroom trying to get my hair to behave itself.

Alex has asked me at least twice already if I want to have a bite to eat before we leave. My answer's been no both times. Even though I don't feel overly anxious yet, as I told him earlier, my stomach isn't really settled. At all. And I'm pretty sure if I have anything to eat right now, it'll come right back up.

I exit the bathroom, giving up on getting my hair to do what I want. He's sitting on the edge of the bed, maybe sending a text or something. He looks up at me with a small smile, shoves his phone into his pocket, and pats the bed next to him.

"Almost time to leave. You know where you're going?" he asks as I sit.

With a short nod, I lean against him, pull out my phone, and open up my maps app. It's already zoomed in on our location. "Her office is inside Urban Arts," I explain, pointing to the screen. "It's a small art gallery just a block over. She wants me to meet her there at eight thirty."

Alex nods and rests his hand on my lower back. "Perfect. Any idea how long the meeting will last?"

"No fucking clue."

He laughs, takes my phone out of my hand, and tosses it on the bed behind us. Then he pulls me in for a hug. And even though I thought I wasn't really feeling anxious, some tension leaves me as I melt into him, wrapping my arms around his waist and resting my forehead on his shoulder. He breathes a kiss on my cheek, and it's so gentle and so soft that I can't help but sigh.

"Remember that she already knows about your anxiety, and she already knows about your work experience and your skills. She just needs to meet you in person. That's all," he assures me. I nod but hold him a little tighter, and, just as I wanted, he kisses my cheek again. "And remember that this is as much about giving you the chance to make sure you'll be comfortable with the job, too. That's important as well—that you feel you'll be able to work there and with her."

I nod once more. Alex's mom had explained that to me, too—that it would be okay if I decide the job Vera might or might not end up offering me isn't what I'm looking for. Given all the details I know so far, I can't see that being the case. But I'm allowed to turn it down if I think I won't be comfortable in the position.

He keeps holding me for another few minutes. I can feel the confidence he has in me giving me strength, and I'm legit almost eager to actually get going. I straighten up.

"I'm ready," I say with a nod that doesn't feel forced at all.

His smile lights up when our eyes meet, and he leans in and kisses me. "Alright. Let's go."

Alex and I part ways at the corner of San Carlos Street and South Market Street. He's heading to the train station, which is about a mile to the west. From there, he'll catch whatever the next train is going north to Palo Alto, and he'll meet up with that professor he's always talking about so they can geek out over stars and black holes and dark energy or whatever for the next few hours.

Me, I turn the opposite direction, shoving my hands into my pockets and keeping my head down as I follow the light Saturday-morning crowd crossing South Market Street.

I'm alone now.

Alone in a new city, surrounded by strangers.

And I'm about to go meet another stranger and try to convince her to pay me much more money than I ever expected I'd really be worth.

I lift my chin as I push away that thought and all the anxiety that wants to come with it. I can do this. I *have to* do this. For myself. And for Alex.

*For us.*

I step up onto the sidewalk on the other side of the street and keep walking. One block over, then cross First and turn right, and there it is. Urban Arts.

I stop, staring at the two-story building, its high glass windows decorated with bright geometric designs and random bursts of color. It looks loud and energetic, especially in the early morning light, but at the same time, it's inviting, pulling me in its direction.

My heart's racing, too, with some mix of eager anticipation and nervousness. It's a different nervousness, though. Maybe just a *normal* nervousness. A normal I'm-about-to-meet-my-future-employer nervousness.

I can almost feel Alex laughing at me for that thought, and I shake my head at myself, then reach into my pocket and pull out my phone to check the time and make sure I'm not too early.

Eight twenty-five. Perfectly on time. And I'm ready.

I take a slow breath, and I'm just about to put my phone back into my pocket when it vibrates and a notification pops up on my screen. It's a text from Alex.

A simple three words.

*I love you.*

My heart stutters, and I feel the most comfortable warmth surrounding me. Like he's here, whispering the words in my ear as he hugs me.

With a deep breath, I silence my phone, slip it back into my pocket, and then get my feet to move, bringing me one step closer to our future together.

# chapter forty-two

## *alex*

Mom (1:44 p.m.): Sounds like such an amazing opportunity! I'm so proud of you! <3

Mom (1:45 p.m.): Are you back in San Jose now?

Alex (1:45 p.m.): just got here

Mom (1:45 p.m.): And Nico?

Alex (1:46 p.m.): havent heard from him yet

Alex (1:46 p.m.): ill let u know as soon as i can

The train slows to a stop at Diridon Station, just a little over a mile from our hotel, and I frown down at my phone and then step off onto the platform as the doors open. My mind's still reeling from the day, all of my excitement and enthusiasm mixing with worry. It's almost two, which is much later than I planned to be back, and I still haven't heard anything from Nico.

That's probably a good thing. At least, that's what I keep telling myself as I grip my phone and start the walk back to the hotel.

Everything about my own experience today was fantastic—my chat with Dr. Ellis, the tour he gave me of his lab on the second floor of the Physics and Astrophysics Building near the main quad on campus, the presentation by one of his postdocs for the entire department. Afterward, Dr. Ellis introduced me to several other faculty members in the department and to Dr. Millan, the visiting professor I spoke with earlier in the summer. Before I left campus, he gave me a formal offer to join his lab as an undergraduate researcher in the fall.

There's a strange feeling of pride in my chest, and it all feels unreal and exciting. I can barely believe it.

I just hope Nico's day has been as good as mine. Or at least good enough.

I break into a jog to catch the light before the crosswalk sign changes, and as I step up onto the curb on the other side of the street, my phone buzzes. Nico's name pops up on the screen, and I stop in the shade of one of the trees lining the sidewalk as I click on the notification.

> *Nico (1:58 p.m.):* Where are you?

The immediate relief of seeing his message hits me square in the chest. I shoot him a quick response.

> *Alex (1:59 p.m.):* almost to hotel. u?

I'm still over half a mile from the hotel, but I start walking again at a decent pace. Several minutes later, as I'm turning the corner onto San Carlos, he texts me back.

*Nico (2:04 p.m.):* I just got back to the room

I can't read a single thing from the tone of his text, which isn't anything new. But the simple fact that he texted me back means he's not in awful shape.

*Alex (2:05 p.m.):* be there in a few

He almost immediately responds with a thumbs-up emoji, and I grin and pick up my pace even more.

Another ten minutes or so later, I pull my keycard out of my pocket, tap it on the door lock, and then push open the door. The room's dark and quiet, and I hesitate just inside, stepping forward slowly. When the bed comes into view, my stomach drops. Nico's lying there under the covers, his back to me. The clothes he was wearing earlier are in a pile on the floor at the foot of the bed, next to the shoes he borrowed from me, and his phone is sitting face down on the nightstand.

"Nico?" I ask softly, not wanting to wake him.

"Hmm?" he answers. Then he shifts over onto his back and opens his eyes partway, turning his head toward me with a weak smile. "You're late."

I narrow my eyes as I study him, trying to figure out what it means that he's lying half naked in bed in the middle of the day after a job interview. And what it means that he's smiling.

"You were late, too," I say slowly.

He nods and then lifts up the edge of the comforter and gestures for me to join him. "Vera took me to see three other art galleries she manages in the area," he explains sleepily as I slip my shoes off and make my way over to the bed. "And then we came back, and she took me to lunch at this café right across from Urban Arts."

I slip under the blanket, gather him up in my arms, and kiss him gently. He smiles against my mouth, and my heart skips a beat.

"Sounds like it went well?"

"Mmm, yeah. I think so." With a deep sigh, he closes his eyes and settles his head against my chest. "I'm just exhausted now."

"Rest, then," I say quietly, and he nods into me. Within a few minutes, he's already asleep, his breathing rhythmic and slow. I kiss the top of his head and close my eyes, letting myself rest as well.

I don't fall asleep, though; my mind's racing with possibilities. And carefully, so I don't wake him, I reach into my pocket, pull out my phone, and open up a new browser tab to start a search for one-bedroom apartments nearby.

"So, what do you think?"

Nico stands next to me, looking up at the newly painted white-brick building sandwiched between a pizza place and a pub. His eyes scan the windows on the second and third floors, and his expression tightens.

"I think it's crazy that a three-hundred-square-foot studio apartment rents for two thousand a month," he says. "But the location is perfect."

"It's less than a mile from Vera's gallery. And it's quiet and private."

"Yeah." He glances down at the brochure he's holding. "All utilities included. And it's fully furnished."

"And there's pizza," I add, nudging him with my elbow and

then hooking a thumb over toward the pizza place on our left.

He laughs and shakes his head. "You're hungry?"

"I didn't have my future employer buy me lunch," I answer, slipping my arm around his waist.

He smiles weakly but then drops his chin. "She's not my future employer yet."

"Eh, technicality." I squeeze him to me, and he laughs again. "Pizza?"

"Yeah, sure."

We step apart just enough for me to drop my arm from around his waist and then take his hand, and together we head into the pizza place. It's not busy right now, but given the atmosphere, I suspect it will be getting busy closer to the dinner rush. We order a few slices each of Detroit-style deep-dish pizza with various toppings, along with a couple of bottles of water, and then head back out to the patio seating and grab one of the open tables, scooting our chairs close together.

While we eat, we talk seriously about his budget. I pull out my phone and open up the spreadsheet we made earlier in the summer, and together, we update everything. Car insurance removed. Monthly passes for the local bus and train services added. Rent cost updated to reflect the cost of the studio apartment we just toured. Utilities removed from the list. A few other tweaks here and there.

And when it's all said and done, Nico looks up at me, his eyebrows arched with a tentative hope.

"So . . . it's doable?" he says. "Maybe?"

"It is," I answer. "Definitely."

He just stares at me for a moment, several conflicting emotions flickering in his beautiful eyes. Then he purses his lips and blinks a couple of times. "I'm still scared to hope. Why am I still scared to hope?"

I reach up and cup his cheek, letting my thumb stroke gently

along his skin, and we come together in a short kiss that's sweet and
tender and loving. My heart is full, and I'm not sure I've ever been
happier or more proud of him. When we part, I rest my forehead
against his, and he shakes his head almost imperceptibly.

"I can do this," he says, though he sounds less than sure.

I nod and kiss his lips again, briefly and softly. "And you're not
alone. We'll be together. I'll help you. We'll support each other."

He closes his eyes, and a single tear slips down his cheek. "*We*
can do this."

"Yes."

He straightens up and brushes the tear from his cheek. Then
he's quiet for a moment before he says, "I like the apartment. As
soon as I get the call from Vera, I'll email them and put down the
deposit. I have enough money saved for that now, yeah?"

Some overwhelming emotion grows in my chest, and all I can
do for several seconds is stare at him. It's real. This is real and
happening, and I'm suddenly so grateful, so intensely grateful, as
I think back on just a little over a month ago.

I thought I'd be losing him at the end of the summer. I thought
I'd be leaving him in Nebraska, my heart breaking more and more
each day as we grew farther and farther apart. I imagined life would
be condensed into a series of phone calls and unanswered texts,
punctuated by infrequent, guilt-filled vacations back home that
wouldn't ever really be long enough.

I've never been so glad to be so wrong about anything in my life.

He arches an eyebrow at my silence. "Alex? It's enough, yeah?
I think I have about twelve hundred now, and the deposit is a
thousand? Right?"

I nod slowly as a smile spreads across my face. "Sorry, yeah," I
say, my voice catching again. "Yeah, that's right. You have enough."

A huge grin spreads across his face, his eyes lighting up, and god,
if that's not just the best sight in the world, I don't know what is.

# chapter forty-three

*nico*

ALEX CLOSES THE HOTEL room door behind us, and with the solid *click*, much of the tension I've been holding all day seeps away. His arms slip around my midsection, and I let myself melt back into him for support.

I'm exhausted. Maybe even more exhausted than I was earlier after I got back from my interview with Vera. The hour-long nap I had wasn't nearly enough, although at the same time, I'm not sure if I could fall asleep right now.

There are too many things still floating around in my brain. Half a worry that I'm not actually going to get offered the job after all. More worry that I won't be cut out for it. Uncertainty about the revised budget we put together over dinner, even though it looked solid and showed that I should have a good buffer every month.

It's normal to be worried about things. Alex told me his mom's always reminding him about that. And I'm sure it is. I'm sure she's right. But it's hard to get everything to quiet down, especially with how tired I am from the whole day of having to manage my anxiety in a new place, meeting new people, talking and being engaged.

I turn around in Alex's arms and lean against his chest. "Hold me?" I ask.

He chuckles and kisses my forehead. "I *am* holding you."

I groan and push away from him, starting over toward the bed. When I reach the edge, I let myself fall face-first onto the mattress, breathing out a long sigh. He flops down on his back next to me, and I turn my head to look at him.

He's grinning—a gorgeous smile that's somehow also soft and kind and understanding. The feeling washes over me with warmth and love, and some of those voices of worry and uncertainty go quiet in my head. I scoot over on the bed until I'm lying partly on top of him, one knee hiked up over his thighs. Then I kiss him, his lips pliant and warm and willing.

His hands roam, too, but gently and slowly, inching under my shirt to run along my lower back and then smoothing up to my shoulder blades and down again. It's soft, like his kisses—like he's trying to soothe me with his touch and tell me he loves me at the same time.

And it's arousing as hell.

"Mmm, Nico . . ." He tugs on the hem of my shirt. "Take this off."

"Only if you say please," I taunt, slipping my own hands up under his shirt too. I shift my leg over him, hooking my foot around his thigh, and he groans, screws his eyes shut, and presses his head back into the bed as his hard length throbs against me.

The next thing I know, I'm on my back underneath him, and he's tossing my shirt off to the side. His lips close over one of my nipples, and he sucks. Hard.

"Oh, fuck me," I hiss, gripping the blanket as a jolt of arousal rushes straight to my cock. He lifts his eyes to look at me, his expression teasing as he continues to pleasure me with his mouth and tongue. I laugh and roll my eyes. "That wasn't an invitation."

"Are you sure?" he asks, pulling away so his lips hover just above my skin.

Before I can respond, he dips back in, taunting and teasing me with his lips and teeth and tongue, and I close my eyes and moan his name. His hands slip down between my legs and hook under my thighs, then he settles between my knees and brings my legs up a bit, running his fingers along my inner thighs. He teases me, his touch burning, scorching. God, it's fucking good.

"Clothes off," I say, but then I tug him back up to me and capture his mouth again in another kiss that starts off soft but builds fast to something much more intense.

He breaks away from me only long enough to rip his shirt off over his head, and then he's back on me, pushing his tongue into my mouth, tasting and exploring, even as he's still undressing both of us. As soon as my shorts and briefs are off, he settles back over me, lowering his hips until our cocks meet.

A soft curse escapes his lips, and his body shudders with what I can only imagine is need and arousal. I close my eyes and bend my knees up, bringing him closer to me. He drops his forehead onto my good shoulder, his breath hot against my skin, and his hips jerk forward.

"Touch me," I beg. My fingers thread through his hair as he flutters kisses on my shoulder and over to my neck.

"Where?"

I'm panting now, my whole body on fire, pleading for more. And I'm not sure how to answer because I'm actually not really sure what I want or where I want him to touch.

Actually, that's not true. I do know.

"Everywhere."

"Mmm. Yeah, good," he murmurs against me, and he doesn't hesitate at all. He kisses my lips gently and whispers, "I'll be right back." Then he disappears for only a few seconds, returning with the bottle of lube and a towel from the bathroom.

He settles back over me, tossing the bottle and towel on the bed next to us, and I reach between us and take his shaft in my hand, stroking him as he moans and curses and says all the little things he never says at any other time, except when we're in bed together. He doesn't let that last long, though, before he takes back control, moving lower, fluttering kisses down my chest.

He's popped open the bottle of lube before I even register what's happening. And then he's stroking my dick, slicing it up. His hand slips lower, and he cups my balls gently before rubbing along my taint and then circling my hole.

Heat courses through me, my cock pulsing. I reach down and stroke myself as I push my head back into the bed with another moan.

"Impatient?" he quips, his slick fingers still teasing the outside of my hole.

"No," I blurt out. "I . . . just . . . need . . ."

His lips close over mine, and he kisses me slow and deep. Then he pulls back. "What do you need?" he asks, his voice low and raspy.

I open my eyes halfway. His gaze is trained on me, intense and fucking aroused. Sexy as hell. I swallow hard and don't look away. "You. Inside me," I say, and as soon as the words are out of my mouth, my face flushes with heat.

He lets out a sharp breath, and he studies me as his tongue peeks out of his mouth to wet his lips. "Are you sure?"

I nod. "Yes."

I *am* sure. But I'm also a tiny bit nervous, and I know he can see it in my eyes.

He holds my gaze for another second, and then he leans in and kisses me again, soft and gentle this time, as though reassuring me he'll take care of me. His fingers circle my hole, and as he slowly pushes one inside, I gasp, a ripple of arousal shooting all the way down into my toes.

I tear my lips away. "Holy fuck, Alex," I rasp, and then I press my hand into his chest, close my eyes, and moan his name.

"I've got you," he says, his voice a rough whisper. "Relax and breathe." His finger pushes deeper, and I try to do what he says, breathing and bearing down. He lets his lips graze my neck. "There you go," he says. "That's it." And he starts moving his finger slowly, in and out, stretching me and opening me up with each careful touch.

It's more than incredible, just like it was a couple of nights ago when we messed around like this for the first time. Before long, I'm begging him for more—a second finger, and then a third—and I'm panting and clinging to him. And when he curls his fingers just right, I turn my head and muffle a cry into his hair as a shock of ecstasy races through me.

"There. Fuck, right—yeah, right there," I stammer, and he hums against me softly before hitting the same spot again and again. "Jesus. Shit. What are you—what are you doing? That's—fuck."

He huffs a laugh, turns his head, and captures my lips in a kiss that's not quite as gentle. Then he sits up, kneeling between my legs, still moving his fingers in and out of my channel. I lift up an arm to cover my eyes as I struggle to keep my breathing steady. My whole body's tingling now.

He lets his fingers slip out of me and then runs his other hand along my thigh. "I think you're ready? Maybe?" he says, adding, "I don't want to hurt you."

I shift so I can see him, my eyes half-lidded, and I nod and then glance down at his erection. It's perfectly long and hard and willing, precum leaking from the tip.

Fuck, I want him.

No, I *need* him.

I lick my lips and nod again, lifting my eyes to meet his. "Yeah, I'm ready."

His cheeks flush an adorable shade of pink, and he blinks and looks down at the bed, where he put the lube. My heart's pounding fiercely in my chest—a mix of anticipation and desire. I watch, holding my breath, as he coats his shaft and then wipes his hands on the towel.

From there, everything seems to go in slow motion. Delicious slow motion.

He leans over me, finding my lips, and he kisses me sensually and gently. When he sits back up, both of his hands caress along my inner thighs and back to my knees. He's looking down at me, smiling, and then he drops his chin and takes a breath.

"I, um, did some reading . . ."

"*Reading*," I echo, grinning crookedly at him. "Right."

He gives me a look, but then he laughs and runs a hand nervously through his hair. "No, seriously. I did. And, uh, anyway, just tell me if it hurts, okay? Or if you don't like it. Or . . . anything."

I know where his nervousness comes from, and I'm honestly still nervous, too. Nervous it will hurt, yes, but also worried he won't like it or I won't like it or it won't be good for him or *I* won't be good for him.

But I trust him more than anyone else I've ever known. And I love him. I reach up with both hands to cup his cheeks, and I tug him down to me for another soft kiss.

When we part, he whispers, "I love you." And then he smiles gently and kisses me again.

He's careful and mindful, positioning me so my feet are off the bed, my knees bent up to expose my hole to him even more. Then his hand caresses my calf as he guides the head of his cock to my entrance. I close my eyes and breathe in deeply, and when I exhale, he starts to push into me.

And god, he's bigger than he looks.

At least, that's the first thought I have as his cock breaches my entrance. I let out a moan that's part pain, part pleasure, and I hear him grunt above me as he stops moving.

"You're . . . god, you're so tight," he says, his voice strained. "Are you okay?"

I'm trembling, but I manage to nod. "Yeah. Just give me a minute?"

"Of course. Does it hurt?"

I open my eyes to look up at him, shaking my head. "A little," I say, "but it's also"—I groan and close my eyes again—"it's also fucking incredible." I reach out and cover his hand on my thigh and then force myself to take several slow, deep breaths. When the burn stops, I squeeze his hand. "Okay, I'm ready again. Go ahead."

Alex lifts my hand to his lips and presses a kiss on my knuckles. Then he pushes in a little more and a little more, slowly filling me. Raw need and pleasure mix with a brief sting of pain as he stretches me to accommodate his size.

I want it. I want more of it.

I press my head back into the bed with a rough moan as he sinks in the last few inches.

"Oh fuck, Nico," he gasps, his hands moving to grip my thighs. "Tell me when I can . . . move." He's trembling now, probably struggling to hold himself still.

"Yeah . . . just a—just a minute," I manage, and he nods.

"You feel incredible," he murmurs, and he slowly leans forward, resting his elbows down on either side of me. He's still shaking, but he buries his head in the crook of my neck and grazes my skin with his lips. "So perfect."

"God, Alex."

"Beautiful and perfect." He breathes sharply, still kissing my neck. "And tight and hot."

He shifts just a little, and I moan and then let out some whimper-whine-groan that would maybe be embarrassing if it didn't make him curse and gasp my name again.

"Fuck, Nico, please tell me you're ready," he begs. His lips find mine, and he swallows any response I might have had. I can feel him clinging to me, and something about that—the fact that he seems about to come undone without even starting to move inside of me—sends another jolt of pleasure and need through me.

My hands slip around his back, and I caress up to his shoulders and back down as he continues kissing me. When he pulls back, he's panting, and he groans and drops his head to my shoulder.

"Please, Nico."

I kiss his temple and whisper, "Yeah. I'm ready."

His body shudders, maybe with relief, and his mouth covers mine as he slowly pulls his cock out and then buries himself inside me again. He does it over and over, gentle and careful with each thrust, but more confident, too. When he breaks the kiss, he's breathing hard, like I am, and he props himself up on his elbows but then leans back in, his breath warm against my ear.

"You're so perfect, my Nico," he whispers sweetly. "Perfect and beautiful and sexy. I love you so much. Let go. Come for me." He brushes my hair back out of my face and kisses my forehead, letting his lips linger there.

And I think it's that touch that pushes me right up to the edge, bolts of pleasure and pressure coiling inside me. I mumble another string of curses and beg him to give me more. He presses his lips to my forehead again, then reaches between us, his fist closing around my sensitive cock, as he thrusts into me again and again. And then I come hard, crying out and clinging to him.

His arms wrap around me, and he holds me through every intense pulse of relief and release and bliss. Just as I'm coming back down, my heart still racing and my body trembling, he pumps into me one last time, burying his head against my chest as he comes with a muffled grunt.

He groans and hugs me tighter and then pulls back just enough to kiss my cheek. "God, that was amazing. I love you. Are you okay?"

How he's breathing and saying words right now, I'm not sure because I definitely can't do either of those things. I nod, though, and he sighs with relief. Both of his hands cup my cheeks, and then his lips cover mine with an earnestness and tenderness that sends more warmth to my chest. He kisses my lips and my cheeks again, then he places a tiny kiss on the tip of my nose before he slips his arms around me and holds me to him.

I finally manage a laugh, and I hug him back, burying my head in the crook of his shoulder. It's perfect, to be here with him, to have this together. Tears slip down my cheeks, but I ignore them and hold him tighter.

He must notice my tears when he presses another kiss to my cheek, because he asks, "You're sure you're okay?"

I let him go and collapse back onto the bed, exhausted. I close my eyes. "Very okay."

He pulls out of me slowly, leaving me feeling strangely empty. But as soon as he falls onto the bed next to me and gathers me up in his arms and starts kissing every bit of me again, the feeling is gone.

All I feel is him, his touch gentle, caring, loving. I feel safe and cherished and so, so loved. And at least in that moment, any and all uncertainties and doubts I had don't seem important anymore. It's just him and me, here, together.

After a few more minutes of his soft, affirming kisses, he stills, resting his forehead against mine. His fingers caress my cheek.

"I'll be right back. Don't move."

"Couldn't even if I wanted to," I admit.

He laughs lightly and kisses my cheek. Then the bed shifts, and he disappears, returning a moment later to touch his lips to my shoulder and then my neck and then my lips. He doesn't speak. Instead, he cleans me up with a warm washcloth he brought from the bathroom. It's oddly intimate, even given what we just did. And when he's finished and put the washcloth back in the bathroom, he pulls down the covers and coaxes me underneath them, and then he's holding me again, flush against his chest.

He nuzzles my hair and breathes in deeply, and I can feel him smiling into me. I love that.

I let my hand settle low on his stomach, and I slide my foot down his leg until I reach his ankle. He hums contentedly and tightens his arms around me.

"Comfortable?" he asks quietly.

"Mmm, definitely." I tilt my head back just enough to see his face. His cheeks are still flushed, his hair mussed and his eyes slightly unfocused. Like he just had the best orgasm of his life. He looks fucking incredible. "I love you," I whisper.

His eyes brighten, and then he grins and says, "You mean that?"

My cheeks heat up, and I nod. "Yeah." I stretch up to kiss him softly. "With all of my heart."

# chapter forty-four

## *alex*

"It's fucking busy as hell here," Nico mumbles, his shoulders tightening more as he slams to a stop to let a wave of loud, rowdy college athletes pass by us. My hand finds his lower back, and he leans into my touch.

The airport is definitely much busier now than when we arrived here in San Jose on Friday evening, and though he *is* handling himself, I probably should have expected that traveling today would be harder on him.

"We're almost to the gate," I reassure him, and though he nods stiffly, I can feel him shaking. "You're doing great. We'll find a quiet place to sit until it's time to board. Okay?"

He nods again, and we start walking. I stay just behind him, my hand on his back, and I hope that helps him feel at least a little safer. He hesitates and starts and stops a few more times, clenching his hand into a fist when another person cuts in front of him, almost bumping into his bad shoulder.

"Can't they watch where they're going? Jesus," he complains, and then he grimaces. "Sorry. Sorry, I'm just not feeling good. Wh-which gate again?"

"Nineteen. Just ahead on the left there. And you're fine. You're doing great."

"I'm not doing great. I'm gonna puke." He glances back at me over his shoulder, frowning.

I give him a small smile and rub my hand up and down his back. "Come on," I say, tipping my head toward the gate. "There's plenty of seats over by the window. It's quieter over there."

He swallows and nods, then starts walking. Again.

A moment later, he drops his backpack on the floor next to one of the open seats along the window and nearly collapses into the closest chair. With a groan, he leans forward to rest his elbows on his knees, which is a bit awkward with his arm back in the sling. I take the seat next to him, and he immediately falls into me, his arm stretching out across my midsection.

"It's better over here, yeah?" I rub his back gently, and he nods into me, though he doesn't otherwise respond. So I start talking quietly, telling him all of the things about the tour I had yesterday at Stanford that I haven't had a chance to tell him yet. He listens, and gradually, his shoulders loosen up and he relaxes. At least a little.

We fall into silence again after a few more minutes, but it's a comfortable silence. He's lifted his eyes and is looking around, watching people walk past, his expression taut.

"I hate that I'm like this," he says finally, and he shifts a bit to sit up more. I start to protest, but he shakes his head. "You being here with me, though, it makes everything tolerable. Or, I mean, mostly. Sometimes." I don't even say anything and he's rolling his eyes at me. "Shut up."

I laugh, and he does too. Then he leans against me again. "For what it's worth," I say, "I'm extremely proud of you for everything you've done this weekend."

He looks up at me, arching his eyebrows. "Everything was nearly impossible. And it made me so exhausted."

"I know. I had to wake you up this morning, remember? You

almost took my head off."

He swats at my chest. "Did not."

"It wasn't safe in the hotel room until you'd had *at least* two cups of coffee."

He groans at my tease and rolls his eyes.

"Anyway, as I was saying . . ." I slip my arm around his shoulders and squeeze gently. "I'm proud of you, and I'm glad I was here to support you. I want to . . . always be here to support you."

His chest rises and falls slowly, like he's taking a careful breath, and then he nods. "I want that, too."

My heart stutters, and I close my eyes and rest my cheek against the top of his head. "So I guess you're stuck with me, then."

"Poor me."

I laugh and hug him to me more, and I hope he's feeling the same things I am—warmth, love, certainty. It's such a different feeling than what I had right at the beginning of summer break, when I was having to seriously face the possibility of leaving him behind.

"I don't think I could have done it," I blurt out, and it's only when he straightens up a bit to look at me, confusion in his expression, that I realize he hadn't heard the whole of my thoughts.

"Done what?"

I frown and drop my eyes to where my hand now rests on his forearm. "I don't think I could have left Nebraska without you."

"Alex—"

"I'd have rather stayed and gone to UNO."

"No—"

"I need you, too, you know." I lift my eyes, and he's shaking his head, his jaw clenched. "I need you, too, Nico," I repeat.

He holds my gaze, a million different emotions flickering in his gorgeous green eyes. It's probably several seconds before he purses his lips and ducks his chin, his cheeks turning pink. Then he squeezes me a little and mumbles, "Hopefully Vera calls soon."

I squeeze him back, and when his head settles on my chest again, my heart soars. He's accepted it—that I need him, too—and he wants our future as much as I do.

It's progress. All of it. Him even being here, in this position—waiting on a phone call about a job he's *got*, sitting having a normal conversation at a super busy airport, doing all of these things he maybe never thought he could do because he never believed in himself—it's huge progress.

I glance toward our gate, where they're just starting to board the first groups of priority passengers. No one's paying attention to us, and so I lift my hand to touch his chin. He tilts his head back, and when our eyes meet, he smiles.

Warm fuzziness tickles through me. I bend down and press a brief kiss to his lips, and when I straighten back up, his eyes are gleaming.

"I love you," I whisper.

He bites at his lower lip. "I love you, too."

He rests his head against my chest again and closes his eyes.

Things get louder and a little more chaotic around us as they call the next group to board, and then the next. He keeps his eyes closed, his arm resting on my midsection and his breathing tightly controlled, though I can feel the tension creeping back into his shoulders. Finally, after another fifteen minutes or so, they call our group. Together, we stand and gather our things, then line up behind a mom trying to wrangle her three young children. Several others step into the line behind us, and I rest my hand on Nico's back to reassure him when I see him tense up even more, his hand balling into a fist. That seems to help enough, though, because he twists his head to look up at me, trying for a small smile. He seems like he's just about to say something when he suddenly stops, his eyes wide. He turns toward me, stuffing his hand in his pocket and pulling out his cell phone—which is buzzing with an incoming call.

"Shit, it's her," he says, staring at the phone as all the color drains from his face.

The line starts to move, and I set my hands on his shoulders—gently—and move us out of the way, motioning to the people behind us to go on ahead.

He glances up at me, and I nod. "Answer. It'll be good news. I'm sure."

He looks like he's about to puke, but he nods too and then reaches up and swipes to answer the phone call. His eyes drop to the floor. "Hello?"

I try not to eavesdrop, and all I get are mostly one-word, stilted responses from him anyway.

"Yes . . . Okay . . . Yeah, that's right . . . Okay." He lifts his eyes, but I still can't read his expression. "Yeah." He looks right at me and nods, and the smallest hint of a smile flickers on his lips. "September 15 . . . Yes . . . Yes."

My heart bursts with joy as he nods again, then closes his eyes.

"Thank you, Vera. I'm—I'm looking forward to it . . . Yeah, we're at the airport right now . . . Me too . . . Thank you again . . . Yeah. Goodbye."

Nico ends the call and shoves his phone back into his pocket. He runs his hand through his hair and lets out a sharp breath, and as he glances up at me again, shaking his head, I see the disbelief in his eyes. His gaze darts toward the gate for half a second, where the last few people are boarding the plane. Then he looks back at me, still shaking his head, and he bites his lip as his head shake turns into a nod.

"Yeah?" I ask.

"Y-yeah. Yeah, she . . . she just offered me the job. It's real. I-I can't believe it."

My duffle bag drops to the ground as I throw my arms around him and pull him in for a hug, burying my head in his hair. "I'm so proud of you," I murmur against him. I'm trembling, and I can feel he is too.

He returns my hug, sliding his arms around my waist, and then he's laughing—shaking and laughing and grinning up at me. He reaches up with his good hand and hooks his fingers around my neck, then tugs me down for a kiss, right there in the middle of the airport.

When he pulls back, he's breathing hard. "I can't believe it," he repeats, shaking his head again. "She says she thinks I'm going to be perfect for the job, and she wishes I could start sooner."

More pride swells up in my chest, and I pull him back in for another hug. "You did it. You freaking did it."

He nods into me, holding me as tightly as I'm holding him. "I did."

As much as I want to sit here in this moment with him for a little bit longer, the last call for boarding for the first leg of our flight comes over the loudspeaker, and Nico steps back, glancing toward the gate. The line's gone now, and the airline's staff is standing at the podium right near the doors to the jet bridge, watching us.

"Let's go home?" he says, turning back to me. His face breaks out into a huge grin again. "And then we'll be back here in two months."

He's beautiful, especially with that smile on his lips and all that hope in his eyes.

I nod. "Yeah, let's go."

I bend over to grab my bag, and he waits for me, then takes my hand. Our fingers intertwine in a way that makes my heart feel full and happy and content. And I have the silly thought that maybe there's nothing more perfect in the whole world than the way our hands fit together. I smile and press a kiss to his knuckles, and he grins back.

"Ready?" he asks, tipping his head toward the gate.

"Yeah."

He squeezes my hand, and I think it again—how perfect this is, the two of us, together. He must see me blushing, because he bumps me with his shoulder.

"Stop thinking naughty thoughts," he whispers, "or it's gonna be a *really* long day."

I roll my eyes. "I wasn't—"

"Whatever you need to tell yourself," he cuts in, and then he winks at me, lets my hand go, and pulls his boarding pass out of his pocket to have it scanned.

With a happy sigh and a shake of my head, I hurry to follow him. And a moment later, as we head down the jet bridge to the plane, my hand finds its place on his back.

Another spot made just for me.

It's perfect. We're perfect like this, together.

And he's right—it's gonna be a *really* long day.

*Two months later...*

# epilogue

## *nico*

Mom,

I'm not sure how to start this letter or exactly what to say, but since I'm leaving for California today, I needed to say something.

I guess that something is this - I miss you.

Or maybe it's that I miss who I thought you were.

I thought you were someone who loved and supported me. Who defended me and cared about me and my well-being. I thought you were someone I could count on, especially after what happened with Patrick the first time, when you told me "never again."

I miss that person - my mom.

I don't know what made you make the decisions you did - to let that man back in your life, accept the lies *he told you, and then kick me out and abandon me. I can't reconcile that with the person I thought I knew.*

*So if you ever find that person again, please tell her that I love her and miss her.*

*I'm not leaving my new phone number or address, because as much as it hurts, I can't trust that you won't give that information to Patrick. But I hope things change for you. And if they do, I hope we find our way back to each other again.*

*Goodbye, Mom.*

*-Nico*

"IT'S AWFUL, ISN'T IT?" I grab the paper back from Alex and frown as I scan the words I finished writing only a few minutes ago. Guilt weighs heavy on my shoulders, and I shake my head and look back up at him. "I-I can't . . . I can't give this to her."

He's not smiling, but his expression stays soft, and he gently takes the letter, folds it up, and sets it on his desk. Then he pulls me into his arms and holds me tight.

"It's honest and real and your truth, right?"

I close my eyes and nod. "Yeah. It is. I just . . ."

"I know," he says quietly. "I know."

"I don't want to leave without saying goodbye to her. But I can't face her," I admit. I hate how my voice sounds fragile or something. But Alex nods against me, and it gives me more strength. "I really do hope that one day, she'll realize what she did and . . . and what that did to me."

Alex nods again, and his hand rubs up and down my back.

Then he says, "I'll go with you to drop it off."

I want to tell him he doesn't have to—that I'll go by myself. But I probably shouldn't do that. Last time I went to that house alone, bad things happened. Patrick is still in jail, and he will be for another several months. But the truth is, I don't actually *want* to do this alone, either.

So instead, I step back from him, swallow back all of my uncertainty, and then tell him, "I'd appreciate that."

I pick the letter back up and refold it so it'll fit in my pocket. Then he and I sneak downstairs together, trying to be as quiet as possible since it's not yet six in the morning and his mom is still sleeping, grab the keys to the truck, and head out. He drives, which is good because I'm fretting, my leg bouncing up and down and my hands wringing in my lap.

Within only a few minutes, he turns into the driveway to my mom's house, flipping the truck's lights off. There's just enough illumination from the sky barely starting to brighten, so I know he can see as we drive slowly down the long dirt driveway.

I wonder if I'll ever be back here again.

We're leaving today, in just a couple of hours, actually. His mom is driving us to California, all of his stuff (and what little I have) already packed in boxes sitting in the garage. We just have to load up and go. My job is waiting for me there. My job and my tiny apartment and my new life with my boyfriend, whom I love very, very much.

And I can't see ever having any reason to come back, except maybe to visit Alex's mom.

So this goodbye feels final to me, and despite the fact that I've had two months to come to terms with everything, it still hurts that my mom never even tried to reach out to me again or to apologize or anything at all. It still hurts. A lot.

Alex sets his hand on my thigh as he stops the truck next to my mom's car. "You want me to walk up there with you?" he asks gently.

I shake my head. I'm not alone, but I have to do this part myself. "I'll be right back."

"Okay." He squeezes my thigh and then lets go.

And I don't give myself any time to think. I quietly open the door, step out into the warm, humid September morning, and shove my hand into my pocket as I start toward my childhood home. I don't let myself stop until I reach the door. Then I pause, blink back the tears I'm refusing to let fall, and pull the letter out of my pocket.

The screen door doesn't creak like it used to. Maybe she got the hinges fixed.

For some reason, the thought makes my chest feel tight, and I hurry to slide the folded letter into the thin slot between the door and the doorframe. Then I turn and jog back to the truck.

Alex has us heading back down the driveway before I can even really process that this is it. We're halfway back to the road when I twist around and look behind us.

That house.

It's nothing special at all. A tiny, old house with dead flowers and peeling paint outside and a broken story inside. I'm not really going to miss it.

But I might miss what I wanted it to be.

Just like how I'll miss who I thought she was.

I screw my eyes shut against all the painful emotions and face forward again, leaning my head on the cold window. "Can we not go straight back?" I ask quietly, glad when my voice doesn't tremble.

The truck bumps around at the dip at the end of the driveway and then stops.

"Uh, yeah, sure," Alex says. "Where do you want to go?"

I open my eyes and glance out the window, out to the east. The sky is mostly dark, but right at the horizon, it's starting to change colors. Deep pink and orange, spreading out across the line of trees.

"To the river." I turn and meet his gaze, and I manage a tight smile. "Let's go to the river one more time."

His expression softens. "That sounds perfect."

It really does. I nod, then close my eyes again and settle my head back against the headrest as Alex pulls out onto the road.

Not more than fifteen minutes later, he's holding my hand as we navigate the narrow trail through the woods, mostly in the dark, and emerge along the riverbank at our spot. The narrow stretch of sandy beach ends in the shallow river ahead of us, flowing quietly along. We stop together and sit silently, and his arm loops up around my shoulders.

Far out ahead of us, over the tops of the trees on the other bank, the sky lightens a little more, the deep pink and orange spreading upward. It's beautiful and almost feels magical, which is silly. The sun rises every day. It's not magic.

It still feels special to experience it, though. And maybe it's even extra special because Alex is with me and because today is the start of our new lives together.

I smile and lean my head against Alex's shoulder. "I've never watched a sunrise before," I admit, keeping my voice low for some reason.

Alex hums softly. Then he turns his head and kisses my temple. "I have, but it was a long time ago," he says, "when my mom took me camping up north. I can't really remember where."

"Hmm."

"This is better, though." His arm tightens around me, and I find myself smiling again, a pleasant heat in my cheeks.

Out across the river, the sun finally peeks up over the trees. It's just as amazing as I imagined it would be—the light slowly inching up into the sky and bringing a hopeful warmth with it. Shadows from the trees form, stretching all the way across the river at first, then beginning their gradual recession as the sun lifts higher and higher.

I almost wish we could stay here all day. Just him and me, here at our spot on the river.

Or maybe that's not what I actually wish, because I'm ready. I'm ready to start the next phase of our lives together. I'm ready to let this be a memory—to let *all* of this and everything that happened to me at my old house with Patrick and with my mom just be a memory.

And I'm ready to see what the future holds. Our future. Together.

I'm looking forward to it.

I'm not sure I ever thought I'd say that.

Alex seems to be thinking much the same as me, because he lets out a quiet, contented sigh and then says, "Ready? My mom wanted to get on the road early."

"Yeah."

Neither of us moves right away, though. We sit there for one more short moment, soaking it all in. Then I turn my head and look up at him, and he lifts a hand to cup my cheek, his thumb stroking my skin. He smiles and leans down to kiss me. It's a soft kiss. Hopeful and bright in the way all of his kisses are.

When he pulls back, he's still smiling, and he tips his forehead to rest against mine.

"I love you," he tells me, his voice catching.

My heart stutters, the extra beat fluttering in my chest, and I quickly capture his lips again, kissing him back. It's another short kiss, but more intense, and this time, when we part, we're both breathing hard.

He shakes his head with a laugh. "It's going to be a really long drive to California. Promise me you'll be good."

"Me?" I arch my eyebrows at him with a smirk. "I'm always good."

"Right." He grins back at me, his eyes sparkling in the morning sunlight, and then he pushes himself to his feet and offers me his hand. "Ready to get out of here?"

I stare up at him for a second, then I nod and take his hand. "Yeah, let's go."

Three and a half

years later...

# epilogue

## *alex*

"So, it's officially official, then?" Nico asks. He slips off his loafers and joins me on the bed in our tiny studio apartment, which we've shared since the end of my freshman year almost three years ago. With a grin, he straddles my hips. Then his hands settle on my stomach, and he starts inching up the hem of my T-shirt, his fingers grazing playfully along my skin.

I laugh and nod, turning the letter around so he can see. "Yep. Officially official."

His hands stop moving as he leans in to read the letter with a proud grin. "'Dear Alexander, Congratulations! On behalf of the Department of Physics, we are pleased to inform you that you have been admitted to our PhD program beginning in Fall Quarter of the 2029–2030 academic year. Your research achievements during your undergraduate studies truly set you apart from the other candidates, and it is our privilege to invite you to continue pursuing your education here at Stanford in our department. An additional letter will be forthcoming, which will provide you with your financial aid offer.' Oh, fuck, yeah."

I laugh again, set the letter on the nightstand on top of the rest of our mail, and then wrap my arms around Nico and roll us over so he's on his back underneath me.

"Were you worried?" I ask. My lips press against his neck as I flutter kisses along his skin.

"Mmm."

That's not really an answer, so I pause and lift my head. "John told me months ago that I had nothing to worry about, especially since he got his grant renewed for my research project," I remind him before dipping back down to suck gently at that sensitive spot right at the base of his neck.

Nico groans. "Yeah, but—" His hands find my chest, and he pushes just enough to make me sit up a little. He studies me for a few seconds, and I'm surprised I can't really read his expression. Then he drops his eyes and says, "I, um, have some news, too, but I didn't say anything last week because I didn't know if it was going to work out."

There's a spark of recognition in my chest, and I sit up all the way. "Last week . . . ?"

He nods slowly and looks up at me, his gorgeous green eyes now dancing with amusement. "Last Thursday, actually."

"Last Thursday . . . That was the day you came home in a really, *really* good mood." I run one hand down his chest and then dip my fingers lower, skimming under the waistband of his slacks. I lean in and brush a kiss below his ear. "You teased me *all night*. It was torture."

"Torture, huh?" His hands slip back to cup my ass, and I feel him grin. "I seem to recall you enjoying yourself. Quite a bit, in fact."

I groan as he rocks his hips up into me, squeezing my ass cheeks at the same time. His dick throbs against me, and my fingers inch lower under his boxer briefs until I meet the hot, smooth skin of his erection. He moans, the rough sound making my body burn with an aching want.

"You were fucking amazing," I whisper against him. "I loved

every second of it. Torture or not."

It's true. I *definitely* enjoyed myself. Usually I top, but that night last week, he took me instead—bringing me so, so close to the edge of coming undone, then backing off. He did that several times, actually. First with his mouth on my dick, then with his tongue and fingers in my ass, and then with his cock inside me, stretching me and filling me and pounding into me before he finally, *finally* let me come.

I'm suddenly warm all over, and I shift my hips up, unfasten both his belt and the button on his pants in quick succession, and then push down the zipper.

"You never did tell me why you were in such a good mood," I say. My hand wraps around the base of his cock, and he exhales sharply.

"I—*fuck*, Alex." He groans as I start stroking him slowly. "I had to know we were staying here first," he forces out. "If you didn't get into Stanford for grad school, and—holy fuck. Don't stop."

I grin against his skin. I'm curious what his news is, and I briefly consider making him keep talking while I taunt him, bring him right up to the edge but not let him come, like he did to me last week. But then his hand slips under my shorts, his fingers sliding down between my ass cheeks to tease my hole, and that burning, aching need sears me again.

I want him inside me. Now.

We can talk later.

He seems to have the same idea, because his hands shift to my hips and he tugs my shirt off over my head, forcing me to release his cock. Then he's pushing me over onto my back, and within a few more seconds, we're both naked and he's kneeling between my legs, slicking up his cock with lube.

My heart's pounding, and I'm panting, one hand stroking myself as his hungry eyes drink me in. He licks his lips as though what he really wants to do is taste me, and so I tease him, brushing my thumb up over my slit to catch the drop of precum leaking out. I start to bring my thumb to my mouth, and his hand shoots out to stop me.

"Please, Alex," he whispers, deep and husky, his eyes dark with need.

I grin and lift my hand to his mouth instead. "Whatever you want."

My thumb grazes his lower lip, and without any hesitation, he opens his mouth and takes me in, his eyes closing as he lets out a quiet whimper.

"Do I taste good?" I slide my thumb in and out of his mouth slowly, and he moans again as his tongue runs along my skin. It's hot and sensual and sexy, and my dick throbs with want as I watch my thumb disappear into his mouth again and again. When I finally pull it out, he groans and opens his eyes partway, his cheeks now flush and his dark curls falling loosely over his forehead. His hips shift forward, the head of his cock pressing up against my hole insistently, and I exhale a sharp breath and then reach down, hook my hands under my thighs, and pull my knees up higher to expose my hole to him more.

"Fuck," he whimpers again. He stares at me for a second, breathing hard, and then his hand wraps around his hard shaft, and he guides himself in, pushing slowly. My eyes screw shut as the initial pain of his cock breaching my entrance fades into pleasure, fullness, and heat.

He stops when he's all the way in, straining to control his breathing. One hand rubs gently up my calf and thigh before he flattens his palm on my chest. Then, without a word, he leans in, and his mouth covers mine, his kisses wet and messy, as he starts moving. It's slow at first—how he pulls all the way out and pushes back in confidently. His hand sweeps up into my hair, and he grips lightly, just enough to encourage me to tilt my head back so his mouth can trail more wet kisses down my neck. Each touch makes my skin tingle and sends another jolt of pleasure to my cock, the sensation building until I'm crying out with every thrust of his hips.

"God, Nico," I breathe, my hands running up his chest. "More. Fuck, more, please."

I press both palms into him as though I need a counterpressure, and his lips find mine again, but only briefly. Then he pushes up and sits back, his hands hooking around my thighs, and he starts pumping faster and harder. The new angle hits exactly the right spot. For a second, I can't breathe as my whole body tightens, an overwhelming coil of heat and pain and pleasure all pressing against me at once. He's touching me again, both hands running gently up my inner thighs. Then he's stroking my cock, leaning down over me, still driving into me hard.

"You're sexy like this, when you can't control yourself," he whispers into my ear, his breath hot against my cheek. "I love to hear you moan my name when you come. Let me hear you, Alex."

I groan.

"Let me hear you," he repeats, more firmly this time. Then he sits up again, still pumping my cock as he thrusts into me.

And that's it. I'm gone. My hands fall down to the bed, and I screw my eyes shut, and everything turns bright white, bursting with brilliant pulses as I come. His name is on my lips as I gasp for breath, clinging to the sheets to keep me anchored. He strokes me through the last of my release, and then he's leaning over me again, moaning, pressing his cock all the way into me as it starts to throb.

His forehead drops down to my shoulder, and I have just enough energy to bring my hands up to frame his face and tug him back to me. We kiss as his body trembles and jerks with his climax. Then he collapses on top of me, his chest heaving.

"Holy fuck," he mumbles.

I laugh weakly and kiss the top of his head. "Mm-hmm."

"Mmm, don't laugh at me." He pokes me in the side, and I flinch and laugh again, which makes him grunt. "That feels so weird when I'm still inside you."

I purse my lips together, trying not to laugh this time. "I know what you mean."

"Mmm, yeah, you would."

I can feel his dick softening inside me, but I know he doesn't like to move right away. He likes to stay just like this for a while, still connected and close as we catch our breaths. I don't blame him. I think it's kind of perfect, too.

I close my eyes as his fingers thread up into my hair, stroking me gently, and I do the same, letting my hands slide lazily up and down his back.

With a happy, content hum that makes me smile, he pushes up onto his elbows and stares down at me. His eyes are full of love, and even though it's something I've grown used to seeing, it still makes my stomach swoop and my heart stutter. I reach up and brush his hair off his forehead, but it just falls right back down. He laughs quietly, then smiles and lowers his mouth to mine for a soft kiss.

Together, we get up, go to the bathroom to clean up, and then get dressed—me back in the clothes I was wearing earlier and him in the first T-shirt and joggers he pulls out of the basket of clean laundry sitting near the closet. The shirt is mine—a burgundy Stanford shirt that's a size too big on him—and when I arch my eyebrows at him as he tugs the shirt into place, he just shrugs.

"We should probably fold the laundry," he says with a smirk.

"Eh. Maybe." I grin back at him and reach out my hand. He takes it and comes willingly into my arms, resting his head against my chest. I press a kiss into his hair. "So, what's the news you had that depends on us staying here?"

"Mmm, well . . ." He straightens up and pulls back, lifting his chin. His eyes are sparkling with enthusiasm again, and his smile . . . god, it's perfect and beautiful.

My fingers lift up and run along his cheek. "Tell me," I insist.

He drops his eyes with a nod and then pulls away. I stand there and watch as he walks the few steps over to the kitchenette, opens the junk drawer, and digs through the mess until he pulls out a business card. He pauses and stares down at it, nervousness flickering across his expression. Then he turns to me and offers me the card.

It's sleek and black, with a simple logo at the top reads *Bay Area Art Conservation LLC*. Underneath is a woman's name—Greta Hoffmann—and contact information. The address is up in Menlo Park, just north of Palo Alto.

"What's this?" I look back up at Nico.

His expression is almost a cautious sort of hopeful now, and he takes a deep breath and says, "Vera introduced me to this woman last week. She came into the gallery. I've seen her at a few events that Vera's hosted. She, um, she has an opening for an art conservator apprentice at her studio, and Vera thinks it might be a good fit for me."

My brain isn't really processing everything he's trying to say, and I shake my head a little. "Huh? What? I thought you like your job, don't you?"

He nods quickly. "I do. It took me a while to get used to everything that first year, I'm sure you remember. But I do like it, and I'm good at it. It's comfortable now, I guess."

"Yeah, I remember," I say softly. "Getting used to working around people you don't know wasn't easy. You really worked hard for it. And I know we're in a good position financially now, with my financial aid from school helping to pay the rent here the last couple of years. So, uh, I guess I just didn't think you were looking for a change?"

He shrugs. "I'm not, really. But, um, you know, I've just been thinking about what I want to do long-term . . ." He shakes his head a little, and my stomach drops as some of that light in his eyes dims. "Yeah, it's a dumb idea, isn't it? Sorry, I—"

"No, wait, wait," I cut in, lifting my hands to rest on his upper arms. "I didn't say that. I just don't understand. What's the offer? And are you interested?"

He lifts his eyes and holds my gaze for several seconds. Then the corners of his lips twitch up into a tentative smile, and he nods. "Yeah, um, I think I am interested."

"Okay, okay." I pull him into a tight hug and kiss his cheek. "Tell me all about it, then. I want to know how we can make it happen."

"Really?" he asks, wrapping his arms around my midsection. When I nod, he lets out a short breath and then looks up at me. "Okay, so . . ."

Together, we sit at the kitchen table, and he starts talking as he pulls out his laptop and opens up the website for Bay Area Art Conservation LLC. He tells me all about Greta and her business, what art conservators do and how the apprenticeship would work. It would be a lot, he says, almost like he'd be going to school full-time *and* still working for Vera full-time, putting in hours on the weekends and some weekday mornings in Menlo Park, then coming back to San Jose for his regular job. Since he wouldn't be getting an advanced degree, like most art conservators, he'd have to learn everything during the apprenticeship and on his own. Probably by the time I finished with my PhD in five or six years would be about when he'd have enough training and experience to start his own career, either at Greta's company or elsewhere.

*His own career.*

When he pauses after telling me that, I let out a sharp breath, scoot my chair closer to his, and pull him into another tight hug.

"Nico . . ."

"I-I dunno," he mumbles against my chest, shaking his head. "I mean, it honestly sounds really cool and like an actual career, not just a job. It'll be a lot of work, and there's a lot to learn, but I think I could do it. Vera thinks so too."

"Nico, it's perfect." I squeeze him gently. "I love this for you so much."

He pulls back to look up at me. "Yeah? You think I could do it?"

"I *know* you can," I tell him, and I bend down and kiss his lips softly. When we part, I rest my forehead against his. "I believe in you, Nico. I always have."

I feel him nod, and after a few moments, he straightens up, glancing back at the computer screen. There are tears in his eyes, but he blinks them away and smiles. "You're sure about this?"

"Absolutely."

He sits there for a few seconds, still staring at the computer screen. When he turns to me, his entire expression is lit up with excitement. "Okay, then. I'll call Greta tomorrow and let her know. And then I'll talk to Vera."

I nod and lean toward him, and he meets me halfway in another short, sweet kiss.

"I love you," I whisper, and then I kiss him again, his lips silky and soft.

When he pulls back after a few seconds, he's grinning, his eyes dancing like they were earlier, and my heart skips a beat at the sight. His smile is so warm, so full and bright. It's that smile of his I just love—the one that disappeared for so long after all that awful stuff happened back in Nebraska.

He's changed a lot since then, and I see that smile more and more now. But it's still special every single time.

And I don't think he knows just how much it gives me strength.

"What?" I ask, grinning back at him.

He shakes his head. "It's nothing. Just . . . I'm happy," he says quietly. "I'm happy and excited about this and about our future."

"I am, too." I set my hand palm up on his thigh, and he lowers his eyes to watch as our fingers intertwine.

Then he looks back up, and his smile softens. "You've always been there for me," he says. "You've always supported me, even when things were hard. You're my best friend, and I love you. And god, this sounds corny as fuck, but I . . . I want it to be like this, you and me, forever. Can you . . . can you promise me that?"

My chest tightens at the tiny bit of uncertainty in his voice, and I nod without hesitation. "Yes." I reach up to touch his cheek with my free hand. "My heart belongs to you, Nico. It always will. I promise."

He gifts me that beautiful smile again, and I feel all his hope and love and the depth of the promises we just made to each other.

It feels like the beginning of something incredible. And god, I'm all in.

# extended epilogue

*Two years later...*

# chapter one

## nico

FLAKES OF OLD, BRITTLE backing paper crumble, lifting off the back of a 1902 Stanisław Masłowski watercolor as I gently scrape the thick wove paper with a small metal spatula. The painting doesn't look like much now—it's covered in dark red and brown splotches known as foxing, which I've learned commonly occurs due to ageing and humidity—but after I'm finished removing the backing paper, our senior paper conservator, Susan, will start the careful process of washing the paper to eliminate the spots.

It's a slow, tedious job, and the success of the entire restoration depends on me being thorough. So I am.

The studio is quiet now, like it usually is on Saturdays. My boss, Greta, who owns the studio, is sitting at the workbench behind me, retouching surface cracks on an oil painting from the 1860s, and her wife, Sabine, is finishing up filing their taxes at the computer on the other side of the room. Most of Greta's other employees are only in on weekdays unless they've got a project that's time-sensitive, but I'm usually working at least one weekend day since I have to fit in as many hours as I can outside of regular business hours.

It's an exhausting schedule—working thirty-five to forty hours a week for Vera in San Jose and then another fifteen or so for my apprenticeship here at Greta's Menlo Park studio. I love the work, though, just like Vera thought I would. The long, quiet hours of careful attention to detail are ridiculously rewarding when each job is finished, an old painting slowly brought back to life.

The morning passes, and by the time Greta and her wife disappear around noon to go to lunch, I've finished removing about a third of the old backing paper on this painting. The goal is to have it finished by Monday, so Susan can get started on the next steps, but I need a break, too. So I set my tools down, stand up, and stretch, and then I head out of the main studio to the employee lounge, pulling my phone out of my pocket to check on my boyfriend.

I'm not surprised to see a slew of missed text messages, all from Alex. He's been panicking for the last week or so about a presentation he's giving to the entire physics department later today, *and* his mom just flew in from Nebraska last night so she can attend. When I left our apartment at eight this morning to catch the train to Menlo Park, he'd already been up for hours, going over his notes and fixing little things here and there in his slides. He's been nervous before, especially the first time he had to present at one of the department's smaller meetings last year. But I don't think I've ever seen him quite as nervous as he was this morning.

I grab a bottle of water from the fridge and then collapse onto the couch along the far wall and click to open the string of texts.

> *Alex (9:15 a.m.):* dude have u seen my nice sweater?

> *Alex (9:15 a.m.):* the black one with the v neck

> *Alex (10:22 a.m.):* nvm i found it

> *Alex (10:25 a.m.):* what about my shoes?

> *Alex (10:33 a.m.):* nvm i found those too

> *Alex (12:01 p.m.):* im gonna puke. what the hell is wrong with me

I'd laugh if I didn't know he was serious and really, honestly so nervous he was making himself sick. Frowning, I push myself up to sit, and I text him back.

> *Nico (12:12 p.m.):* Hey. I'm on a break. Do you need to talk?

He responds almost immediately.

> *Alex (12:13 p.m.):* no i just need to calm the f down

> *Alex (12:13 p.m.):* we're on campus. taking my mom to see the lab and meet John

A selfie comes through then—a picture of him and his mom in front of the physics building where Dr. Ellis's lab is. Alex is holding the phone out as far as he can, grinning, his arm wrapped around his mom's shoulders as she hugs him. It's probably meant to reassure me that he's fine. But I can see how off he's feeling. He looks pale, and his hair's out of place, a lock streaked with dark blue falling over his forehead. His smile isn't his typical easy smile, either. It's forced and tight.

> *Nico (12:14 p.m.):* You're gonna do great. You always do. I love you <3

I stare at the phone for a moment, waiting for him to respond. But he doesn't.

With another frown, I look up toward the main studio just across the hall. I've still got a ton of work to do, and so I shouldn't even consider skipping out on it to go support my boyfriend. He already told me he doesn't need to talk, and he's got his mom there and his whole lab, after all. It couldn't possibly help him for me to be there as well. Could it?

I glance down at the phone again, his not-real-smile staring back up at me, and my chest tightens.

I can take a longer break. Come back afterward and stay late here to finish my work. Maybe it won't really help. But then again, maybe it will.

Mind made up, I click out of the text chain with Alex and scroll through my other messages to find Greta's number. I send her a quick text letting her know I had something come up and I'll be back later in the afternoon. Then I head out, locking the studio behind me.

It's a short walk to the train station and then a very short ride to the Palo Alto stop. But it's a busy Saturday afternoon, and I spend the majority of the train ride huddled against the wall in the back of the train car, doing my best to ignore all the noise and bustle around me. By the time I get off the train and start walking toward campus, my heart is going about a million miles an hour and I feel like *I'm* the one who's about to puke.

I pull up a map of campus as I walk, keeping off to the edge of the sidewalk so people can pass by me. It's a long walk—a little over a mile—and by the time I make it to the building where Alex's presentation is, it's two minutes to one o'clock. I hurry inside, following a group of students who look like they know where they're going up a few steps and through a set of automatic double doors. The lobby is mostly empty, thank fuck, and I jog up a set of stairs to the second-level entrance for the auditorium. I quickly slip in as the doors start to close, and then I collapse against the back wall to catch my breath.

The auditorium is massive. Stadium-style seating that's already nearly full leads down to a large stage, and on that stage, standing next to a podium and talking with Dr. Ellis and another professor I don't recognize, is my boyfriend.

Even from all the way in the back, I can see how nervous he is. He's smiling and nodding at whatever Dr. Ellis says, but his shoulders are tight, and he keeps glancing out at the crowd as though he can't believe how many people are here.

I step away from the wall and scan down the aisle ahead of me, hoping to find Alex's mom or at least an open seat on the edge of some row. I'm not that lucky, though; the entire auditorium is packed, and the only unoccupied seats I see are in the middle of the second row from the front. I can't find his mom anywhere.

I start down the steps anyway, forcing myself to ignore the fact that there are probably hundreds of people in the room, and I somehow make it down to the second row and across to the middle, shrinking down as small as I can to fit through the narrow

space between the back of the seats in front of me and the knees
of the other people in the audience. My heart's pounding, though,
and as I finally manage to slip into one of the few open seats, my
head's pounding too. I slump down, crossing my arms over my
chest, and glance up toward the stage.

Alex is staring directly at me, his lips pursed as though he's
not sure what he's seeing. He blinks and shakes his head, then he
mouths "what are you doing here?" I smirk at him and shrug, and
he holds my gaze for another few seconds before grinning broadly.
Dr. Ellis touches his shoulder, and he turns away, nodding.

"Yeah, I'm ready to go," I hear him say, his voice as steady and
confident as ever.

Dr. Ellis steps up to the podium on the stage, Alex right behind
him. The lights dim, and the room goes silent as he adjusts the
microphone and then looks up around the crowd.

"Good afternoon, and welcome, everyone, to the third session
of our spring semester's *What If* series, hosted by the Physics Department," Dr. Ellis says. "Today's talk is on a topic everyone here
should appreciate, even if the complexities of the research aren't
in your wheelhouse: gravity and space-time. Alexander Hayes is
a second-year PhD student in my lab, and although he's new at
this, he already has quite an impressive resumé." Next to Dr. Ellis, Alex's face flushes bright red. "Alex graduated top of his class
here at Stanford in 2029, with a bachelor's of science in physics.
His undergraduate research yielded not one, but two research papers, both published in the *Journal of Cosmology and Astroparticle
Physics*. He's got a third paper currently in the revision stage with
*Nature Astronomy*, and his research is included in an Astronomy
and Astrophysics Research Grant from the US National Science
Foundation. On top of that, he's a Knight-Hennessey Scholar and
just an all-around good guy. Please welcome Alexander Hayes for
his talk today, titled"—Dr. Ellis glances down at Alex's laptop, sit-

ting on the podium in front of him—"'Quantitative Measurement of Dark Matter, Gravity, and the Warping of Space-time.'"

Damn. That's an introduction if ever I heard one.

I'm grinning with pride as I clap along with the rest of the audience, and when Alex's eyes land on me as he steps up to the podium, I mouth, "Holy fuck, man." His cheeks turn an even deeper shade of red, and he shakes his head lightly, holding back a smile.

I'd like to think me being here does actually help him in some way, because he absolutely knocks it out of the park. I mean, I can't follow much of the science—I only know bits and pieces from what he's tried to explain to me over the last several years—but he sounds perfectly confident as he first introduces the concept of dark matter and then goes on to show how he and his colleagues in Dr. Ellis's lab are using some new approach to measure dark matter by looking at the warping of space-time. Or something like that. Whatever it is, he does well, and by the time his final slide comes up on the projector screen behind him about forty-five minutes later, everyone in the audience is still listening and engaged. Hands lift up around the room with questions, which spark a lively discussion lasting another twenty minutes or so.

I stay in my seat as the audience starts to file out around me, and it's several minutes later that I see Alex's mom heading to the front of the room. Alex is still up on the stage, taking questions and talking, and his mom stops back a bit, watching with a proud smile on her face.

I know how she feels.

When the rest of the room finally clears, Alex steps down off the stage, slipping his laptop into his backpack. He's smiling and happy and still looks just as confident as he did when he first started his presentation. His mom wraps her arms around his waist in a big hug, and I finally stand up and start down toward the end of the row, shoving my hands in my pockets.

". . . so impressed. I can't believe you've done all that, and—oh, Nico! I didn't know you were here!" Laina Hayes's eyes light up when I approach, and she lets Alex go long enough to offer me a hug too.

Despite the anxiety still lingering from my unplanned train ride and then having to sit next to too many strangers for over an hour, I step right up into her arms and let her hug me. It's warm and soothing, as it usually is now, although I remember a time when it was difficult to let her touch me.

"I barely made it on time," I say when she pulls back. My eyes shift to Alex, who looks about ready to cry.

"You didn't have to come," he says, shaking his head softly, "but I'm really glad you did."

I shrug. "I just wanted to learn all about dark matter and gravity and stuff. No other reason."

He gives me a silly smile, then steps up to me, settles his hand on my hip, and places a light kiss on my cheek, lingering for an extra second with his lips against my skin.

"Thank you," he whispers, and he kisses me again before straightening up. "Can you come to lunch with us? I couldn't eat beforehand, but John and a bunch of others are headed over to San Agus, and we were planning to go meet them."

I wish I could say yes, but I know the group—while his advisor and lab colleagues are all nice people, they also tend to get loud and rowdy, and I'm constantly on edge when I'm around them. I shake my head and frown. "I should get back to the studio."

"Of course, yeah," Alex says. He purses his lips and then turns to his mom. "Uh, can I meet you outside in a minute?"

"Sure, sweetie." She smiles at me, too, and a few seconds later, Alex and I are alone.

He sets his backpack down on the ground next to him and then loops his arms around my waist and hugs me to him tightly. "Oh my god, man, I'm so glad you were here. As soon as I saw you . . ."

He trails off as he buries his head into the crook of my neck, blowing out a long breath, and I slip my arms around him and hug him back.

"You were fucking brilliant."

"I was fucking *nervous*," he corrects with a laugh. He straightens back up, shaking his head as he bends over to grab his backpack. "Did you see how many people were here? It was insane."

"Did you see where I had to sit? Every seat was full. It was torture." His smile falters, but I shake my head and slip my hand into his as we start toward the exit. "I'm fine. And I'm glad I was here if it helped you."

"It definitely did," he says.

I squeeze his hand, and he reaches ahead of us to push open the door. His mom is waiting in the lobby, and she smiles softly and puts her phone away in her purse when she sees us.

"I looked up the restaurant, and it seems like the train station is right nearby. So we can all walk together?"

Alex nods, still holding my hand. "Does that work for you?" he asks me, and when I agree, we start on our way, out of the building and then back across campus.

He and his mom talk most of the way, and he seems so happy and at ease that I'm reluctant to say goodbye when we get to the train station. But then he kisses me and tells me he loves me and that he's so thankful I came. And he says he can't wait to see me at home later.

Something about that makes my heart full.

We kiss again, and I hug his mom goodbye, though I'll see her later, too. Then they turn and continue walking on to the restaurant while I make my way over to the platform to wait for the next train.

Not more than ten minutes later, I hop off the train at the Menlo Park stop, clenching and unclenching my fists as I try my hardest not to let anyone bump into me. When I'm through the small crowd of people entering and exiting the train, I take a left and make the rest of the short walk back to the studio.

Greta's here again, though she's at her computer rather than working on the painting still sitting on her workbench, and when I walk in, she looks up with a kind smile.

"Welcome back. Everything okay?"

I nod. "Yeah. Alex had a presentation today, and he was really nervous, so I went to support him."

Her smile broadens. "How did it go?"

I sit in the swivel stool at my workbench and spin it around to face her, and then I briefly recount how amazing and genius-level smart my boyfriend is. The whole time, Greta watches me with that same knowing grin. When I finish, she nods and stands as she picks up a piece of paper from her desk.

"It's so important to be supportive like that," she says, starting over in my direction. "You two sound like you have a strong relationship. How long have you been together?"

"Five years. Almost six now, actually," I say, and I look down at my hands in my lap. "But, uh, we've been best friends for as long as I can remember. He's been there for me so much. It's, um, usually me who's in need of support. It's nice to know I can be there to help him when he needs it, too."

I glance up. Greta's at her workbench now, half sitting on it while still smiling softly at me. She nods in understanding.

"Relationships aren't one-sided, even if it seems sometimes like they are. And, contrary to what some will say, they're not fifty-fifty, either. Sometimes one partner gives more, sometimes it's eighty-twenty." She drops her eyes for a second and shrugs. "Hell, I remember days when I couldn't give anything, and Sabine . . . well, she carried the weight until I could again. It's all about being kind and understanding and communicating. And being there when you can, like today."

She and her wife have been married for almost fifteen years now, but they've been together for even longer. Twenty-five years, I think.

*I hope Alex and I make it there someday.*

My breath catches at the thought, and I look back down at my hands in my lap as I nod. Moments from the last few years replay in my head—times when I've helped carry that weight for him without even realizing it. Like that time he got really sick during finals week his freshman year and I spent hours calling and emailing all of his professors to reschedule his exams. And the time he forgot his student ID, which he needed to take his advanced physics midterm during his fourth year in undergrad, and I took a long lunch to bring it to him so he wouldn't miss the exam. And all the times he would have forgotten to eat if I hadn't made dinner, not had clean clothes if I hadn't done the laundry.

He supports me; he's there for me when I need him in all the ways that count. But he needs me, too, just like he told me that morning at the airport in San Jose nearly six years ago now. And I'm suddenly so glad for the reminder.

After a few seconds of silence, like Greta knows there's something big going on in my head, she clears her throat. "Here, this is for you. There was a phone call for you just before you got back. I took a message."

I look up, and she's offering me the paper she picked up off her desk minutes ago. "Ah, thanks," I say.

She smiles at me, then tips her head toward her workbench. "Back to it, huh?"

I nod and swivel my stool back to face my workbench. The Masłowski watercolor sits right where I left it, covered with a thin sheet of plain white paper for protection. I need to wash my hands before I get started, so I stand and start toward the sink, unfolding the paper on the way.

The words on the page stop me in my tracks before I even round the corner of my workbench.

*For Nico—*

*Please return call to Cindy @ 402-555-7765*

That's my mom's name. And my mom's phone number.

And this is the first time she's reached out at all in nearly six years.

I quickly crumple the paper up and toss it in the trash can. Then I force myself to move toward the sink again so I can get back to work.

# chapter two

## alex

THE REST OF SATURDAY and Sunday is busy; since my mom's only visiting for the weekend, we try to fit a lot in. The three of us go to dinner and a show at a theater near our apartment in San Jose on Saturday night. Then my mom and I head up to San Francisco on Sunday and do all the touristy things—Fisherman's Wharf, Alcatraz, the Golden Gate Bridge. Nico works all day, says he has a deadline he needs to meet on a project, and so it's just my mom and me.

It's not until the train ride home from San Francisco late Sunday evening that I finally tell her what's been on my mind for months now.

And since I'm nervous as hell about it, I just randomly blurt it out without any lead-in as soon as I've gathered the courage.

"So, um, I want to ask Nico to marry me."

My mom looks up from her phone, her eyebrows arched. "Sweetie—"

"It's crazy, right? I mean, I'm still in school, and he's working full-time and has his apprenticeship, and everything's good but we're so busy. So it doesn't *really* make much sense. But, Mom, I love him so much, and—"

She reaches across the small table between us and sets her hand on mine. She looks so calm, smiling with amusement at my rambling, and I shake my head.

"It's crazy, right?"

"No, sweetie," she says softly. "It's not crazy. Actually, I'm surprised it's taken you so long."

I huff a weak laugh and drop my eyes. "I've been thinking about it for a while."

"Have you talked to Nico about it?"

Heat floods my cheeks, and I immediately shake my head.

"Well, don't you think that should be the first step? Does he want to get married?"

I lift my eyes again, and she's watching me with such a gentle expression that I can't hold her gaze. "We've talked about the future. About *our* future, I mean. What we're going to do when I'm finished with school, where I'm going to try to get work, what he's going to do when he's finished with his apprenticeship. We're saving money together. We've lived together for almost five years now. We budget and plan. And we've already, um . . . promised each other we're going to be together forever." I swallow and force myself to look at her.

"Sounds like commitment."

"Yeah." I nod a little. "I want to spend the rest of my life with him. I want him to be my husband."

Her eyes are dancing now, and she squeezes my hand, then releases me and leans back into her chair. "Did you buy the rings already?"

"No . . . But I looked." My heart speeds up at the admission, but her grin only grows more.

"Let me guess . . ." She tilts her head sideways, like she's thinking. "Titanium bands in a medium gray, matte, not a shiny finish."

My face gets even hotter, and I look down and pull out my phone, then scroll through the tabs in my browser until I find the rings I picked out.

"There's a jeweler near campus. I stopped in last week." I hand her my phone. "These are the ones I want."

They're pretty much exactly as she described—plain dark titanium bands with a brushed matte finish.

"A-and not that it really matters, but, um, they're having a sale through next weekend. I have the money from my savings, and I was thinking, um . . ." I trail off when she lifts her eyes again and slides the phone back toward me across the table.

"What, sweetie?"

"Um, well, there's this Japanese garden—it's near that little zoo. We've been there quite a few times, and he likes it a lot because it's quiet and peaceful. It's not really like the river back home, but I think it kinda reminds him of that."

"Is that where you're thinking of proposing?"

I frown. "It's stupid, isn't it?"

"No, no, not at all." She reaches out again and takes my hand. "Honestly, sweetie, it sounds absolutely perfect, for both of you."

My heart is pounding now, and I nod slowly as a smile finally forces its way out. "I love him so much, Mom."

"I know you do." She sniffles and pulls her hand away to wipe a tear from the corner of her eye, though she's still smiling. "Just make sure you invite me to the wedding, okay?" she says, trying to make herself sound stern. "Even if you just elope or get married in the courthouse in front of a judge, I want to be there. Promise me!"

I roll my eyes but agree, and she huffs "good" and then grins at me again before turning to look out the window, reaching up to swipe at her eyes.

Nico's alarm goes off at just after six on Monday morning, the jarring notes of "Radiance's Theme" from *Hollow Knight* startling me out of a comfortable dream. Nico groans and rolls away from me to hit snooze. Then he scoots back until he's flush against me and settles his head on the pillow.

"Mmm, too early?" I slip my arm around his waist and hold him to me tighter.

"No."

I don't have to be at school for journal club until ten, but Nico starts at Urban Arts early on Mondays—some weekly meeting with his boss, Vera, to organize their schedules and goals for the week. He's usually dragging himself out of bed by six thirty at the latest.

"Can I make you breakfast?" I ask, and I'm still groggy and tired and not fully aware, but I feel him stiffen up.

"No."

"Okay."

Something's bothering him, but I'm not sure exactly what. He did get home quite late last night, so maybe he's just tired. He works so much and rarely takes a full day off. It seems like more than that, though.

I let my hand drift lightly up and down his forearm, and I flutter tiny, slow kisses along his bare shoulder. After a moment, he inhales deeply and breathes out a long sigh, his body relaxing back into me.

"Mmm, better?" I murmur against his skin.

"Yeah . . . Thanks."

"Want me to stop?"

He mumbles a no, and so I keep gently rubbing his arm and then his back with soft, long strokes while my lips caress his shoulder and neck. He's silent, except for the occasional quiet sigh, but after a few more minutes, most of the tension in his shoulders is gone.

Of course, that's when his alarm goes off again. I quickly prop myself up and reach over him to shut it off before he can move. He groans and then rolls onto his back, one arm coming up to cover his eyes.

God, he looks exhausted.

"You need a day off," I say softly. I lower my mouth back to his neck and trail a path of kisses down to his collarbone. Then I pause with my lips barely brushing his skin. "Things have been hectic lately. You've been working so much."

I glance up and see him frowning, his eyes half open as he looks at me.

"I . . . have to," he says, and I nod.

"I know. But you need some downtime, too." I reach up and touch his cheek with just the tips of my fingers, and he closes his eyes, then lowers his arm and shifts onto his side so he's facing me.

"Yeah, you're right."

"I'm always right," I tease, and he grins and swats my arm. Then he's silent again, and his expression turns serious, like he's thinking about something important. Quietly, I start caressing his arm and placing tiny kisses on his forehead and cheeks. "So, hmm, what about this weekend, maybe Sunday? We can relax and spend the day together? Go somewhere?"

A buzz of eager excitement rolls through me, my mind already racing with possibilities, even before he's answered. I know exactly where I want to take him. And Sunday . . . Sunday would be perfect. Morning, so it's not busy or too hot. We can have breakfast at the café he likes—the one by Urban Arts. Then take a bus over to the garden, it's not too far. And the cherry blossoms are just starting to bloom; they'll make the perfect backdrop. Afterward, after he says yes and we're engaged and I've made sure he knows exactly how much I love him and how much he means to me, we can come back home and just relax and hang out, play video games like we used to or maybe go to the movies. Whatever he wants to do.

It'll be perfect. Like him.

I drop my head down to his shoulder and smile against his skin, and he hums and sets his hand on my chest.

"Hmm, yeah, maybe? I mean, I'll have to check with Greta," he says, but I feel him shake his head slightly. "Wait, won't you be studying for your qualifying exam? It's the following week, isn't it?"

My stomach drops at the reminder, and the beautiful, idyllic scene I painted in my head poofs out of existence. "Ugh. Yeah, you're right. The exam is Tuesday afternoon. I'll need to study all weekend."

The two-hour-long oral qualifying exam is a requirement for formal advancement to candidacy for my PhD in the Physics Department. I'm prepared and ready—John has been making me practice the first part of the exam, which consists of a prepared oral presentation on my chosen topic, during our weekly lab meetings—and I'm fairly confident I'll do well. But it's stressful anyway, especially because the committee selected to administer my exam includes two faculty who will also be members of my dissertation committee.

I sigh. "Well, what about the following weekend, then?"

Nico shakes his head. "That's the weekend Vera's overseeing the opening of that new gallery up in San Mateo. I'm working there both Saturday and Sunday."

"Oh, right." I let out another resigned sigh. "When did we become such an old, busy couple?"

He laughs, his breath hot against my chest, but he shakes his head and hesitates a second before he says, "Six years together this summer."

My heart stutters, all my disappointment forgotten. I lift my hand to cup his cheek, and he smiles softly as his eyes meet mine.

God, he's so beautiful and so perfect.

I have to be the luckiest guy in the world.

"Six *amazing* years," I murmur, and I lean in for a short, sweet kiss.

When we part, he laughs lightly as he looks up at me. "I've loved you a lot longer than that, you know," he says.

And my darn heart skips another beat. I wrap my arms around him and pull him up against me and nuzzle my face into his hair. "I've loved you for so long, Nico."

I've got the stupidest urge to just blurt it out right now, like I did with my mom last night.

*Marry me, Nico. Be my husband. Just you and me. Forever.*

But then he sighs, tilts his head back, and kisses me again, long and deep and slow, and the urge passes.

That's okay, though. I want to do this right, anyway.

I want to have the rings and get down on one knee and see his eyes go wide with surprise. I want to hold his hand while I say everything I'm feeling in my heart. Then I want to hear him whisper *yes, yes, of course*, barely holding himself together, and I want to slip the ring on his finger and stand up and wrap my arms around him and kiss him.

He hums into the kiss with a quiet contentment that makes my heart flutter *again*, and then he pulls back, smiling. "I should get ready. And you should go back to sleep." He touches his lips to mine one more time. Then he rolls over and drags himself out of bed.

I watch him shuffle across the room to the dresser and then disappear into the bathroom to get ready for work, and when the bathroom door shuts, I collapse back onto the bed. I'm fully awake now; there's no way I'm falling asleep, despite how early it is.

So, instead, I grab my phone from the nightstand, spend a few minutes texting with my mom, who's at the airport already, waiting for her flight back to Omaha, then pull up the same tab I showed her last night—the one for the wedding bands I picked out. A grin stretches across my face as I stare down at the dark metal band on the screen, and I close my eyes for a beat, trying to imagine what it will feel like on my finger and what it will look like on his.

God, I just can't wait.

I mean, I *will* wait, because, again, I want to do this right. He deserves for me to do this right. But I'll definitely be making a trip to the jeweler's at some point today, maybe even right after journal club is over. And then I'll have to figure out when—a day we both have off; a day we can spend all day together, no distractions or work or anything else. Just the two of us.

It'll be perfect.

I just know it.

# chapter three

*nico*

Sunday night after the two-day event at the new gallery opening, Vera pulls me aside and tells me, under no uncertain terms, that I'm to take the next two days off. I would argue, because I still have a ton of work to do both for her and for Greta, but the weekend was long and taxing, and I'm barely holding myself together as it is. My job for the weekend consisted mostly of managing things from the back office—yet the number of phone calls I had to make or take and the number of strangers I had to meet were both impossible for me.

On top of that, ever since I got that message from my mom two weeks ago, I've been in a bit of a downward spiral. Sleep has been difficult and filled with nightmares, and work has been one challenge after another, every little thing making me second-guess myself. Honestly, I'm surprised I made it through this weekend.

I pack up my stuff, thank Vera, and say good night to the owner of the new gallery and several other colleagues. Then I step out into the brisk spring evening and start the walk to the train station. It's not until I'm alone that I really start to feel all of the tension and anxiety I've been holding all day, all weekend, all of the last *two weeks*. I've been ignoring it as best I can, pushing through, going, going, going. But it suddenly hits me like a brick wall, and I nearly stumble as all of my energy seeps away and a vaguely familiar lightheadedness makes me wobble on my feet.

Fuck, this isn't good.

There's a bench along the sidewalk, and I stagger over and collapse onto the seat, dropping my head down between my knees. Long, slow breaths help a little, as does closing my eyes and covering my ears to shut out all the noises echoing around me. But the world keeps swaying for what's probably several minutes.

I should have stuck around and asked Vera for a ride back to San Jose. Or I should have called Alex and asked him to meet me here. Or I should have taken that day off last weekend, like he suggested.

My chest tightens, and my shoulders ache, and everything around me feels like it's shrinking, closing in, suffocating me, even though I know I'm outside, out in the open, and perfectly safe. And I *should* be able to breathe.

Shaking, I reach into my pocket and pull out my cell phone.

He'll be mad at me. That's the first thought that pops into my head. He'll be mad at me because I should have known this was going to happen, and I should have listened and taken a day off, and I've overworked myself into this panic. And if he's mad, maybe that'll be it. Maybe that'll be enough, and he'll leave me.

I know it's not true. I know it. But these types of thoughts have been fucking with me for the last couple of weeks as well. It's almost as though the note from my mom brought back all of my insecurities—the awful reminder of how she turned on me and abandoned me that summer six years ago—and those insecurities are now bleeding over into my relationship with my boyfriend.

I grip my phone tighter, my eyes screwed shut, and I focus on my breathing for a few moments. Alex isn't like that. He won't be mad at me. If anything, he'll be worried, and he'll be glad I called to get help. I *know* that. I do.

Still, I hesitate, my indecision fueled by uncertainty and the icky feeling that my heart's not beating right.

"Goddamn fucking anxiety," I curse under my breath.

I force my eyes open, and I glance quickly to my right—the way to the train station. It's really not too far. I should be able to make it on my own.

Clenching my jaw, I grip the arm of the bench with my free hand and use it to push myself to my feet. And I manage to get myself moving again. The world's still spinning, and everything's loud and too bright, even in the darkness of the night. I keep my head down, staring at the sidewalk in front of me as I walk, still holding my phone tightly in my hand.

The tension in my jaw turns into an irritating ache that starts to work its way upward, into the back of my skull, and before I make it to the train station, I have a pulsing headache—the kind I know isn't going away until I've gotten enough sleep and a hefty dose of Tylenol.

When I finally sit down on the bench at the platform to wait for the next train to show up, I'm weak and shaky, and the air around me feels hot, like it's tinged with anger and irritation. I know the feeling; it's not new or different. But it *has* been a while since it's been this bad.

The next southbound train isn't due for another ten minutes, and so I pull out my phone and immediately open up my text message app and click on Alex's name.

> *Alex (5:08 p.m.): <3*

It's the last message he sent me, nearly four hours ago now—just a heart emoji. I never had the chance to respond earlier, but even just seeing the text now seems to take the edge off the worst of my anxiety. I take a slow breath and then click on the phone icon to call him as I pull my feet up onto the bench.

It rings twice before he answers.

"Hey, Nico!" His voice surrounds me like a warm blanket, and I close my eyes and let the feeling settle.

"Hey, yeah, um—"

"Are you okay? What's wrong? Where are you?" He must hear the hoarseness of my voice, because he cuts in before I can even start to tell him what's going on.

I take a slow breath. The air isn't quite as hot or stale now, though the acrid smell of exhaust fumes lingers. And suddenly, I want nothing more than to be at home, with him. "We finished with everything a bit ago," I say. "I'm at the station in San Mateo, waiting for the next train."

"Alright, okay. But that doesn't answer my question. Are you okay?"

A tiny huff of a laugh escapes me. "You asked me *three* questions! I answered the last one, which was the easiest."

"Yeah, well, you should have answered them in order of importance," he teases back, his tone playful but still worried.

I grumble a nonresponse and open my eyes to look down the train tracks. "I'm tired," I say quietly, but I know he needs a little more than that, so I continue. "I started feeling exhausted and lightheaded when I left the gallery. Um, I think it's just from all the stress and going nonstop, and today and yesterday were busy, you know? But I made it to the station, and . . . and now that you're on the phone with me, I'm feeling a lot better."

It's the truth—I am feeling better just hearing his voice. But it's not the whole truth, and maybe that makes me an awful boyfriend.

Even if I *wanted* to tell him about my mom, about how sharp the reminder of her abandonment has been stinging, about how deeply bone-tired I am, especially with all the extra stress of working so fucking much—which I don't—I'm not sure I could anyway. He's been so happy lately—all cute and lovey and sappy, holding me longer when we're in bed together, sending me those little heart emojis all the time. I would *hate* to see his joy drained for even a second.

I close my eyes and lean back against the bench again, one arm wrapped around my knees.

The line is silent for a few seconds, and I feel my shoulders tightening. But then he says, his voice soft with concern, "Do you want me to come meet you? I'm at home, so it'll take me some time to get there. But I can leave right now, and you won't have to be alone."

It's nearly an hour by train from San Jose to San Mateo, and I know if I need him to, that's exactly what he'll do—leave home right now, catch the first train he can, and meet me here. He's amazing like that.

"I love you," I say.

"That's sweet of you. But that doesn't answer my question, *again*."

I smile weakly and shake my head. "I know. I'm thinking."

"I'm leaving now. Are you safe?"

My heart does something funny, rejecting all the negative stuff that's floating around in my head and replacing it with gratitude and love for my wonderful boyfriend. "I'm safe," I say quietly. "Don't come, please. The train will be here in just a few minutes, and I just need . . . I just need you to stay on the phone with me for a bit."

"I can do that," he says without hesitation. "Oh, you'll totally appreciate this! So, I was on campus earlier studying with Garrett and Parker, and we decided to go to that taco place, you know, the one with the giant cactus mural on the wall . . ."

I lower my head to my knees and listen as he talks, taking me through most of his afternoon and evening. When the train arrives a few minutes later, I stand up without swaying at all, and I find a seat in the closest car. Alex keeps talking the whole time—the entire fifty-minute train ride. It's exactly what I need, and somehow, he knows it.

It's after ten when the train pulls up at Diridon Station in San Jose, and I see him standing there before it even stops. He's still holding the phone up to his ear. Our eyes meet through the window on the train car, and he smiles a big, gorgeous smile that makes my heart flutter.

"Hi," he says into the phone, like we haven't been talking to each other for nearly an hour.

A smile finds me, too, and I shake my head as I stare at him, a million things running through my head.

*What are you doing here?*

*You didn't have to come.*

*God, it's good to see you.*

*I love you, Alex. I love you so much.*

Instead, I just echo back, "Hi."

His smile widens, and he tilts his head toward the doors to the train just as they open. We both hang up, and I meet him outside the train a moment later, immediately melting into his arms. He hums as he hugs me to him, and he kisses my cheek.

"Are you okay?" he asks softly.

I nod. "Yeah. I am now."

# chapter four

*alex*

"THIS IS RIDICULOUS. WHO the hell thinks these things up? New Guinness World Record for the most number of rhinestones stuck to the human body? Why?" Nico scoffs.

I glance over from where I'm standing at the stove to see him shaking his head as he stares at his phone. He's lying on his stomach on the bed, naked except for his boxer briefs, his hair still damp from the shower he just took. He shakes his head one more time and then looks up at me as he tosses his phone down on the bed.

"Remember Shane, from high school?" I ask, and when Nico nods, I turn back to the stovetop and flip the grilled cheese sandwich I'm cooking for him. "He's the current world record holder for most paper airplanes thrown into watermelons."

"Sounds super useful."

I laugh. "Right?"

With a groan, Nico rolls over onto his back and covers his eyes with one arm. He looks much better than he had an hour ago when I met him at the train station, but the dark circles under his eyes and tension in his jaw haven't entirely disappeared. He needs to eat and then sleep.

"You have tomorrow off, right?" I ask quietly. I turn off the heat for the burner on the stove and move Nico's sandwich to a plate, and when I glance over at him, he's turned his head to look at me, his eyes half open. His exhaustion is so clear, and it makes my heart ache.

"Tomorrow and Tuesday. Vera made me promise not to come in." He grimaces. "I think Vera mentioned something to Greta, too, because Greta texted and said not to come in until Friday morning."

"Good." He arches his eyebrows at me, and I frown. "You're exhausted. You've been working so much. You need a break."

Something in his expression shifts, but he turns his face away before I have time to figure out what it is. "Yeah, I do," he says.

I pull out a knife to cut his sandwich into quarters, and then I move the plate to the table for him. Without a word, he pushes himself up to stand and then takes his seat at the table.

"OJ? Or milk?"

"Nah, this is fine. Thank you."

I get a napkin for him and then start cleaning up the kitchen as he eats. He's quiet, and not that that's anything unusual, especially with how tired he is, but I can't shake the concern that there's something deeper going on.

I've been busy—last week, I took my qualifying exam, which I passed easily, and I have a deadline coming up for revisions for the research article John and I submitted to *Nature Astronomy* plus homework for my classes and exams to study for.

And I've also been distracted for other reasons.

I bought the rings. They're hiding in a box in the back of one of the drawers in our dresser. And I scouted out the Japanese garden to make sure I know exactly the spot to take him to. I've also written and rewritten what I want to say to him probably a hundred times by now, and I've been keeping an eye on both of our calendars, hoping a day pops up that'll work for both of us. Actually, if he's off work on Tuesday . . . maybe I could make that work.

But I've been so busy and so distracted . . .

I close the fridge after putting away the cheese and butter, and by the time I finish washing and drying the dishes, he's done eating. He brings his plate to the sink to wash it, and I take it from him with a small smile.

"I've got it. You can go lie down, okay?"

His expression tightens, and he seems like he's about to object, but he stops himself. "Then you're coming to bed, right?" he asks.

"Yeah."

With a nod, he loops an arm around my waist, hugs me, and then shuffles over and collapses onto the bed, not bothering to crawl under the covers. I finish up, turn out all the lights and lock the front door, and then undress and join him in bed. He's already almost asleep, but he has enough awareness to scoot under the covers when I pull them back. Then he mumbles something incoherent and cuddles up against my chest, resting a hand on my stomach.

I drop a kiss on the top of his head and close my eyes. "Good night. I love you, always," I whisper. I don't expect a response; I figure he's drifting off already and probably didn't even hear me. But I must be wrong because he stiffens up in my arms and presses his cheek against my chest harder.

He holds himself still for several seconds before letting out a shuddering breath and forcing out, "Good night."

No *love you, too*, like he would normally say. And I hope I'm imagining it, but he suddenly feels like he's trembling, even as he clings to me.

"Nico? Hey, what's going on?" I ask softly, letting my hand rub up and down his back.

He blows out a quick breath and shakes his head. "Sorry. Sorry. I'm so tired."

"I know." I wrap my arms around him and turn over onto my back, bringing him on top of me. Then I tug the comforter all the way up to his shoulders and resume rubbing his back. He sighs deeply against my neck. He loves lying on me like this; he says it makes him feel close to me and comfortable and safe. I hope that's the case right now, too. "That's all, though, right? You're just tired? Nothing else?" I ask gently.

Tension returns to his shoulders, but he doesn't answer right away. I guess that *is* his answer, though.

"Whatever it is," I say softly, "you can tell me."

The last couple of weeks start to replay in my head when he still stays quiet. Little things I shrugged off. A flinch here, a frown there. Going to sleep early, skipping a meal. Things that now seem out of place but that I didn't really pay enough attention to at the time.

"Nico," I murmur again, and I kiss the top of his head. My hand stops on his lower back as he inhales a deep breath and then lets it out slowly, his body trembling. "Talk to me, please. Whatever's bothering you . . ."

I trail off as he shakes his head against me.

"It's nothing. I don't want to talk about it," he mumbles, but then he buries his head into the crook of my neck, and I feel dampness on my skin, like he's been crying. "I just wanna go to sleep. Please. I'm so tired. And it's not . . it's not urgent. It's nothing, really. It's nothing, and I—dammit."

My stomach drops as he pushes away from me, rolls over, and sits up, swinging his legs off the bed. He doesn't stand or talk or move, and I'm scared if I say or do anything, he'll retreat further. So I don't move, either, not even to reach out and comfort him. After several seconds, his shoulders slump, and he lowers his head into his hands. Shaking, he turns back around and crawls into bed again and back into my arms, and he clings to me, his cheek pressed against my chest.

"She called," he says, his voice muffled and low and broken.

"She? Who? Vera? Or Greta?"

He shakes his head. "My mom."

"Your . . . oh, god." I understand now. Maybe. I hold him tighter. "When?"

"The Saturday you gave that presentation at school."

That long ago. Two weeks and a few days. And he's been keeping it to himself the whole time.

A twinge of hurt stabs my heart, but I quickly push it away. He has to be hurting much more than I can even imagine.

I'm not sure whether to ask him the billion questions I have or to just hold him and comfort him. He doesn't make me decide, however.

"Sh-she called Greta's office number when I was gone," he says, and he shifts just enough that he's not mumbling into my chest anymore. "I-I'm not really sure how she found me, but I'm listed on Greta's website as her apprentice. That's my only guess. She left a message with Greta asking me to call her."

"Did you?"

"No," he chokes out. "No, I didn't. I don't know what to say. I don't know why she called. I'm not sure I can talk to her. It's been six years, and she's never reached out at all. She has your number, she knows your mom. If she really wanted to, she could have called you or talked to your mom. She could have tried anytime. Why now? Why wait so long? Was I not—" He cuts himself off, shaking his head angrily.

Or, actually, maybe it's not anger. Maybe it's sadness mixed with frustration and doubt and anxiety.

I start rubbing his back again, as I did earlier, and he sucks in a breath and then buries his face against my chest. He starts crying softly, his body shuddering with each quiet sob.

"I had no idea." I kiss the top of his head and close my eyes, willing myself not to cry right along with him. "I'm sorry I didn't realize sooner—"

"No. Please don't," he cuts in. "It's not your fault I didn't tell you."

"Nico . . . you're my boyfriend and my best friend." I squeeze him gently. "I feel like I should have realized something was wrong and made sure you were okay."

He shakes his head. "You were busy. We were both busy. Please don't blame yourself. I . . . deliberately didn't tell you. This is on me."

That twinge of hurt pulses again, but again, I push it away. "Still, I'm sorry you had to deal with this on your own for the last two weeks. Do you want to talk about it now? Or do you want to sleep and talk about it in the morning?"

He doesn't answer. Instead, he closes his eyes and takes controlled, careful breaths in and out until he's no longer shaking. Then he silently climbs on top of me, back into that position he was in a few minutes ago. He reaches behind him and pulls up the comforter, and he settles his head on my chest.

After a few moments of quiet while I rub his back softly, he shifts a little and sniffles. Then, his voice unsteady and tight, he says, "Can we talk in the morning? I really *am* exhausted."

"Yeah, of course."

His breath shudders, and he mumbles a shaky "thank you" against my chest before he starts crying softly again.

No alarm goes off, but I'm awake before the sun's up the next morning. Nico's deep in sleep now, though that wasn't the case much of the night. He moved around a lot, woke up out of unsettling dreams several times, and though he always came back to my arms when he realized where he was and who I was and what was happening, he did push away from me, startled, more than once when he woke.

I don't even want to guess what his dreams were about.

I continue holding him, his back flush against my front, until light streams in around the edges of the curtains on the window. Then I slowly slip my arm out from under him, turn over to grab my phone from the nightstand, and pad quietly across the room to the bathroom. It's still only a little after six thirty, and honestly, I hope he keeps sleeping for a while.

I take a quick shower, brush my teeth, and shave, and when I sneak back out to find some clean clothes, he's still sleeping, still in the same position he was when I left, which makes me happy. After dressing in a pair of gray joggers and an old sweatshirt, I try to keep myself busy. I study for a bit, finish reading the article we'll be discussing today in journal club, and check my school emails. Then, as quietly as I can, I start breakfast.

Pancakes are still his favorite. Pancakes with a ton of syrup. And they're easy to make. So that's what I do.

He finally wakes up with a groan about ten minutes later when I set our plates on the kitchen table. His eyes are puffy and red, probably from crying last night, and seeing that as he rolls over and looks up at me makes my stomach sink.

"Hey," I say softly, trying for a smile. "I made breakfast."

He manages a smile back as he props himself up on one elbow, his gaze shifting to the plates on the table. "Smells amazing."

"It *is* amazing. Only the best for my man."

His smile turns crooked, which looks adorable, and he rolls his eyes, which also looks adorable. With a yawn, he sits and glances at his phone. "Eight fifteen?" His smile fades. "You should have woken me up."

"You needed to sleep," I argue, and although his frown deepens, he doesn't argue back. Instead, he pushes himself off the bed and heads over to the dresser to find some clothes. A minute later, he scoots his chair as close to mine as he can at the table and then leans over and rests his head on my shoulder.

"I hope I didn't keep you up last night. Sleeping sucked. Fucking nightmares all night long," he mumbles. Then he swallows hard and adds quietly, "Most of them were about Patrick. It hasn't been that bad in a really long time."

I slip my arm around his shoulder and press a kiss to his temple. "I figured."

He stiffens a little but doesn't say anything more. I lean forward slightly and slide the syrup across the table in his direction.

"Eat."

He laughs weakly. "Yessir."

"Damn right." I grin at him, and he just shakes his head, then straightens up and reaches for the syrup.

After he's thoroughly drenched his pancakes, I drizzle some syrup over mine as well, and we both start eating. He sets his fork down after just a few bites, however, and he leans against me again.

"What time do you have to leave?" he asks quietly, picking at a small scratch on the edge of the table.

"Nine. So, about a half hour."

He nods and pulls his hand away from the table. When he speaks, his voice is more steady than I expected. "I've been going back and forth about whether I want to call her back. What do you think I should do?"

"Me? What do I think?"

"Yeah," he says, tilting his head to look up at me. "Who else would I ask? You know the situation and her and what happened. And you have a more, um, objective view than I might."

"But it's not up to me."

He laughs humorlessly and sits up. "I know that. I just want to know what you think so I can decide what to do."

I don't know how to answer, so I shake my head. "I'm not sure, honestly. What have you been thinking?"

"I miss her," he says immediately. "I know we were never as close as you are with your mom, or, hell, as close as *I* am with your mom now. But . . . but she's my mom, and I want to have her in my life. I want to be able to share things with her. Like . . . I honestly don't even know if she knows about us. And what if, someday . . ." He trails off and closes his eyes, and then he leans into me again and his hand comes to rest on my chest. Quietly, he says, "What if someday we get married? I'd want her to be there. What if someday we have kids? I'd want . . . I'd want her to know them."

My heart clenches, and I wrap both of my arms around him, pulling him up against me as best I can. I kiss his forehead, and he continues.

"I never wanted what happened between us. It hurt so much then. I-I know it was what I had to do at the time. It was necessary for my safety and well-being. I don't regret it. But . . . but, god, Alex, if she's changed . . ."

I let out a short breath and kiss his forehead again. Then I say the words I know he's thinking. "And what if she hasn't? How much *more* will that hurt?"

"That's why I don't know what to do," he admits. His hand slips out to my waist, and he squeezes me as though he needs to be even closer. "She . . . abandoned me once before, and if she lies or hasn't really changed or doesn't see anything wrong with what she did back then . . ."

I feel his jaw tighten, and he exhales a sharp breath before pushing away and looking up at me. His whole body shrinks a little as he blinks back a flash of what looks like uncertainty. And despair.

His eyes drop to where his hand now rests on my chest.

And it hits me, hard. It's not even anything he's said, really. It's just a sudden understanding of what his anxiety's probably been telling him—not about his mom, but about *me* and about *us*. And it's dead wrong.

"Nico," I breathe, shaking my head, "you know that I'd never, ever . . . do that."

I can't even say the words; it hurts too much to even acknowledge that he'd think I might leave him. But when he doesn't refute it right away, I have my answer for that, too.

It's immediately painful—a sharp sting square in the middle of my chest—and it takes all of my effort to not react outwardly. I'm sure that would just make things worse. Just like I'm sure he's already feeling awful and uncertain and scared enough.

"Sorry," he mumbles, and his hand slips down my chest until it falls away from me completely, breaking the contact. I suddenly feel cold and vulnerable, and it's not a feeling I'm used to. I don't particularly like it. "Sorry," he continues, "I-I don't *really* think that. I . . . just . . ."

A voice in my head retorts something not so nice, but I hold it back, trying to reason it out. Of course he doesn't really think I'd leave him. Right? Of course he's just struggling because his mom, who was supposed to be the one person he could always trust to be there for him, unconditionally, played fucking awful games with his mental health.

*She* abandoned him. *She* chose her abusive ex over him. *She* lied to him.

But I've *always* been here for him. How could he think—

"Alex." His hand cups my cheek, and he turns my face toward him. His eyes are pleading with me, and he shakes his head. "Sometimes my anxiety tells me things. That doesn't mean I really believe them or that they're true."

I close my eyes briefly and nod. I've known that about his anxiety for a long time, and I hate that I'm feeling doubt about everything like this. I've never doubted before. I nod again. "I know, I know. I'm sorry." I laugh weakly. "Apparently I have some anxiety, too."

He gives me a tight smile and leans in for a short, reassuring kiss. I want more, so I chase his lips as he goes to pull away. That earns me an actual smile and a cheeky shove with his hand on my chest. When our eyes meet, my heart stutters, and I reach up and brush his hair back from his forehead.

"I love you," I say softly. "Always."

"I love you, too." He lets out a long, slow sigh and falls against me one more time, his head settling on my shoulder.

After a moment, he starts talking again, picking back up where we left off before *my* anxiety got the best of me. "The last couple of weeks have been really hard because her call did remind me of all that shit I've tried so hard to forget. And part of that was the fact that she abandoned me. And, yes, that reminder . . . it really fucked with my head." His hand finds my stomach, and he sighs again. "But I knew it was just my anxiety. I knew you wouldn't do that to me."

I nod, and he continues.

"Um, so, it's like you said—there's this huge part of me that wants to call her back, but then, fuck, what if . . . what if she hasn't changed? What then? I don't know what to do."

I press a kiss into his hair, wishing I had advice for him, but I really don't. It's a choice only he can make.

"I'll be here for you, whatever you decide," I assure him, and he huffs a laugh.

"You got nothing, really? No words of wisdom or five-step plan of attack?"

I shrug. "Sorry. I mean, I'm sure you'll make the right decision, whatever that is, and—"

"You know," he cuts in, straightening up with a teasing smirk, "sometimes I like you better when you just boss me around." He pokes my side with a wink, and when I roll my eyes, he laughs. Then his expression tightens again. "Seriously, though . . . if you were me, what would you do?"

I hesitate, studying his eyes for a second. Then shake my head. "I really don't know. Although . . . um, I think . . ." I force a small smile and take one of his hands in mine. "I think you'll be okay."

His eyes narrow in confusion. "What do you mean?"

"I mean if you call her and it turns out not to be what you expected . . ." I squeeze his hand. "I think you'll be okay. You're not the same person you were six years ago. You're stronger. And you're stronger than you think. And you won't be alone. I'll be here with you, and you'll get through it."

His cheeks redden, and he looks so perfect that I need to kiss him again. I lean in, and he meets me halfway. The kiss is warm and sweet, and when he smiles into it, I feel all his love and hope.

We part, and he's still smiling. "Thank you," he whispers.

I grin and nod, and I can't help myself. I pepper more kisses on his lips and then his cheek and his forehead. "I meant every word I said," I tell him, and I plant another kiss right on his nose.

He laughs, his cheeks still flushed. "I know."

# chapter five

*nico*

WHEN ALEX LEAVES JUST before nine, I swear the temperature in our apartment drops at least ten degrees. I pull on his sweater—the one he was wearing before he changed clothes to head to campus—and I crawl back under the covers on the bed, scooting over to his side so I can sleep on his pillow. Bundled up in his sweater with my head on his pillow, I feel warm and loved and cared for.

"*. . . you won't be alone. I'll be here with you . . .*"

I close my eyes and imagine he's still here, his arms holding me tight. I don't fall asleep, but I get a lot of thinking done. More back and forth, except now with a bit more perspective and maybe a tiny bit of confidence. And I make a decision, finally.

I'll call her, and I'll do my best to listen and be open to whatever she has to say. But I'll make sure Alex is with me when I call, in case it doesn't go well. It's too easy to remember where I was at that summer nearly six years ago—the devastation of knowing she chose Patrick over me, the hopelessness, the dark thoughts, fleeting but terrifying.

I haven't been back to the top of those metaphorical stairs since. And a huge reason for that is Alex.

He says I'm stronger now than I was, and he's right. I am. But I've also learned to lean on him when I need to and that it's okay to need to. That's why I'll wait until he's here with me to call. Maybe tonight, even.

I'm still in bed, not sleeping, several hours later when my phone vibrates from the nightstand. With a groan, I roll over to grab it.

Text messages. A string of them.

> *Alex (11:48 a.m.):* so

> *Alex (11:48 a.m.):* i did a thing

> *Alex (11:48 a.m.):* and i hope u dont hate it

> *Alex (11:49 a.m.):* also

> *Alex (11:49 a.m.):* dont freak out, ok?

> *Nico (11:50 a.m.):* What?

> *Alex (11:50 a.m.):* ;)

> *Nico (11:51 a.m.):* Winky face emoji tells me nothing

> *Alex (11:51 a.m.):* i know ;)

There's a knock at the front door, and even though Alex *literally* just told me not to freak out, I instinctively flinch and flip over to face the front door.

"Who is it?" I call out. There's no answer, which doesn't help but also doesn't surprise me.

> *Nico (11:52 a.m.):* Who is at the door?

*Alex (11:52 a.m.):* shrug

*Alex (11:53 a.m.):* ;)

> *Nico (11:53 a.m.):* Ugh. You know I don't like surprises

*Alex (11:53 a.m.):* i know

*Alex (11:54 a.m.):* thats y i warned u

I roll my eyes at the phone, wishing he could see me, then I push the covers back and drag myself out of bed, still gripping my phone in my hand. A quick look through the peephole shows nothing; whoever was there is now gone. So I unlock the door and inch it open.

The fragrance hits me first—floral and fresh and strong. Then I see the mass of dark-red blooms, at least a dozen of them, arranged perfectly in a clear glass vase.

Roses.

He bought me roses. Beautiful, perfect, gorgeous red roses.

Hands shaking, I type out a quick message and send it as I kneel down.

> *Nico (11:55 a.m.):* Holy fuck, Alex

There's a plain white card stuck right in the middle of the flowers and a small box sitting next to the vase. I shove my phone in my pocket and then carefully lift the vase and box and head back inside, kicking the door closed behind me.

I set both things on the table and then sit down, overwhelmed. He's randomly done a few sappy things like this over the years, like our first Valentine's Day together when he attempted to bake and decorate a heart-shaped cake (I have photo evidence of how spectacular that fail was), but this is hitting different today. It feels like much more than just a show of support and love.

My phone vibrates, and a string of red heart emojis greets me when I pull it back out of my pocket. I really don't want to cry again—I did enough of that earlier—and so I blink back the tears and send him a short reply.

> Nico (11:59 a.m.): You didn't have to do this

> Alex (12:00 p.m.): u havent opened the card yet have u?

> Nico (12:01 p.m.): =P

> Alex (12:01 p.m.): ;)

> Nico (12:02 p.m.): They need to invent a better eye roll emoji

> Alex (12:02 p.m.): open it <3

Sighing, I set my phone back down and pick the card out of the flowers. Inside the envelope, there's a single piece of white cardstock embossed with a red rose. I run my finger over it, then flip the card over.

*I love you*
*with all of my heart.*

*- Alex*

Just like the flowers, the words hit hard, and I screw my eyes shut, willing myself not to cry. Tears slip out anyway, and I shake my head and wipe them away so I can see well enough to text Alex back.

> *Nico (12:04 p.m.):* Fuck you

> *Alex (12:04 p.m.):* ah

> *Alex (12:04 p.m.):* thats the reaction i was expecting

> *Alex (12:04 p.m.):* also im free tonite

> *Nico (12:05 p.m.):* Jesus

I swipe at my cheeks again, laughing through the tears, and then I open the small box. Inside, two very large chocolate-covered strawberries drizzled in white chocolate sit on a plain rectangular plate, a little pink heart-shaped candy with *luv u* stamped on it positioned between the strawberries.

I close my eyes and laugh again, and then I pick my phone back up.

> *Nico (12:06 p.m.):* These strawberries are massive. Guess I don't have to worry about making lunch

> *Alex (12:07 p.m.):* perfect

> *Alex (12:07 p.m.):* just takin care of my man

> *Nico (12:08 p.m.):* Again, need a real eye roll emoji

> *Nico (12:09 p.m.):* But seriously, thank you so much. You don't know how much I appreciate this. Really

> *Alex (12:09 p.m.):* I love you <3

> *Nico (12:09 p.m.):* I love you too

> *Alex (12:10 p.m.):* c u l8r

> *Alex (12:10 p.m.):* ;)

Shaking my head, I wipe the tears from the corners of my eyes, and then I just sit there, staring at the flowers and card as I let my heart settle. The gratitude and love I feel are overwhelming, an intense warmth spreading outward from my chest, and it's only after a few minutes that I'm finally able to breathe.

I send him one more text—a short row of red heart emojis followed by a rose emoji—and then I push back my chair, pick up the box of strawberries, and move to the bed again for an afternoon of wasting time playing video games.

"Ready?"

"No."

Alex laughs, and then he scoots closer to me on the edge of the bed, kisses my cheek, and wraps me up in a tight, warm hug. "You can do this," he whispers into my ear. "I'm here with you, and no matter what she says, she can't hurt you anymore. You're stronger than that."

I nod, trying to feel the truth in his words. "You're right."

I straighten up and glance down at my phone as Alex's hand finds my lower back.

"One step at a time. She called you, she's—"

"—the one who should do most of the talking," I finish for him, and he nods. We talked about this earlier, so I'd hopefully have some idea of what to expect. But that doesn't stop me from being nervous now. "Okay."

I blow out a short breath and slowly type in her phone number—the same one she's had for as long as I can remember. Then I pull my feet up onto the bed, lean against Alex, and press the call button.

It rings. And rings again.

"Hello?"

Her voice sounds exactly as it always has—slightly annoyed, like she's in the middle of something and has somewhere else to be and something else to be doing. It's familiar but also just as painful as I expected it to be.

I close my eyes as Alex's hand rubs up and down my back. "Um, hi, Mom." Once the words are out, my chest tightens, and I shrink into myself a little, curling up against Alex. His hand slips around my shoulders, and he gives me a gentle squeeze.

The silence on the other end of the line is suffocating, like it's taking up all of the space around me, sucking the air out of the room. Then there's a sharp sound, followed by my mom's voice again, different this time, softer but strained with disbelief.

"Nico?"

"Yeah." When she doesn't respond, I add, "You left a message for me a couple weeks ago."

"I did. I did," she says, and she sniffles, though I can hear she's trying to cover it up. "God, I—god, it's so good to hear your voice. I-I didn't—I didn't think you were going to call me back."

I'm not sure whether to say I almost didn't, and I can feel my shoulders tightening up, my jaw clenching, my teeth grinding. So instead, I just skip that and any other pleasantries that might normally be considered appropriate, and I get right to the point. "Why did you call, Mom?"

Alex kisses the top of my head and whispers, "Breathe."

And I shake my head and pull the phone away from my ear. "I am breathing." Then I take a long, deliberate breath as I bring the phone back up.

My mom is still quiet, sort of. I can hear her sniffling and taking short breaths, like she keeps trying to say something but nothing comes.

"Mom?"

"Yeah, sorry, sorry. I'm . . . I wasn't expecting . . ." There's a clearly muffled sob this time, and her voice trembles as she says, "I called because I—I needed to hear your voice. I've missed you so much. And I . . . I *know* how much I messed up. I know that now. I hope you'll let me apologize, and I hope we can try again."

I've wanted to hear those words for so long that it almost doesn't seem real. I turn and press my forehead against Alex's chest, and his arm squeezes my shoulders again. "It's been six years, Mom."

"I know, I know," she says. "Please, please, can I explain?"

I take another slow breath in and out, and I nod into Alex. "I'm listening."

There's a short pause, and then she says, "Thank you." In the background, there's some rustling and then a jingling, like keys being set down on a counter. "Um, so . . ."

She hesitates again, and in the silence, I pretend that I can picture her as she is now. Probably much the same as she was, maybe with a little gray hair and a few more wrinkles. And maybe she's standing in the kitchen, still wearing her work uniform, one hand resting on the counter while she closes her eyes, trying to figure out what to say.

I open my eyes and shake my head. "Mom?"

"I was selfish that summer," she finally blurts out. With a sad sigh, she continues, her voice wavering as she speaks. "Just before you graduated, Patrick came back to town. He told me all sorts of things, how it would be different this time around, how *he* would be different this time around. And I believed him. I believed everything he told me. When I found out how he hurt you again, I kicked him out, but I . . . I still didn't . . ." She pauses, and there's another sniffle and a quiet sob. "Nico, baby, I messed up so much. I had myself believing things that weren't true, about you, about me, about everything. And I kept digging myself deeper into that hole. Patrick went to jail after what he did to you, but he was out again after a year, and he came back, *again*, a-and I . . ." Her voice catches as she stutters through her next words. "I-I . . . I let him, *again*. But the winter before last, around your birthday when you turned twenty-three, it finally really hit me, how much all of my decisions had hurt you and me and us. I . . . I became depressed. Patrick left me, moved down to Florida or something, I don't even care anymore. And everything got so bad I was almost fired. Melinda, my boss, finally convinced me to get help."

"Get help?" I echo, and I feel Alex's fingers brush my cheek softly, wiping away a tear.

"Yeah." She lets out a ragged breath and says, "I . . . I started seeing a therapist in Omaha. Twice a week at first. Now I go once a week."

My heart clenches in my chest, and I cling to Alex and force out a weak "oh."

With what sounds like renewed conviction, she continues. "It was the first step I needed to take to get my life back," she says. "And I've been working very hard on myself every day. I . . . know I hurt you, Nico, and—and I'm your mom, and I shouldn't have done that. Ever. I can't take back what happened, but I'm working hard, still, all the time, to be sure I'm no longer that person. I hope . . . I hope you'll believe me when I say I'm so sorry for everything I did to hurt you. I also understand if you can't trust me, but I would really, really like the chance to show you that I've changed—that I'm working to be who you need me to be."

I'm shaking, my breathing fast and stilted, and I bury my face against Alex as he holds me tighter. "I want that," I say, and I sniffle and turn so I'm not mumbling into my boyfriend's chest. "I missed you, too, Mom."

She breaks down then, crying, and she doesn't try to hide it. She repeats a lot of what she just said—how sorry she is, how much help therapy has been. And she tells me that she loves me and that she'll do everything she can to show me that.

When she finishes, I'm still shaking, but Alex hasn't let me go. He holds me gently, kisses my cheek, and whispers in my ear that he loves me and that I should breathe again. I laugh and elbow his side.

"Ow," he complains, but he's smiling when I look up at him. I close my eyes and settle my head back on his shoulder.

"Who are you with? Was that . . . Alex?" my mom asks, though her tone is almost reluctant, like she's scared to say anything that might make me hang up. Or maybe like she knows she's not entitled to any information about my life if I don't want to share.

But I do want to share. I've wanted her to know how happy I am, how this life I've built with Alex is everything I ever dreamed of. So I nod, curl up against him, and give her just a little bit.

"Yeah, it's Alex. We live together out here in California. He's my boyfriend."

# chapter six

## alex

THE SMOOTH SKIN OF Nico's stomach caresses my lips as I trail a path of kisses slowly down past his navel. He smells of warmth and vanilla, and I pause to breathe him in as my fingers draw lazy circles on the inside of his bare thigh.

Morning lovemaking wasn't on my list of to-dos today, but he woke me up a bit ago, teasing his fingertips down over my nipples and wedging his knee between my legs. Now he's on his back, naked, his eyes closed and his hands stroking my hair as I kiss my way up and down his body.

He's quiet, as he sometimes is on mornings like this. No words, no crying out my name, no fast panting or loud moans. It's him needing me in a different way. And so everything is slow, sensual, tender. It's soft kisses, gentle touches. Usually he wants my mouth to bring him to his climax, but he'll let me know exactly what he needs when he's ready.

We take our time.

My slow kisses find their way out to his hip and then back up along his side and inward again until his nipple is in my mouth. I suck gently on the stiff bud, and he encourages me, his hands still in my hair. When I switch to the other side after a few moments, he lets out a soft sigh, and his hands slide down my upper back to rest just below my shoulder blades.

"Alex," he breathes.

I swirl my tongue around his nipple and suck lightly as I lift my eyes to meet his. He's watching me, bliss on his face, and he smiles softly and brings a hand back up to run through my hair.

I close my eyes again and continue fluttering kisses up to his neck, along his jawline, behind his ear. And all the while, I continue to stroke his inner thigh, down to his knee and back up, the tips of my fingers teasing just high enough to graze the base of his cock. There's a quiet hum of approval, and so I repeat the touch, my flat palm running down to his knee and back up again.

"How's this?" I ask, my lips hovering just above his skin along his jawline. In response, he turns slowly onto his side, hooking his leg around my thighs to give me room to keep touching him, and his mouth finds mine. His lips are as warm as his skin and so soft and pliable.

We kiss more and touch more, all with this sensual, slow tenderness. When he finally pulls back from our kiss, his cheeks are flushed, and he's breathing heavily. He closes his eyes and falls onto his back on the bed again.

"Alex," he says, and this time, there's a neediness to his voice. "Please . . ."

"Mmm." I caress up to his hip and then his chest and neck and chin until I'm cupping his cheek in my hand, and I turn his face so he's looking at me. I lower my mouth and kiss him again, softly. "You're so beautiful," I whisper against his lips before I start downward one more time, trailing my tongue along his skin as I go.

He whimpers, and his fingers thread into my hair as he gently encourages me lower. "I . . . I want . . ."

"Shh, I've got you."

He shudders and lets out another quiet breath, and I reposition myself between his legs and continue kissing down his stomach. It's still slow and sensual, even as I wrap my hand around his shaft and take him into my mouth—just the tip at first. I suck gently, tasting him, and then flatten my tongue down along his slit and tease a low moan out of him. And it stays slow and sensual, even as I take him in all the way to the back of my throat.

I slide up and down his length again and again, but it's not fast or hard or with any urgency at all. And that's how he wants it now—a slow build to the edge. His breathing changes with each bob of my head, and the next time his cock hits the back of my throat, he makes a small sound, like another whimper. He stops stroking my hair, and his hands find my shoulders just before his cock starts pulsing with his release.

I swallow everything he gives me. Then I let him slip from my mouth, and I push myself up on the bed to lie next to him, gathering him up in my arms. He's warm and soft and feels weak and tired as I hold him, and yet, he clings to me and frames my face and then kisses my mouth.

"I love you," I whisper when he pulls back, burying his head down into the crook of my shoulder. He nods into me and closes his eyes, quiet again as we lie there.

Mornings like this, moments like this, they feel comfortable, deep, important. He asked me once if it bothered me that sometimes—that on mornings like this—he's unable to reciprocate, to make me come how I made him come. And I remember telling him no, it didn't bother me in the slightest and that I was glad he trusted me enough to let me love him like this.

Outside, the sunlight grows stronger, peeking in around the edges of the curtains on the window, and sounds of a busy Tuesday morning in downtown San Jose begin trickling in. Footsteps from the apartment above us, cars driving along Santa Clara Street, the occasional honk of a horn. But he doesn't move, and so I don't, either.

"What time do you have to leave?" he asks after a while longer, though he stays curled up against me, holding onto me.

I kiss the top of his head. "I don't. No class today, and John said I can have the day off."

Nico tilts his head back and looks up at me with sleepy eyes, his mop of dark hair falling over his forehead. He's adorable and gorgeous, and I can't help it when my heart skips a beat.

"So you're staying home?" he asks, and when I nod, he says, "Did you already plan to, or are you just staying because of last night? Because I'm okay. I mean"—he pushes away from me a bit and props himself up on one elbow—"the conversation with my mom went better than I thought it would, and I think I'm . . . I'm really fucking tired but I'm also okay, you know? I might just, I dunno, stay in bed all day and play video games. I don't think I'll be great company."

By the time he stops his ramble, I'm grinning and shaking my head, and I prop myself up, too, and scoot over to kiss him. When we part, I rest my forehead against his.

"We can do whatever you want," I tell him quietly. "I just want to spend some time with you. I already planned to stay home."

"Are you sure?"

I nod. "Whatever you want."

In my mind, today is *the day*. I can see it— us getting up and out of bed, heading on the short walk to Sunrise Café to have breakfast, then taking a bus to the Japanese garden. Me getting down on one knee, the words I've been practicing, all the promises and I love yous and forevers right on the tip of my tongue. I almost let my eyes dart over to the dresser where the rings are hidden.

But when I straighten up and our eyes meet, there's an exhaustion in his expression that I know all too well. It's not a physical exhaustion, but an emotional one. Our lovemaking, too, was proof that he's okay, but he's hanging on by a thread. Yesterday took *a lot* out of him.

And as much as I *want* it to be today, I also want him to be feeling good and happy and to have the energy to smile and laugh with me. I want him to want to come out, not for him to say yes just because he knows I want to.

So, maybe today will be the day. But maybe it won't be. I can't be sure yet.

Regardless, I *do* want to be here with him, even if it means staying home all day. Cuddling. Streaming a movie. Playing video games and generally just being together.

"Let me go grab us breakfast from Sunrise?" I suggest, letting my hand rub up and down his arm.

He smiles weakly and nods. "Yeah, that sounds good, actually." And then, as though he's run out of energy altogether, he closes his eyes and plops back down onto the bed with a quiet sigh.

I start to pull away so I can get dressed and get going, but he stops me, his hand lifting to my waist. He tilts his head toward me and opens his eyes halfway, then he shifts his hand and tugs gently on my hip.

"A few more minutes first?" he says.

My stomach swoops, and I immediately nod and settle back down on the bed next to him. "Of course."

"No, no, no! Don't go in there, Jenna! We should go around!"

"Oh, don't worry. I got this. How many times do I have to tell you? I can tank *anything*!"

Nico groans in frustration, but he pushes the knob on his game controller forward, guiding his character to follow Jenna's through a doorway and down a hall.

I follow with my character, too, casting a regeneration spell on our whole group, but I also keep arguing with her. "Not *this* boss, you can't. He'll one-shot you, and then I'm dead next, and—"

"Trust me, guys!" Jenna's voice comes through the speaker from my laptop, and then, on the TV in front of us, we watch as her character rushes in, axe and shield raised, to meet the massive minotaur waiting at the opposite end of the room.

Nico groans again. "I'm gonna kill her."

"I heard that!" Jenna laughs. "Look, see, guys, it's easy! All I gotta do is not let him—"

Her character's health suddenly drops from nearly full to nothing as the giant beast's two-handed battle-axe drops right down on top of her.

I didn't even have a chance to cast another healing spell.

Nico boldly holds his position, spamming fireballs at the boss until it takes him out as well, and I turn and run, morphing my character into a sleek black panther as I dash toward the exit.

Jenna's laughing and teasing me for running, and Nico nudges my leg with his foot.

"Just let him kill you," he says with a smirk. "You can rez and then get me. We can let Jenna run back, though. Give her time to think about how her actions affect others."

"I heard *that* too!"

With a sigh, I stop, and the beast catches up to me within seconds. He raises his axe, stomps a foot, and bashes my character just once, draining all my health.

"I'm kinda tired of dying," I complain, hitting a few buttons to resurrect my character once the monster is gone. I backtrack to find Nico's character first and bring him back to life, and then inch my way forward just enough to reach Jenna's warrior and bring her back to life as well.

"Yeah, I've gotta run, actually," Jenna says. "My Con Law class starts in about an hour, and I need to finish writing this case brief still."

"Procrastination is still the key to success, even in law school?" I tease, and Jenna laughs again.

"Maybe. I've gotten by so far, but this class is killing me. Anyway, it was nice to *finally* catch both of you online at the same time. It was fun!"

"It was, totally," I agree.

Nico adds a quick thank you, and we all sign off. I take our controllers and put them away, back in a drawer in my nightstand, and Nico shuts my computer and pushes it over to the other side of the bed. Then he collapses onto his back with a dramatic groan.

Grinning, I crawl over and cuddle up next to him to nuzzle his neck. "So, how are you feeling now?" I ask softly, and I press a series of kisses up from his collarbone to his jawline. When I reach his mouth, he smiles and meets me halfway, his hands coming up to frame my face. He feels good. Happy. Not as tired as he did earlier.

"Mmm, better. And hungry. Is it lunchtime yet?"

My heart leaps in my chest, and I glance toward the kitchen. The clock on the microwave says it's one fifteen. I nod and lean in to kiss him again. "I have an idea. You can veto it if it's too much. Okay?"

He eyes me with a cautious half smile. "Yeah, okay. What?"

"How about"—I kiss the tip of his nose—"we grab a couple slices of pizza, and then, if you're up to it, we can catch the bus to the Japanese garden. The weather's perfect today, and it shouldn't be busy."

I'm *sure* he can see right into my brain and just *knows* what I'm planning or at least that I'm planning *something*. But his expression just softens and he nods.

"Yeah, I think I can handle that."

"Great," I say, and I kiss his lips, lingering there for an extra few seconds, before I roll over and away from him to stand up. "We can get dressed and leave in five?"

When I glance back at him, he's nodding and pushing himself up to sit. I get that sense again that he's comfortable and happy and that whatever weight had been on his shoulders this morning, making him so exhausted, has lifted a bit.

And seeing that makes my heart stutter.

Maybe today *is* the day, after all.

# chapter seven

*nico*

SOMETHING'S UP WITH ALEX.

He's been jittery since we left home, and he barely ate lunch, even though he swears the pizza place right near our apartment has the best pizza in the world. He's also been alternating between talking my ear off and completely silent, and right now, he's walking just slightly faster than normal, which is a bit awkward considering he's gripping my hand and having to almost pull me along next to him.

Ahead of us, a large, dark-stained wooden gate underneath a gray pagoda-style roof marks the entrance to the Japanese Friendship Garden. Besides Vera's art gallery, it's probably one of my favorite places in San Jose. The first year we lived here, the garden underwent a massive restoration and renovation to update and repair the ponds and bridges. I remember Vera telling me about how the park used to be and how happy she was that they finally did all the planned work. The garden fully reopened, better than new, just shortly after Alex moved down from Palo Alto to live with me in San Jose his second year of undergrad.

I slow and stop as we reach the entrance, and Alex stops half a step ahead of me. When he turns around to look at me, his eyes are bright and eager, and he's grinning this huge, silly grin. I smile back and tug on his hand lightly. "Where's my kiss?"

I didn't think it was possible, but his smile lights up even more. He closes the distance between us and lowers his mouth to mine for a short, sweet kiss. It's silly, but it's become a bit of a thing—for us to kiss under the entrance here. We did it the first time we came, although I can't really remember exactly why, and now, we do it every time right when we enter.

"I didn't forget," he says, smiling sheepishly. He kisses me again, as though to prove his point, and then he tips his head toward the garden. "I'm just a little distracted because I saw the cherry blossoms."

"They're still blooming? This late in the season?" I glance past him into the park, and it's like he said. Several of the cherry blossom trees are still in full bloom, even though we're well into early May.

He squeezes my hand gently, and together, we start walking again. The rough cobblestone path leads us to the edge of a large pond, and we pause there, too, his arm slipping around my waist. Where the water meets the edge, a small group of colorful koi fish congregate, swimming close to the surface, and then farther off in the pond, a couple of geese float along, basking in the sunlight.

It's so peaceful, and for a second, I lean into Alex and close my eyes, and I just let myself feel the freshness in the air. It's this clean, crisp feeling, everything alive and growing around us, serene and calm. The sweet fragrance of the cherry blossoms, the cool breeze, the quiet sounds of leaves fluttering and birds chirping.

"I needed this," I say softly, and Alex's arm tightens around my waist. "The whole day, I mean. We haven't spent a day together like this in a while. Thank you for staying home with me."

Our lives have gotten so busy, especially with all the hours I'm putting in for my apprenticeship, and even when I do have days off or half days off, they rarely coincide with his.

"We're going to be busy like this for a while, I think," he says, as though he's reading my mind. "So we have to take what we can, right?"

I nod and open my eyes partway. The geese are still floating in about the middle of the pond, and the koi have started to move on, the water rippling here and there as bright white and orange shapes weave about below the surface.

I smile and tilt my head back. Alex isn't watching the geese or the koi; he's looking at me, his eyes shining and happy. God, I love this.

"I love you," I whisper, letting my hand come to rest on his stomach.

He purses his lips to rein in his smile, and then his eyes dart off across the garden to the other side of the pond for just a second. "Let's walk?" he asks quietly.

I narrow my eyes at his redirect but then nod, and his cheeks turn bright red. He quickly looks away again, and together, we start walking at a leisurely pace along the edge of the pond, his arm still around my waist.

He guides us down the path until it curves back around on the far side of the pond, where the ground is littered with cherry blossom petals. The slight breeze that picks up plucks a few more from the trees, and they flutter around us, light and airy, until they come to rest on the path. His steps stutter then, and he pauses and tightens his arm around me. His eyes are focused ahead, where there's a little red bridge that rises up to cross over a portion of the pond.

I follow his gaze and smile, pulling out my phone. "Here, your mom would *love* this picture," I say, and then there's a twinge in my chest as I add, "And maybe I can send it to my mom, too."

He sucks in a breath and nods, and then he holds me even closer as I lift the phone up in front of us to take a selfie. He's grinning, his huge smile and bright blue eyes complemented by the vibrance of the cherry blossom tree in the background. I smile just as wide as I capture one picture, and then he turns and kisses my cheek as I take another.

"Oh yeah, you should send them that one," he mumbles against my cheek, and I fake-scoff, then laugh and shove him away.

Both of his arms wrap around my waist from behind, and he bends down to kiss my neck. "Here, take this one too," he says. I hesitate for only a second before I lift the phone up again. On the screen, I see him—I see us. He tilts his head a tiny bit to rest against mine, and he smiles that same brilliant, bright smile.

"You're gorgeous," I breathe.

He shakes his head a little and murmurs, "Take the picture."

"'Kay, yeah."

We both smile, and I snap the photo. Then he does the same thing he did with our first pose, kissing my cheek, and I snap that one, too. I lower the phone and look down at it, scrolling through the pictures. They're perfect, each and every one of them. He's happy, and, fuck, even *I* look happy. I close the camera app and start to open up my messaging app to send the photos to his mom (and *maybe* to my mom, too), but he stops me, his hand covering mine.

"Wait, one more thing first before you send them," he says, though his voice seems to waver. "Come on."

Rather than waiting for a response, he takes my free hand and gives me another grin, tipping his head toward the bridge. With a shrug, I slip my phone back into my pocket and follow as he leads me the rest of the way up the path to the bridge. The wood creaks under our feet as we step off the path, and he stops us right at the top of the slight arch.

"You want another picture from here?" I go to pull my phone out, but Alex intercepts my hand and pulls gently until I'm facing him. He has this smile on his face that's soft and hopeful and eager all at once.

"Um, not quite yet, actually. First . . ." His smile deepens, and then he ducks his head as his cheeks turn bright red.

And it's not until he squeezes my hand and then starts to lower himself down to one knee that I finally realize what's going on and why he brought me here. My heart jumps in my chest, and I think I stop breathing as he lifts his eyes up to meet mine.

"Nico . . ." He smiles again, and it's still soft and hopeful and eager, filled with all of his love.

He brings my hand slowly to his lips and kisses my knuckles, the gesture sweet and loving, and before he's even said more than my name, this wave of warm, bright joy hits me. I swallow and shake my head, but his smile just widens.

"Nico . . . you're my best friend," he says softly, and I swear his eyes are now glistening with unshed tears. He blinks them back and continues. "There's not a day that goes by that I'm not grateful for you, for what we have together . . . for this life we've built."

I smile and drop my chin as a tear slips down my cheek. "Alex . . ."

He squeezes my hand. "I love you, Nico. I love you with all of my heart, and I will love you for all of my life. And—" His voice falters as he lets my hand go long enough to reach into his pocket. He pulls out a small black box, and, with a shuddering breath, he opens the box and lifts his eyes to mine again. "Nico West, will you marry me?"

My gaze drops to the two matching dark metal bands in the box, and I'm suddenly laughing and crying and nodding and blubbering something incoherent all at once. Whatever I say must sound like the *yes* that I mean, because Alex's face lights up like the sun, and then he's standing and my arms go up around his neck, and he kisses me, his tears mingling with mine. We kiss and kiss until I'm breathless, and then he steps back and takes one of the rings out of the box, his hands shaking.

"I-I hope it fits, I had to guess at your size," he stammers, and I can't talk, so I just nod again. The ring slips on my finger easily, and it's just fucking perfect.

I tell him that, and then we kiss again, his hands finding my waist as mine slide up his chest to rest on either side of his neck.

"I love you," I whisper against his mouth.

"Mmm, I love you too," he hums. He kisses me one more time, but it's an awkward kiss because we're both grinning. When he pulls back this time, I lower my hands to his chest, and he glances down and then takes my left hand in his, running his thumb over the band. "It is perfect, isn't it?"

"Yeah," I breathe. Then, wordlessly, I take his ring out of the box he's still holding, and I kiss his hand before I slide the ring on his finger. "Perfect."

I lift my eyes to look up at him, and he's watching me too. I shake my head. "I knew something was up."

He laughs and lowers his eyes. "I thought you might have."

We're quiet for a moment, and then I laugh and hand him back the ring box before taking my phone out of my pocket.

"So, now you want that picture, right?" I say.

He nods.

There are still tears on my cheeks, and I'm sure my face is as flushed as his, but I lift up the phone anyway as he steps behind me and wraps his arms around my waist. He threads the fingers of his left hand through mine and rests both of our hands on my chest so the rings are visible. Then he tilts his head against the side of mine, and I snap the selfie.

"Perfect," he whispers in my ear, and he kisses my cheek as I snap another.

# chapter eight

## *alex*

*He said yes.*

Through a wonderfully beautiful jumble of tears and smiles and laughter, Nico said *yes*, he'll marry me.

Even almost a week later, I still feel giddy and weightless and warm all over every time I think about it or see the ring on his finger. It's gotten so bad—how I randomly smile or laugh or just have this urgent *need* to kiss him—that he's started teasing me about it, flashing the ring just to get a reaction out of me.

I absolutely adore all of it.

With a lovesick sigh, which naturally earns me an exaggerated eye roll, I slip an arm around him and kiss his cheek while I continue stirring the pasta sauce on the stovetop. He steps away momentarily to drain the noodles but moves right back into position—close enough that I can wrap my arm around his waist again—as soon as he's transferred the cooked pasta back into the pot.

"So, you'll be home late tomorrow night?" I ask, turning off the heat on the burner and setting the spoon aside.

Nico nods. "Yeah. Greta wants to show me this technique she'll be using to remove an old layer of varnish on an oil painting that was previously restored, so I'll head up there in the afternoon when

I'm finished with my day at Vera's. She said the process takes a few hours."

I start pouring the sauce over the pasta, and my heart does that same thing again where it feels like it's skipped a beat. I'm so damn proud of him.

He nudges me with his elbow. "Stop it."

"Stop what?" I retort, but I know exactly what he means. I'm grinning like an idiot, and he's seen the look on my face.

"It's not a big deal."

"It's a huge deal." I set the pot back down and pick up the spoon to stir the pasta and sauce together. "It's a huge deal because when you talk about anything to do with your apprenticeship, your voice changes, and you sound eager and happy, and I just love it."

He slips both arms around my waist and tugs on me until I turn to face him. Then he stretches up to kiss me, his lips soft and warm.

"Mmm," he hums against me, smiling, and his arms tighten around me. When he pulls back, his cheeks are tinged pink, and he ducks his head. "I'm so grateful Vera suggested it and Greta took a chance on me. The work—it's perfect for me, I think." He glances back up at me, and he seems about to say something else when his phone chimes from the pocket of his slacks.

He shrugs and pulls it out while I finish mixing the pasta and then get us each a bowl from the cupboard.

"My mom, um . . . says hi." He turns so he's leaning back against the counter, now staring at his phone, his shoulders tense.

I set the bowls down and watch as he takes a deep breath, then taps out a message on his phone. After he sends it, he looks up at me, his face contorted in a grimace.

It's just a little too much, sometimes, he told me. It's only been a week since he reconnected with his mom, and she's been maybe a little bit more eager than he was ready for. Not that there's been anything bad. It's just been a lot. She's been sending him multiple text messages a day sometimes, and she's already tried to call him again twice. Both times, he wasn't at home or with me, and so he made the decision not to answer, which I think was the right call.

"You don't have to respond," I remind him, and he almost sort of smiles but then drops his eyes to his phone again as another message comes through.

With a weak laugh, he shakes his head. "She just asked if your hair is still blue." He pauses and continues reading whatever else is on his phone screen.

It seems like he needs me now, so I abandon our dinner and step over to him. My arm slips up around his shoulders, and he immediately leans against me with a sigh. I press a soft kiss to his temple.

"I haven't sent her the pictures we took last week. I guess I wasn't quite ready yet," he says quietly.

I nod but don't say anything.

He lets out a long sigh and sets his jaw. "Maybe . . . maybe I'll send them now. That would answer her question, yeah?"

"Only if you want to."

"I think I do." He snuggles up against me more, and I squeeze his shoulders gently as he types out a short text message that reads *"Dark blue now. And this happened last week. <3"* Then, he attaches one of the photos we took on the bridge at the Japanese garden—the one where my hand is partially covering his on his chest, showing off our matching rings—and hits send.

He quickly hits the power button to black out his screen and shoves his phone in his pocket like he doesn't want to see whatever her response is. Then he turns back around and reaches across the stove to the pot of pasta. His phone chimes almost right away, but this time, he ignores it.

"I just need a minute," he explains.

My hand finds his lower back. "I know. You're so strong for talking to her like you have been. But it's okay to need some space too. If you need help telling her that . . ." I trail off as he shakes his head.

"No, it's okay. I . . . I can do it if I need to." He gives me a tight smile and then sighs. "Let's eat?"

I nod, smile softly, and lean in to kiss him gently on the lips, letting my hand rub low on his back.

Together, we portion out the pasta and then move to the kitchen table, his phone chiming a few more times before we get seated. He laughs and makes a comment about how he shouldn't have opened the floodgates right before dinner. And he scoots his chair as close to mine as it can go, leans up against me, and closes his eyes.

After a few long moments, he sets his hand on my thigh and straightens up. Then he reaches out to pick up his fork. I copy him, and we start to eat. The meal is a simple one—a recipe of my mom's that she calls chicken pot pie pasta. It's easy and one of Nico's favorites, and I'm glad to see his appetite when he digs in.

"So . . ." He nudges me with his elbow, and when I glance over, he's grinning, his eyes sparkling with eagerness. "Big or small?"

I narrow my eyes in confusion. "I'm gonna need a bit more context, because, you know, big or small, it *really* depends . . ."

He giggles and shakes his head. "For the wedding. Big or small? Outdoors or indoors? Here or in Nebraska? Soon or wait a while? Do you have any preferences?"

I'm suddenly all choked up. The mention of the wedding sends a rush of emotions through me, and it's a moment before I can speak. "Um, yeah . . . I don't think I have any preferences. We can get married at the courthouse for all I care. I just want to be your husband. So, actually, um . . ." I pause, and a huge grin spreads across his face. God, he's gorgeous.

"So you *do* have a preference?" he teases.

My face heats up. "Maybe . . . I mean, just that maybe sooner would be better?"

"Like over the summer sooner?"

I nod. "And outdoors, definitely."

"Here in California, but small. Just family and a few close friends?" he says, with a bit less certainty. "Unless you were thinking—"

"That's perfect," I cut in, and I lean in to kiss him again. "Whatever you want, it's perfect."

He's quiet for a moment, but the tension in his shoulders seems to gradually fade as his smile returns. He gives a small nod and slides his hand over to take mine, intertwining our fingers. My heart clenches as I feel the cool metal of his ring.

"I love you, Alex," he says softly.

And for whatever reason, his admission, which I've heard probably hundreds of times now, completely overwhelms me. A wave of some warm, pleasant buzz rushes through me, and I shake my head, laugh-sobbing or something, as I pull him in for a hug. I kiss his cheek and then his lips, and I repeat the words back to him.

"I love you, too."

His lips find mine again, and we kiss, the weight of everything else gone for those few precious seconds. My heart is as full as it was the first day we kissed, nearly six years ago now, and when I straighten up and our eyes meet, that feeling only intensifies.

He's my everything. My best friend. My lover. And now, my soon-to-be husband.

And I love him, with all of my heart.

The End.

Wondering what happens at their wedding? Check out the bonus chapter, *All of My Life*, along with other freebies at my website (https://www.beccaneil.com/freebies)!

# note from the
## author

THANK YOU FOR READING *All of My Heart*. I hope you found Nico and Alex's journey sweet and heartwarming.

Nico's struggles with severe social anxiety stem from the actions of his abusive ex-stepfather. Unfortunately, situations like Nico's are all too common. According to statistics cited by Prevent Child Abuse (PCA) America (https://preventchildabuse.org) using data published in the medical journal *JAMA*, 18% of adolescents between fourteen and seventeen years of age report having been physically abused by a parent or caregiver at some point in their life.[1] Moreover, nearly half of all child fatalities are the result of child physical abuse.[1] Though the causes of child physical abuse vary, research has shown that some of the most effective prevention efforts focus on "strengthening economic support to families, changing social norms to support parents and positive parenting, providing quality care and education early in life, enhancing parenting skills to promote healthy child development, and intervening to lessen immediate and long-term harms."[1] I hope that further research, promotion of support services, and effective public policy change will lead to better outcomes and protect the most precious members of our society—our children.

As with my other novels, I will be donating the proceeds from the sale of this book to charity. Because of Nico's situation and challenges, I have chosen to donate to PCA America. Thank you for helping me support them. You can visit https://preventchild abuse.org for more information on PCA America's mission or to find other ways you can help.

[1]PCA America. Child Physical Abuse Prevention. https://preventchildabuse.org/what-we-do/child-physical -abuse-prevention/. Accessed December 18, 2025.

# acknowledgements

THIS BOOK WAS DIFFICULT to write. After I poured so much of my heart into *Pieces of Home*, I really thought I should probably write something lighter, and while I suppose this story *is* lighter than *Pieces of Home*, there's still a lot of heaviness to it. Nico is so very special to me, and Alex is just a beautiful soul. I love their story so much and how it came together.

I couldn't have written this without the cheering from my wonderful team, KC and Logan and Kristi, or the support of my husband and my children, as always. I want to thank you all from the bottom of my heart. I also want to thank all of my readers, the wonderful artists I've worked with (especially @angki.s_! WOW, this cover art is just gorgeous! Probably my favorite so far!), and everyone else who has supported me on this journey.

Thank you, and thank you for reading! I hope you loved it!

-Becca

# about the author

BECCA NEIL WRITES CONTEMPORARY romance, heavy on the hurt/comfort and angst but always with plenty of fluff and swoons and an uplifting happily-ever-after. She enjoys crafting character-centered stories of love and healing and forever. When she's not writing or thinking about writing, she might be off hiking somewhere or lost in the beauty of a sunset.

*All of My Heart* is Becca's fifth book. To check out her other books, sign up for her newsletter, or get your hands on some freebies, visit her website at www.beccaneil.com.

To find out more about Becca and her upcoming projects, visit or connect with her on social media on the following social media platforms:

Facebook (Becca Neil and Becca and KC's Book Nook)

Instagram (@beccaneilauthor)

TikTok (@beccaneilauthor)

www.ingramcontent.com/pod-product-compliance
Lightning Source LLC
Chambersburg PA
CBHW020457020726
47493CB00001B/67

* 9 7 8 1 9 6 4 0 4 1 2 1 6 *